Cassie grit

Hysteria was imminent, guaranteed, if this jerk didn't get out right now. "No, no, I'm fine. Will you please just leave!"

"Well," Caleb drawled, the word easing slowly through his lips. "If that's what you want." He grinned at the blush that was stealing over her collarbone. Her face must be the color of a fire hydrant by now, he thought with unholy amusement. He couldn't resist torturing her just a bit more. "I hope we'll be seeing more of each other in the near future."

He turned, heading for the door, pausing one last time with his hand on the knob. "By the way, you're a real knockout. See you around, Slim."

Laura Moore

Ride a Dark Horse

POCKET STAR BOOKS

New York   London   Toronto   Sydney   Singapore

This book is a work of fiction. Names, characters, places and incidents are products of the author's imagination or are used fictitiously. Any resemblance to actual events or locales or persons, living or dead, is entirely coincidental.

An *Original* Publication of POCKET BOOKS

 A Pocket Star Book published by
POCKET BOOKS, a division of Simon & Schuster Inc.
1230 Avenue of the Americas, New York, NY 10020

ISBN: 0-671-04292-0

First Pocket Books printing March 2001

10 9 8 7 6 5 4 3 2 1

POCKET STAR BOOKS and colophon are registered trademarks of Simon & Schuster, Inc.

Cover design and illustration by Carlos Beltran

Printed in the U.S.A.

QB/

to Charles

Ride a Dark Horse

Prologue

The pounding of the stallion's hooves broke the quiet of the afternoon. Horse and rider gained momentum as they rounded the end of the ring and headed toward the last row of jumps. Closer and closer the rider neared, gathering and steadying his mount. Ten yards, five yards, and then it happened. Again. The two men leaning against the fence winced.

"Hell. The stupid bastard's eating dirt again. How many times does that make it now, Caleb?"

"Eight, nine . . . I think I've lost track. Tell me, Hank, when are you going to find a real rider to work with Orion? I'm getting damned tired of these jokers. If we don't find someone who can stay on his back long enough to finish the course, I think I'll take over. I couldn't do any worse than these chumps."

Hank Sawyer looked at the man he considered a second son and grinned. He had watched Caleb grow from a gangly, wiry kid into a six foot two inch, one hundred eighty pound man. At thirty-two years of age, Caleb Wells was solid muscle. Broad shouldered and lean hipped, he radiated power and grace—even when shaking his head in disgust at Hank's soon-to-be former rider. The long, curling ends of Caleb's dark hair brushed the collar of his navy blue flannel shirt. He'd rolled his sleeves up, exposing strong, sinewy forearms. Even in the chilly March air, Caleb preferred to be in shirtsleeves. He rarely wore coats, at most slipping on a heavy fisherman's sweater and a denim jacket should the Virginia weather turn really cold. His casual attire suited his lifestyle. As a veterinarian, specializing in equine medicine, he wore clothes that could withstand the wear and tear his profession demanded.

Hank leaned his elbows against the top of the rail and turned his attention back to the fallen rider, watching closely as the man rose shakily to his feet, caught the stallion's reins, and awkwardly remounted.

After reassuring himself that the rider wasn't too rattled by his spill, he called out, "All right, take him over that line again. Then you can warm him down. And try to stay on top of him this time!" This last bit was muttered under his breath. No point adding insult to injury.

Rubbing a hand over his lined face, Hank turned once more to the younger man. "Listen, Caleb, I know you've got the ability to continue Orion's training, but we're going to need someone who can show him this coming season, too. You're just too damn busy. You know how much time it takes. Do you really want to give up your practice to train and show him? After all these years of hard work? I know it's frustrating to watch these riders get on Orion and make a hash of it, but there's got to be somebody out there." He grimaced as he turned to observe the rider circling around the ring on the horse that was his and Caleb's pride and joy. "Preferably someone with a modicum of talent. That's what we need if we want Orion to win and be sought after as a stud. Look, I'll start calling around. Get out some mailings. Maybe we'll get lucky."

"The hell of it is, even if we find someone halfway

decent, Pamela will probably come up with a way to nix it. Jesus," he bit out in frustration as he raked his fingers through his thick, dark brown hair. "You'd think she *wants* Orion to end up finishing last in every class, the way she keeps shoving these nobodies down our throats. Damn her and her lawyers."

Hank made no reply, knowing Caleb would brush aside words of sympathy. The boy had been chastising himself over the debacle of his marriage and his divorce for far too long now. He watched Caleb's eyes flash with self-contempt and the lines around his mouth deepen as if forcing down a bitter taste.

Caleb leaned his tall body into the fence, shoved his hands in his faded jeans' pockets, and considered his friend's advice. As a rational argument, Caleb knew Hank was right, that they should once again resume the tedious process of trying out potential riders for the stallion. Perhaps this time they might luck out and find someone gifted enough to ride Orion. But as Caleb lifted his head and watched his stallion take a large double-oxer in an effortless leap, resentment and anger filled him. Because of his appalling lack of judgement, his stallion, a horse he had helped foal, had helped train, a horse filled with such incredible potential was, figuratively speaking, being left to rot. Such a stupid waste.

For the thousandth time, Caleb cursed the day he laid eyes on Pamela, his ex-wife.

But to give up would mean that Pamela had won whatever twisted game she was playing. No way would he let her have that satisfaction, too. Technically, she might be the owner of Orion, but Orion was Caleb's horse, one hundred percent. Come hell or high water, he was determined to regain rightful ownership of his stallion. And when that day came, Caleb intended for that slip of paper the lawyers and the judge had written, giving Pamela full ownership of Orion, to have as much value as a piece of

toilet paper. Then Pamela could stick it where the sun
didn't shine.

"Okay, Hank, we'll do it your way," he agreed finally.
"Find another rider to give it a go. But make sure he knows
how to ride a spirited stallion like Orion." Caleb shook his
head skeptically. "I hope to hell we can find someone with
balls enough to do it."

1

As Cassie Miller drove the Jeep Wagoneer down the sloping hill that led to the farm's driveway, she caught herself chanting, "I think I can, I think I can." Glancing ruefully at her reflection in the rearview mirror, she prayed that her nervousness wouldn't ruin her interview.

The entrance to the driveway was marked by the sign Five Oaks. Pulling in, she steered the Jeep over to the side of the well-graded dirt road, cut the engine, and twisted around to face the backseat.

"Okay, kids, time for a face and hands check." Two small children looked back at her with matching deep blue eyes and golden curls. They waited expectantly.

"All right, you guys, stick 'em up!" Cassie said in her best James Cagney voice. The two giggling five-year-olds raised their hands to the level of the front seat and showed them to Cassie for inspection. Cassie took Jamie's and then Sophie's, examining each in turn.

"Excellent! We've got two clean pairs of hands here. Now, Jamie, how many fingers have you got? We don't want any missing."

Jamie looked down, wiggling his fingers. "One, two,

three, four, five," he began and rushed on, "six, seven, eight, nine, ten!"

"That's terrific. Now I know you'll be able to shake hands politely with Mr. and Mrs. Sawyer."

"What about me?" clamored Sophie, eager to be included in the game.

"Have you got ten fingers, too, Pumpkin?"

"Yes!" crowed Sophie triumphantly. "Just look!"

"Why, imagine that! You're right! What luck. You do have ten fingers." Cassie pretended to wipe her brow. "Whew! I was so worried! But what about your faces? Are those peanut butter and jelly sandwiches you had at lunch in your tummies or on your cheeks?"

"In our tummies!" cried both children, this time a little doubtfully.

"Hmm, I guess they look clean enough."

In fact, both Sophie and Jamie's faces fairly glowed, Cassie having taken the precaution of arming herself with packets of moist towelettes for the trip. She leaned over and kissed their soft cheeks, marveling once again at the beauty of her two little imps. She was so proud of them. Had been from the day they were born.

"You two certainly look smart to me. But let's make sure of one last thing. Your shoes. Are they on the right feet? We can't have you going off to an interview with shoes on the wrong feet!"

"But Mom," cried Jamie in an aggrieved tone. "*You're* the one who's gonna get the job. We're just kids."

"I don't know about that. If I get this position at Five Oaks, you two will be my assistants."

"We will?" Jamie's small voice rose with excitement.

"Of course. And I'll also need both of you to take care of Topper and Pip. Those ponies are a big responsibility."

"Yes, Mommy, we know."

"And, kids, I need you to be on your best behavior. Mr.

Sawyer was super nice about letting you two tag along while I talk with him about working here."

"We know Mommy, Uncle Alex and Thompson told us that, too."

"About a zillion times."

"No, it was a *quadrillion* times."

Cassie smiled. "Right, well, don't forget. I'm counting on you. Now that that's settled, how do *I* look? Any muck on my face?"

Now it was the children's turn to inspect Cassie. Treating the matter with utter seriousness, they leaned forward, bending at the waist to look at her more closely.

Sophie pronounced judgement. "You're the most beautiful mommy in the whole wide world!"

A bittersweet lump formed in Cassie's throat. She swallowed hard before attempting to speak.

"Thank you, Pumpkin. I love the two of you very much. You're so wonderful to me."

"But Mommy," interrupted Jamie, who already knew he didn't like gooey kisses and hugs and wanted to stop things before they got out of hand, "Your hair is coming out again."

"Oh, dear," cried Cassie in mock dismay. "Mr. and Mrs. Sawyer will just have to see the wild side of me." As a child, Cassie's hair had looked like Jamie's and Sophie's, but over the years the corkscrew curls had softened, so that now they more closely resembled riotous waves that flowed down to the middle of her back. But whenever she tried to tame it, pulling it back into a knot at the nape of her neck, as she had done for the upcoming interview, strands escaped and framed her face with golden curls.

"Well, we'd better get a move on before I lose my courage and drive us straight back to New York. I faxed the Sawyers and told them to expect us at about three o'clock. It's just three now."

Cassie turned the key in the ignition and pulled the car back onto the driveway. The farm, she already knew, was spread out over two hundred acres of prime Virginia horse country. When Cassie had seen the job announcement, offering a dual position as trainer and rider for Five Oaks, she'd immediately faxed her résumé and crossed her fingers. Professionals from all over the country would be responding to the ad.

She'd been thoroughly elated, as well as a bit astonished, when she received a call from Hank Sawyer asking her to come down for an interview.

The driveway stretched for nearly a quarter mile with white wooden-fenced pastures on either side. Cassie and the children could see horses grazing on the new grass. As they reached the horse barns, pastures gave way to riding rings with brightly colored jumps set at various heights. Behind them, Cassie noticed a large indoor ring. The driveway ended in a wide circle around which stood five enormous oaks.

Cassie parked, opened her door, then let the children out of the back. They clambered down from their seats, chattering excitedly. Cassie stood silently, taking a moment to gaze at the beauty of her surroundings.

There were four barns in all, two attached together to form a T shape with the third one off to the side. As Five Oaks was a breeding farm, Cassie assumed that the separate barn was used for the brood mares. A fourth barn was set off at a distance. She noted with approval the pristine condition of the buildings. Painted white with dark green trim, they shone invitingly in the afternoon sun. Muffled noises and the occasional whickering of horses floated out on the air.

"Come on kids, take my hands and let's go find Mr. Sawyer."

They entered the shaded interior of the larger barn. Rows of box stalls flanked a wide concrete aisle. The barn smelled of horses, leather, hay, and creosote, a scent that was as familiar to Cassie as the smell of her own home. As familiar and as loved. Hooked up to a pair of cross ties, a large bay was being groomed by a man wearing an Orioles baseball cap. He looked to be about thirty, and from his dark olive complexion Cassie guessed him to be Mexican.

"Excuse me. Could you please tell me where I might find Hank Sawyer?" The man stopped brushing but continued to lay his hand on the horse's shoulder in a soothing gesture. A smile spread across his features when he saw the young woman holding the hands of two almost identical children.

"He's in the office. Follow this aisle down and then make a right. His office is around the corner." From the man's slight accent, Cassie knew that her guess had been right.

"Thanks a lot."

The trio moved past the horse and Cassie ducked her head under the cross ties.

"Mommy," Sophie whispered excitedly as they began walking past the long line of stalls. "Can we say hello to the horses as we go by?"

"Yes, a couple, but let's not be late for our appointment." Cassie knew only too well just how much time it might take two five-year-olds to say hi with this long a row of box stalls. Many of the horses standing with their ears cocked forward and their necks arched gracefully over the stall doors, seemed as inquisitive as the two chidren. They observed the humans' progress down the aisle toward the office.

The door to the office was shut, so Cassie let go of Jamie's hand and knocked. From within, a voice called out instructing them to come in. Cassie, Jamie, and Sophie stepped inside. Behind a large desk piled high with stacks of papers and books, a man stood and came forward to greet them.

"Hello, you must be Cassandra Miller. I'm Hank Sawyer. You're right on time. Hope the trip down from New York wasn't too exhausting."

He paused a moment, his glance lighting on the two small children standing at her side. "And what are your names?"

"Hello, Mr. Sawyer, I'm Jamie Miller." Jamie stretched out his small hand. Hank shook it with a solemn smile, his large hand engulfing the tiny one. Sophie thrust out her hand, too, determined to be as grown-up as her brother.

"Hi, Mr. Sawyer, I'm Sophie. Jamie and I are twins. He was born before me. But I can count to twenty faster." She boasted proudly.

"That's true for the moment, Sophie, but Jamie's catching up to you. I'd keep practicing." Cassie glanced at Hank Sawyer. "Thanks again, Mr. Sawyer, for letting us impose on you this way. Sophie and Jamie learned all about the Baltimore Aquarium in school this year. They were desperate to come, so we've turned the trip into a three-day cultural adventure."

"The aquarium's a fascinating place, and the harbor, too. You'll enjoy it. We've taken our grandchildren there quite a few times. Just let me telephone my wife so that she knows you've arrived." Hank turned to his desk and picked up the phone. As he dialed, he looked up, "Make yourself comfortable. On the wall over there are photographs of some of our horses."

Sophie and Jamie scrambled over to the wall to peer excitedly at the pictures of horses soaring over fences; horses standing in the judges' circle, blue ribbons hanging from their bridles; riders smiling as they leaned down to shake hands with women in sequined gowns. Cassie thought she could make out the younger features of Hank Sawyer as well as another, unidentified man.

As she waited quietly while Hank spoke into the phone, she took the opportunity to observe him unobtrusively. He

looked to be somewhere between fifty-five and sixty. His
full head of hair was silver, cut short to reveal the strong
bones of the face. It was a kind and open one, with laugh
lines bracketing the corners of his mouth. The lines etched
into his brow and the deep gold tone of his skin, even this
early in spring, attested to the hours he spent under the sun.
Cassie liked the way his eyes had crinkled up at the corners
when he'd smiled at Sophie and Jamie. She'd also seen the
shrewdness and intelligence in them, something she'd
expected to find. One couldn't survive in the horse business, let alone run such a clearly successful establishment
as Five Oaks, without those qualities.

She hoped Hank was also a bit of a gambler, that he'd
be willing to take a chance on her.

Hank interrupted Cassie's thoughts. "Melissa will be
here in just a few minutes. She was wondering whether the
kids might be interested in a snack."

"That's very kind of you. For the moment though, they
seem pretty taken with your photo gallery. I noticed you
rode at Devon, Mr. Sawyer."

"Call me Hank. Everyone does. I hardly know who
they're talking about when I hear Mr. Sawyer." His gaze
skimmed the photographs on the wall. "Yes, a couple of
those pictures are from Devon. I'm just glad I wasn't riding
against you when those were taken."

At Cassie's startled look, Hank smiled and continued,
"Of course you didn't realize this, but I saw you compete
both at Devon and Washington the year you were racking
up points to qualify for the national team. You were
amazing. And the way you handled that stallion, On The
Mark, was incredible. You were what, barely nineteen,
and you could hardly have weighed more than one hundred and ten, but had him flying over those fences in
the jump-off as if he were a merry-go-round pony in
Mary Poppins."

The image of On The Mark being like a carousel ride

brought a wide grin to Cassie's face. "He was a great horse, a great teacher. I was lucky to ride him so early on in my career. He taught me how to listen. And he taught me how important it is to figure out what makes each horse tick. In On The Mark's case, it was his pride."

"Interesting. How did you come to that conclusion?"

Cassie's hands lifted, gesturing as she explained. "He had such natural ability and he *knew* it. He was a cocky son of a gun. I realized that it really bothered him if he even so much as nicked a fence. He hated it, it threw off his whole performance. So I did my darndest to set him up perfectly for each and every fence. Then I tried not to mess around too much and let him do the rest of the work. By the end of that season, he was in a class by himself. Nobody could beat him."

"Well, when I got your résumé, your name rang a bell. It didn't take long to remember what you achieved with that horse. Those were some remarkable rides, Cassandra."

She felt a blush stain her cheeks. "Thank you. And please call me Cass or Cassie. I don't think I've quite grown into Cassandra yet."

That might be true enough. Although he knew from her résumé that Cassie Miller was twenty-four, there was a youthfulness to her face, especially with that charming blush that made her look hardly out of her teens.

Far too young to be the mother of five-year-old twins.

But the children looked a lot like her, he noted. Deep blue eyes and blond curly hair. It was like seeing the finished product when you looked first at the twins and then at Cassie. Even though Cassie's hair was pulled back from her face, accentuating her wide, high cheekbones and her full lips, he figured that in about ten years, Sophie would be a close copy of her mother. Jamie, too, looked like he would be equally good looking.

Cassie Miller stood an easy five foot eight—good, she'll be big enough to handle Orion—and her body looked strong and fit. His glance next took in the long legs and well-defined arms revealed by the ribbed cotton top she wore under her jumper.

Hank would have been deeply embarrassed if someone had pointed out to him that he was cataloging Cassie's attributes much as he might a horse he was interested in acquiring. But he would probably have argued that he had no use for a rider who wasn't physically up to the challenge of riding their stallion, any more than he would be interested in purchasing a swaybacked, knock-kneed horse. Luckily, she had the look of a rider who kept her body in peak condition.

Hank motioned for her to take one of the seats near his desk as they waited for his wife. As Cassie rested her elbows against the wooden arms of the chair, Hank noticed there was no wedding band on her left hand. Interesting.

He was on the verge of broaching the awkward topic of why Cassie Miller's bid for the national team had come to a disappointing nothing, when his wife, Melissa, and their housekeeper, Mrs. Harris, came into the office. As he stood up to greet the women, he gave his wife a fond smile.

Melissa had been his wife for thirty years and Hank loved her even more now than he had when they first married. She was his mate, partner, best friend, and his lover. She was also as good a judge of human character as she was of horseflesh. Hank wanted Melissa here for the interview with Cassie. Even with her excellent résumé and the memory of her skill with horses, Cassie was nevertheless something of an enigma.

Why hadn't she continued competing, trying for the national team? After the Olympics, being a member of the U.S. equestrian team was most riders' greatest ambition, so what had prevented her? Riders with the kind of talent and skill she had just didn't drop off the face of the earth without a trace. As Hank remembered it, after that dazzling year, Cassie had vanished from the show circuit as if her

season as the hot young rider to beat was just a dream. The
question had been bugging him ever since he'd recognized
her name at the top of her résumé.

He glanced at the twins, considering.

No, not even a pregnancy should have kept her away
from the circuit for so long. Pregnancy would have side-
lined her for a year, eighteen months at most, but she'd disappeared and hadn't come back. He wondered if perhaps
the twins' father might have tried to discourage Cassie in
her riding career, but if that was the case, what was she
doing applying for the job at Five Oaks?

Thank heaven for Melissa. Hank had no doubt that a
few subtle questions from his wife would provide them
with answers to whatever had been going on in Cassie
Miller's life.

2

$\mathcal{H}$ank introduced Melissa and Mrs. Harris first to Cassie and then to the twins, who were still inspecting the photographs on the wall, arguing quietly between themselves over which horse they would most like to ride.

Melissa Sawyer listened to the heated debate for a moment, a smile playing across her lips. Crouching down to the level of their faces, she managed to draw their attention.

"Well, aren't you big kids! You seem to know so much about horses. It must have taken you a long time, years and years. Let me guess, you must be seven years old. No, you're only five?" She shook her head as if in disbelief. "I can't believe how very grown-up you are."

Cassie smiled as she saw Sophie and Jamie's faces light up at Melissa's compliment.

"You know, Mrs. Harris just finished baking some chocolate chip cookies. I was going to bring them over but they're still a bit hot, and I thought you might enjoy a glass of lemonade. If you'd like, Mrs. Harris can take you up to the house and you can have your snack there. Then, when your Mommy's finished talking to us, we can take a tour of the stables. I'll show you my favorites."

Jamie and Sophie looked up at their mother for permission. A smile and a nod from her had them scampering off with Mrs. Harris, already chattering like magpies.

"Thanks for providing such a delicious diversion for the children. At times I think they're all mouths. When they're not talking, they're eating so much I get a stomachache watching them. I have to warn you, though, you probably won't have anything but crumbs left for tonight. Jamie and Sophie are regular vacuum cleaners when it comes to freshly baked cookies."

"Oh, don't worry about that. Hank and I eat far too many cookies as it is." She reached up to give her husband a kiss on the cheek. "I thought maybe it would be easier to talk if there were just the three of us."

Cassie nodded in agreement. "Once Jamie and Sophie start talking, it's like being caught on a runaway train."

"Five-year-olds can be like that. They're beautiful, your twins. They must have kept you quite busy when they were born."

Hank hid a smile. This was vintage Melissa. Smooth and easy, she conducted a nice, friendly inquisition. Most people never stood a chance once she got them talking. He'd lay odds his wife was as curious as he to find out more about this young woman with the two adorable children. He even suspected she'd already looked at Cassie's ring finger and noticed it was bare. It hadn't taken him all that long, and Melissa was a woman. They always seemed to zoom in on things like that. Detail oriented, or something like that. If he'd had to ask Cassie these personal questions, he would have felt like a bull in a china shop. He was more than happy to let his wife take over.

Just then, he caught Cassie taking a deep breath, as if bolstering herself. Like she realized full well what sorts of questions Melissa might ask. Abruptly he decided he wanted to make her as comfortable as possible.

"Uh, why don't we all sit down. Here, Cassie, take this chair; Melissa, you can sit in this one."

Cassie lowered herself gracefully into the canvas director's chair opposite Hank's. A hesitant smile lifted the corners of her mouth. "Yes, well actually, Mrs. Sawyer—oh, thank you—Melissa, Sophie and Jamie aren't my natural children. I adopted them. They were my brother Tom's and my sister-in-law Lisa's. When Sophie and Jamie were only ten months old, their parents died, along with my father."

"Oh dear, how dreadful! What happened?"

"There was an accident. I was in college at the time. Tom and Lisa were living in Princeton, New Jersey. Christmas was just a week away. Tom had invited Dad to stay with them for the holidays. Our mother had died several years earlier, and Lisa and Tom wanted Dad to share Christmas with his only grandchildren. I was invited, too, but was planning on joining them Christmas Eve. I was busy getting ready for a trip down to Florida to compete in some shows before the second semester started. Our other brother, Alex, couldn't make it. He'd just started his job at a Wall Street firm that fall. They were working him like a dog. He didn't even think he was going to get Christmas Eve off."

Hank and Melissa didn't bother interrupting Cassie's rambling narrative. It was clear from the tense expression on her face that the death of her brother, father, and sister-in-law was still far too traumatic.

With an effort, Cassie pulled her thoughts together. There were very few times she wished she smoked cigarettes, but this was definitely one of them.

"It happened on Route 1 as they were driving back to their home in New Jersey. An eighteen-wheeler was in the next lane over. The driver fell asleep. Truckers have to log so many miles . . ." Cassie's voice faltered. Hank glanced down at her hands. They were knotted tightly in her lap, the knuckles white under her skin.

"The truck went out of control, careening directly into Tom's car. There was no time to avoid a collision. The force of the impact sent Tom's car through the guardrail, into the oncoming traffic. Another couple were killed besides Tom, Lisa, and Dad. They were in the car that Tom crashed into . . ." Cassie's piercing blue eyes lifted, meeting the Sawyers' sympathetic gaze. "I hate to admit it, but sometimes I wish the truckdriver had died, too. He came out of that wreck with a severe concussion and several broken ribs. A night in the hospital and he was home."

"I'm sure that's a perfectly natural reaction, Cassie. How could you not feel that way toward the person responsible for taking the lives of three members of your family?" Melissa reasoned gently. "I know that if something like this had happened to Hank and our children, I would have tried to strangle the man with my bare hands, deserving or not."

Cassie smiled gratefully at Melissa. Distractedly she combed her fingers through her hair, loosening more strands from her chignon. "You're right, of course. Alex and Thompson both said the same thing. And the truckdriver was filled with grief and remorse over the accident. For a long time he kept calling and writing letters. That almost made it worse."

Hank drew a hand over his face, wishing he could wipe away the harrowing images from his mind. No wonder Cassie Miller had dropped out of sight from the horse show circuit.

"It was a blessing the babies weren't in the car, too."

"Yes. My father had invited Tom and Lisa to go to the opera with him. Dad was a big opera buff. That's why they were driving back to Princeton so late. Jamie and Sophie were at home with the live-in nanny and housekeeper, Bessie Thompson." Cassie gave a small smile. "Thompson—she hates being called Bessie—says it makes her feel like a cow and that at her age that's a double curse: to be old and a cow. Ridiculous, but I'll do just about anything to make her happy. She and Alex really pulled me through some bad times."

Cassie stopped for a minute and gave the older couple a wry smile. "Sorry, I realize this is a somewhat unusual interview. I doubt you expected to hear such a sob story when you asked me down here. But I thought it best to tell you about the accident." Her blue eyes met Hank's squarely. "Since you saw me compete, you've doubtless been wondering why I stopped riding just when I was so close to earning a spot on the national team."

Hank's head nodded in silent confirmation.

"My plan had been to see just how far On The Mark and I could go. We'd had a great season in the Northeast, and I'd been looking forward to the winter circuit in Florida. And some people I'd met wanted me to show their horses down there. But then suddenly, in the space of twelve hours, I had two beautiful ten-month-old twins." Her lips curved. "Looking back, I can only thank God Sophie and Jamie weren't identical. That would have been a real mess!"

Melissa and Hank laughed, wanting to put her at ease, still stunned by her tragic story.

"How terribly sad for all of you. It must have been difficult becoming a mother without any warning," Melissa offered sympathetically.

"Boy, you can say that again! I knew absolutely *nothing* about kids. There were moments after the accident when I wished I hadn't been bitten by the horse bug so early and had spent a little time during my early teens babysitting. Instead, I knew textbooks worth about equine management, yet I couldn't even put on Jamie's diaper properly! When Jamie and Sophie were newborns, I'd held them in my arms and watched Lisa nurse them, but I was in school, caught up in my riding, and all my spare time was devoted to being with my fiancé, Brad. We'd only recently gotten engaged."

Melissa was taken aback when Cassie's delicate features hardened at the word *fiancé*. She'd already noticed the absence of a wedding ring. Had Cassie's engagement, like the rest of her life, taken a sudden and unpleasant turn?

It was amazing how in the short space of fifteen minutes since she had met this young woman Melissa already liked Cassie more than anyone she'd encountered in a long time. From listening to her recount her story, Melissa had learned enough to know Cassie was caring and resilient. Someone who took her responsibilities seriously. If Hank considered her a good enough trainer to work with their horses and a good enough rider to handle Orion, Melissa would do everything she could to ensure she was offered the job at Five Oaks.

Yes, there was something special about Cassie. It had taken courage and strength to tell a tale that tragic to strangers. Cassie had spoken with the kind of dignity that made Melissa want to get to know her even better. Melissa had an intuitive feeling that Cassie would mature into an exceptional woman.

What bothered her, however, was the very wrong note that had sounded when Cassie had mentioned her fiancé, Brad. What had happened between the two of them?

Melissa had always prided herself on knowing when to respect a person's privacy, but this time she was going to succumb to her curiosity, or nosiness, as she was sure Hank would call it. She justified herself with the thought that it was important to know whether this Brad person would play a role in Cassie's decision to accept the position at Five Oaks. So she excused her rudeness at broaching what was obviously an awkward topic.

"I suppose you and your fiancé decided to postpone the wedding until your life was more settled?" As prying went, this lacked subtlety, but Melissa decided a certain amount of directness might prove the easiest path to take.

She didn't need to glance over at Hank to realize he was frowning warningly at her. After three decades of marriage, Hank and Melissa knew each other's thoughts as well as they knew their own. Hank clearly felt that Cassie had already revealed quite enough of her personal life.

Cassie fell silent as she wondered how to describe the aching disappointment, the sense of betrayal she experienced at Brad Gibson's hands. She'd never told anyone the whole story. And however much she instinctively liked and trusted the Sawyers, she wasn't ready to reveal its full ugliness. Not yet, anyway. Maybe never.

She'd met Brad at college in the fall of her sophomore year. Brad, a senior economics major, was bright and ambitious, with plans to enter law school the next year. Boyishly handsome, he'd been a campus star, popular with his frat brothers, and with a grade point average that all but guaranteed his acceptance at any of the law schools to which he was applying.

Cassie had fallen for him hard. When she remembered the depth of her infatuation, she consoled herself with the knowledge that she'd been only nineteen, far too naive and sheltered because of her commitment to her riding.

Brad had been Cassie's first serious boyfriend, and her first lover. His blond good looks, his Connecticut upbringing, his prep school education exuded sophistication. His self-assured charm had dazzled Cassie completely. At the time, Cassie remembered bitterly, Brad had seemed equally enamored of her. And when he'd proposed, Cassie had been radiant with happiness.

Looking back now, Cassie was immensely grateful to her father. He'd insisted upon a long engagement for the couple, that they wait until Cassie, too, graduated for the wedding to take place. How disastrous it would have been if she and Brad had actually married.

She still had difficulty comprehending the underlying roots of Brad's behavior. What she knew for certain was that after the accident, Brad changed. Unfortunately, however, Cassie was oblivious at first. Shock, grief, and the need to be with her family—with Alex, Jamie, and Sophie—were overwhelming. And by the time Cassie began to resurface from the depths of her loss, Brad's feelings had . . . cooled. The quaintness of that expression made Cassie shudder inside. The reality had been to watch, stunned into helplessness, as her lover transformed himself into a selfish stranger.

As Brad's sullenness and increasing coldness became more pronounced, Cassie'd repeatedly tried to talk to him, to get him to explain why he was so unhappy. But it had been like talking to a brick wall. He insisted he still loved her, still wished to marry her, but the words sounded empty and mechanical. Illumination had come one miserable afternoon in February, revealing to Cassie the real target of Brad's hostility. When later it was all too bluntly confirmed, the disillusionment tore at her heart.

Cassie had been unable to confide in anyone what transpired between her and Brad. When she informed Alex and Thompson that the engagement was off, Cassie's expression alone was enough for them to gauge the depth of her hurt. They let her be, allowing Cassie to choose when, if ever, to reveal the details. After all the sorrow they had suffered, Alex and Thompson knew that some pain had to be dealt with privately.

Looking at Hank and Melissa now, Cassie again chose to keep Brad's cruel words to herself. Not for anything would she permit them to sully her two children by speaking them aloud. Instead, she opted for the same clichéd version she recited whenever the need arose, eager to rid herself of thoughts of Brad.

"Some things in our relationship made me realize that Brad wasn't ready yet for both marriage and children. It was too big an adjustment. Once that became clear, and I saw it wouldn't have been fair to any of us to go through with the marriage plans, I broke off the engagement."

Cassie missed the look Melissa and Hank exchanged as well as the muttered "son of a bitch" that tumbled from Hank's lips. The Sawyers had reached their own conclusion about Cassie's ex-fiancé, independent of her carefully worded explanation.

"In a way, I'm really grateful things didn't work out. Our breakup made me rethink my priorities. I filed for Jamie and Sophie's adoption on my own. Then, after I graduated, Sam Waters hired me as an assistant trainer at his stable in Long Island. As you know from my résumé, Hank, I've been with him for almost two years. My dream of competing on the national team hasn't completely evaporated. Who knows, maybe I'll be able to ride full time on the circuit now that the kids are older." Cassie shrugged her shoulders. "It's hard to anticipate, I guess. But I'd really like a chance at this job if you think I'm right for it."

"I spoke with him on the phone yesterday, and he had nothing but praises for you. That's saying a lot, coming from a man like Waters." And now Hank understood better why Sam Waters had been so closemouthed about Cassie's personal background. "Well, I think we've covered everything we need to for now. Why don't we take a tour of the barns. We've got a stallion here I think you're going to be really interested in. After you've seen Orion, we can talk some more."

Melissa stood up and placed a light kiss on Hank's mouth as she hugged him, her heart filled with pride. Hank was clearly taken with Cassie. She turned, keeping one arm looped around Hank's waist and laid her other hand on Cassie's forearm. "Why don't I go see whether those two cookie monsters of yours have left any crumbs for the rest of us. I'll give them a private tour of the barns while you and Hank go see our baby."

3

This was some *baby*. Cassie looked at the dark bay stallion grazing in the far pasture and whistled softly.

"Wow! That's a fine looking horse you've got there."

"Isn't he? That's Orion. He was born here, and is the principal reason why I'd like to hire you. He's the product of the considerable talent of Caleb Wells, my partner."

"Your partner?"

"Yeah, I'm lucky to have him. Caleb's a vet. He specialized in equine medicine in school. Always loved working with horses, ever since he was a kid. Even before he finished veterinary school and started his own practice in town, I asked him if he'd consider working with me on Five Oaks's breeding program. He spent months researching bloodlines for Orion's dam and sire. Everything we've been aiming for in the crossbreed is all there in Orion. Caleb's really attached to him."

Cassie's eyes pored over the stallion grazing in the distance. Excitement was buzzing through her. "Mmm, I can understand why," she offered, unwilling to take her eyes off the horse. "You said he was a vet?"

"Yeah, and a good one at that," Hank replied, the pride

in his voice clear. "It was rough going for a while after he graduated, working full-time as a vet and spending all his extra time here. But in just a few years, he built up his reputation enough so that he had a solid clientele, large enough so he could invite some other vets into the practice. Now he works half-time there and half-time here." Hank gave a small chuckle. "'Course, that means he works about fourteen-hour days. Orion was the first of our babies. He's real special to us. I'll introduce you to Caleb later."

Hank didn't bother to add that he thought Cassie was going to be a bit of a shock for Caleb, an unpleasant one at that. Cassie would find that out all too soon. Ever since his marriage ended in divorce, Caleb had been pure hell on the female sex. Hank was getting a bit fed up watching Caleb go through women like they were disposable razors. Use 'em and toss 'em.

Well, Cassie and Caleb were simply going to have to learn to deal with each other, because Hank knew in his gut that Cassie was the rider for Orion.

"He's big," she murmured. Hardly a word Hank had spoken had registered; Cassie was too busy examining the horse before her. A gorgeous dark bay with four white stockings and a white blaze down his face. "What is he, about 16.3 hands?"

"Actually, he's 17.1 hands. He's bigger up close. He's half Thoroughbred, half Selle Français. Seven years old. Caleb and I want to build a stock of jumpers that have a more solid frame than pure Thoroughbreds. We're going for strength and speed. Our aim is to produce right here at Five Oaks the type of horse that up to now has been found primarily in Europe."

"And you've started showing him." Cassie's eyes were still glued to the magnificent piece of horseflesh.

"Yeah. That's the problem. Conformation's excellent, his bloodlines are top notch. But Caleb and I want people to see him in action. To see how versatile he is. We started showing him last year, but we've never gotten a rider who clicked with him, really tapped his potential." *And Caleb's ex-wife, Pamela, has done everything in her power to keep it that way,* Hank added silently. *For the moment, the less Cassie knew about that particular mess, the better.*

"Here, let's bring him in so you can take a closer look. He's an unbelievable horse, Cassie. Caleb and I are pinning our hopes on him. We think he's got the potential to be Grand Prix material. He's strong, powerful, moves like a dream, jumps just about everything we've shown him so far, and he's smart as hell. Maybe too smart."

Cassie turned her head to look at Hank. "What do you mean?"

"He plays games with his riders. He doesn't suffer fools, and unfortunately, most of the riders we've gotten have been just that. None of them with brains enough to figure out how to stay on him. So Orion teases them. Lulls them into thinking they've got him figured out. Then, whammo! He shifts his weight in mid-air, or takes a fence way too early, and the next thing they know, they're lying face down in the mud. And I swear to God, Orion's laughing his head off." He paused to scratch the back of his neck. "I tell you, it's really hard to place in those jumper classes when his riders can't stay on his back."

She laughed. "Yeah, I've noticed. But he's not unwilling or mean?"

"No, it's not that. I've seen plenty of mean-tempered stallions. Absolute devils. No, I think Orion is just waiting for the right challenge, the right rider. Maybe he's bored."

"Then I guess it'll be my job to entertain him!" Cassie replied with a grin. "I can't wait to try him out. Would you mind if I popped back to my car for a minute? I've got my breeches and boots in the back."

"Sure. Change in the office if you like. I'll grab Orion and meet you in that barn over there." Hank pointed to the smaller barn located in the distance.

"Great. See you in a few minutes."

Cassie ran off to the Jeep, opened the back and grabbed her gearbag, as Hank went off to get a lead rope to bring in Orion. On her way back to his office, excitement bubbled up inside her. *I've got to be dreaming! This is too good to be true! Please, God, let me be able to ride Orion like nobody's business.*

Caleb detested beepers, but he figured they were an unavoidable fact of a vet's life. He'd arrived at Five Oaks barely five minutes ago, and already he was turning around to go back to his car phone and call in. He punched in the number.

"Joyce? Yeah, this is Caleb. What's up? Okay, tell them I'll be there in fifteen minutes and tell Matt I'll need him for the anesthesia. See you in a bit." With an oath, Caleb replaced the phone and ran toward the barn.

Cassie dropped her bag on the floor of Hank's office and unzipped her dress. She'd worn it to look neat and professional, but mainly because Sophie had badgered her incessantly, saying she looked so pretty. *No one like a determined five-year-old to wear you down,* Cassie thought ruefully. Unfortunately, her young daughter's taste in clothes didn't exactly mesh with Cassie's, at least when it came to work clothes. When she was around horses, she hated dressing in anything but jeans or breeches. She was eager to change. She could feel the adrenaline at the prospect of riding Orion thrumming through her as she lifted the hem of the dress up and over her head, pulling her cotton shirt up along with it in an effort to hurry. She'd almost gotten them off when the metal hook on her dress snagged a clump of her curls.

Caleb pushed open the office door and strode in, in a hurry to tell Hank that he'd try to see him later, after he'd performed the emergency surgery. He was already speaking as he entered the room, the door swinging shut behind him.

"Hank, I've got to head back right away. The Holmes's cat got attacked by a dog. Ripped it open. A royal mess, but perhaps I—" He stopped abruptly, staring transfixed at the sight before him.

God, he loved that shade of pink in a woman's panties. Made him think of strawberries and cream. Her legs must be a mile long. Caleb let his gaze wander, taking in the gently flaring hips, the flat belly with skin as silky looking as the scrap of pink she wore, then moving up, to the rounded breasts raised and straining against matching fabric.

It was then that Caleb belatedly grasped the woman's unfortunate situation. His lips twitched as he watched her wriggle and squirm to free herself, her arms twisting and flexing, her head lost in a rumple of cotton print. It was clear from her muffled mutterings that she hadn't heard him enter. That cotton shirt must be like a huge Ace bandage wrapped around her head. *What a terrible predicament,* Caleb thought cheerfully. He took a long, last, and thoroughly appreciative inventory before clearing his throat.

"Uh, excuse me, could I be of any help?"

Cassie stilled immediately. Actually, she felt literally glued to the spot. Utter mortification swamped her. *Just great.* Her first major professional break, and she had to unveil herself in front of some groom. Summoning as much poise as she could under the circumstances, Cassie decided to play it cool.

"Uh, no thanks . . . I think I've got it." She'd raised her voice to be heard through all those layers of fabric, but it came out sounding strangled all the same—with embarrassment. She had no idea whether her blasted hair was untangled or not, but she'd sooner give herself a Mohawk than stand here for a second longer with this man watching, amusement lacing his smooth southern accent.

She tried again. "If you're looking for Hank, I believe he's in the stallion barn."

"Thanks. But, you know, I really hate to leave you here like this. You sure I can't help? Maybe hold the dress up for you?"

Cassie gritted her teeth. Hysteria was imminent, guaranteed, if this jerk didn't get out right now. "No, no, I'm fine. Will you please just leave!"

"Well," Caleb drawled, the word easing slowly through his lips. "If that's what you want." He grinned at the blush that was stealing over her collarbone. Her face must be the color of a fire hydrant by now, he thought with unholy amusement. He couldn't resist torturing her just a bit more. "I hope we'll be seeing more of each other in the near future."

He turned, heading for the door, pausing one last time with his hand on the knob. "By the way, you're a real knockout. See you around, Slim."

The door shut behind him with a soft click. Caleb left the barn, chuckling to himself. Holy Mother of God, what a body. Too bad he hadn't gotten a chance to see her face. No way could it be as great as the rest of her. . . . A shame, but what the hell, he decided philosophically, he'd just keep his eyes focused on her neck on down and he'd be in heaven.

Shit, he'd forgotten to ask her name. Caleb was certain, however, that he'd recognize her again anywhere. Then he'd make sure they were properly introduced.

Caleb glanced at his wristwatch. Entertaining and pleasurable as the encounter with his little stripper had been, Caleb had used up the five minutes he'd had to spare ogling instead of talking to Hank. He'd have to catch up with him later and find out how the search for their new rider was progressing. Caleb yanked his truck door open, climbed in, gunned the motor, and was gone.

Within three minutes, Cassie was fully dressed in her breeches and field boots. She stared balefully at the tangled clump of hair attached to her dress. The spot on her head still stung like the dickens. What a way to go prematurely bald. She shoved her clothes into her bag, muttering a few choice words about creeps who barged into rooms without knocking. As silently as possible, she opened the door of the office, cautiously peeping her head out. She wouldn't put it past that jerk to be hanging around, waiting to humiliate her further. To her relief, she saw the corridor was empty and hurried on outside. Now she just had to hope he wasn't in the rear barn talking to Hank.

On the way to the stallion's barn, Cassie dropped her gear bag into the Jeep and exchanged it for her saddle. Propping it against her hip, she continued on, eager to meet her new mount.

"If it's okay with you, Hank, I'd like to school Orion on the longe line, first. It'll give me a chance to see how he moves. Then I'll hop on him for a bit, find out how we feel about each other."

"Sure, that'd be fine. Let him work off some steam, too."

"Another goal I had in mind."

She and Hank had already groomed Orion. Whenever time permitted, Cassie preferred to work with her mounts herself rather than having one of the stablehands take over. It helped forge bonds between rider and mount, and she learned far more about the horses she rode when she worked with them on the ground as well as in the saddle.

Already, Cassie was impressed by how well-mannered Orion seemed to be, standing quietly at the cross ties, waiting to be saddled. Plenty of stallions were just too unmanageable to work around without extra grooms helping. She had to give credit to Hank and this Caleb person. They must have begun handling him as a young foal to have him this well behaved as a mature stallion. "Let's get his tack on, Cassie, and then we'll take him out." Hank threw her a boyish grin and disappeared into the tack room to fetch Orion's bridle and a longe line. Taking the opportunity to give Orion a final going over with a soft brush, she watched the stallion's muscles ripple beneath his glossy coat.

As she brushed, she spoke quietly to the horse, giving him a chance to hear her voice's tone and timber. "What a beauty you are, Orion. I think you and I are going to do just fine together."

She reached for her saddle, propped against the stall wall, and laid the fleece saddle pad over the gentle slope of the withers. Next came the saddle, but Cassie realized that her girth would never get around a horse of this size.

"Hank," she called, "could you grab his girth, too? Mine's way too short."

She didn't have to wait long. Hank returned, his hands full of leather and cotton webbing. "Here you go, grab the bridle, I'll tighten the girth."

Cassie relieved Hank of Orion's bridle and unsnapped the cross ties from his leather halter. With the ease of practiced movements, she slipped the bridle's reins over his neck and unbuckled the halter. Stretching sideways, she hung it on a nearby hook and then lifted the bridle to his head, the bit resting against the flat of her palm as she pressed it to Orion's muzzle. Orion took the bit without hesitating and Cassie praised him in her low, gentle voice. She stroked his nose and brought the reins back over his neck as Hank joined her side.

As Cassie and Hank led the stallion toward the exercise ring, she noticed Melissa and Mrs. Harris standing with Sophie and Jamie at the far end of the ring. *Oh great, a peanut gallery. I hope I don't land on my head in the middle of the ring.*

While Cassie wasn't thrilled by an audience, she knew she needn't be concerned that the twins would distract her or make any noises that might cause Orion to spook. They'd been around horses so much now that they already conducted themselves like miniprofessionals. Cassie had drilled into them the importance of proper behavior around horses. Moreover, the twins knew that if they didn't behave, they wouldn't have the pleasure of riding their ponies, Pip and Topper, for a long time.

After they'd entered the ring, Hank turned to make sure the gate was securely closed behind them. Standing next to each other, Cassie eased the longe tape so that Orion could walk in increasingly wider circles around them.

Her eyes fixed on the stallion as he moved. She offered short, telegraphic comments. "Nice carriage. I like the way he studies his surroundings. Seems confident and alert." Hank merely grunted in agreement. Both were far more interested in studying the horse than in talking right now.

Cassie let Orion walk in the circle around them for a few minutes before she lowered the line slightly, gave the whip a quick flick, and spoke to the stallion in a clear carrying voice, asking him to trot.

God, he moves beautifully on the flat. That back's so nice and rounded, Cassie thought to herself. *If he's a klutz over fences, maybe I can convince Hank to try him as a dressage prospect. On the other hand, if he's as good in the air, I'm going to be riding a champion.*

Impatient as she was to get on Orion's back, Cassie nonetheless finished his longeing session, asking the stallion to canter, and then repeating the process once more in the opposite direction.

"Let's bring him in so that you can get on him. I don't want you losing the light when you jump."

Cassie looked at Hank, then at the sun's distance from the horizon, surprise showing on her face. "Sorry. I lost track of time. He's so gorgeous, I could stand here for hours watching."

A small laugh escaped her lips as she approached

Orion, reeling in the longe line as she walked. "And the way I'm feeling now, so pumped, it's like I have x-ray vision. Everything's crystal clear. I can't believe a little thing like the sun setting would make a shred of difference!"

Hank smiled. "Well, let's not take any chances. I want you and Orion to get on like hotcakes." *That'll make it a hell of a lot easier for me when I tell Caleb I've hired you,* he added to himself, *'cause the shit sure is gonna hit the fan then.*

Hank held the reins lightly while Cassie lifted her left foot and placed it in the stirrup. She swung herself up in a graceful, fluid movement, gathering the slack in her reins as soon as her right leg was over the saddle. Hank stood watching her a moment before ducking under the ring to join Melissa and the others.

"Hello, love," Hank said softly as he gave Melissa a kiss on the forehead. He looped an arm around her waist. "You never got a chance to see Cassie ride at any shows, did you?"

Melissa smiled at him, shaking her head.

"If she hasn't lost her touch, you're in for a treat. She looks damn fine on Orion, doesn't she? Question is, whether she's still got it?" A small laugh escaped him when both Sophie and Jamie turned and shushed him, their fingers pressed to their mouths. No idle chitchat to break their mother's concentration permitted.

Properly chastised, Hank and Melissa watched silently as Cassie began Orion on flat work. Yes, thought Hank. This is what we need. A rider with a great classic style, quiet hands, and the athleticism and agility to match Orion. He watched with intense satisfaction as Cassie took Orion through his paces: gradually increasing the complexity of her demands; extending his trot; moving him into a controlled, steady canter; bringing him to a halt within a matter of steps. They looked natural together.

Hank reentered the ring as Cassie reined Orion to a walk. She patted his neck enthusiastically. "Good going, Orion." Cassie believed in always letting her mount know she was grateful for the ride. And Orion was definitely a great ride. "Hank, which fences do you want me to try him on? How high has he been jumping, by the way?"

"Height's never been a problem with Orion so far. I'll set them at around four feet. I don't care so much about how high he goes right now as I do seeing you jump him over a variety of combinations and distances."

Cassie and Hank decided on a number of fences, schooling Orion first over one or two and then adding on more with each attempt. After the first couple of jumps, bubbles of excitement had him rocking on the balls of his feet. Whoa there, he cautioned himself. Let's see what happens with the trickier combinations. He held his breath as Cassie took Orion over a double-oxer, a wall jump, a roll back, and then finally a triple. Hank remembered that it was the triple combination that had, literally, thrown Orion's last rider so many times.

As Cassie cleared the last three fences, Hank heard the excited gasps of Melissa, the twins, and Mrs. Harris. Cassie had balanced Orion beautifully for the last three jumps, setting him up so that with each takeoff, Orion soared like a bird in flight. After she'd landed her last jump, she reined Orion to a walk. Hank could hardly stop from grinning like an idiot.

Melissa had latched onto his arm, squeezing it to death, talking excitedly. "She's fantastic. Gosh, she looks so young and fragile. Orion's other riders were all strong men, but they had as much luck staying on as Humpty Dumpty!"

"That's the wonderful thing about riding," Hank replied, his face still stretched in a wide smile. "It doesn't depend on brute strength. In fact, now that I've seen Cassie ride, I realize that's probably where the other riders were making their mistakes. Stupid of me not to catch it earlier."

At Melissa's puzzled expression, Hank explained. "They were trying to muscle Orion over the fences. Consciously or not, they probably thought a big horse needs big-time muscling. Orion simply showed them that they were fools to be pushing him around. He muscled them right back. Cassie's different. She's able to finesse it. She's got such good form and balance. And she can spot those distances for takeoff like nobody's business. That's a true gift." He paused, his glance straying once more to the young woman astride the stallion. "And I bet she could beat quite a few men in an arm-wrestle, anyway."

Hank and Melissa turned to Cassie as she rode over to the group. "Hi, kids, did you have fun with Mrs. Sawyer? Isn't this a beautiful horse? Yes, after I've gotten off, I'm sure Mr. and Mrs. Sawyer will let you pat him."

Cassie's face was glowing like a hundred-watt bulb as she addressed Hank and Melissa. "He's terrific, Hank. Smooth as a dolphin jumping through waves. Just great. You got anymore like him kicking around?"

Hank laughed. "You did good, kid. The job's yours, if you want it. I've got some other horses for you to work with, too, real promising. You can meet them later. But so far, Orion's our star. Let's cool him down."

Cassie nodded and nudged Orion forward, walking him easily around the ring. She shivered slightly and lifted her hunt cap off to wipe her brow. Now the sun was sinking behind the rolling hills and though the sky was a spectacular wash of pink, orange, and blue, the temperature was dropping. The sweat on her brow and down her back was already cooling.

Cassie inhaled deeply, enjoying the rush she always felt after a good workout. She bent slightly at the waist, rubbing her hands along the stallion's neck. Orion's ears flicked back and forth, registering every move she made, listening to her praise him. She knew she had a long way before winning Orion's trust, but at least she hadn't made a lousy first impression. *Not like with that cretin who caught her in her underwear,* Cassie thought sourly. She hoped she wouldn't run into him any time soon.

Cassie dismounted smoothly and led Orion back toward the barn. The horse's neck was arched gracefully, his ears pricked forward, his eyes alert. Still plenty of beans left in this fellow, Cassie thought. He could probably have gone another couple of rounds and still not be winded. She'd have to figure out how to use all that energy to her advantage in her training, yet keep him safe from strain or injury.

Melissa walked up to Cassie and Orion, reaching out to stroke Orion's nose affectionately. She remembered the night he'd been born, and how she, Caleb, and Hank had celebrated far into the night with champagne. It was a sweet memory. Caleb had looked so happy, the happiest he'd looked in years, especially since his marriage with Pamela had crumbled. She looked closely at Cassie and smiled as an intriguing thought crossed her mind. A little matchmaking might be in order here.

"Cassie, we'd like to invite you and the twins to dinner tonight. Just a casual family meal. Would you and the children feel up to it? It'd be an opportunity to iron out all the remaining details with you."

"We'd love to, thank you. I was planning on hunting down a diner before we returned to the bed-and-breakfast we're staying at. This would be wonderful. I've got a lot of questions for you."

"Great. Hank and you can finish up with Orion while the twins keep me company. Come on kids, let's see whether we can fix something really special for dinner."

"You mean pizza?"

"Hot dogs!"

4

*H*ank pushed his dessert plate to the side and poured some cream into his coffee. Now and again, the sound of the trumpeting of wild elephants drifted in from the den. Sophie and Jamie had been excused from the table and were watching a nature program on TV. He wasn't sure whether he could distinguish the real elephants' calls from the ones Jamie and Sophie were making. They were getting pretty good. A little more practice and the grown-ups would have to take cover. Hank grinned, remembering Cassie's adamant refusal to allow them to turn on a sitcom. It was a good thing she wasn't afraid to be strict with these two youngsters. They seemed quite a handful, if the pleading antics the children had tried on Cassie were anything to go by.

He studied Cassie over the rim of his coffee cup. She'd showered upstairs and changed back into her dress and added a sweater to her outfit. He was struck again by the beauty of her features. Yes, Caleb was going to be mighty interested when he got a good look at her. Difficult to imagine a man *not* interested in a woman who looked like Cassie. Hank was somewhat surprised that Caleb hadn't been by the farm today. Probably for the best, he reflected wryly. He wanted Cassie all settled in before the two of them met. He knew Caleb well enough to predict what his M.O. would be: bed her, then boot her off the farm. Hank was going to have to figure out a way to slow Caleb down long enough to give Cassie a fighting chance.

"So, Cassie, how long will it take you to pack up and move yourself and the kids down here?"

Cassie shifted in her seat and took a sip of her coffee. She'd been daydreaming a bit, going over the day's events in her mind, imagining how life would be, living down here in Virginia. She thought a bit, before responding to Hank's question. So much had happened today, no sense making rash promises.

"If it were just myself, Hank, I'd be here in thirty-six hours." Cassie smiled. "But I've got to think of Sophie and Jamie, and then there's Thompson and Alex. Could you give me two weeks? I need to inform the twins' school we're moving, and find a school here. Can you tell me anything about the schools?" She asked Melissa, who was sitting quietly across from her.

Melissa nodded. "Well, the public schools here are quite good. This area around Charlottesville has plenty of academics, so there's a vested interest in maintaining a high standard. Our kids, Robbie and Kate, both went to the schools here. Caleb, too." She laughed. "What a terror he was! Caleb gave those teachers a devil of a time, always full of pranks. I expect some of them still wake up at night in a cold sweat because of him."

Cassie couldn't help but be intrigued. Hank's veterinarian partner was beginning to sound quite entertaining. She was looking forward to meeting him.

"Do you think it'll be a problem, enrolling Sophie and Jamie this late in the year?" Cassie asked, her mind backtracking to the subject of her children. Things could get so complicated, with so much to organize when raising two kids.

"I'll give John Perkins a call tomorrow. He's the elementary school principal. He'll know. We'll get the details sorted out so that you're not bogged down. In this town everyone knows each other pretty well. And Perkins is a horse person. He bought his last horse from us."

Cassie smiled, relieved. Melissa's last comment spoke volumes. "Well, I guess after the kids' schooling, the next major hurdle is finding a place to live."

Melissa rushed to answer Cassie before Hank could respond. "I'm sure Hank said that living accommodations were included in the job offer."

Cassie nodded. Often large horse farms provided lodgings for some of their staff, the relatively modest wages they received reflecting the free housing.

"Unfortunately, the cottage our trainers use only has two bedrooms. You, the twins, and your housekeeper would all be too cramped for space. So I think we'll have to find you a bigger place. Of course, we'll give you a housing allowance to compensate."

Cassie shifted uncomfortably in her chair, reluctant to admit to the Sawyers that she had more than enough in her bank account to cover buying a house, let alone renting one. Her brother Alex's genius with money had made it so that if she chose, she could spend the rest of her life lying about, popping chocolate bonbons into her mouth. Not that she was remotely interested in that kind of pampered lifestyle. But admitting to that kind of wealth was simply too awkward.

She asked instead, "Would you know anyone who might be renting, or is there a broker I can call?"

Melissa checked to see if Hank had been paying close attention to the conversation. Clearly not. He was leaning back in his chair, savoring the last of his coffee, leaving it up to the women to handle the problem of living arrangements.

"Actually, it just so happens I've come up with an idea that'll be a great solution. You can rent Caleb Wells's house." Ignoring the sudden sound of Hank choking on his coffee, Melissa continued brightly, "Caleb's parents were our next-door neighbors. They live about a five minutes' drive from here. Did Hank mention to you what good friends we are with Caleb's parents?" When Cassie shook her head, Melissa elaborated, tucking her feet under her chair to avoid Hank's repeated attempts to nudge . . . no, kick—her shins.

"Well, we've known Mark and Susan forever. Our kids and Caleb all played together, even though Caleb's a few years younger than Robbie and Kate. He tagged along just like a kid brother. It was great for Kate. It gave her someone to boss around after she'd been on the receiving end from Robbie."

Cassie smiled. She'd been the youngest of three so she remembered well what it was like to be tormented by older siblings.

"Anyway, the Wells's house is just down the road a bit. A lovely place, with lots of room for the kids to run around, both inside and out."

Melissa didn't give a fig if she sounded like a real estate agent with a hard sell on her mind. This afternoon, she'd decided that Cassie might just be the woman for Caleb. And she was determined to do what she could to set things in motion.

"But don't they live there anymore?"

"Oh, no. They decided to move to a retirement community in Arizona last year. Both Mark and Susan are golf crazy."

"What about Caleb?"

"He and his wife, Pamela, were living on the other side of town during their marriage. After they split up, Caleb moved into the carriage house that his parents had converted. It's just behind the main house, but very private. He says the main house is too big for him all alone. He's been meaning to rent it for some time, hasn't he, Hank?"

"Well, yes," Hank admitted, with all the enthusiasm of a man facing a firing squad. "He has mentioned it. But I'm not sure it's—"

"I'm sure Caleb will be more than happy, he's Hank's partner after all. But if there's a problem, we'll let you know." Melissa finished, drowning out her husband's words.

Hank rolled his eyes. Great. Melissa was setting them up for a mess of trouble. She was dreaming if she thought Caleb would appreciate Melissa interfering in his private life. He wasn't about to bring up Caleb's character faults in front of Cassie now, but Hank fully intended to talk Melissa out of this harebrained scheme the second he got her alone.

"So you think he might consider renting it to us? Should I call him?"

"Oh, no. When Hank talks to him tomorrow and tells him he's offered you the job, I'll be sure and ask him about the house. It should be just what you need."

"That sounds wonderful. What a relief it'd be not to have to waste time house hunting." She grinned. "I'd rather be riding. I want to thank you both. I'm really looking forward to working here."

Hank and Melissa smiled in return. Hank spoke for the two of them. "We're really pleased you're taking the job. You'll probably have a ton of questions for us over the next two weeks. Don't hesitate to call. By the way, are you bringing any horses with you?"

Cassie blushed. She'd completely forgotten to ask. What professionalism, she groaned to herself.

"I've got the twins' two ponies. It's no problem if you want to pasture them outside during the summer months.

They're both super easygoing." Cassie paused and raked her fingers through her hair. "I've also got my mare, Hot Lips." At Hank's raised eyebrows, Cassie grinned. "Sorry. I can't take the credit for naming her, though actually it suits her to a tee. I bought her about six months ago off the racetrack. She's got more go than a locomotive. If I can just iron out her rough spots, I think she'll have great potential."

"Well, we've got room for all three of them. I think we can even find a couple of box stalls for the ponies. I'm sure they're pretty special if you got them for the twins."

Cassie gave Hank a smile of gratitude. Hank Sawyer was a good man. Moreover, he seemed to her to be a true horseman: He was interested in all horses, not just his own. Cassie had had enough dealings in the horse world to recognize Hank was a rare breed.

Melissa wondered idly to herself whether Hank would continue talking even if she turned off the light, snuggled into his chest, and began to snore. Loudly. She sighed. Sometimes her wonderful, adorable husband was like a dog with a bone. He'd started about thirty seconds after they'd waved goodnight to Cassie, Sophie, and Jamie. He'd continued through the washing up, as they'd turned off the lights and locked up, and during the time it had taken Melissa to clean and smooth moisturizer over her face.

Hoping to distract him, she shifted onto her side and placed her hands on either side of his face. She pressed her lips against his, silencing him at least for the moment.

"Hank, darling," she offered soothingly. "I know you're worried about how Caleb's going to react to Cassie."

"That's putting it mildly! I finally find a decent rider to work with Orion, and the whole thing's going to come flying apart!" Hank grumbled, his hands moving instinctively to stroke her soft, round shoulders.

"Why do you think that?"

"You moving Cassie into Caleb's house, that's why. I've been racking my brains, figuring how to keep them apart, and you send her off to live next door! That's tantamount to sending a lamb into the lion's den. He's going to swallow her whole."

"Hank, honey, I have a feeling you're underestimating Cassie. She strikes me like she might be one tough cookie. I don't think Caleb's going to have such an easy time seducing her. Just look at the way she handled that jerk."

"What jerk?"

"Brad the Cad," Melissa replied, slightly exasperated. Hank didn't always zero in on the complexities of relationships. "You remember, the man she was going to marry. A person doesn't have to be Einstein to figure out he balked at taking on the twins. Can you believe it?"

"Definitely a creep. Didn't I say so earlier?"

"Yes, love, you did. Anyway, it's clear Cassie's no lightweight. Caleb's smooth talking isn't going to turn her head like these fluff balls he's been seeing. And it's darn well time Caleb learned the difference. There's no way I'm going to let that blood-sucking witch Pamela destroy Caleb's chance at finding a real woman."

"Still isn't a good idea."

"Hank, really, there'll be a housekeeper. I'm sure things will work out fine. Better than fine when you consider Cassie's added ammunition."

"What? Woman, I've lost you," Hank said, shaking his head in mild aggravation.

Laughing softly, Melissa planted a lingering kiss on his lips, before whispering softly in his ear. "The twins, Hank. You know what a softie Caleb is when it comes to children. He won't be able to think of a young, beautiful mother as one of his playthings."

Deeply satisfied with how well things were working out with respect to Cassie Miller, Melissa settled back against the plump pillows. A sigh of pleasure escaped her as Hank reached for her, pulling her into his embrace. Linking her arms around his neck, her mouth nuzzled the warm flesh at the hollow of his neck. In response, Hank moved his hands slowly down the gentle curves of her back, molding her close to his body.

Quickly losing any interest in conversation, Hank reached out, extinguishing the bedside lamp. Turning back to his wife, he began trailing kisses along her neck. "So, you think Cassie's got ammunition? Well, sweetheart, I'm armed and dangerous."

Her soft laughter enveloped them in the dark. "Oh, Hank, I love you so."

With a happy grin, Hank settled himself over his beloved wife. Caleb and women be damned. He had his own woman to tend to.

5

Caleb stared, furious. "Let me get this straight. You mean you've gone ahead and hired this girl without my even meeting her, without my seeing her ride Orion? That's a hell of a fucking partnership we've got, Hank."

With a sad sigh Hank rubbed his hand along his jaw. He looked at the younger man wearily. Caleb's anger was evident in the taut line of his body, and the hard glitter of his dark eyes. This was one of the few times he and Caleb had ever had a serious disagreement, and Hank was sorry for it. Moreover, Hank knew he was in the wrong, a feeling he disliked intensely. Problem was, he hadn't, not even with all of Melissa's suggestions and strategies, figured out an easy way to break the news to Caleb that he'd hired Cassie.

So he'd stalled. For two long weeks.

Now he had not only to convince Caleb that Cassie was the rider they were looking for, but also that he hadn't deliberately gone behind Caleb's back in hiring her. To top that off, he had to inform Caleb that he had a new tenant for his house. Jesus, what a mess. His temples throbbed mercilessly.

"Look, Caleb, I know you're angry." He chose to ignore

Caleb's snort of disgust. "When Cassie came for the interview, you were nowhere around. I wanted you to have a chance to meet her, but there just wasn't time." His hands rose in a helpless gesture. "She's been living up in New York and was heading off early the next morning. Here—" He broke off and rifled among the papers on his desk, shoving a stapled sheet eagerly toward Caleb. "Take a look at her résumé, the classes she's won. She's had plenty of experience for someone her age, but that's nothing compared to how she rides. You're going to love her," Hank said, deciding that he'd be damned lucky if Caleb was even willing to tolerate her.

"Jesus Christ, Hank, she's only twenty-four. She's a *baby!* What the hell's the matter with you? Just how much *experience* could she possibly have?"

Caleb simply couldn't believe it. Hank was usually as level-headed as they come. Somehow this Cassandra Miller had managed to turn Hank into a complete idiot. It was tempting to demand that Hank fire her immediately, but the truth was he valued Hank and Melissa's friendship too much to jeopardize it.

Shit! In all fairness, he supposed he had to give this girl a chance. But if she wasn't everything Hank promised and more, he'd throw her out on her ass, and to hell with friendship.

With a defeated sigh he dropped into the chair facing Hank's desk and shot him a baleful look. "All right," he agreed grudgingly. "We'll give her a try. When does she get here?"

"Thanks, Caleb. I owe you one. Cassie should be arriving this afternoon sometime." Hank grinned, deeply relieved that Caleb had let him off the hook so easily. "She's bringing down some horses with her, so I don't know exactly when she'll be arriving. We've invited her to sleep at our house. Why don't you come by in the morning and I'll introduce you?"

"What do you mean, sleep at your house? Isn't she moving into the cottage?"

"Er, no. Melissa and I have decided to let Raffael have it. As barn manager he really deserves to have more than the studio over the garage. He was having trouble finding anything suitable close by, and Melissa and I don't want to do the late evening check on the horses anymore." Hank paused. Time to lay it on a bit thick. He gave Caleb a regretful smile. "I don't like to admit it, but we're not feeling quite so young these days."

Caleb stared at Hank. What was going on here? Hank had more stamina than most of the thirty-year-olds Caleb knew. This conversation was beginning to feel like something out of the *Twilight Zone*.

"So where's this Cassie going to be staying? Have you found her a house?"

"Well, as a matter of fact, Melissa came up with a nifty plan. Hey, you know what? She's up at the house. Why don't we go get a beer from the kitchen and she can tell you all about it." So, he was chickening out. At least he'd managed to convince Caleb to give Cassie a shot. Hank wasn't about to press his luck further. He'd let Melissa go a few rounds this time. Caleb had always had a soft spot for her.

"Sure," Caleb said, his eyes narrowing with suspicion. "I could use a little fresh air. This room's beginning to reek of B.S."

Caleb and Hank were seated around the kitchen table. Both men had opted for coffee as it was still only ten o'clock. The sheepish expression on Hank's face when he'd looked at the clock over the stove had been a sight to see. Unable to resist a crack about premature senility, Hank scowled, restoring much of Caleb's good humor.

He stretched his long, booted legs in front of him. The cup of steaming black coffee was cradled in his hands. His eyes were trained on Melissa, regarding her with curiosity. In all his life, he'd never known her to be a hoverer, but here she was, moving around the kitchen, alternately sitting, the next moment standing up, acting like some sort of deranged butterfly.

Suddenly it struck him. Melissa was nervous. This woman who had paddled Caleb's behind more than once during his mischievous childhood, who had always appeared as calm and tranquil as a mountain lake, was fumbling about like a self-conscious teenager. What in the world was going on? Caleb normally considered himself pretty bright, but right now he was experiencing the annoying sensation of being two steps behind the game. The feeling had been creeping over him ever since he'd sat in Hank's office listening to the crock Hank had been dishing out. It was starting to irritate the hell out of him.

"All right, Melissa, spill it. What have you cooked up in that devious mind of yours?"

Melissa swallowed, wiping damp palms against her slacks. Her thoughts had been racing, frantically rehearsing various approaches in her mind, discarding one after the other. She took a deep breath. Okay, she'd simply tell Caleb Cassie's story and appeal to his protective side. Despite the damage Pamela had done, Melissa knew that Caleb was still a caring and compassionate man. Of course he'd want to help out. The fact that Cassie had kids might sway him, too. Melissa remembered how she'd thought of the twins as Cassie's secret ammunition. Caleb had always had an incredible affinity with animals and kids. Melissa was trusting that his nobler sentiments would rise to the occasion when he heard children were involved.

Melissa pulled out the chair next to Caleb and sat down. She reached over and plucked one of the wildflowers out of the vase placed in the center of the table. Twirling it back and forth between her fingers as she spoke, she recounted the tragic accident that had struck Cassie's family, leaving Cassie and her brother with the care of two small infants.

"Cassie's adopted the twins, Caleb, so they and the housekeeper will be coming down in a week. They were all supposed to come down together, but Cassie wanted her brother Alex to have a little extra time with them. They seem to be very close. Alex is driving the children, Thompson, and all their stuff down."

"Tough break. It must have been hard on both of them," Caleb offered grudgingly. It was difficult to maintain his resentment toward Cassie Miller now that he'd heard about the accident. But, he reminded himself, that still didn't mean she was skilled enough to handle Orion. No matter how hard her life had been recently, she had to be able to do the job.

"What does all this have to do with where Cassie's going to live?" he asked, looking at Melissa and Hank.

Melissa cleared her throat. "Well, I thought that you might be interested in renting her your house." She hurried on, before Caleb could begin protesting. "You've been talking about renting the place for some time now. A house like your parents' needs someone living in it. Otherwise, it gets neglected."

"Mrs. Trapp comes in once a week, as you're well aware," Caleb replied curtly, his jaw clenched at having been maneuvered once again by Hank and Melissa. "What makes you think I want a couple of screaming four-year-olds living fifty yards away from me? Personally, I was envisioning something more along the lines of a quiet professional couple."

"They're five, not four, and absolutely adorable," Melissa corrected with asperity. "Honestly, Caleb, do you think I would have even made the suggestion if I thought Cassie and her children were going to be a nuisance?"

"Well, now, Melissa," Caleb drawled, anger lacing his voice. "It seems to me that an awful lot of decisions have been made here recently without my having any say whatsoever. I guess choosing the tenant for my house could just be one I might want to make all by myself."

"Cal dear . . ."

Caleb stiffened in affront. Now Melissa was shooting below the belt. Nobody dared to Cal-dear him except his mother and Melissa. They were the only two people who got away with it, but even they had the sense to reserve it for special occasions. Or when they wanted to make it clear that he was being unforgivably obstinate and selfish. And they always succeeded in making him feel as if he were a naughty ten-year-old again. He hated it.

"Just think how happy your parents will be when they hear children are living in the house again. I was planning on calling Susan in Arizona tomorrow, and telling her all about it."

Caleb threw up his hands in utter disgust. And defeat. He was turning into a regular doormat, letting Melissa walk all over him like this. But he figured it was easier to give in now than have Melissa badger him for the entire week.

"Fine. Great. They can live in the house." Caleb glared at Hank and Melissa. "But no more going behind my back. Is that agreed?"

His friends laughed in relief and Melissa sprang out of her chair to hug Caleb, kissing his cheeks soundly. Caleb smiled ruefully as he returned her embrace, unable to stay mad at Melissa for more than thirty seconds.

"Now I know why the pair of you are so successful in the horse business. You two could sell water to a drowning man."

It was nine-thirty the next morning when Caleb parked his truck and made his way directly to the barns, avoiding Hank's office. He'd decided last night that he was going to get a jump on Hank and Melissa and corner Cassie Miller alone. He didn't want Hank running interference for her.

Caleb started at the larger barns, moving slowly through them, checking to see whether anyone he passed looked like an overgrown pony camper. He was still incredulous that Hank had hired a twenty-four-year-old girl to be Orion's rider and trainer. Hank may have lost his wits when he hired her, but that didn't mean Caleb had. He wanted to judge for himself just how good she was before she stayed on another day. He wasn't about to sacrifice his stallion for some starry-eyed twit who wanted to mess around with horses.

Caleb traveled the length of the barn, saying good morning to the stablehands he passed. As he exited the barn and stood in the morning sunshine, his gaze moved between the two barns in front of him: The brood mares' barn, or the smaller stallions' barn? *She's probably all eager to get started on her new charge,* Caleb thought sourly and veered off toward his stallion's barn.

The interior of the stallions' barn was designed differently from the larger main barn. There were fewer stalls, and each was a good bit bigger than a normal box stall, allowing for a stallion's natural tendency to pace. The barn was constructed so that the stalls were spaced widely apart, standing as isolated units. This was to prevent the studs from trying to tear each other apart. Stall walls were heavily reinforced to withstand the kicking and pounding of hooves. Double doors permitted the stallions to pass by each other with a minimum of fuss.

At the moment, Five Oaks had three stallions: Orion; Orion's sire, Kenyon; and a newly purchased Selle Français named Gaspar. In Orion's stall, Hank and Caleb had given him a donkey as a stallmate, believing that its presence helped calm the stallion. They'd also installed speakers so that music played quietly in all the barns. In addition to it being soothing for the horses, the staff liked working with the songs playing softly in the background.

At the far end of the barn, with Orion hooked up to a pair of cross ties, Caleb saw her. She stood with her back to him, her tall, slim figure illuminated by the light streaming in through the barn doors. Her hair was pulled into a thick braid down her back, but the escaping tendrils formed a golden halo around her head. Trick of the light. Must be dust motes in the air, Caleb muttered to himself, annoyed with the fanciful image. Nonetheless, he felt strangely shaken without knowing why.

The girl turned sideways and Caleb felt a kick in the gut. A jolt of recognition speared him.

His stripper!

He'd spent enough time staring at those breasts in Hank's office to commit them permanently to memory. Hank wanted *her* to ride Orion? Well hell, he thought cynically, now he knew how she'd gotten the job. Just a shimmy of her delicious body would have most men's tongues hanging on the floor. Poor Hank's brains had probably turned to mush within three minutes. Never mind that he was old enough to be her father. She'd probably have that effect on a ninety-year-old.

He stopped and propped his shoulder against the barn wall so he could watch her from a discreet distance. He didn't want thoughts about her body clouding his judgement, although even from this distance his eyes locked on her slender waist and her impossibly long legs encased in breeches and boots. He remembered only too well how she'd looked wearing next to nothing. Today she had on some sort of tight-fitting turtleneck, and when she lifted her arms high to curry his horse's neck, Caleb found himself swallowing like a schoolboy. Get a grip, you jerk. It's not like you haven't seen a pair of breasts before. You're here to see if she's any kind of a rider, not whether she should enter a beauty pageant.

Caleb watched. Cassie Miller had obviously just begun

grooming Orion, for she went from curry comb, to bristle brush, and finally to the soft brush, covering the horse's body in slow, even strokes. She was always touching Orion: stroking, brushing, scratching, rubbing, always keeping contact, even when she exchanged one grooming tool for another.

And she used her voice. Sometimes she spoke, low crooning sounds, murmurs he could not decipher from where he stood. But when she began to sing to the radio songs coming over the speakers her voice rose and harmonized, flowing smoothly from one song to the next. It could have been ten minutes or two hours that passed as Caleb watched Cassie weave her spell on his horse. Caleb knew for certain that some sort of enchantment must be involved because he himself felt positively bewitched. And he could tell by Orion's twitching ears, shifting back and forth as the horse followed both the sweet cadence of Cassie's voice and the movement of her hands against his velvet coat, that Orion, too, had fallen under her spell.

Caleb stepped forward as the last notes of Van Morrison's "Moondance" ended and a Bonnie Raitt song began to play. "Moondance" had been one of his favorite songs when he'd been in high school, and he had to admit, Cassie Miller did a fine job harmonizing. She had a low, throaty voice that flowed like thick golden honey out of a jar. But, he reasoned to himself as he approached her, she couldn't be nearly as entrancing close up. It was the softly lit interior of the barn and the nostalgia of hearing a lovely voice singing one of his favorite tunes that had created this atmosphere. When he looked her in the face the illusion would be shattered.

He was dead wrong.

It was tempting to come to a complete standstill, just so that he could stare, focusing all his energy on absorbing the perfection of her features. But he forced himself to put one foot in front of the other until he stood a short yard away.

As the sound of his footsteps reached her, he watched her face register his presence.

Cassie's hands slowed their work on Orion as the man came forward out of the gloom of the barn's interior. A big man, she thought distractedly, even taller than her brother Alex. Her eyes traveled quickly over him as she took in his lean hips clad in stained, faded blue jeans. Momentarily mesmerized, she watched the fabric strain and shift as he came toward her with the grace of a big cat hunting its prey. Embarrassed at the prospect of being caught, she jerked her eyes upward to the faded sweatshirt he wore over his broad shoulders, and finally to his face. It wasn't smiling.

Cassie was taken aback. This was the first person she'd encountered at Five Oaks who hadn't immediately offered her an easy smile of welcome. Instead, the man who stood staring down at her had his lips pressed together in a forbidding line. *He looks like a wrathful angel,* Cassie thought a bit wildly to herself.

Damn, she's utterly beautiful. Caleb was annoyed at how strong the temptation was to reach out and touch the soft wisps curling about her face, to feel their silkiness beneath his fingertips. His eyes roamed over her face. He let the silence between them grow, fascinated by the way her eyes widened into deep blue saucers as nervousness betrayed her.

The man's dark, penetrating eyes were making her feel absurdly self-conscious. A deep rich brown, his irises were almost indistinguishable from his pupils. His gaze was intense, the eyes of a preacher. With a single look, he could show me heaven or damn me to hell.

But who *is* he? Uneasy, she tried to place him, explain his presence, his stare. He must be one of the grooms I haven't yet met, and he's angry that I'm handling Orion.

Eager to break the tension that engulfed them, Cassie tried to speak, only to find her mouth had gone dry. That'll teach you, she chastised herself. First you stare at a gorgeous man's pants, and then you practically drown yourself in his deep, come-hither eyes. She swallowed and watched the man's thickly lashed lids descend as his gaze lowered to her throat. Oh my God, he's watching me swallow.

Her tongue was suddenly a foreign and awkward object in her mouth. She tried to speak. "Uh, hi. I'm Cassie Miller. I've, um, been hired to be the new trainer here."

"Hi," Caleb paused for a few heartbeats. "I'm Caleb Wells."

Oh, no, she thought, utterly flustered. Not her other new boss! Why couldn't he look like a normal guy, maybe twenty pounds overweight and sporting one eyebrow?

"You've got a great singing voice. That one of your training techniques?"

He'd heard her singing, too? How embarrassing could this get? Cassie swallowed again, searching for a dignified response. "Not exactly . . . it's just that I've listened to so many songs on the radio in so many barns since I started riding—I was five when I started—that I know most of them by heart. Half the time I don't realize I'm singing. But I do think that horses like music. Orion seems to, at least. . . ." Cassie's voice trailed away. She sounded like an idiot. An earnest idiot.

"Yeah, he certainly seemed to be." Caleb's hand reached out to stroke his stallion's head. Orion dropped his nose down, nuzzling Caleb's flat stomach, searching for a treat. Caleb grinned, flashing straight white teeth. Out of the corner of her eye, Cassie saw his other hand disappear into his blue jeans' pocket and fish out a treat. With truly impressive willpower, Cassie succeeded in keeping her eyes above Caleb Wells's waist, although the pull she felt to follow the path of his hand was almost irresistible. No! She would not start looking at just how and where Caleb Wells's jeans bulged.

"You've got a beautiful horse," Cassie offered a bit desperately, determined not to succumb to her new boss's out-

rageous good looks. It suddenly occurred to her she didn't
know how to address him. Mister seemed ridiculous. He
couldn't be too much older than herself, Cassie thought.
Calling him Caleb seemed far too intimate, dangerous
even, given the bizarre effect he had on her. She decided
she'd stick with *you*.

"Orion's got the makings of a great jumper," she continued. "Big, athletic, and quick. He seems to have the character, too."

"Yeah," Caleb drawled, his voice deep and lazy. "I think
it must have been his *character* that was sending so many
of the riders we hired sailing through the dust."

Cassie laughed. "Well, that goes with the territory."

"That's not what one of Orion's riders thought. He
ended up with a broken collarbone after his first week with
Orion, and wimp that he was, washed his hands of him
after that." Caleb looked steadily at Cassie, a challenge in
his dark eyes. "I'll be interested to see how you handle
him."

Cassie smiled brightly, aware that Caleb had thrown
down the gauntlet. Well, lots of other big, strong men had
doubted her abilities because she was a woman. Just
because he was better looking than any man she'd ever
seen in her life, didn't mean he wasn't like many of them
inside: a chauvinist pig.

"I guess you're in luck then. I was about to pick out
Orion's hooves and tack him up. Hank had suggested that I
ride at around ten o'clock. He had some work to do with
the yearlings, but wanted to watch me work out."

And stick close by you to act as a guard dog, thought
Caleb. I'm one step ahead of you this time, old buddy.

"That's fine. I've got to head off to the hospital later this
morning. When I come back, I can take you to see my parents' house. Melissa told me you might be interested in it."

"All right," she returned hesitantly. Now that she'd met
Caleb Wells in the flesh, she wasn't so sure it was a good

idea for her and the kids to move into his house. The mental image she'd painted of Caleb Wells didn't match the man standing next to her one iota. This man was too intimidating, too big, too sexy, too much. It might be best if she reconsidered.

"Of course, if renting your house is inconvenient at all, it's no problem for us to find another place." Cassie hedged, racking her brain to come up with a polite excuse.

"Oh no." Cassie could have sworn Caleb's voice dropped even lower. It caressed her like warm velvet brushing her skin. "I'm delighted to have you and your children at the house." As he spoke, his hands stroked Orion's neck with his long, lean fingers.

A delicate trembling started, traveling from her head to her feet. Her body felt electrified. As if it had been she rather than the stallion Caleb had touched, caressed.

He watched her face change before his eyes, subtly softening, as if slipping into a dream. He had an overwhelming urge to learn the texture of those slightly parted lips, then bring her body close to his, ease her down into the fresh straw and make slow, endless love to her.

Jesus. With a shake of his head, Caleb tried to banish the erotic image from his brain. He'd known this girl for five minutes and already he was thinking with his pants. She was tying him up in knots without even trying. He felt the anger grow inside, that her looks could so easily affect him. *Hadn't he learned his lesson after Pamela?* he thought with self-disgust.

Well, he'd best make it crystal clear to Cassie Miller he wasn't the type of man to grovel at her feet the way she was probably used to. If she wanted to play, it would be on *his* terms.

"You know," he observed, his voice different now: harder, slightly mocking. "If working as a trainer doesn't pan out, you might want to consider a career change." He paused as his eyes locked with hers. "Singing, perhaps, or maybe even a strip show. Believe me, you've certainly got the talent for it. See you at the ring, Slim."

Cassie yanked her saddle off the stand, her breath coming out in angry pants. She was trembling from self-righteous anger. His words kept repeating themselves over and over in her mind, each time like a bucket of ice-cold water dashed in her face. What a royal jerk that Caleb Wells was. Insufferable moron. Just the sort of snide comment she'd expect from an arrogant SOB. Cassie shook her head in disgust as she pulled Orion's bridle from its hook and bent down to grab his bell boots from the tack box. She must have been born under an unlucky star, she thought bitterly. Of all the people to catch her one flimsy garment away from her birthday suit, she had to get stuck with Caleb Wells. How typical, she muttered under her breath, my boss and my supposed landlord. Not that she had any intention of moving in there now.

She'd rather commute from Timbuktu than live within spitting distance of that creep! Good thing she wasn't attracted to him at all. He could be as drop-dead sexy as he wanted. Dr. Caleb Wells was the one who could drop dead, for all she cared.

Feeling slightly calmer, Cassie proceeded to tack Orion. She wasn't going to give that jerk of a vet the pleasure of screwing up her training session. She was a professional, and she worked damn hard. She deserved this job. No way was it going to slip through her fingers on account of some lascivious peeping Tom.

As Cassie led the stallion out to the exercise ring, she saw Hank and Caleb standing together by the entrance gate. *Bet he's probably telling Hank what bra size I wear,* thought Cassie sourly. Resolutely, she pushed Caleb Wells out of her mind. Approaching the men, she schooled her features into a polite, emotionless smile. Hank beamed at her and started toward her, Caleb following more slowly.

"Cassie, let me introduce you to my friend and partner, Caleb Wells. I've been telling him how lucky we are to have you riding for us."

So, Cassie thought, he hasn't told Hank about our previous encounter. Must be waiting for some golden opportunity to embarrass me publicly. She nodded coolly in Caleb's direction, her eyes glittering like sapphires.

Caleb returned her look with a small smile. He'd been wondering how she'd react to that last comment he'd made. He'd surprised himself a bit. He didn't ordinarily go out of his way to make people uncomfortable, especially not beautiful women. Women he had every intention of making love to.

He dismissed his rudeness, easily convincing himself that Cassie's beauty hadn't been the equivalent of a sucker punch to the gut, leaving him rattled and off balance, but that instead he was still royally ticked off she'd been hired without his say-so.

Just because he'd wanted a taste of that delectable body from the moment he'd seen her, didn't mean she'd get the job. Hank might fall for those beautiful eyes and that killer body, but Caleb was a bit wiser than his partner. Until Cassie Miller proved her worth, he wasn't going to give her an inch.

Caleb could tell by the deep-freeze look she was giving him that he'd just taken on the role of Public Enemy Number One.

Hank's gaze was darting between the two of them, bewildered by the lack of response from either Cassie or Caleb. Caleb's smile widened lazily, amused when she stiffened up like a poker in response.

"Actually, Hank, I introduced myself to Cassie earlier in the barn. I wanted to have a chance to chat a bit before she rode. If Cassie rides nearly as well as she, uh, sings, your praise will be justified."

Hank shot a worried glance at Cassie. Damn, it was clear as rainwater that Caleb had already said something to set Cassie off. It would be just great if Cassie quit before Caleb even had a chance to see what a superb rider she was. And knowing Caleb, he'd probably be too stubborn to apologize for whatever dumbass remark he'd made.

Cassie directed a withering look in Caleb's direction, refusing to acknowledge his comment. "If you'll excuse me, Hank, I'll hop on Orion now. Don't like to waste the day yapping."

"Yapping," Caleb muttered, shaking his head in bemusement as he watched Cassie lead his horse to the center of the ring. Little terriers yapped. Boy, she sure knew how to dish out insults. He felt positively wounded.

"Good going, Caleb," Hank commented sarcastically, "What'd you do back there in the barn? Pour on some of your renowned charm?"

Caleb shrugged his shoulders helplessly. "What can I say. She finds me irresistible."

"Yeah, right. I could see just how much she liked you. If you'd gotten any closer to her, I'd have had to treat you for frostbite."

Caleb gave Hank what could only be described as a feral smile. "You know Hank, you haven't been straight with me yet with respect to Cassie Miller. I suppose it escaped your notice that she's beautiful enough to make a saint sweat?" He paused, watching the guilty flush stain his partner's cheeks. "Right. You know, of course, who else is going to notice? My lovely ex-wife. We might have gotten away with this scheme if Cassie Miller had looked like a close relative of Barney, the donkey. When Pamela gets a load of your little rider there, she's gonna have a shit fit. Then it'll be, 'Do not pass go, do not collect two hundred dollars.'"

"Hell, Caleb, we'll deal with Pamela when the time comes. With any luck, she'll be so busy with her social calendar she won't even know we've switched riders. Swear to God, Caleb, just wait 'til you watch her ride. Then you'll see I made the right decision. Come on, she's already up."

An hour later Caleb had that sick sensation in the gut when you've eaten humble pie. *To top it off,* he thought, *he might just have a couple of busted ribs from Hank poking him excitedly each time Cassie brilliantly negotiated Orion over a fence.*

Okay, so Hank was right. Cassie was an outstanding equestrian. For the first forty-five minutes, she'd taken Orion through involved flat exercises, working on his balance and response. Hank had explained that Cassie's idea was to refine Orion's flat work, using that as a foundation for his success over fences.

She rode smoothly, adjusting Orion's gait and form with a magician's touch. Orion was moving, for all his size and power, as if his hooves were barely skimming the ring's dirt surface. When Cassie began taking him over jumps, Hank and Caleb walked to the center of the ring, so that they could watch Orion's take-offs from a closer vantage point.

Caleb had seen his fair share of great riders, both at shows where he'd competed himself and the times he'd been on call as a vet. It didn't take long for him to recognize that Cassie's talent shone as brightly as anything he'd ever seen. Her riding style was classic, elegant. With perfect balance and perfect form. The way she moved with Orion reminded Caleb of an intricate ballet duo performed where strength, grace, and timing become art.

Afterwards, as Cassie slowly walked Orion around the ring, letting the stallion warm down, Caleb stared thoughtfully at her. Her posture was erect and alert even though the workout was finished. She looked like she never allowed for sloppiness while on a horse's back.

His mind made up, Caleb made his way over to her and

began to walk alongside. He figured she might be more forgiving while perched on top of *his* horse.

Cassie eyed Caleb warily as he approached.

She was still furious but some of its red-hot intensity had dissipated. She always felt such a high after a good training session (the pleasure center of her brain tingling with neuron-firings or whatever) so that she could even feel mellow and forgiving toward first-class jerks. She hoped he wasn't going to start up again, because she was feeling pretty great just now.

"I can see that my reservations about you were unnecessary, Cassie. You and Orion move like clockwork together."

"Thanks." Cassie inclined her head coolly. She wasn't simply about to forget Caleb's earlier comments. "We've got a lot of work to do if we want to be ready to show him by late spring."

"We can talk with Hank about which shows he wants to enter Orion in," Caleb offered, steering the conversation to safe, neutral ground.

"I think we should look for as much exposure as possible without stressing him too much," Cassie replied, following his lead. "He's still like a new kid on the block, even with the shows he's competed in."

"Sounds good. I want to keep him injury free." Caleb broke off and ran his hand through his hair.

From her higher vantage point, she could see how silky and thick his hair was, his fingers lost in the dark locks. The color reminded her of rich coffee beans. His curls brushed the edge of his collar. He probably cuts his hair himself, Cassie thought, unwillingly comparing Caleb's negligent style with her ex-fiancé Brad's meticulously groomed appearance. Caleb's hair begged to be touched, to have a woman's fingers entangle themselves around those careless curls. The sound of his throat clearing broke into her thoughts. Quickly, Cassie's eyes darted away to fix on Orion's ears.

"Look, I'd like to apologize for the way I behaved." From his stilted voice, it was abundantly clear to Cassie that Caleb was a man who hated apologizing. It was probably something he practiced as little as possible.

"Don't worry about it," Cassie replied, equally stiffly. "People are always suggesting to me that I keep my career options open." She paused and looked down her nose at him, a pretty easy feat considering that she was still astride Orion, Caleb noted sourly. "Of course, this is the first time *stripping* has been offered as a possible choice."

Caleb grinned, abandoning his air of repentance. "It could just be that you're multitalented, Slim."

"Very funny," Cassie snapped, her temper coming quickly to the boil once more. "Gee, you're a regular comedian." Eyes flashing, she continued. "Sorry to cut our conversation short, but I've got to get back to the barn. I want to do some massage techniques on Orion. Then I've got three other horses to ride. After that I've got to work with my mare as well as a few other things Hank mentioned." Cassie decided that she didn't give a fig if this guy was her boss. He was the most obnoxious person she'd had the misfortune to run into in a long time. No way was she going to play the polite, deferential employee role.

Caleb appeared unfazed by her tone. The twinkle of amusement in his eyes told her he was lacking any remorse over his stripper comment. He gave her a devastating smile, showing his strong white teeth. Apart from his character, just about everything concerning Caleb Wells was devastating, she acknowledged peevishly.

"Well, I'll let you go, so that you can be finished in time to come and see the house."

"Don't trouble yourself, Dr. Wells. The twins and I will

find another place in town to live," Cassie replied in her haughtiest tone.

Caleb only laughed. "Man, you sure do give freezer burn, Ice Case. The Dr. Wells is a nice touch. I sound kind of like one of those soap opera villains about to be sued for malpractice." He stepped closer to her, his chest inches away from her booted leg. "Or am I the evil doctor that drags innocent young nurses into the supply closet to have my wicked way with them?" Before Cassie could tell him that she'd vote for the latter, he continued. "I'll be back around five. You know, for your kids' sake at least, you should definitely come by and see the place." With a casual pat to her knee, Caleb Wells sauntered off, whistling Van Morrison's "Moondance" just loud enough to reach her.

6

Caleb was inordinately pleased with himself that morning as he saw patients in the examining room. He'd zeroed in on the key to foiling any attempt by Cassie to extricate herself from living at his house: her kids. Sure, it was emotional blackmail, but after all, the house *was* made for kids, with grounds and space enough for them to run free. If Cassie tried to resist, Caleb wouldn't hesitate to lay a major guilt trip on her. She'd come away feeling as if she was going to be handed the title of lousy parent of the year. And if she dreamed up any other excuses, he was confident he'd be able to overrun them, too.

Caleb wasn't sure why, in the space of a few short hours, he'd undergone such a radical and irrational transformation with respect to Cassie Miller, but he did know that he was damned if she was going to slip away before he'd figured it out. And if he was going to rent his house to someone, Cassie Miller was, without a doubt, a whole lot more interesting to look at than some happy yuppie couple.

Caleb's list of patients was fairly typical that day: Three dogs, five cats, as well as two trips to neighboring farms.

The first to check on a horse with an acute case of laminitis, and the second to a mare in foal. Caleb loved his work. Animals had been his passion since childhood, and he'd studied hard to get his degree and start his own practice. Hank had been right when he said that Caleb wouldn't want to give it up to take over Orion's riding and training. While he'd always loved riding and competing, there was no way he wanted to give up the work he did here and at Five Oaks. Caleb realized that for him, his work as a veterinarian was what was ultimately the more fulfilling.

It had been his work that kept Caleb together after Pamela had left him jilted and betrayed. By concentrating on the animals in his care, Caleb had managed to block out the pain and anger of her desertion and manipulation—and salvage his soul and pride piece by piece.

Caleb allowed thoughts of Pamela to intrude as infrequently as possible. His greedy bitch of an ex-wife should have been a closed chapter of his life, one he wished had never been written, or on which he could press the delete button. Instead, she remained far too present, like a festering wound that refused to heal.

All because she'd managed to rob him of the single good thing that had happened to him during their years of marriage. The court had awarded her ownership of his stallion Orion, and now she used that position to torment and thwart him at every turn.

God, he'd been so green, so foolish. What had he known of the damages a vindictive spouse could wreak upon entering the hallowed halls of the Juvenile and Domestic Relations Court? He'd been nothing but a damn fool, thinking his marriage would be anything like those of his parents, his sister, or that of Hank and Melissa. A marriage that would endure and grow stronger with the test of time. It was only now as he looked back that Caleb recognized that his and Pamela's marriage had about as much chance of success as a tin shack did of surviving a direct hit by a twister. None at all.

He could still remember how optimistic and brash he'd been back then. He'd recently finished veterinary school and had returned to his hometown eager to begin building a clientele. His principal goals in life at that point had been his work and paying off the student loans that he'd taken out. That and having a kick-ass time at the parties he went to on the weekends.

He and Pamela had met one night at just such a party. Thrown by a close school friend, the party was pretty much a typical vet school bash: noisy, crowded, and wild enough to shake the walls. Pamela spotted Caleb right away. Her bold eyes never leaving his, she made her way across the crowded room, not stopping until her body was pressed against his.

Splaying one hand across his chest, while the other stroked the beaded bottle of beer in his hand, her fingers trailing up and down its length suggestively, Pamela rose slowly on her tiptoes and lifted her lush, red mouth to whisper in his ear.

"Why don't you take me home and we can make this party more private."

The feel of Pamela's sinuous body rubbing against his was like a sleek cat demanding attention, her perfume filling his head, her eyes making hot promises. Too hot to ignore. Caleb grabbed the hand that had abandoned the bottle and was now making an unerring journey down to his crotch. Dragging her behind him, they'd made a hasty exit.

Even before they reached his house, Pamela had begun tearing at his clothes, eager to have him at her disposal. Caleb smiled bitterly at the memory. That's exactly what he'd been to her: disposable.

That she'd used all her sexual wiles to capture him, he

could forgive. For Pamela was an intensely sexual creature. What he couldn't ever pardon was having duped him into believing she loved him. Only him. And then for giving him one final royal screw to remember her by.

A mere three months after they met, they were married. Caleb bullheadedly ignored the worried looks and anxious comments of his parents and Hank and Melissa. Caleb shook his head at the memory. Christ, he'd been so young at the time. Wet behind the ears. Pamela hadn't been any older, but far wiser and equipped with all the treachery of Delilah. She'd spun a sexual cocoon around him that left him blind to her faults. Blind to just about everything except for the intoxicating lure of her body.

Their marriage had lasted a little over three years. Enough time for Pamela to go through her sexual repertoire and begin hankering for greener pastures. Enough time for Caleb's head to clear and for him to realize just what a shallow creature she was.

From the word go, his marriage with Pamela seemed to be based on one colossal mistake after another. If he and Pamela had been contestants on one of those TV game shows, Caleb would have been the one standing around looking stupid as a bucket of ice water was dumped on top of him. The loud gong would be sounding for the audience, with Pamela laughing and clapping.

Pride and stubbornness had kept him from ending the marriage as soon as it started to stink as bad as last week's garbage. His second mistake had been to throw himself into his work so much that he didn't keep track of exactly how green his wife liked her pastures. Which in Pamela's case translated into a nice fat bank account, a mansion, and a shiny Lamborghini in the garage. A sweet package when combined with a slick new hubby who apparently didn't mind if his wife was shallow, vain, and utterly incapable of holding a conversation that didn't revolve around herself.

It was one of life's little ironies that the man Pamela

dumped him for was one of Caleb's clients. Stuart Ross III, a multimillionaire with a stable full of polo ponies.

Ross had called Caleb's animal hospital frantic for his help. One of his best ponies had come down with a life-threatening case of colic. After locating the blockage using x-ray, Caleb had injected the pony with a saline solution to the intestine, thereby eliminating the need to operate and remove a large section of the pony's intestine. An operation that would have meant, in all probability, premature retirement for Ross's prized starter. Afterwards, Caleb had written up a whole new regimen for the pony, a complete overhaul of its diet and feeding routine hoping to prevent a recurrence of the colic.

Ross, overcome with gratitude, had invited Caleb and Pamela to be the guests of honor at one of Ross's dinner parties. An "intimate" affair of fifty friends seated at two long banquet tables. Pamela had been thrilled by the invitation. In the three years of marriage, life as a young vet's wife had disappointingly lacked in glamour. With a zeal she usually reserved for purchasing overpriced designer clothes, Pamela had set about convincing Caleb of the advantages a party like this could present. How great an opportunity for him to make contacts and generate new clients. Caleb had finally agreed, and Pamela rushed out to buy an evening gown.

Caleb arrived at the party in black tie, and Pamela in a long black crêpe de Chine dress that clung to her luscious curves like a second skin. She'd spent the entire afternoon at the beauty salon, luxuriating in a facial, a manicure, and hair treatment. The stylist had pinned her deep chestnut hair at the back of her head so its shiny mass tumbled down the length of her back. That evening she glowed like the exquisite creature she was, with all her sexy beauty. A single glance at the shell-shocked expressions of every man and woman at the party told Caleb that once again his wife's stunning sensuality had hit its mark.

Pamela had been awed and thrilled by the splendor of Ross's mansion. Like a sponge, she'd absorbed every detail: the lavish furnishings, the marble fireplaces, the enormous dining room, the proportions of which almost dwarfed the massive banquet tables laden with candles, silver, fine china, and clever floral arrangements set before each lady's place. As the wife of the guest of honor, she was seated on Ross's right. Caleb, a few places down, next to a bejeweled society matron, watched his wife flirt with their host, inclining her head and body so that each exchange became more intimate.

Occasionally, he still wondered why he hadn't put a stop to the way she was carrying on right then. The only answer he could give was highly unflattering. Even with their marriage on the rocks, he'd simply been too bloody arrogant to imagine the possibility that Pamela would be unfaithful.

Seventeen days later, she informed him she was filing for divorce.

The bitter arguments, the hateful words they'd thrown at each other so quickly, so easily, revealed only too well the emptiness of their marriage. Although she refused to admit she was leaving him for another man, Caleb was left with little doubt that Ross was behind her every step of the way. She wouldn't have been able to afford that slick fancy New York lawyer otherwise.

Pamela should have been an actress. She'd played the role of her life in front of the judge, her eyes glistening with unshed tears as she described Caleb's cruel neglect. Her shoulders had bowed gently, overcome with shame, her voice small and breathless, telling the patrician, silver-haired judge how Caleb never came home, how he'd cut off her credit line simply because of a few too many over-drafts—merely harmless errors—how he wouldn't make love with her . . .

The judge had eaten up Pamela's words like they were little after-dinner mints set before him on a fussy sterling silver tray. It was quickly obvious to Caleb that the presence of his lawyer, seated next to him, was useless.

The lawyer's protests had fallen on deaf ears, most likely because the judge's eyes were glued to Pamela's oh-so pathetic figure, outlined to mouthwatering perfection in a dove grey woolen dress, so modest and so revealing. The crying, too, had been a nice touch.

Pamela had sat in the Moroccan leather in the judge's chambers sobbing as if her heart had been shattered in a million pieces. She managed, however, to quiet down long enough to listen to the judge admonish Caleb as if he were a piece of pond scum for not taking better care of such a lovely woman. For not honoring his vows. Then the judge pronounced it only just and fitting that a woman who'd devoted herself to such a heartless partner be recompensed accordingly. Truly miraculous how those tears had dried up the second Pamela was handed a deed giving her full ownership of Orion.

The debacle of his marriage and the travesty of his divorce left a deep, festering wound. However, the experience taught Caleb a vital lesson. Ever since the divorce, he had only let himself be involved with women who were easy. Easy to get into bed, easy to say good-bye to. His considered opinion was that he'd sooner get a lobotomy than another wife. Good, hot sex was all he was after. No strings attached.

So, it came as a somewhat unsettling sensation when he left the animal hospital that afternoon and drove back to Five Oaks to find himself already anticipating what new excuses Cassie Miller might have concocted to avoid moving into his parents' house. He was surprised at how eager he was to see her again. Perhaps it was because she'd been so easy to rile. He hadn't enjoyed teasing anyone this much in a long, long time. He was curious, too, whether Cassie would still be mind-blowingly lovely. Or could her extraordinary looks have been merely a product of his heated imagination?

After parking his truck, Caleb headed toward the exercise ring, figuring that, if Cassie was still working, this was where he'd find her. He stopped as if he'd slammed into an invisible wall, eyes widening in disbelief.

Cassie was astride a fiery red chestnut who was doing its damnedest to hurl her straight into the setting sun.

He watched, stunned, as Cassie rode the alternately bucking, crow-hopping ball of fire around the ring. Gone was the exquisite poise he'd witnessed when she'd been on Orion. Her riding style now looked like someone trying to stay on top of a comet bouncing off earth's atmosphere.

It was a hell of a balancing act.

As far as he could make out, Cassie's game plan was to keep the horse moving forward, no matter how badly it tried to shy to the side or throw her to the ground. He spotted Hank, hanging over the side rail, grinning from ear to ear. Caleb laid a hand on his shoulder.

"So Cassie also does bronc busting, Hank? Looks like a western rodeo out there."

"Hey, Caleb. Glad to see you, son. That's Cassie's new mare, Hot Lips."

"You mean, she actually paid money for that ball of fire?"

"Yeah. Apparently the mare's got this nasty trick she plays every time someone gets on her. For the first fifteen minutes, she's wilder than a tornado. Then she starts to settle down a bit."

"How many minutes have I missed?"

"About five. Doesn't appear to be slowing down yet."

Caleb whistled under his breath. "She's a nice looking horse, when she isn't hopping like a Mexican jumping bean. Classy mover." Caleb looked at Hank out of the corner of his eye before shifting his gaze back to the spectacle before him. "Tell me, Hank, you get any work done, or have you been sitting on this fence all day watching Cassie ride?"

"Hell, yes!" Hank replied, his tone offended. "I've been going over stud books all afternoon. There are a couple of entries I want to go over with you. And I've been writing up a list of shows I think we'll want to enter Orion in. Not too many small shows nearby, but I've found a couple we can start him on. Even better, I think they're so small, Pamela wouldn't be caught dead at them."

"Beneath her dignity."

"Of course." Hank grinned. "Now with respect to Cassie, I've been out a couple of times a day, half an hour at a time, tops. Just to see how she's doing with the other horses, fill her in a bit on how we've been working them. I do like how that girl rides. Got a nice way with the youngsters, too."

"Well, tomorrow it's my turn. I know you'll want to be down in the south pasture, checking the fields." The south pasture was where the mares and their new foals were grazed during the warmer months. The weather was just beginning to turn fair enough to allow the new foals to stay out during the day.

"By the way, did she mention me?" Caleb asked casually, his eyes still locked on the red mare Cassie was finally managing to quiet.

Hank laughed. "I wouldn't want to damage your ego by telling you, Caleb. Let's just say I get the feeling she's a bit doubtful you'd be providing a healthy atmosphere for her two kids."

"Healthy atmosphere? I'm a doctor, for Christ's sake," Caleb protested, grinning.

"You're a vet, moron."

A groan of relief escaped her lips as she slipped off Hot Lips's back. Her mare had finally calmed down, and Cassie had been able to work her over the flat for about forty minutes. She'd opted against jumping her, however, unwilling to subject her horse's legs to any more pounding. Anyway, Cassie's gas tank was on empty.

She was beat.

Those crow hops, rabbit leaps, and bucks played havoc on her lower back. Hot Lips had better mellow out soon or her owner would be a cripple. She was going to have to spend some time stretching tonight if she didn't want to be stiff and sore in the morning. She pulled off her hard hat and wiped the sweat off her brow. Lord, she could drink a gallon of water. Her water bottle had better be near the tack room, she seemed to remember leaving it there. The inside of her mouth felt like sawdust.

She led Hot Lips out of the ring, sighing in resignation as she saw Caleb Wells coming toward her with Hank at his side. She felt his gaze sweep over her sweaty face and clinging shirt. An eyebrow lifted challengingly.

What did he think? That women didn't sweat? She'd been riding for close to six hours, with only lunch as her real break. The rest of the time she'd been grooming, tacking, or massaging horses. Did he think she'd be ready to serve tea and cucumber sandwiches?

Caleb wondered how it was possible that Cassie could look even more breathtaking now than she had this morning. With a start, he realized that it was precisely because she was sweaty and disheveled that she looked so beautiful, so desirable. She was alive and full of color, as though she'd been wrapped tight in the arms of a man, making passionate love. She looked the way he wanted to make her feel.

He cleared his throat, his body hard at the turn his thoughts had taken. He hoped Cassie's eyes didn't chance to stray to the fly of his jeans, or she'd run screaming, convinced he was the pervert of the county, if not the century. And blow his chances with his potential tenant for good.

"Hi, Cassie."

"Hello," Cassie returned in a clipped voice. She didn't want to be churlish, but he was beginning to annoy her big time.

"I thought you might want to come and check out the house, if you've got the time."

Cassie seized the excuse. "Gosh, I'm sorry, Caleb, but I have to cool down Hot Lips and then give her a rubdown. She's not moving as smoothly as she usually does. I want to check her legs for swelling. And I need to take a shower." She sighed and shrugged her shoulders. "I just don't think I'll have the time." She didn't even make a token effort to look chagrined.

Caleb smiled a slow, knowing smile, telling her he'd been expecting some kind of excuse. Just watching the way his lips stretched across his even white teeth made Cassie's heart start beating as if it had been given shock treatment. Her pathetically tired body felt the tingles race through it.

"Okay, so why don't you give me Hot Lips. Catchy name, by the way. I'll cool her off and rub her down for you." Caleb continued before she could form an objection. "Come on, Slim, don't give me the deep-freeze treatment. I *am* a vet. I may even throw in a free examination for her because we're friends."

Caleb fought back a laugh at the look of horror that crossed Cassie's face at the term *friend*. Guess he hadn't earned enough Brownie points yet for that.

All right then, time for the knockout punch. "That way, you can go up to the house and have a cool glass of iced tea and then take a long, hot shower. We'll probably both be finished at about the same time. You can meet me back at Hot Lips's stall and make sure I've done everything right."

Cassie's brain had turned to mush at the thought of a cold drink and a hot shower.

"Oh, fine. Whatever," she grumbled ungraciously, not

caring that she was as close to bitchy as she'd ever come. Slapping the reins into his hands, she waspishly instructed, "Her stall is in the large barn at the far end. Left side. My tack box is labeled CBM. Don't mess things up."

"Sure thing, boss. I live to serve," Caleb said cheerfully, giving the reins a gentle tug as he led the mare away. "By the way, Slim, I like you all rumpled and hot. It suits you."

Cassie stormed into Hank and Melissa's house, complaining volubly about arrogant know-it-alls and insufferable vets. Holy God, that man really rubbed her the wrong way. *Nobody* had ever had the nerve to talk to her that way before. And she had just stood there, like a dumb cluck, taking it!

Melissa, in the kitchen slicing vegetables for dinner, heard her angry muttering and grinned into the pile of diced carrots.

"Don't worry, Cassie, when Kate was still living at home, Caleb used to tease her mercilessly. It's a sign of affection."

"Great," said Cassie. "I can see why your daughter moved away! I guess it was either that or kill the wretch."

Melissa laughed and laid the knife down on the cutting board. "Actually, Kate learned to dish it out pretty well, herself. Caleb used to blush bright red at some of the things she said to him."

"That I'd have liked to see," Cassie said spiritedly. "I'm going up to take a shower. Would you mind if I brought a glass of iced tea with me?"

"Go right ahead. We'll be eating dinner at seven-thirty, if you want to join us."

Cassie glanced at her watch as she opened the refrigerator door. "I'm sure to be back in time. Can't take too long to tour a house. And I want to get back in time to call Alex and the twins."

Melissa smiled to herself as she finished slicing the zucchini and reached for a clove of garlic. Knowing Caleb, she didn't think he'd be in any hurry to let Cassie go too quickly. He'd have her inspecting every floorboard and closet in the place.

"Why don't you call them now, then you won't have to worry about calling too late. You can use the upstairs telephone for privacy."

Cassie smiled. "All right. Thanks. I miss them so much, and it's only been a day and a half!"

"I understand. I used to be a nervous wreck whenever Hank and I went on buying trips for horses. Even though Mrs. Harris was with the kids, I was sure everything would fall apart without me." Melissa smiled wryly at the memory. "Never did. Actually, I think those short trips were good for us. Gave us all a bit of a change in schedule and a little vacation, too. Take advantage of it, Cassie."

Cassie nodded doubtfully, then made her way upstairs. She was sure Melissa's suggestion had merit, but Cassie wasn't sure whether *she* was ready to be separated for a whole week yet. She had no doubt the kids were in heaven. Her brother Alex had decided to take an unprecedented ten days off so that he could devote himself to the kids and then drive them and Thompson down to Virginia. He wanted to make sure they were comfortably installed before he returned to New York. Cassie knew the decision stemmed from his reluctance to see them go, even though Alex had loyally encouraged her to apply for the job. Cassie and the children's departures would leave an enormous hole in Alex's life.

She treated herself to a long, soapy shower, working the kinks out of her neck and shoulder muscles as she washed the dirt and sweat from her body. After she'd patted herself dry with a towel, she smoothed body lotion over all her skin, enjoying the silky smoothness the moisturizer gave her. She dressed, grabbing a pair of ivory silk panties and a matching bra. Over that she pulled on a pair of faded blue jeans, a baggy blue lamb's-wool sweater, socks, and a pair of paddock boots. She let her hair hang down her back to dry in the air. *At least Dr. GQ vet can't claim that I've dressed to stun him with my good looks. This is what I wear when I'm mucking out stalls.*

Cassie straightened up the room and went into the bathroom to hang up the towels and brush her teeth. Feeling entirely rejuvenated, she went into the upstairs sitting room to call her brother.

A short while later, she joined Caleb at Hot Lips's stall. The mare, hooked up to the cross ties, whinnied while Caleb went over her with a soft brush. He turned his head at Cassie's approach and smiled.

"Hi. Feeling better?"

"Yes, thanks. Sorry I took a bit longer. I called my brother, Alex. Spoke with him, Jamie, and Sophie."

"Everything's fine? I'm looking forward to meeting your kids. Melissa and Hank tell me they're great kids."

Cassie smiled broadly, relaxing a bit in his presence. She said proudly, "Yeah. They are great kids. As we speak, they're enjoying a Disney festival. Alex has allowed them to rent one for every night." Cassie laughed. "They're in heaven. But I can't wait for them to get here. I miss them."

He liked the way her face lit up when she laughed. Her eyes were still twinkling as she reached up to stroke Hot Lips's nose.

"So how's my other baby doing?"

Caleb dropped the brush he'd been using back in the carry-all, and came to stand beside her, his hand resting on the mare's shoulder. Cassie couldn't help but notice again how tall he was, his body lean, his shoulders broad and strong. She wondered distractedly how long she would continue to be dazzled by his masculinity, by his sheer male beauty.

"She's a beautiful horse, Cassie. Her conformation is excellent, so that's not where the problem lies. Is this the first time you've noticed her moving stiffly?"

"I bought her this fall up in Saratoga. She was fine for about three months. Since then she's been slightly inflamed. She's never shown any lameness, but I've been turning her out a lot and riding her pretty lightly. But you've seen what she's like."

"Yeah," said Caleb rubbing his jaw with his left hand. "She's a real firecracker. Her owners at the track didn't mention any previous injuries?"

"No. They were almost desperate to get rid of her. Apparently, she used to pull that bucking bronco stunt when the starting gate went up. They were becoming the laughing stock of the track." Cassie grinned. "I got her for a song."

"I bet," Caleb said dryly. "What are you going to do with her?"

"Oh, I thought I'd work on her a little, then sell her as a pleasure horse." Cassie laughed delightedly at the appalled look on Caleb's face.

"Just kidding." A smile still hovering on her lips. It was a nice change to have Caleb be the one off balance. "I've got to see how she develops once she settles down. She's still really green. I think of her as sort of my long-term project. I was toying with the idea of entering her in a few prejumper classes this summer if she comes along well. She's got the spirit and the drive."

"You sure seem to like challenges." He kneeled beside the mare's slender thoroughbred legs. Cassie did the same.

"I'm fairly certain Hot Lips's problem results from a strained tendon. It's just barely swollen, but I can feel some heat just below the fetlock joint, running down to the ankle." He paused, allowing Cassie a chance to run her fingers down the leg. "I'll bring my ultrasound machine tomorrow, so we can take a better look. In the meantime, let's cold-pack and wrap the leg to keep it from swelling as much as possible. While you were at the house, I rubbed liniment on the other legs. With all that bucking and crow hopping, they need it."

"Do you think she injured the tendon this afternoon?" Cassie asked anxiously.

"It's difficult to say whether the stiffening you noticed in her gait is from an old racing injury that went undetected or from the damage done by her bronco routine. That much twisting and pounding puts a lot of strain on ligaments and tendons."

"Do you think you can make her sound?" Cassie asked, a frown marring her brow. She knew that a badly injured tendon or a bowed tendon could easily take weeks, even months, to heal.

"I think so." His tone reassuring. "We can start with a couple of things. I'll go get some sodium hyaluronate from my truck right now. That'll keep the inflammation down. Unless the ultrasound turns up something totally unexpected, laser therapy will probably be the most effective treatment for her. I've seen terrific results using it."

Cassie nodded her head in agreement, as Caleb continued, his voice calm, his manner professional. "And if it is a strained tendon, you'll have to restrict her to total stall rest. After a couple of weeks, perhaps three, you can walk her on the lead for about fifteen to twenty minutes a day. But no turnout time in the pasture. You don't want her pulling any funny stuff and injuring herself even more severely. But let's begin with the cold wraps. I have some special bandages you can borrow, they should be around here, somewhere."

"Thanks, Caleb. I appreciate your help." Cassie was amazed at how comfortable she felt with Caleb in his professional mode. He must be a terrific vet to make her forget completely how annoyed she'd been with him only half an hour earlier. Maybe if she could keep thinking of him as a vet, he wouldn't get under her skin so much.

"All right then, let's cold-wrap her leg. Might as well put some bandages on her other legs, too. It can't hurt."

"I've got everything we need in my tack box."

Caleb nodded. "Okay, I'll go ask Raffael if he can watch her, check on the leg in a bit, and change her wrap. That'll give us a little daylight left before we head over to my house."

7

Cassie was obliged to ride with Caleb in his truck. She'd driven the trailer down from New York to transport Hot Lips and the ponies, leaving the Jeep for Alex, Thompson, and the kids. Caleb had argued her out of the idea of borrowing the farm's truck, insisting that it would be no problem for him to return her to Five Oaks later.

It was unsettling, the effect his presence in the close confines of the cab had on her, but then again, she'd never met anyone who possessed such blatant masculine appeal. Even Brad, who was undeniably handsome, fell to the ranks of a mere pretty boy in comparison.

As they turned onto the road from the driveway, Caleb began describing the surrounding region.

"We're on the road that leads back to town, if you drive in the opposite direction. From my house, it's about a fifteen-minute drive. All the shops and markets are located either in town itself or in the small mall that's just on the edge of town. Luckily, enough of the stores in town are doing a strong enough business that the mall hasn't taken over all the commerce."

"Does the school bus stop by your house?" Cassie asked, thinking of the twins.

"Yes. It used to pick me up at the end of our driveway. There are still kids living in our area, so the bus route can't have changed. If you prefer to drive them, it's not a long drive."

"Well, they were terribly excited about riding on a school bus. Like the big kids."

"Yeah, I can see that. Still, I remember how nervous I was that first morning, standing at the end of the driveway with my mom. I tried to talk her out of the whole school thing entirely." Caleb grinned at the memory, and Cassie felt herself relax a little. It was easy to picture Caleb as an adorable five-year-old, dark brown hair enchantingly curly, clutching his mother's hand.

"Don't you have brothers or sisters?"

"I have an older sister, Emily. But she's twelve years older. My parents tried for years after my sister's birth to have a second child. Then they kind of gave up." Caleb glanced at Cassie, his eyes filled with wicked delight. "I was what you might call an unexpected surprise. Anyway, Emily and I never went to the same schools. By the time I entered first grade, she was a senior, driving herself to high school."

"Does she still live nearby? Melissa told me your parents moved to Arizona."

"No, she got married and moved away. She and her husband bought an enormous house up in Portland, Maine, and run a bed-and-breakfast. It's a nice place. Sometimes I go up and stay with them for Thanksgiving when I'm not on call."

"Sounds lovely. I've only been to Maine once, I think. Not too many A-rated horse shows up there," Cassie explained.

Caleb chuckled. "Even if there are some, it's an awfully long haul." Caleb lifted a hand from the steering wheel and pointed ahead.

"Here's the driveway. It's a little shorter than Hank and Melissa's, but the house is set back far enough that you won't have to worry about the kids playing too close to the road. You've got fields in front and behind the house."

Cassie saw a sign posted at the foot of the driveway: Hay Fever Farm.

"Unusual name."

"A family joke. My grandfather bought this farm from the cousins of the people who owned Five Oaks. The wife of the farmer had absolutely terrible allergies. She forced her husband to sell the farm so that they could move to the city. Pollution was easier on her system than ragweed and hay."

"Why didn't they sell the place to their cousins?"

"Oh, they hated them because Five Oaks is a bigger parcel of land. They preferred selling the land to strangers, namely Grandpa Wells, than to their own kin."

"Nice people," she said dryly.

"Charmers," Caleb cheerfully agreed. "Anyway, it all worked out in spite of them. My father became a doctor, and when Hank and Melissa bought Five Oaks about twenty-five years ago, Dad asked Hank to work the land. A large portion of the hay used at Five Oaks comes from Hay Fever Farm."

As the pickup truck rounded a corner, Cassie caught her first glimpse of the house. White, with a dark shingled roof, and navy blue shutters framing each window, it looked like a classic colonial farmhouse. An open porch extended the front side of the house, with a walkway leading to its steps. Caleb turned off the ignition and stepped down from the truck, coming round to open Cassie's door.

"How lovely." She took in the picturesque setting before her, enhanced by the rays of the setting sun bathing the house in golden tones. There was a calm peacefulness to the house nestled among the green fields.

She didn't even have to walk inside to know instinctively that she was going to love it. So much for any token resistance, she'd be willing to be neighbors with the devil himself for a chance to have Sophie and Jamie grow up in a setting this beautiful.

"My mother did a lot of work on the inside of the house, and then turned her attention to the gardens. She became the town's unofficial landscape designer after she'd finished this house. First, all her friends wanted her to redo their own gardens. Word spread after that. It kept her busy once Emily reached school age."

Caleb waited politely as Cassie climbed down from the pickup. He shut the truck door behind her. Placing his hand lightly against her back, he guided her around to the house. The warmth of his fingers penetrated the layer of her sweater. She blamed the tiny shocks that coursed up and down her spine on the gentle friction of Caleb's hand pressing wool against bare skin.

"Mom planted lilacs and climbing roses on the sides of the house. From springtime on, the air is full of their scent. Over by the front porch she chose clematis and smaller shrub roses."

"Who keeps up all the gardens? It must be a lot of work," Cassie inquired. She knew Thompson liked gardening, but she didn't know how much time or energy the older woman wanted to devote to the task.

"Mom used to do it all herself. So she stuck mainly to perennials and shrubs. Now I've got Sam Jaffe, an elderly gentleman in his sixties who comes once a week. He's pretty good, my mother recommended him, and at this point the garden's fairly low maintenance: lawnmowing, some weeding. There's a housekeeper who comes once a week, too. She does both houses, mine and my parents."

"Thompson, the lady who works for me, also does housekeeping. Will that be a problem?"

Caleb shook his head. "You can always arrange it so that Mrs. Trapp comes in on your housekeeper's day off.

I'd kind of like to keep her on, if it's all the same to you. She worked for my parents and the extra money helps her."

"All right, just let me know how much to pay her."

"Okay." He smiled. It was pretty clear from her questions that Cassie was already a goner when it came to the house. "We'll work that out once you're settled in." Caleb bent down to the ground and plucked a small, bell-shaped, white flower that bordered the edge of the house. He offered it to Cassie. "Here. It's a snowdrop. We've had an early spring, so the crocuses and daffodils will be out soon. Tulips a bit later. It's a beautiful time of year here."

Touched, Cassie smiled shyly in thanks. "I don't think I've ever met a man who knows the names of so many flowers."

Caleb laughed. "Ah, the bane of my youth. Mom used to make me work for her once a week in the summer when I wasn't over at Five Oaks. Lawnmowing and gardening was how I earned my allowance. Sometimes even flower arrangements. It was positively mortifying when I was a teenager. I convinced myself I'd never get a girlfriend because of all those hours I was forced to spend working in the garden or picking flowers. But now, it comes in pretty handy." He paused and his dark, mesmerizing eyes locked with Cassie's blue ones.

"For instance," he murmured as he dipped his head and slowly brought his mouth down to her throat, his lips a soft whisper against her skin. "You're wearing honeysuckle. You smell like a summer's day by the sea. Divine."

His words, the nearness of his lips, sent Cassie's heart hammering, her breath caught in her throat, excitement and desire flooding her. Thoughts skittered around in her head, barely forming before they disappeared as quickly. Will he kiss me? Oh, please, yes. I mean, no, it's too soon. Oh, but I want to so.

Against his lips Caleb felt the frantic fluttering of her pulse as he bent over her. With sensuous delight he watched how her silky lashes drifted downwards and felt her body lean fractionally closer to his. His own heart thundered in anticipation. Knowing she could be his, he hungered for a taste. He wanted her kiss.

Then, summoning a self-control he hadn't bothered or needed to exert in years, Caleb straightened, settling instead for a light kiss on the tip of Cassie's nose. There was no point in rushing a good thing. Instinct told him that if he pushed Cassie too fast, he might very well scare her off. Exhaling deeply, he tried to ignore his body's growing arousal.

A crooked smile shaped his lips at the bewildered expression on Cassie's face as her eyes opened once more. Desire lingered, at war with confusion.

"Come on Cassie, let me take you inside."

Determined not to show how disoriented she felt, Cassie succeeded in following Caleb up the steps to the front porch. Sheer force of will had her making an appreciative murmur, even though her brain scarcely registered the porch swing and the comfortable rockers set beside it. By the time she'd reached the landing she'd managed to regain control of her body, if not her racing thoughts.

Why hadn't he kissed her? she wondered, slightly irritated. She'd certainly made it plain that she was agreeable—gosh, she'd almost melted into a puddle at his feet. Cassie was still amazed that she'd responded so strongly to what amounted to no more than a nuzzle of the throat and a brotherly kiss on the nose.

She must be really desperate if that was all it took to set her off. Maybe, she reasoned, it was because she'd hardly dated since her engagement to Brad. It had taken her a long time to get over the pain of their breakup. Then, she'd either just been too busy or, on the few dates she'd accepted, hadn't been even remotely interested in the men who'd tried to kiss her. It must be her lack of practice that was sending her senses reeling each time Caleb came near.

Determined to forget the incident and focus instead on the house, where her thoughts should be, Cassie took two extra steps into the front hall, distancing herself from Caleb.

It was next to impossible to take his eyes off her as she stood there, a flush still delicately staining her cheeks. She was so lovely, dressed in a baggy cable-knit sweater and jeans that it was all he could do to stop himself from taking her into his arms once again. Perhaps she truly had bewitched him earlier this morning in the barn. He ached so badly, he wondered why she couldn't see the waves of desire he felt rolling over him.

Reminding himself of the point of their visit, Caleb began rattling off specifics, hoping the details would bore him into a near comatose state.

"Downstairs, there's the living room, dining room, study, kitchen, pantry, and a bathroom. My parents took a few pieces of their furniture with them. If you think you'll need anything, just let me know."

Cassie had already entered the living room ahead of him, noting the smaller study that adjoined it. She shook her head, her golden hair brushing against her shoulders.

His eyes watched as its thick mass swept back and forth across her slender back. He imagined her golden hair against her naked skin. Against his skin, wrapped around him.

Cassie's voice forced an end to his erotic daydream.

"I wouldn't have noticed a lack. Everything is so perfect." A note of skepticism crept into her voice as she admired the simple, clean lines of the furniture. Dark brown oak chairs and tables stood in the living room. The couch, a deep blue, was placed against the wall between two windows. A muted blue and cream floral-patterned rug covered the wide-planked floors.

"Are you sure you want two five-year-olds running through this place? They can be more destructive than a hurricane."

Caleb laughed. "You wouldn't believe it, but most of this stuff was here when I was a kid, and I was pretty incorrigible. My mom was forever dragging me off to pick up some disaster I'd left behind." He shrugged. "If it worries you, you can have the twins keep the crayons in the kitchen. But my parents always intended for there to be children in the house."

"What about you?" Cassie asked impulsively, her curiosity about him overriding discretion. "Surely your parents would be thrilled to know their son is living in their home?"

Caleb stiffened slightly and was silent for a moment, but he didn't ignore her question. "When I married, my parents were still living here. We could have moved into the carriage house, but Pamela preferred to live closer to town. Our marriage didn't last long enough for this house to become an issue."

"I'm sorry." Cassie felt extremely gauche, annoyed with herself for having pried into Caleb's private life.

"Don't be," he bit out harshly, then softened his voice when he saw Cassie's startled expression. "It was a bad marriage for far longer than it was good. We weren't right for each other."

The understatement of the century, he thought cynically to himself. But he wasn't about to go into the sordid details of his marriage to Pamela.

Cassie wished she had the courage to ask him more questions and she wished she could think of something else to say other than, I'm sorry.

So, she said nothing.

For long moments, silence reigned. At last Caleb seemed to shake off his pensiveness. He motioned for Cassie to precede him through the doorway.

"The kitchen's through here. Then I'll show you the upstairs. There's something you're going to go wild over."

Glad that thoughts of his ex-wife were no longer haunting him, Cassie replied jokingly, "What, a king-size waterbed that vibrates?"

Caleb laughed, the rich sound filling the room. He gave Cassie a devilish grin, his teasing mood restored. "What a kinky mind you have, Slim. I love that in a woman." Caleb raised his hands, halting any further questions. "No, no. I'm not going to tell. I think I'll surprise you."

After they'd toured the kitchen, Caleb led Cassie upstairs. "There are six bedrooms in all. Two on each side of the hall and then two larger bedrooms on either end of the house. If I were you, I'd stake my claim on this one. It was my parents'."

Cassie entered the room. A cherry wood double bed was set against one wall. Opposite the bed, there was a large bay window with a window seat and cushions arranged invitingly, offering a view of meadows and rolling hills, still visible in the deepening dusk. Cassie smiled with pleasure at the sense of coziness and comfort the room gave.

"You're right. The room's lovely. The entire house is incredible."

"Slim, you ain't seen nothing yet," Caleb said. He opened a door that Cassie hadn't noticed in her enthusiasm over the view. With a Cheshire cat grin, Caleb let her pass. Curious to see what Caleb could find so noteworthy in a house that already bordered on the marvelous, Cassie stepped inside. Only to stop. Enchanted. Enthralled. In heaven.

Cassie stared at the sunken jacuzzi in silence, already envisioning easing the day's aches and pains in a whirl of hot, pulsing jets. The muscles in her lower back and thighs, brutalized after her roller coaster ride on Hot Lips, cried out at the sight of the deep, massive tub.

She didn't hear Caleb approach. She hardly registered the fact that he was standing in front of her. Until he began talking. Heatedly, fervently.

"Sweet Jesus, Cassie, I thought I was going to be able to keep my hands off you, but I can't resist that look on your face. Like an angel in a dream." He reached out and gently drew her toward him, flush against the hard planes of his body.

Cassie didn't think to protest. His hot, whispered words, his hands, his mouth flowed over her, caressing all her senses. "Cassie, sweet Cassie, do you have any idea of what you do to me? I'm losing my mind."

Unable to reply, Cassie could only moan helplessly. Caleb rained warm kisses over her face, brushing eyelids, cheeks, jaw, trailing his mouth down the slender column of her neck before returning again and again to plunder her soft lips. Hungrily tasting her.

Her skin might never have been touched before. The sensation of his hands sweeping down the length of her body, learning the shape of her breasts, the narrow indentation of her slender waist was so devastating, so new. His mouth continued its erotic assault, his teeth gently tugging the soft flesh of her earlobe, sparking a wildfire in her nerve endings.

Desperate to experience the feel of his mouth against hers once more, Cassie's fingers closed, fists digging into his hair, guiding his lips to hers. Her body quivered, her knees weakened as Caleb responded, his tongue entering, seeking the heat of her mouth.

His blood had turned to fire, coursing through him, setting him ablaze. Like a blind man searching, he fingered the hem of Cassie's sweater and slipped underneath. The intense pleasure that flooded him at the satiny warmth he found there made him groan. He needed more, more heat.

"Christ Almighty, Slim," Caleb's voice was strained, his words rushing with the force of his breathing. "I've been thinking about your sweater since you walked into the barn. What I could do with it. Did you know? How easy it would be to slip my hands inside and find you so soft and sleek. Like warm silk. Do you like the way I touch you?" At her moan of pleasure, Caleb's hands moved, cupping the gentle swell of her breasts. "Your breasts have been in my dreams since I saw you in Hank's office. The way they looked. How they would feel in my hands if I could touch them, caress them. Like now . . . perfect."

Wrapped in the sensual spell Caleb wove so skillfully, so effortlessly, Cassie's hands clutched his muscular shoulders, her legs too weak to support her. She could no more resist him than she could stop the tremors that were enveloping her body.

His body was screaming for release. Never before could he remember feeling this degree of fevered urgency for a woman. He needed to see her naked, her glorious hair spread out like a golden halo about her.

"Sweetheart, let me take you to bed," Caleb murmured urgently in her ear. "I don't want to make love to you here." He moved to scoop her into his arms, but stopped when Cassie stiffened abruptly and hastily stumbled back, freeing herself from his embrace.

His whispered words had the same effect as if her body had plunged into an ocean of ice. Cold shock washed over her, her mind numbly taking in the scenario of the past. . . . God, she wasn't even sure how much time had passed while Caleb had been kissing her like a starved man at a banquet. With her equally famished. She couldn't believe it. Here was a man she'd known for perhaps three hours, the first man she'd even kissed in *months,* and she'd been close to begging him to make love to her on—wildly, she looked around, no longer even sure where she was—on the bathroom floor. Next to a jacuzzi, of all things. Dear God, what had possessed her?

Caleb watched her withdrawal with deep frustration. That's what he got for opening his mouth. He should have just kept kissing her senseless. Then he could have picked her up, holding her close against him, and carried her to the bed. Slowly, he'd have undressed her, caressing her flesh inch by inch as he uncovered it. He groaned in silent frustration at the image so clear in his mind, knowing from the look on Cassie's face that there wasn't a snowball's chance in hell she would let him touch her again any time soon. His errant thoughts were interrupted by her voice. It was strained with tension.

"I don't know what kind of impression you have of me, but I want you to know that I don't usually do this."

"Do what, kiss? Surely you've been kissed before?" Caleb replied, hoping to tease a small smile from her. No success.

"Very funny. You know perfectly well what I mean. But if you want, I'll spell it out." Her spine straightened with the rigidity of a marine. She glared at him defiantly. "I'm not fast. I'm not easy. And I don't hop into bed with men I've known for a total of three hours. If you're thinking that having me live in this house means that I'm going to sleep with you, you can think again. I have two small children to take care of. And my job at Five Oaks is far too important to me to screw it up because you can't control your overactive hormones." Knowing it was unfair, she nevertheless forced the last bit out, unwilling to acknowledge the depth of her attraction, either to herself or to Caleb.

There were few things he hated as much as hypocrisy, especially when it came to sex. They both knew damn well he wasn't the only one suffering from overactive hormones. Cassie's prissy righteousness nettled, provoking him.

"If I remember correctly, Slim, you seemed to be enjoying yourself just fine, if those throaty moans you made were any kind of gauge." His gaze held hers. "You were with me every step of the way. Moreover, I've never once thought of you as easy or fast. Ninety-five percent of the

time, you've got more prickles than a porcupine. The rest
of the time, though, we seem to get along pretty well. And
for your information, I don't want you here as a convenient
fuck." He use the word deliberately, angrily. He was mad
enough not to care whether he offended her delicate sensibilities.

Her outraged gasp was loud enough to be heard in the
next county.

Unmoved by the sound, Caleb stepped closer, his arms
pulling her stiff body flush with his. With his head lowered, his lips were merely inches away, and she looked up
to find his eyes dark with angry passion. His breath
brushed over her lips as he spoke once more.

"But just to make everything crystal clear for you,
Cassie, we *are* going to make love. You want to and I'm
damn near dying to. And when we do, it won't have anything to do with where you live, your kids, your job, or the
fact that I'm your boss. It'll just be the two of us. You and
me. Alone. Together."

The rest of the tour passed in a thick fog for Cassie.
Caleb, as she was coming to learn, could shift moods with
mercurial swiftness. As quickly as it had come, his anger
vanished, replaced by his usual teasing self. Cassie however, remained off balance, still dazed by the passion he'd
so easily ignited.

On the way out of his parents' house, Caleb had led her
through the back door, via the kitchen, and pointed out the
carriage house where he lived. The exterior was painted in
identical colors to the main house. Cassie saw two large
mullioned windows set on either side of a huge barn door.

"Wow. Is that your front door?"

"No, it's over on the side of the house. What you're seeing used to be the original entrance for the carriages and
wagons. My parents decided to transform it into an enormous window. There's a matching one at the back. They

both have screened wooden frames, In the summer when it's hot, I can swing the doors open and latch them to the house. All that open space provides a good cross breeze and the view out the back is amazing."

"It must be lovely in the summer."

"Yeah, they did a terrific job on it. It still has the space and feeling of a barn inside, but it's also comfortable." Caleb paused and looked at Cassie. In the darkening evening, it was difficult to read his expression.

"I'd invite you in, but the way I'm feeling right now, I'm not sure I'd let you leave without trying to convince you to stay the night."

Cassie said nothing, but she felt a blush stealing over her features, suddenly grateful now for the concealing darkness. Caleb laughed softly at her mute response.

"I guessed as much. Come on, Slim. I'll take you back to the farm. You'd best keep your fingers crossed that Hank hasn't eaten all your share though, or you might have to go out to dinner with me."

"At least in public you'd keep your hands to yourself," she replied, waspish and annoyed that he could tease when she was still reeling from the aftershocks of their embrace.

Caleb's laugh rang out in the night. "You never can be too sure. Let's go out together tomorrow and test that idea."

"No thanks, I'm sure I'll be busy. I generally wash my hair at night."

"Slim, you've wounded me," Caleb protested, his hand clutching his chest in a theatrical gesture. "Passed over in favor of a shampoo. I thought that line died in the sixties."

Cassie made a sound of utter disgust as Caleb continued to shake with mirth. Determined to have the last word, Cassie yanked open the truck door.

"You should forget the vet business. Maybe you should consider a career change, too. I read somewhere they're

filming *Dumb & Dumber II*. You could easily get the third
lead role: Dumbest."

When the pickup truck pulled into Five Oaks, Cassie
futilely attempted to scramble out of the truck before Caleb
could get to her side. For such a big man, he moves
awfully fast, she reflected disgruntedly, as he opened her
door and helped her out. Taking her by the elbow, they
walked together to the steps of Melissa and Hank's house.

Caleb could sense Cassie's eagerness to flee into the
safety of the brightly lit house. Perversely, he slowed his
steps.

"I'll give Mrs. Trapp a call and have her come in and
give the house a thorough cleaning. She can make the beds
up for you. I'm glad you're going to take the house."

Was it her imagination, or could she really feel the heat
of his body from where he stood? In contrast, the night air
was bitingly cool at her back. Vivid memories assailed
her—of his heat, of all the wonderful things Caleb could
do with his hands and mouth. Unable to help herself, she
swayed, like a reed in the wind, closer to his seductive
warmth.

That tiny, infinitesimal movement was enough. His lips
swept lightly over hers, once, twice, and then a third time,
their weight as heavy as a butterfly's wings. She rose on
her tiptoes to meld her lips closer to his.

At her instinctive response, Caleb groaned, wanting
nothing more than to deepen the kiss. Reluctantly, he made
himself remember where they were. She'd probably faint if
Hank or Melissa were to come upon them now, and Caleb
didn't want to risk it. Cassie was skittish enough already.
Withdrawing his mouth from her lips, he stood, his forehead resting lightly against hers, breathing deep lungfuls of
the cool evening air. His hands lifted, stroking her hair,
gently smoothing the curls against the side of her head. He
allowed himself the pleasure of a final kiss, chastely

pressed against her brow. "Good night, Cassie sweet. See you tomorrow."

Caleb turned and slipped off into the dark, leaving Cassie to stare after him with troubled eyes.

The sky was still an unrelieved black when Cassie rolled out of bed the next morning. In a way, she was grateful that she'd set her alarm clock for five. At least she didn't have to continue her futile pretense at sleep. Her night had been tormented with images of Caleb—his teasing dark eyes, his firm lips, his strong, sensitive hands. No matter how much she tossed and turned, how determinedly she tried to block him from her mind, Caleb was there, mocking her, kissing her, delighting her. What mysterious power did he possess that he could invade her dreams, disrupt her thoughts?

She tried to reassure herself with the thought that maybe now that she knew what kissing him was like, she'd be better equipped to resist him. Yeah, right, Cassie replied mockingly to herself. She'd like to see any woman resist Caleb Wells's seduction. The man gave a whole new meaning to the term *sex appeal*.

Cassie pulled on her running tights, a running bra, and an old sweatshirt. Brushing her hair in quick, impatient strokes, she pulled it back into a ponytail and, sneakers and socks in hand, made her way quietly downstairs to the kitchen.

The linoleum felt cold against her bare feet as she moved around the kitchen, pouring herself a cup of coffee and a glass of water. Cassie never ran well if she ate too soon beforehand. But she couldn't run a step if she didn't have a bit of caffeine jolting her system awake. She sat staring through the window while the sky turned to a gun-metal grey, a narrow wash of red and gold coloring the horizon. She loved this time of the day when she could watch the dawn unfold in peaceful solitude. She tried not to wonder whether Caleb Wells also enjoyed waking up for sunrises.

Coffee finished, she pulled on her socks and running shoes, her movements quick and efficient. She wanted to get her run in, eat breakfast, and begin her training sessions as early as possible. That afternoon she had an appointment to meet with the principal of Sophie and Jamie's school. In spite of Melissa's reassurance that the principal, John Perkins, was a horse person, Cassie felt nervous about the meeting, anxious that Sophie and Jamie make a smooth transition into their new school and their new life. Was she uprooting them too much by moving down to Virginia? They were going to miss Alex so much. He was the closest thing to a father the twins had.

She gave a mental shake, banishing her worries as she went out the front door and set out at an easy jog down the road. She'd make sure the twins were fine, Cassie thought determinedly. They were the most important thing in her life and she'd move heaven and earth to make them happy and secure.

Cassie set the chronometer on her watch. She planned to run twenty-five minutes in one direction and then turn around and head back to the farm. She estimated that she'd get in a little over a five-mile run that way. Running was a key part of her training schedule, as was weightlifting. Cassie was convinced she rode better when she knew she was strong both physically and aerobically. She couldn't understand riders who wanted their horses to be in top physical form, but from themselves demanded little, as if merely grabbing hold of the reins and hanging on, helpful as a sack of potatoes, was sufficient exercise. The best riders she knew were as diligent about their own fitness as they were about the training routines of their mounts.

Whether consciously or not, Cassie headed out in the direction of Caleb's house. True, she didn't know that many routes yet and she'd remembered the drive yesterday as being picturesque, full of gently rolling hills and trees bordering the side of the road. She certainly wasn't running down the road to his house at five-thirty in the morning because she was feeling like some lovesick fifteen-year-old with her first crush. She wasn't even sure she liked him.

Cassie ran on, her bent arms swinging rhythmically at her sides, her breathing deep and easy. There were a lot of hills, but none had really made her start to burn yet. Perhaps she'd try to pick up the pace on the way home. She glanced at her watch. Ten more minutes, then she'd do a U-turn and head back to the farm.

The sky was lightening, with streaks of bright blue pushing back the darker grey overhead. It was promising to be beautiful, though the air was still quite chilly. Cassie thought wistfully how great it would be to ride in a T-shirt and feel the warm sun on her skin.

Then she saw him.

She recognized him immediately. How many men over six feet, who moved with the grace he did, would be running down this stretch of the road at this hour of the morning? Cassie could tell the moment he recognized her, too. His pace changed, eating up the ground between them. Propelling him forward, his long legs lengthened their stride as the distance between them closed. Cassie continued at her even pace, refusing to acknowledge his quickened pace by changing her stride. Let him show off if he wants to, he'll probably be totally winded by the time he reaches me.

He wasn't winded.

He was furious.

He grabbed her arm and pulled her to a halt. "Don't you have a lick of common sense? Where have you been living for the past twenty years? Shangri-la?"

"Good morning to you, too! What in the world are you talking about? Actually, forget it. I'm not interested," Cassie bit out, now angry herself at Caleb's domineering tone. Impatiently, she shook off his arm and started running. Hoping he'd take himself and his bad mood away.

Behind her, she heard him mutter a curse. A second later, he fell into step alongside her. "Don't you know it's dangerous for a woman to run alone? This may seem like bucolic countryside but there are crimes around here. Rapes. You shouldn't be out here alone this early in the morning."

"Excuse me, but I've lived in New York, I know how to be alert to danger."

"Does Hank know you're out here?"

"No," she shot back tersely. She'd been having such a wonderful run until Caleb had come and made her feel like a reckless fool. She was used to her independence and hadn't really thought about the possible dangers in running alone this early with no one aware of her whereabouts.

"Jesus!"

Cassie blocked out the other oaths that poured from his mouth. "Look," she finally said, exasperated. "I'm sorry that I came out alone. Believe it or not, I'm not totally irresponsible. Back home, my brother Alex used to run with me, but here I don't have a partner. And I wasn't about to knock on Hank and Melissa's door at five-thirty in the morning to tell them I was going out. It might surprise you to learn that I have managed to reach the age of twenty-four without a baby-sitter. So, good-bye. See you later." She picked up her pace, hoping he'd get the message that despite his concern, she preferred to run alone.

He didn't. Obtuse man.

His long legs kept pace with hers, his feet hitting the asphalt in a steady rhythm as they jogged side by side. Cassie glanced at him out of the corner of her eye, annoyed that he didn't find the pace uncomfortable. She'd been hoping to see him start to wheeze and lose his form, but he looked utterly relaxed, breathing easily, his arms loose at his sides.

He was dressed in baggy grey sweatpants and a University of Pennsylvania sweatshirt. Perspiration had darkened the neck of his sweatshirt. Lines of sweat trickled down the column of his neck. She could imagine its taste, its saltiness on the tip of her tongue. She wished she weren't thinking about what his stomach might look like if she were to run her hands against it. Sweaty and hard. Her pace increased a little more.

"How much farther are you planning on going?" Caleb asked, trying to make a stab at normal conversation. He'd been repeatedly telling himself to calm down for the last five minutes. It certainly hadn't been his intention to jump down Cassie's throat, but when he'd seen her all alone, on an empty road, in the half-light of dawn, he'd lost it.

He couldn't figure out why Cassie was eliciting these bizarre and foreign responses from him. Sure, she was beautiful, sexy, and drove him nearly mad with desire, but that didn't explain why he felt this need to be near her. Or to protect her. Hell, if he were honest, most of the women he'd slept with recently he couldn't wait to say good-bye to. And he certainly wouldn't have gone ballistic if he'd seen one of them running alone. Whatever the reason, he was sure this wasn't a healthy condition. Cassie's voice broke into his thoughts.

"I was planning on going for another five minutes or so in this direction and then turning back and heading to the farm. It's getting quite light now, so feel free to head on back. I wouldn't want to tire you out," she added cattily.

He laughed. "Oh, don't worry about me, Slim. I'll just huff and puff along with you if that's all right. Wouldn't want to get a tire around my middle. How often do you run?"

"I try to run three or four times a week. I do light weight lifting on the other days with a set of free weights I have."

"As one of your employers, I can't tell you how pleased

I am that you keep yourself in such good shape." The grin on his face was both devilish and admiring. And those crinkles at the corners of his eyes when he smiled were far too appealing.

"Thanks. I try to keep the bosses happy," Cassie replied lightly, his smile erasing their confrontation like the sun dispelling the clouds from the sky. Perhaps running with Caleb Wells wasn't really so unpleasant after all. After you got used to it.

They ran on in a strangely companionable silence, turning around when Cassie indicated she was ready. On the way back, Cassie was sure Caleb would leave her at the foot of his driveway, but he surprised her by continuing on, seeing her to Five Oaks's drive.

"There, now I'm back safe and sound. Thanks for keeping me company." Cassie was walking around in small circles, shaking her legs out to keep the muscles loose.

"My pleasure. When are you going again?"

"Tomorrow. Why?" Cassie inclined her head up to look at him.

"It would make me feel a whole lot better if I knew where and when you were running. Just in case."

He couldn't be serious. Cassie was about to protest until she saw the look on his face.

Caleb continued. "If you want, I can try to join you some mornings, depending on my schedule. Think of it as a way of keeping me in shape."

A bubble of hysterical laughter rose inside her at the idea of Caleb Wells needing to keep in shape. She didn't even want to contemplate what his body might look like *improved*. It was already ruining her peace of mind.

"I'll think about it. See you." Cassie turned, intending to jog slowly back to the house. She'd started a few steps when suddenly, she felt herself grabbed by the middle and swept around in an arc, her legs skimming over the ground like a doll twirled in the air by a little child. Caleb turned her effortlessly in his arms and set her down in front of him.

"Don't go yet, Slim." Caleb's voice was suddenly husky. "I haven't had a chance to say good morning yet."

Still breathless with surprise, Caleb's mouth swept down and captured hers. He tasted hot, salty, and sweet, from exercise and toothpaste. Irresistibly delicious. Cassie returned his kiss, matching his intensity and need with her own. Her fingers raked through his damp hair, holding him close as her tongue entwined feverishly with his.

He was ready to burst, his blood pounding in his veins. Cassie felt like heaven in his arms. He wanted, was dying to bury himself deep within her. Why, he asked himself in frustration, did he keep grabbing her in such inconvenient places? First a bathroom and now the middle of a frigging road. He was sure he had more finesse than to make love to Cassie on a gravel driveway. Maybe there was a tree he could prop her up against. *Damn it!*

The blast of a horn as an amused trucker passed them had Caleb and Cassie breaking apart, guilty as teenagers caught necking in public. Moments later, when Caleb could breathe without feeling as if he'd just sprinted the last mile, he shrugged his shoulders, a smile tugging at his lips.

"Guess our secret is out. It'll probably make the headlines in the local paper."

Cassie looked at him aghast. Was he kidding or did this place really operate like an overgrown grapevine? She wanted time to settle in with the kids and get to know people on her own without having her name romantically linked with the local vet and partner of Five Oaks. She wanted to be Cassie Miller, mother of Jamie and Sophie, trainer at Five Oaks, not Caleb Wells's new girlfriend, one in a string of many, no doubt.

Caleb's smile slowly evaporated as he read Cassie's expression. Right. So she didn't mind a little private neck-

ing, but heaven forbid she should have to own up publicly
to her desire.

"Sorry the idea offends you so much." His pride hurt, he
turned away and bent down to adjust his laces. Cassie
stood awkwardly, staring down at the dark head of curls,
not knowing how to explain her feelings, not knowing if
she should try. He didn't give her the chance.

"Look, I'll see you later. I've got to shower and head
over to the hospital to see some patients. Would you mind
waiting to ride Orion until about eleven? I'd like to watch
your session." Caleb's tone was overly polite, a stranger's,
his head still lowered.

Within the space of a few seconds, he'd succeeded in
erecting a wall between them that Cassie didn't know if
she should try to breach.

"That's fine," she replied equally stiffly, her formality
matching his. "I'll work with the three-year-olds, first. I
just have to be finished by early afternoon. I've got an
appointment with the head of the elementary school, John
Perkins."

"Fine. I'll take a look at Hot Lips's tendon before you
go off. So long." Straightening, Caleb barely glanced in
Cassie's direction as he turned away, his long legs carrying
him off, fast and effortlessly. Confused and uncertain,
Cassie stood, staring at his retreating figure.

How was it possible that the arrogant Caleb Wells could
be so hurt over such a minor blow? Should she care? She
was still trying to sort out the reason for her overwhelming
attraction to him. There were his obvious good looks. But
then she'd been around lots of handsome men before. The
horse world was chock full of them. And she'd never lost
her head so completely. Certainly never been tempted to
kiss them as if the world were going to end. True, the
majority of the men she'd met had been conceited and
shallow bores. Caleb might be arrogant, but he didn't seem

conceited. No, he was charming, clever, and arrogant. And too seductive by half.

And he was her boss, which was proving far too complicated, no matter what Caleb might say to convince her otherwise. If she were smart, she'd steer a wide berth around Dr. Caleb Wells.

8

*H*ank and Melissa were at the breakfast table when Cassie walked in. Glancing up from his paper, Hank took in her sweaty face and running gear, inquiring mildly before returning his attention to the morning paper, "Have a good run?"

So much for Hank's concern over rapists and molesters, thought Cassie dryly.

"Lovely in an odd sort of way. I ended up running with Caleb for part of it." She paused for effect. "He seemed a mite concerned for my safety. Are there many escaped convicts on the loose that I should know about?"

Hank laughed, folding the newspaper in half. Melissa merely smiled. Cassie moved about the kitchen, fixing herself toast, cereal, juice, and coffee. When at last she sat down beside them, Hank explained. "Funny thing about Caleb, he's quite the gentleman. You know, always holding doors for women, getting up when a lady enters the room. That sort of thing. Doesn't surprise me that he decided he needed to protect you from any bad guys lurking about at six o'clock in the morning. Mark and Susan drilled his manners into him pretty well." Hank took a slow sip from

his coffee cup. "All that was probably wasted on Pamela."
Melissa nodded, but remained silent.

Cassie swallowed the bait whole. Unable to resist, she
pretended to be raptly absorbed in the morning ritual of
slicing her banana and pouring milk over her cereal as she
casually inquired, "What was she like? I gather the marriage didn't last long?"

Melissa and Hank exchanged a smile over Cassie's bent
head.

"What was she like? Well, beautiful enough to make a
man's head rotate a full three hundred and sixty degrees
just to get a better look. But hard. After a while you tended
to notice that even more than her looks. How would you
describe her, honey?"

Melissa didn't hesitate an instant. "She's the kind of
woman who wears a silk blouse and open-toed, high-
heeled sandals into a barn full of horses."

"Oh dear. That's awful." Cassie tried not to snicker too
loudly at the scathing characterization.

Melissa smiled, shaking her head. "Caleb was awfully
young. Pamela simply broadsided him. She had him at the
altar before he knew what was happening. Or any of us
could talk him out of it. In a way, I guess I feel sorry for
her, too . . . at least a little bit, and only on my *most* compassionate days. I think she had this fantasy image in her
mind of how exciting and glamorous the life of a vet might
be, especially for a vet living in these parts who specializes
in horses. Like something out of a made-for-TV movie.
And she was so greedy, not even Caleb's success—and
he's done quite well in a short amount of time—satisfied
her. She left him for some fat cat with a huge bank account
and a string of polo ponies."

Cassie's eyes widened. She sat, stunned by the information. Her cereal quickly turned to sodden mush, forgotten
in its bowl. "You mean she left Caleb for another man?"

"No, I think she actually left Caleb for a bigger bank

account and a purse full of gold cards. Because even now, with all her wealth, married to another man, she's still hovering about trying to lure Caleb back. See whether he'll bite. I certainly don't like the way her eyes eat him up whenever we have the bad luck to cross her path. She hurt his heart and his pride and doesn't even have the decency to leave him alone so that he can heal. Although Caleb tries not to show it, the divorce left him foundering. Her popping up every other minute just makes it all the more difficult."

"But if they're divorced, why would Caleb need to have anything to do with her at all?"

Melissa mumbled a vague reply, something about a divorce settlement, in any case difficult to hear as Hank succumbed to a loud coughing spasm that filled the Sawyers's kitchen.

Suddenly both Melissa and Hank remembered tasks that required their immediate attention, abandoning Cassie to her soggy cereal and her thoughts. She glanced down at the bowl in distaste, shoving it aside. The toast, though cold, was still edible. She picked up a slice.

How awful for Caleb to have discovered too late just how ill-suited he and Pamela were for each other. In comparison, Cassie realized she'd been far luckier. She learned fairly early that marrying Brad could only end in disaster. And the pain that might have been inflicted on Sophie and Jamie was avoided.

That bitter month of February when Brad revealed the true source of his antagonism remained all too clear in her mind, as if it were yesterday.

First, that snowy grey afternoon when Brad had come by her family's home to pick her up. College friends were visiting the city and wanted to get together for the evening. Brad had arranged to meet them at one of his favorite hangouts. But when he arrived, he found Cassie wearing a path into the living room rug as she attempted to soothe a shrieking Sophie. Brad had looked at Sophie cradled in her arms with impatience.

"What's going on? Why aren't you ready?" His gaze moved over her, taking in her threadbare sweatpants and rumpled turtleneck.

"Oh, Brad, I'm sorry! Things have been so chaotic here, I forgot to call. Sophie's not well."

"Why isn't Thompson taking care of it? Isn't that what she's paid for?"

"Thompson's upstairs with Jamie, giving him a bath."

Brad muttered something Cassie couldn't catch. His eyes narrowed on the baby once more.

"I really am sorry, Brad, but please understand. Sophie's been like this off and on since yesterday. She's got a cold and her teeth are bothering her. The pediatrician's given her drops, but they don't seem to help. He said there's not much we can do except to make her as comfortable as possible."

"Well if there's nothing you can do, then let's go. Thompson can deal." He glanced at his watch. "I told Greg we'd meet him at six. We'll be late if we don't hustle."

"Brad, just look at her! Sophie's sick! And Thompson was up all night with her. She's exhausted. I'm the twins' guardian, as well as their aunt. I *can't* leave. I'm sorry, you'll have to go without me. I'm sure they'll understand."

Before her astonished eyes, Brad's face darkened to a deep, ugly red. Without another word, he stormed out, the front door shuddering in its frame seconds after his departure. Leaving Cassie dazed and sick at heart.

She didn't hear from him for more than a week.

Their engagement was over on the evening of the fourteenth, Valentine's Day. It would have been far more fitting had it been Halloween, because even now that final scene played inside her head like a nightmare.

Cassie had been an emotional wreck when Brad finally called. His behavior the afternoon of Sophie's sickness was one reason for her increasing nervousness. Too, Cassie realized it was imperative she broach the idea of the twins' adoption with Brad. Adopting them was a decision Cassie had made as she'd struggled with her grief over Tom's and Lisa's deaths. She was convinced of its rightness. She'd always assumed Brad would agree.

Subconsciously, however, Cassie must have guessed what Brad's reaction to her idea would be. Because when Brad finally called, suggesting they make up and celebrate Valentine's Day with a candlelit dinner at their favorite French restaurant, Cassie had deliberately dressed to please him. Her navy blue silk shift emphasized the slimness of her figure and enhanced the midnight blue of her eyes. She left her hair down, allowing the riotous curls their freedom. Her shoulders were bare, and she'd chosen the tea rose scent Brad said he loved on her skin.

It was over a dessert of raspberry mousse and champagne that Cassie managed to gather her courage and bring up the subject of Sophie and Jamie. "Brad, I've been thinking about the babies."

"Babies, what babies? Oh, your brother's kids." Brad took another sip from his champagne glass. He'd been drinking steadily since they'd arrived at the restaurant. "Yeah, I've been thinking, too. Mulling over ideas about what to do with them."

Determinedly optimistic, Cassie smiled, the candlelight adding to its brilliance.

"You have? That's wonderful!" She reached out to stroke his hand wrapped around the stem of the champagne glass. "You know, whenever I look at them I'm overwhelmed. They're so beautiful. I love you and them so much. Brad, wouldn't it be perfect if we could adopt Jamie and Sophie? We'd be a family. In my heart, I know that's what Tom and Lisa would have wanted."

"Yeah, well, they're gone and we're alive," Brad countered flatly as he lifted his glass, breaking the contact of their hands. The glass stem twirled between his fingers. "Adoption. That's a pretty big assumption you're making, Cassie. What makes you think I'm going to jump at the chance to raise someone else's children? Why should I? The way you've been acting, it's like those kids are the most important thing in the world. Well, they're not to me."

Right then, Cassie'd had the awful sensation that she was going to be sick all over the white damask tablecloth. "But . . . but, Brad!" she'd stammered. Taking a deep breath, she'd forced herself to begin again, to appear calm. Surely Brad's attitude was champagne induced.

"Jamie and Sophie are my nephew and niece. They're barely eleven months old and are orphans. Of course I'm trying to give them as much attention as possible. I'm their aunt and guardian. Wouldn't adopting them be the right thing?"

"And I'd get to assume the financial responsibility. Terrific. I hate to break it to you but I had other plans for my money. You probably don't have any idea how much it will cost, do you?"

"That is unfair and untrue, and you know it. Alex has devoted a lot of time and thought into investing my inheritance and managing the funds in the children's trust."

"And what if your hotshot brother's investments fail? I've had it up to here with how terrific he is. Let me tell you something, from where I see it, I'm the one who's doing all the giving: my name, my house, my protection. So, how about this for a plan? Let's get Alex to adopt the twins. Let him shoulder some *real* responsibility."

"Brad, you said you *loved* me." Cassie hated the pleading note she heard in her voice, but was frantic to find the person she loved.

Not this stranger sitting across from her.

Fear, too, made her voice quaver. She could no longer pretend that this was just the effect of one too many glasses.

"I do love you." Brad leaned forward and grabbed her cold hand, massaging hers roughly. "Come on, Cassie," he cajoled. "We don't need those kids. You and I can make our own babies. Lots of beautiful babies." His gaze dropped to her breasts, lingered, then slowly returned to her face. She cringed at the slight smirk on his lips. "I taught you how, didn't I?"

Abruptly, Cassie stood, trembling from head to foot. She fumbled for the engagement ring on her left hand and pulled it off, feeling the gold scrape her flesh. Carefully, deliberately, she laid it on the table in front of his dessert plate. The raspberry mousse was like a ghastly wound against the white porcelain.

"Good-bye, Brad. Please don't try to call." Cassie gathered her evening purse and left the table. She managed to reach the ladies' room before she was violently ill. Afterwards, she sat huddled in the bathroom, afraid to leave, afraid she might see Brad.

But as brutal as her experience had been, at least she had walked away from the ruins of her relationship with her pride and her sense of self intact. Remembering Melissa's description, Cassie wasn't sure Caleb had fared as well. What kind of a woman would leave someone as dynamic as Caleb for mere wealth? Cassie found it difficult to imagine that life for Caleb and his wife had been too uncomfortable financially, which meant that if Pamela really did leave him for someone richer, Melissa's harsh assessment was amply deserved. She *was* greedy. And stupid to boot.

By the time eleven o'clock rolled around, Cassie had worked with two of Five Oaks's younger prospects, a gelding and a mare, both just four years old. The youngsters had been started by Hank and Caleb together. Hank had explained that it was the part of the training he enjoyed most, working with the young horses, seeing they were gently and properly schooled from the beginning, so that they'd be on the right track for other trainers and riders later. He and Caleb always worked as a team: Hank on the ground advising, Caleb in the saddle.

Both the young mare, Silverspoon, and the gelding, Arrow, were from the same sire as Orion, Five Oaks's stud, Kenyon. Though their dams were different, Hank and Caleb hoped they would develop as impressively as their older half brother.

Hank had dropped by to observe Cassie and had set up some ground rails, known as cavalettis, and a couple of low fences for her to try them on. At this stage in their training, Cassie was careful not to demand too much too soon. Young horses were a lot like small children. They had short attention spans and were easily distracted. The most important thing in their development was for them to remain focused and willing. They had to like what they were doing, or else they'd never be champions.

Caleb arrived after Cassie had already begun warming up Orion, trotting him in large circles around the ring. She knew the instant he appeared. The intensity of his gaze on her was an almost palpable thing. She didn't pause to acknowledge Caleb's presence, nor did he interrupt, as Cassie continued working Orion on the flat, communicating to him with the light pressure of her hands and legs.

The workout over fences Cassie had devised for Orion was based on taking him over a group of four low jumps, split up into two on either side of the ring. By cantering in a large figure eight over the same four jumps again and again without stopping—as she might if she were working Orion on a larger and more difficult course—Cassie was able to zero in on any potential problems with his form. After she set him up for the jumps on one side of the ring, she cantered Orion through the center of the ring, checking his flying changes, making sure that he was able to switch his lead in midair smoothly in both directions and approach the oncoming fence properly balanced. By jumping over the same fences from different directions, she could see if Orion were equally comfortable at flying changes on the right and the left lead. It was an exercise Cassie often employed when she was just beginning to know her mount. Not terribly fancy, but it paid off when show season started.

Orion settled quickly into the rhythm of the exercise, neither rushing the fences, nor getting sloppy because they were set low. Relief swept over her. A few horses Cassie had ridden had the frustrating habit of nicking the fences with their hooves, because they weren't tucking their knees or hocks up high enough as they cleared the fence. Sometimes this happened because the jump was too difficult or too high, which was understandable, but sometimes it happened over easier or lower fences. A sign of boredom, a lack of care on the horse's part. At the major horse shows, where the jumps were supported by shallow cups, a nick that was a hair too hard would bring the pole tumbling down and penalty points tacked on.

When Cassie felt Orion's attention begin to wander, she used her voice to redirect him. It was important for him to realize that they were partners now, that they had to finish the work together. Letting a stallion like Orion think he was calling the shots would be disastrous.

"Come on now, Orion, these last four, and then we'll call it a day."

When the stallion had cleared the remaining jumps neatly, Cassie slowed him to a walk, reaching down to pat his gleaming neck. She circled the perimeter of the ring, conscious of Caleb standing by the gate, making no move to approach.

Shy and uncertain, Cassie admitted to herself that she lacked the necessary experience to handle the situation with Caleb Wells. In her mind, she accepted that it was far better to stay uninvolved. She had a new and challenging job, and she was the single parent of two small children.

She didn't need and couldn't afford the emotional complications Caleb Wells presented, and she knew she wouldn't be able to handle a one-night stand or a casual fling with him. She wasn't sophisticated enough or tough enough to walk away unscathed.

Oh, God, she wondered, why couldn't she get along with men as easily as she did horses? With horses, Cassie understood what they wanted and needed and she knew how to make them understand what *she* needed. But with men, it seemed as if they might as well be aliens from outer space. Alex, her brother, or Hank she could communicate with easily enough, but as soon as she became attracted to a man, her sense of self and her sense of direction just flew right out the window. Brad was a case in point. If it hadn't been for her instinctive need to protect Sophie and Jamie from any more pain and unhappiness than they'd already suffered, she might possibly have done whatever Brad suggested without thought of resistance.

Well, she resolved fiercely, *Brad taught me a lesson. I've got to think of the kids and myself first, not lose myself in a passionate affair with Caleb Wells. If I can keep my distance, I might be able to pull it off.*

And when we're together, I'll simply treat him as I treat Alex. Yeah, right, her inner voice replied. *That should be a piece of cake.*

Dismounting from Orion, she slipped the reins over his neck, gathered them in her hands, and led the stallion toward the gate where Caleb stood watching. He'd changed into black jeans, work boots, and a white cotton button-down shirt. His body looked whipcord lean and strong, but when Cassie looked into his face, her heart sank a little.

Caleb's expression remained identical to the one she remembered from this morning when he'd left her standing at the foot of Five Oaks's driveway. Chillingly polite, his dark, intelligent eyes shuttered. Gone was the teasing glint, the masculine admiration that turned so quickly to sexual hunger that she had seen in them before. That in a mere thirty-six hours Cassie had come to expect, to anticipate.

So much for kidding herself she wanted merely a fraternal relationship with Caleb Wells.

Nevertheless, this was surely for the best. She was here to ride, not to flirt. Caleb could doubtless, at the snap of his fingers, have women lining up for his personal amusement if he wished. She just happened to be around and convenient, no matter what he'd said to the contrary at his parents' house.

Well, good for him. She was happy with her life the way it was: her children and her horses. There was more than enough love for her there.

"Hi," she began guardedly. "Orion did well today. Has Hank told you about the list of shows he's drawn up?"

"Yeah, he asked me to tell you to come over to the office after you've finished with Orion and the three of us can discuss it."

Caleb allowed his gaze to rest briefly on Cassie. She looked incredibly lovely, standing slim and reserved by the large dark stallion. His fingers itched to reach out and finger the silky, golden curls that had escaped her braid. He wanted to lower his mouth to hers and sample once again the sweetness he'd found there. Stronger, though, was the memory of Cassie's look of chagrin when she had thought Caleb's sexual interest in her might become public knowledge.

He knew it was vain of him, but he wasn't used to having a woman upset or humiliated because she was caught kissing him. She'd made him feel as if their mutual attraction was a dirty little secret she'd rather die than admit to. Now his irrational pride dictated that the next time they kissed, it would be up to Cassie to make the first move. For some crazy reason, he was determined to wait her out—and he was equally determined to have her.

He was pretty much resigned to the fact that he was going to find his experience of chastity a bit hard.

Deliberately, Caleb shifted his attention to the stallion. "Hey, big guy, you looked sharp out there. Must be a nice change to have someone who knows how to ride on your back." Cassie's cheeks warmed at Caleb's indirect compliment. But she couldn't help but notice that as they walked back to the barn, Caleb positioned himself on the other side of Orion so that the horse's large head and neck was between them, making conversation impossible. It wasn't until they reached the barn that he addressed her.

"While you're putting Orion away, I thought I'd take a look at your mare. I'd like to see if the swelling's gone down. If not, we can discuss some procedures and treatments you might want to consider."

"Okay. Thanks. I'll try to finish quickly so that I can come see her myself."

He veered off to the main barn where Hot Lips's stall was, while Cassie led Orion back to the stallions' barn. Both Gaspar and Kenyon, the other two stallions owned by Five Oaks, were turned out, grazing in separate paddocks, enjoying the spring weather. The barn's interior was quiet, except for the rustling of Barney's hooves in the straw.

Orion's stallmate, Barney, the donkey, wasn't much to look at. With a tiny, grizzled brown body, he had massive ears that jutted out at a comical angle. When he saw Orion, he brayed a loud welcoming and poked his nose through the bars at the top of the stall door. Cassie dug her hand into the pocket of her breeches and pulled out a dried apple treat and gave it to the donkey. Orion dropped his big head to nuzzle Cassie's hand, smelling the sweet scent of the treat on her flesh.

"Not yet, Orion," Cassie said smilingly at the feel of the warm, velvety soft nose brushing against the palm of her hand. "We've got to get your bridle off first. Then you can have a bunch of treats."

Cassie grabbed Orion's halter from the hook outside his stall, and proceeded to untack him with quick, deft movements. Grabbing brushes from a nearby carryall, she currycombed his sleek coat, following it with a soft brush, her voice lifting to the notes of a Natalie Merchant song playing on the radio.

This part of her life was so good. Professionally, she felt comfortable with her new life at Five Oaks, confident that she was up to the job's challenges, thrilled at the opportunity to work with such great horses. If she could just get her feelings for Caleb under control, everything would be perfect.

After she'd finished brushing him down, Cassie offered the promised treat to Orion and threaded a lead line through his halter. For the rest of the day, Orion and the donkey Barney would be outside in their pasture. Cassie slid the bolt open to Orion's stall as she and the stallion passed. Barney ambled out, trailing after them. Cassie didn't bother with a lead for him, knowing that the donkey would follow at his own pace.

As they made their way to Orion's pasture, Cassie passed Raffael, the man who'd been busy grooming a horse when she and the twins had their first visit; she later learned he was Five Oaks's barn manager. When he discovered Cassie was familiar with some of the stables in Florida he had worked at before he'd moved up north to Virginia and Five Oaks, they'd immediately hit it off. They'd talked shop, trading stories of horses and horse people. Hank had hired Raffael as manager almost a year ago, and Cassie liked his quiet, calm manner around the horses.

"'Morning, Raffael," Cassie said cheerfully, having only seen him at a distance earlier in the morning. She paused with Orion so they could walk together. "Such a beautiful day. The spring breeze has got Orion all pumped up."

"Yeah." Raffael grinned. "All the stallions are feeling their oats. He's going to be a wild one outside today, for sure." He nodded to Orion's flared nostrils pulling in the fresh spring air and to the tail that streamed out behind him. "He's just waiting for some pretty lady to come along, maybe your mare."

Cassie laughed. "What a pair those two would make! He'd have his work cut out for him with a saucy one like Hot Lips."

"Yeah, but that's what makes it fun."

Cassie smiled. "Well, they'll both have to put it on hold for a while. I've got plans for my mare. In the meantime, Orion can run off some of his excess energy."

She led the now prancing stallion through the gate of the paddock while Raffael urged Barney in and shut the gate behind them. Cassie turned the stallion toward her and unfastened the lead line's chain from around his nose.

"Just a minute, then you'll be free to play." Her voice was calm, unhurried, in contrast to the stallion's rising excitement. She released the halter, lowered her hands, and stepped back.

Cassie watched in delight as the stallion pivoted on his muscled hindquarters and sprang away, galloping down the long line of the pasture's white fence. She ducked through the bars of the gate and joined Raffael, and the two watched together as the stallion came tearing back up the field, head and tail held high. The donkey, already nibbling at the tender shoots of grass, ignored the stallion's antics completely.

"The ultrasound's set up. We'll be able to judge how much damage there is to the tendon now."

Cassie had found Caleb with Hot Lips hooked to the cross ties. He'd removed her bandages and was kneeling by the injured leg. He motioned her to join him.

Off to the side, the ultrasound machine looked somewhat like a small television set. Resting on top of it was the head, a mechanism that looked like a cross between a microphone and an electric razor. It had a short antenna that protruded from the top.

"Just hold her lightly by the halter, Cassie. I doubt this will bother her, but I'd rather be safe than sorry. You'll be able to see the image on the screen from where you're standing."

Caleb reached for a tube of KY jelly that was lying near him and smeared some over the mare's leg, coating it from the knee joint down to the pastern. The jelly allowed for the sonic reading of the tissues and bones inside the leg to be transmitted onto the screen.

Wiping his hands on a small rag, Caleb reached for the small device resting on top of the monitor screen. Flicking the switch on the base's monitor, the screen lit up, turning a bright medium blue, much like the color on a computer screen. He brought the sensor's head to Hot Lips's injured leg, running it slowly up and down, across that area of her leg.

"The ultrasound will enable us to see what areas of tissue have been damaged and to what degree."

Caleb's eyes were fixed on the screen before him. Hot Lips stood quietly with Cassie at her halter, speaking softly to the mare.

"Yeah, that's it, at the superficial digital flexor. You see that area right there on the tendon? The strain's down low, just above the fetlock. There's no sign of a bow in the tendon, which is good news, but she's clearly suffered a strain in the tendon."

Caleb reached over, flicked off the machine, and then stood up next to Cassie. "Sorry, Cassie. I'm afraid you'll have to stick to stall rest. I'll start some laser therapy on her tomorrow. I wish I could get to it today, but I've got to go to the hospital right after our meeting with Hank. I've got more patients scheduled."

"That's all right, Caleb. I really appreciate your taking time for her. Should I ice her this afternoon?"

"Definitely. Ask Raff to do some, too, while you're in town. And give her some more sodium hyaluronate."

"Caleb, do you think we can make her sound again?"

"Yeah, I hope so. But it will take some time. What really concerns me is that she might hurt herself all over again if she keeps going wild every time you ride her. We'll have to come up with a strategy to keep her quiet enough so that she doesn't re-injure herself."

"I hadn't thought of that. I guess the first step is to heal the tendon, though. I'll wrap her now and meet you in Hank's office."

"Okay. You need help?"

"No, thanks, I've got it."

From the tightness in her voice, it was easy to tell that she was struggling to master her anxiety for her mare. She obviously wanted privacy until she could get her emotions under control. Caleb had to respect her wish.

People got so involved with the animals they owned and worked with. Sometimes that was the most difficult aspect of being a vet. Experience had taught him that when an animal was in desperate pain from illness, injury, or sometimes simply old age, for the sake of the animal, putting it down was the best course of action, the kindest thing to do.

It was the owners, filled with memories and love for these creatures, that Caleb felt at a loss to help, to console. In all likelihood, Hot Lips would be completely cured with proper treatment and rest, but Cassie clearly took her horse's pain and injury as seriously as a mother would a sick child. *Soft hearted,* thought Caleb sympathetically.

An image flashed before him of Pamela laughing in disbelief when he'd suggested during the first year of their marriage that they try to make a baby. In a voice still trembling with laughter she'd explained, as if speaking to a not particularly bright child, "You don't really expect to me to gain all that weight, lose my figure, and then spend my days changing dirty diapers and wiping milky drool off my clothes? What a revolting idea."

Caleb could only thank God he'd been too disgusted to push her on that one.

"Here's a list of shows I think we should consider for Orion. I've started off with a few smaller ones for the end of May. We can see how he does, get his feet wet, so to speak. By July, we'll be showing him almost every weekend, entering him in the bigger Grand Prix if he's coming along. In the fall we can shoot for the top shows in Maryland, Delaware, and Washington. That's about as far ahead as I want to plan right now."

Hank handed the sheet of paper to Caleb, who was seated next to Cassie in Hank's office. He held the list to his side, so that they could look at it simultaneously. As she leaned over, their eyes locked.

It was no use trying to block the memory of the first time she and Caleb had been in this office. Her eyes jerked away from his as embarrassment washed over her once again, staining her cheeks. Boy, she'd really given him an eyeful then. She didn't doubt that Caleb remembered that afternoon, too. The warmth of his body as he leaned closer with the list pressed against her like a brand.

"These seem fine to me, Hank."

"What's your opinion, Cassie?"

Her shoulders lifted in a small shrug. "Other than the International Horse Show in DC, I've never shown in this region. Some of the big shows, like Roanoke and Charleston, I know by reputation." She paused, going over the list once more. "However, perhaps you might want to consider skipping one or two of the shows you've got down for the end of August and substituting one really big one at the end of the summer."

"Like what? You got a particular one in mind?" Hank asked, his bright blue eyes resting on Cassie's face.

"Well, to tell you the truth, I've been toying with this idea since the first day I saw Orion. How about the Hampton Classic?"

"Jesus." Caleb exclaimed with a heavy drawl, his tone a mixture of astonishment and admiration. "You sure don't lack ambition."

"Well, why not?" Cassie turned in her chair to face him, her voice slightly defensive. "It's a great A3-rated show. You've got some of the best riders and some of the best horses from all over the country. The Grand Prix there is terrific. Really challenging. I think it'd be a great opportunity. And it'll get him ready for the competition he'll see in Washington." The Hampton Classic was traditionally held during the final week of August, right around Labor Day.

"Yeah, but, Cassie," Caleb countered, "it's highly unlikely that Orion will place with that kind of competition. He might not even get past the qualifying class to go on to the Grand Prix."

Out of the corner of her eye, Cassie saw Hank nod his head silently in agreement. In the big Grand Prix events, like at the Hampton Classic, horses had to enter preliminary qualifying events and place high enough to be able to proceed to the Grand Prix. Out of a class of perhaps fifty riders, only thirty would move on. The rest eliminated.

In a restless movement, Cassie sat straighter in her chair, leaned forward, crossing her legs. As if with a will of their own, Caleb's eyes shifted, wandering from her face to follow the enticing contour of her breasts, her gently curved hips, to the seemingly endless line of her legs encased in breeches and field boots.

Did she have any idea at all just how distracting her beauty was? He prayed to God she didn't realize that she was pure dynamite to his senses. He didn't want her knowing how susceptible he was to her. He'd been through enough of that with Pamela. Belatedly, he realized she'd begun speaking again, and quickly pulled his attention away from the entrancing curves of her body.

"Obviously, I can't predict how Orion will do at the Classic." Cassie gave a sidelong glance at Caleb before shifting her gaze back to Hank. "Although I wouldn't be surprised if he did better than any of us expect. But what Orion will get at the Classic is exposure. *Everyone* goes to the Classic. Owners, riders, trainers. Buyers. Money. Word spreads like wildfire during that week of jumping. Just having people see Orion in action is going to generate a lot of interest in him and in Five Oaks. If he does well, so much the better."

Hank and Caleb looked at each other in silence, weighing the merit of Cassie's argument. To compete at the kind of show the Classic represented was what they'd always dreamed of for Orion. The trick would be pulling it off without Pamela's knowledge.

What the hell.

At Caleb's small shrug of surrender, Hank turned his hands palms upwards and gave his partner a lopsided grin. "Shoot, Caleb, we might as well have some fun. Let's go hobnob with the rich and famous."

"Great. I can't wait," Caleb replied, his voice filled with sarcasm. He knew all about the rich and famous. So did his dear ex-wife. Intimately. He wanted to mingle with the kind of society you found at the Classic like he wanted a hole in the head.

"Looks like you've talked us into it, Slim. I hope you know what you're doing, and this idea of yours doesn't backfire."

"It won't," Cassie replied, a brilliant smile pasted to her face. She wished, however, that she felt as fully confident as she sounded. She and Orion certainly had their work cut out for them this spring if they were going to pull this one off.

9

*H*ow was it, Cassie wondered irritably, that Caleb Wells seemed to have taken on the role of personal chauffeur? It had been her plan to borrow Hank and Melissa's car, but when she'd gone to ask Melissa for the keys, the older woman had recollected an urgent errand that she had to run in the opposite direction from town. Then, when Cassie had asked whether she might take the farm's truck instead, Melissa had shaken her head worriedly. The truck wasn't running too well. She thought it best if Cassie wait until it was taken to the garage so George, the mechanic, could look at it.

Well, she could always call for a cab, Cassie decided. But Melissa had foiled that plan, too. Before she could even locate the blasted telephone book, Melissa had turned to Caleb, who was seated at the kitchen table grabbing a quick bite before heading off to the animal hospital. His dark head bent over the newspaper, a mug of hot coffee in his hand, he'd been studiously ignoring the conversation around him. As if the thought had just occurred to her, Melissa announced brightly that she was sure Caleb could wait a few extra minutes while Cassie changed for her meeting with John Perkins. Then he could drop her off at the school on his way to the hospital.

Caleb looked up and shot Melissa a thunderous scowl, his dark eyebrows drawn together in a forbidding line. Blithely, Melissa ignored him, oblivious to Caleb's foul mood. Cassie wasn't unaware, however, but when she quickly protested, mentioning the word *taxi*, Melissa scoffed, declaring loudly how much she hated to see gas wasted unnecessarily. Surely, as a young mother, Cassie felt the same? Then, she somehow managed to hustle Cassie into showering and changing in ten short minutes, making Cassie leave for her appointment a whole two hours early.

Cassie descended the stairs just barely within the allotted time, having selected a deep blue-and-purple-print gauze skirt and a simple white scoop neck cotton blouse.

Caleb gave her one long, brooding look. "Sure hope you don't catch cold," was all he had to say. Then, with a terse, "Let's go," Caleb stood, only to have to wait some more while Cassie searched for her bag. Melissa was all smiles, telling Cassie she looked lovely. She waved them off cheerfully, but not before calling out to Caleb that he should show Cassie around town. The curse he'd muttered in response to Melissa's suggestion made Cassie blush with embarrassment.

So here she sat, in the cab of his truck, feeling miserable, a total imposition. And a bit chilled. She'd planned on grabbing her fleece jacket, but after Caleb's snide comment about her choice of dress, had stubbornly changed her mind. She refused to ask him to turn up the heater, knowing he'd just give her that superior smirk of his. What was wrong with him, she wondered. Was he angry over her idea to enter Orion in the Hampton Classic? Or was there something else bothering him that he was too pigheaded to discuss with her like an adult? *She couldn't wait,* she thought fiercely to herself, *until Alex brought her Jeep next week.* She was darned if she was going to let herself be dependent like this for much longer. Maybe while she was in town she'd look into leasing another car, so that Thompson, too, would have a car as soon as she and the kids arrived.

Caleb remained infuriatingly silent in the confines of the truck, refusing to make even a token effort at small talk. As if he were alone. Cassie was tempted to enter into the game with a vengeance and make it a competition of absolute silence. What did she care if he didn't want to talk to her? But she decided that nothing could be more self-defeating, silly, and immature. One idiot in the car was bad enough.

Therefore, she broke the silence, her voice cool, her words spare. "Is there a car dealership in town that's not too far from the school?"

"Yeah. What for? Wait, let me guess. You'd rather buy a car than get a ride back from me." Just glancing at her was dangerous. He'd been careful not ever to do so since she'd descended the stairs, dressed in that simple, yet shatteringly sexy outfit. Even thinking about it, having her next to him was pure torture. No way was he going to let her know.

"Maybe you're worried I might jump you, lay you down against the seat here, toss that filmy skirt of yours, and have my wicked way with you?" The smile he gave her was thoroughly obnoxious, in contrast to the voice that promised as much as it threatened.

The look she cast was utterly contemptuous. "What *is* your problem? Do you try to be a jerk or does it just come naturally to you? I guess you haven't heard about sexual harassment. You must be a real hit with the women around here. They must love all these sweet nothings you whisper in their ears."

"Absolutely. They think I'm Prince Charming."

"Well, you remind me of a particularly nasty creature I once saw crawl out from under a rock," she retorted hotly, ignoring the deep laughter that erupted from him. "And don't blame me just because Melissa has a screw loose and wouldn't let me borrow the farm truck. I'm hardly thrilled myself at the thought of having a Neanderthal like you drive me around."

"Aw, Slim, how could you think that I'd be anything but delighted to have your delectable presence in my truck. So, you going to tell me what you need the car for? Got a hot date tomorrow? Or do you always like to go shopping for things that cost thousands of dollars?" His smile had Cassie's palms itching.

"Not that it's any of your business, but I need to get a car for Thompson. She'll need one while I'm at the stables during the day. What if the twins hurt themselves and she needs to get to a hospital? I thought I might as well look into it before I meet with Mr. Perkins at three o'clock. Seeing it's only one now, I have a *little* time to kill."

"There's a Ford dealership in town. They're about as honest as you'll get around here. I'll drop you off and point out the street where the animal hospital is. After you're done with Perkins, you can walk on over. I should still be there, unless there's been an emergency call."

He gave an ironic smile. "Then your chauffeur will be ready and waiting, Madam."

"Gee, thanks. I feel so lucky."

"Pleasure's all mine, Slim."

Caleb watched as she walked away and stopped opposite the street from Chuck Jones's Ford dealership, waiting for a break in the traffic to cross. The churned air of the passing cars made her skirt float up, revealing tempting glimpses of calves and knees. A large truck passed in front of her and the air rushing behind it caused the skirt to flatten against her, the thin fabric wrapping around her legs as she moved. The cotton shirt hugged her gently rounded breasts. Every line of her body was revealed.

Caleb closed his eyes. Wishing fervently it were five o'clock and he could have a shot of whiskey. Perhaps a whole damn bottle. In a burst of frustration, he punched the heel of his hand against the rim of the steering wheel. What an ass he'd been to her. Once more he cursed Melissa's transparent and deliberate maneuver to get him and Cassie together. What he needed was to keep away from Cassie, not to have her close, mere inches away, smelling like a lush summer garden, driving him crazy with need.

The afternoon had gone well, Cassie thought with quiet satisfaction. She was the proud new lessor of a Ford Taurus station wagon. Really, it had been quite thrilling, almost liberating, to walk into the dealership and come out with a lease agreement in hand a short eighty minutes later. She'd had enormous fun haggling over the terms and bargaining for extras in the model she chose. This was the first car she'd ever gotten by herself; her father had bought her Jeep for her when she went away to college. Other than Hot Lips, this car was her first major acquisition. From what she'd read in the automobile magazines her brother Alex received each month, Fords were dependable cars. She wanted Thompson comfortable and the twins safe.

The meeting with John Perkins had been successful, too. He'd listened patiently while Cassie briefly described the twins' history; he'd seemed extremely accommodating, nodding agreeably when she'd requested that Sophie and Jamie be put together in the same classroom. A few sympathetic words made it clear he understood her anxiety that the twins might feel lost without each other's presence.

At the end of their meeting, Perkins took Cassie to the kindergarten classroom, where he introduced her to the head teacher, busy straightening up the empty room and preparing for the next day's activities. The teacher, Miss Springer, a pretty woman with long, dark hair and a cheerful smile, seemed full of enthusiasm and goodwill, even at the end of the school day. Cassie tried to picture in her mind what she'd look like after a day spent with a class of fifteen five-year-olds and decided that this woman was a true professional and probably had the stamina of an ox.

Feeling vastly reassured as she left the school, Cassie followed the directions Caleb had given her to the animal hospital. She walked along the tree-lined street, observing with delight the small nubs forming on the tips of the branches. Cassie loved springtime. It thrilled her that she would be able to catch it unfolding moment by moment here in the Virginia hills. She felt sorry for her brother Alex, tied to the financial market of New York. She wished there were some way he too could get out. Perhaps he'd start visiting on weekends. He'd miss the kids so much. She hated to think of him alone in the city, without the twins' noise and constant energy filling their home.

At the end of the street she saw it. Her steps quickened. Though she was loath to admit it, curiosity filled her at the chance to see Caleb's hospital, how he looked in his professional setting.

The hospital was a low, ranch-style building, painted a light grey with white trim. A white wooden sign hung suspended by a short chain over the threshold, with Animal Hospital inscribed in black. As she reached the short walkway that led to the door, she noticed a sign with the names: C. Wells, D. Cole, and M. Winterer—all DVMs. Cassie entered through the white front door, and into the reception area.

The front office of the animal hospital was clean and brightly lit. The floors were covered in a terra-cotta tile-style of linoleum, and on the walls, large prints and posters of animals added decoration and color. Set against the walls, an assortment of wooden garden benches and chairs were being used by a handful of people with their family pets on their laps, seated next to them, or at their feet. Cassie counted three dogs and two cat carriers. The animals' excitement was obvious in the panting of dogs and in the mewling within the sturdy plastic cat carriers. The reassuring murmurs of the owners speaking to their pets, trying to keep the animals' anxiety to a minimum made a nice background noise. A few people glanced up at Cassie curiously, making her realize she was the only person in the waiting room without a pet in tow.

The receptionist was busy speaking into the phone, entering an appointment onto the computer screen in front of her, nodding her head as she listened to some worried owner describing symptoms. When Cassie caught her eye, the receptionist gave a distracted smile.

"Right, Mrs. Sherman," she returned calmly, "you can bring Bubbles in on Thursday morning at nine o'clock. Well, it will either be Dr. Wells or Dr. Cole, depending on which one is out on call. No, I'm afraid Dr. Winterer has the day off on Thursday. Yes, I'll make sure Dr. Wells gets the message and returns your call. Good-bye, Mrs. Sherman, we'll see you and Bubbles on Thursday at nine."

With a small sigh she placed the phone in its cradle and looked up at Cassie. "May I help you?" Her voice had a rich Virginia accent.

"Hello, I'm Cassie Miller. I'm here to meet Dr. Wells."

The receptionist looked at her with sharpened interest, and her smile grew friendlier. "Oh, yes, Caleb told me to expect you. I'm Joyce, the office manager for the hospital." At Cassie's answering smile, Joyce cocked her head to the side and asked inquisitively, "So, you're Caleb and Hank's new trainer. How do you like it over at Five Oaks?"

"So far, it's great. The horses are outstanding, and I really love the country here. It's incredibly beautiful. Are you from around here?"

She nodded. "Born and bred. I only went away for college, and that was just fifty miles away. My husband, Dan, he's from Tennessee. When we first married, we discussed moving back to his hometown, but I just couldn't.

Practically all my family is still here. And Dan's found a good job in an electronics company, so I guess we're here for the long haul."

"Will Caleb be busy for much longer? I can take a walk around town, explore a bit, and then come back later."

"You don't have to do that, unless you want to. Caleb's got three patients left, and two of them are just routine checkups and shots. It shouldn't take long. Caleb's such a doll, isn't he?"

Cassie looked at Joyce, hoping her astonishment at Joyce's characterization wasn't utterly transparent.

"Yes," she replied, smiling faintly, "I guess you might say that."

Cassie sat down on a bench next to an elderly gentleman. His tawny boxer, named Finnegan, sat on the floor between them, his head on his owner's knees in a silent plea to be scratched. The gentleman happily complied. Then the dog's soulful dark eyes fixed on Cassie as if to ask why she, too, wasn't giving him this delightful attention. Cassie was enchanted.

"May I pet your dog?" she inquired, wanting to be sure that she hadn't misinterpreted the dog's seeming friendliness.

"Oh, sure. Finnegan's a bit confused, thinks he's a Pekinese. He'd like nothing better than to jump in your lap and be stroked and petted all day, the big lug." The man grinned, affection for his dog clear in the helpless shrug of his shoulders while his fingers continued to stroke the sleek tan coat.

Cassie reached out and laid her hand against the crown of Finnegan's head, feeling the warmth and softness of the dog's coat against her palm. Finnegan turned his head up to her face and gave her what Cassie could only describe as a grin, obviously thrilled to have the two humans' attention centered on him.

"He especially likes to have his ears scratched, Miss," his owner said helpfully. Cassie immediately shifted her hand to the side, following the fold at the back of the dog's ear. Finnegan responded by lifting his head and shifting his body fractionally so that Cassie's lap now became his pillow. Both Cassie and the owner laughed, and the man said with mock despair, "No sense of loyalty whatsoever."

For the next five minutes Cassie sat happily while Finnegan warmed the tops of her thighs, his eyes half closed. A door opened. Finnegan raised his head and looked toward the noise. A split second later, he was bounding across the floor, his leash trailing behind him.

Caleb, absorbed in the sheet of paper in his hand, glanced up just in time to see Finnegan charging across the room. Dropping to a kneeling crouch, Caleb opened his arms wide as the dog came barreling toward him, with all the speed of a bullet train. The paper fluttered into the air on impact. Cassie heard a small "Oof!" as Finnegan slammed into Caleb and grinned at the sight of the dog's body wriggling with excitement inside the frame of Caleb's bent knees and long arms.

"Yes, yes. That's a good boy, Finnegan. Easy now. What a big bruiser you are." Smiling, Caleb looked up in the direction Finnegan had come from and spotted Cassie and the owner watching with amusement the ecstatic dog's antics.

"Too bad Finnegan doesn't play football, Mr. O'Mally, the 'Skins could use a good tackle."

"I apologize for letting him go, Dr. Wells. But Finnegan would have probably dislocated my shoulder if I'd tried to hold onto that leash. I figured you stood a better chance at recovering from any injury. Bones take longer to heal at my age, you know."

"Don't worry about it. To tell you the truth, I'd be disappointed if I didn't get my usual hello from Finnegan." Giving the dog a vigorous scratch around his thickly muscled neck and shoulder, he continued. "What never fails to amaze me, though, is that Finnegan continues to like me despite all the shots and, uh, procedures I've done on him."

"He's got a forgiving soul, Dr. Wells."

"That he does." Caleb smiled in agreement. Retrieving the sheet of paper that had landed a short distance away and holding Finnegan's leash in his left hand, he approached the bench where Cassie and Mr. O'Mally sat. His eyes were trained on Cassie.

She wondered when her heart rate was going to quit skyrocketing every time those dark brown eyes settled on her. Quickly she averted her own gaze, and fixed it on Caleb's hand firmly wrapped around the exuberant dog's leash.

"Hi. How'd it go with Perkins?"

"Fine." Cassie looked up, her blue eyes hesitantly meeting his for a moment, resisting the urge to lose herself in his dark, compelling gaze. "Would you like me to come back later? I can see you're busy."

"No, not unless you mind waiting a bit. Finnegan's just here for his annual shots, right Mr. O'Mally?" At the older man's nod, Caleb continued. "There are some magazines over on that small table in the corner. Horse journals, too. After Finnegan, I've only got two patients. Joyce will handle closing up."

True to his word, twenty minutes later, Cassie was saying good-bye to Joyce and being ushered out the door by Caleb, his large hand pressed against the small curve of her back. The truck was parked just to the side of the building. They walked together, Cassie already accustomed to Caleb's habit of escorting her to the car door. As Caleb closed his fingers around the door handle, Cassie vaguely registered the sound of a car pulling in the lot, its horn honking.

At the noise, Caleb looked up and muttered, "Damn it all," in tired resignation.

Cassie glanced at him curiously, her mind conjuring up images of annoying clients and vicious cats. Then she took in the flashy, low-slung sports car, her eyes widening as sleek long legs clad in sheer stockings emerged gracefully from its interior. Caleb's hand dropped from the pickup truck's door and she heard him expel a small sigh. But when she looked up at his face it was expressionless, his firm lips set in a straight line, his eyes carefully blank.

The woman approached, her attention fixed on Caleb as she made her way toward them. She was dressed in a light pink wool suit, the miniskirt revealing practically the entire length of her shapely legs. Dark, glamorous, with shoulder-length chestnut hair styled in thick waves around her face, the woman was stunning. Blessed with a complexion as light as cream, her eyes appeared darker than night. Her brightly painted mouth was parted wide, smiling at Caleb with a thousand-watt force.

"Hello, Pamela. What brings you here?"

Cassie's eyes quickly darted back to the outrageously glamorous woman. *This was Caleb's ex?*

"Oh, I just dropped by to see you, to make sure you're all right." Her lips pressed forward into an enticing little pout.

Cassie wondered whether she practiced that often in the mirror.

"It upsets me when I don't hear from you," Pamela continued, advancing until not more than a foot separated them. "You know how much I enjoy our little chats."

Caleb snorted, shaking his head, but didn't deign to respond. Instead, he asked, "Where's Stuart?"

"Off to London on a buying trip. Some duke or other is selling off his string of polo ponies."

"And you didn't accompany him?" Caleb smiled cynically. "You were always such an avid buyer."

Pamela took a step even closer to Caleb. "Oh, I've already got my spring wardrobe picked out. English fashion is so conservative, and you know me, Caleb," she began as she trailed a perfectly manicured nail down the front of Caleb's shirt, "polo ponies are not my thing. I prefer owning really big horses."

Filled with a kind of sick fascination as she watched this woman flirt so blatantly with Caleb, Cassie couldn't tear her eyes away as Pamela flashed yet another practiced smile.

"By the way, how is Orion doing?"

"He's fine." His eyes flashing briefly with impatience and something else Cassie couldn't quite decipher.

"I should drop by some time and see him, just to make sure."

"I don't think that's necessary. Anyway, you might get your shoes dirty."

"Oh, Caleb," Pamela breathed, shaking her head gently, so that her hair swished softly back and forth across her shoulders. "You're always so amusing. Well if you don't want me to see him at Five Oaks"— her fingernail flicked experimentally against the fabric of Caleb's shirt—"you could tell me all about him over a drink, keep me abreast. Like old times."

The nail polish on Pamela's long-tapered finger was an exact match with her lipstick. Cassie thought of her own ruthlessly pared, unvarnished nails and felt about as attractive as a slug. The lip gloss she'd applied earlier for her meeting with John Perkins had probably worn off, too. And she was going to punch this Pamela's lights out if she didn't get her hands off Caleb, *now*.

Caleb had turned as if to stone as Pamela's red-tipped finger playfully meandered across the soft cotton of his shirt. With cold deliberation, he took a step backwards, leaving Pamela's slender finger poised in midair. Her smile vanished as her lips thinned into an angry line.

Good! Cassie said fiercely to herself, her own mouth curving into a smile at the sight of Pamela's finger left dangling ridiculously. She was pleased Caleb wasn't falling for such an obvious sexual come-on, though she'd bet the farm that most men's tongues would be hanging past their knees after being treated to a performance like Pamela's.

She must have made some sort of movement, because Pamela turned her head suddenly, as if only just now aware of Cassie's presence. The look she gave Cassie appraised and rejected in a matter of seconds.

"And who's this, Caleb? You haven't introduced me. Where are those impeccable manners of yours?"

Resigned, knowing there was no way to avoid an introduction, he spoke. "Cassie, this is Pamela Ross. Pamela, this is Cassie Miller." Cassie nodded. If Pamela noticed the gesture, she didn't bother to acknowledge it, shifting all her attention back to Caleb.

"A little young, isn't she, Caleb?"

"Cassie works at Five Oaks."

"And what exactly does she do for you at the farm? Or need I ask?" she inquired archly, her eyes cold. The barb was painfully obvious.

Determined to put Pamela in her place with an equally cutting remark, Cassie opened her mouth. But Caleb spoke first.

"Careful, Pamela, not everyone shares your approach to getting what they want. Some people actually work for it. Keep talking that way and Cassie might guess what your specialty is." Looping an arm casually over Cassie's shoulders, he offered his ex-wife a bland smile.

Pamela's eyes narrowed in anger, watching his every move.

"But yeah," Caleb continued cheerfully, as if unaware. "There's a real youthfulness about Cassie. Very young and sweet. I was telling her the other day how multitalented she was, too. A rare gem. It's getting late, so if you'll excuse us, we'll be on our way." He inclined his head with a mock politeness, dismissing her. "So long, Pamela, I hope Ross still has some money for you to spend after he's through buying those ponies."

"Don't worry about that, Caleb," Pamela shot back with a smile as cold as ice. "He has *plenty*. And how are your finances, by the way? I hope you're not feeling a little strapped for cash?" With a last, disdainful glance at Cassie, Pamela got into her car, revved the motor, and roared away.

She fumed, sitting in the passenger seat as Caleb shifted the truck into reverse and headed toward the parking lot exit. With an abrupt curse, he hit the brakes, and with a jerk of the key killed the engine. Motionless, he stared blindly through the windshield, his fingers wrapped around the steering wheel. The truck's cab was utterly silent for several minutes, until finally Caleb expelled a deep breath and turned his head to look at Cassie. When he spoke, his voice was tense with frustration.

"Damn it all, Cassie. I'm really sorry you had to witness that. I try to avoid Pamela as much as possible."

Cassie's head whipped around to stare at him, her hair flying across her face. Impatiently, she shoved it away. She didn't try to conceal her fury or her hurt. "How could you talk like that about me? I assume that was your ex-wife?" At Caleb's terse nod, she continued. "She had the nerve to imply that I was some sort of stable bunny, there for your and who knows who else's pleasure. You couldn't even bother to tell her I was the new trainer at Five Oaks?"

He felt like an utter bastard for having treated Cassie like a pawn in the vicious chess game he and Pamela played whenever he had the misfortune to run into her. He stared down at his knuckles, white with tension, still clenched around the steering wheel. He forced his fingers to relax.

"Look, I'm really sorry," he repeated. "I can imagine how hurt you must feel. Please don't believe that I meant to insult you. I think you're excellent for the job at Five Oaks,

I really do. I was trying to get Pamela where she was vulnerable. It's an ugly, nasty by-product of our divorce. I do it even when I should know better. I'm ashamed that I let you get caught in the cross fire." And Caleb had no doubt that even now, Pamela was planning some sort of revenge for having lost this last skirmish.

Cassie refused to let him off the hook so easily. "Well, what about those stupid cracks about my age? You made me sound as if I were two. I'm surprised you didn't tell her I had to go back because it was my nap time."

Her outraged tone brought a small smile to his face. "Yeah, I'm sorry about that, too. But, Cassie, to someone as jaded as Pamela, you look hardly eighteen." He raked a hand through his hair in an unconscious gesture of frustration. "And I encouraged her to believe that you're barely old enough to vote, let alone buy a drink. It was petty and I thoroughly enjoyed it."

"Why on earth should she care about how old I am?"

"Pamela's vain enough to be worried about getting old, worried that the competition is getting younger and younger."

Cassie gave a loud, inelegant snort. "Don't try to snow job me, Wells. A woman who looks like that doesn't have to worry about her looks *or* any other woman's until she's in the grave."

Caleb's bitter smile acknowledged the truth of her comment. "Nevertheless, she was worried about you."

"For heaven's sake, why?"

He smiled. "Fishing for compliments, Slim?" Pivoting slightly to face her, his expression changing like quicksilver as he looked at her. His eyes hot, possessive. Cassie felt the temperature inside the truck shoot up several degrees.

"Come on, Cassie, hasn't anyone told you how beautiful you are?" He ignored her embarrassed sound of denial. "You're incredible. Like some golden angel sent down to dazzle us mortals. I'm actually surprised Pamela didn't go directly for the jugular and try to wipe you out on the spot."

Cassie tried not to show how moved she was by Caleb's compliment, telling herself that he was only trying to make her feel special after that awful episode. She didn't see how anyone could be even in the same ballpark with Pamela in terms of looks, but his words helped soothe the hurt of the unpleasant encounter.

"Well, I'll forgive you for the crack about my age, then. I can understand your desire for petty revenge. I've often wished I could have had a few minutes of it myself."

Caleb looked at Cassie intently, considering. He remembered Melissa mentioning that Cassie had broken off an engagement. Had he heard the full story, or was there unfinished business between her and her fiancé? What was his name, again? Did she still love him, have feelings for him? He sincerely hoped not, because he wasn't about to share Cassie with anyone, no matter what previous claim they had on her. For some inexplicable reason, he felt extremely possessive about Cassie.

Cassie spoke again, interrupting his thoughts. "Caleb," she began tentatively, "I still don't understand why you didn't tell her that I was hired as a rider and trainer for Orion and Five Oaks."

Oh, Christ, he'd been dreading this moment. Should he tell her the truth? That Pamela was Orion's actual owner? Yeah, he'd made a dent in the payment schedule he'd arranged with Pamela for buying back his stallion from her avaricious hands. But Orion was still hers. And according to the agreement he'd been forced to sign, Pamela was to be kept informed of Orion's training, with the right to veto any arrangement she opposed.

So far, Pamela had only succeeded in being a real pain in the ass, but Caleb suspected that once she got wind of Cassie's official position at Five Oaks things were going to turn nasty. Did Cassie deserve to go into a situation like that blind? She'd accepted this job in good faith. If he misled her, didn't that make him the same sort of opportunist as someone like Pamela?

He couldn't do that to Cassie.

"She owns Orion, Cassie." There. He'd said it. He supposed he felt marginally better.

"What?"

He let out a long breath. What a mess. He guessed this was it, she'd go back to Hank and Melissa's and start packing.

"That's right, Slim, you heard me correctly. She owns Orion. She and a high-powered New York lawyer screwed me to the wall. The judge gave her Orion as part of the divorce settlement."

"Didn't you appeal?"

"After listening to the performance she gave in the judge's chambers, I knew I didn't stand a chance against her."

"But couldn't you have hired another lawyer, requested another judge . . ."

"Money, Cassie," Caleb interrupted bitterly. "She had it and I didn't. We both knew the precariousness of my financial situation. I'd already taken out loans from the bank to start up the animal hospital. I couldn't take the risk of defaulting. People were counting on me, my staff, my partners."

"But if she owns Orion, then why . . ."

"I cut a deal with her to buy him back. Took out a second mortgage and I pay her monthly installments."

"Oh my God," Cassie said, her voice dazed, still sorting out all the ramifications. "And what will she do when she finds out I'm riding her horse?"

"Oh, the shit'll hit the fan big time," Caleb predicted with absolute certainty. "Look, I know you're going to want to reconsider our offer. I'll understand completely if you wash your hands of this mess. I know I'd be tempted.

Hank didn't feel right talking about it with you because it's my mess, my responsibility. But I promise you I'll do everything I can to prevent Pamela from screwing up the works even more. With any luck, she won't get wind of your riding Orion anytime soon. It's not as if she'd figure it out on her own."

"What do you mean?"

"Pamela's not like you, Cassie. It wouldn't occur to her a woman *could* be hired for a job as a trainer. Hell, she doesn't even like horses." Certainly not to ride. Pamela had only been interested in riding one thing, but it hadn't been a horse. Caleb, however, wasn't about to share that with Cassie.

"Well, then, why in the world did you marry her?" Cassie asked in exasperation, the idiocy of her question dawning on her the second the words were out. She looked down at her fingers twisted together in her lap and wished with all her might that she could grab the words she'd uttered out of the air and swallow them.

Caleb stared at Cassie in astonishment. It was too bad she wouldn't be sticking around. She was truly a breath of fresh air. A grin spread across his face and his eyes lit with unholy amusement. His fingers reached forward, turning the key once again. "Bookkeeping, Slim. Pamela was a truly excellent bookkeeper."

10

The silver Lamborghini responded with a leap of speed as Pamela pressed down hard on the accelerator. The car was all engine, rushing down the road with a satisfying roar. Her hands gripped the steering wheel, relishing the powerful vibrations beneath her palms. Her husband, Stuart Ross, had purchased the car for her last month after she'd awakened him in bed in his favorite way. She knew just the right way to ask for things with Stuart, Pamela thought with a satisfied smile.

Like the sudden twists in the road, Pamela's thoughts turned to Caleb. The sports car lurched forward, trees along the side of the road diminishing to the size of matchsticks.

Anger blurred her vision.

She'd never forgive him for the way he'd spurned her. She still didn't believe Caleb actually took such an old-fashioned view of marriage, of fidelity, seriously.

So what if she'd been unfaithful to him? Who wasn't in this day and age? Anyway, Pamela had had every intention of welcoming Caleb back into her bed just as soon as she married and became Mrs. Stuart Ross III. It had simply been a matter of timing.

She'd never planned to lose such a virile and exciting a lover as Caleb. And the fillip of excitement, having her ex-husband cuckold her brand new one, had only added to her determination to lure Caleb back.

But Caleb had refused. The arrogant son of a bitch even had the unspeakable gall to laugh in her face. She'd been so sure he'd fall right in line at the prospect of tasting her charms again. That he'd still be hers to tempt and to lure.

It would have sweetened their little arrangement so. If he'd just done as she'd wanted, if he'd been extra, extra nice to her, perhaps she'd have relented, letting him buy Orion back a little faster.

But, no, he'd laughed, not even deigning to reply. Then he'd written that first of many checks and walked out the door as if he didn't have a care in the world. As if it didn't matter that she held the winning hand. She could still remember how she'd stood there, the heat of her fury and humiliation staining her face an unbecoming red.

Since his rejection that humiliating afternoon, Caleb had become like an itch she couldn't scratch. Taunting memories of how it had been between them, of the feel of his hard body moving over her, inside her, made her crave him obsessively. Yet he remained just out of her reach. She wanted him back.

She'd get him, too. It was just a matter of timing, like everything. The blond cutie who'd been with him in the parking lot didn't stand a chance.

And after Pamela had sated herself with Caleb's delightfully hard body, she would make him pay all over again.

She'd decided to stay. It hadn't been a difficult choice to make. She already loved it here. Hank was great to work with, she had some good, young horses to train, and there was the chance to ride Orion for however long it lasted. Cassie had been around horses for too many years not to recognize a truly special one when she saw it. No way was she going to let a chance to ride Orion slip between her fingers.

And then there was Caleb. It was time to be honest. The intensity of her attraction for Caleb compelled her to offer what help she could. But her decision was based on more than physical attraction alone. She kept picturing the expression on Caleb's face as he recounted how Pamela had come to own Orion. A horse that meant so much to him.

It was humbling to contemplate how much Caleb had already sacrificed on behalf of his stallion. Not just money, loads of money, but his pride, too.

She couldn't forget, either, that Caleb had been decent with her. He hadn't tried to trick her or sweet talk her into staying on at Five Oaks. In fact, she suspected that he was more than half-convinced she'd run straight to the Sawyers and start packing up her bags. But Cassie wasn't a quitter, and she'd always liked rooting for the underdog.

Cassie'd known she'd done the right thing when she approached him the following morning and said simply, without preamble, "I'll stay."

He'd looked at her silently, his expression carefully guarded. Finally, he'd given her a short nod. "Thanks."

The word had come out a kind of rusty croak, surprising them both. "Thanks," he'd repeated, his happy grin making him look years younger.

And now, almost a week later, it was difficult to keep from jumping up and down with excitement. Alex, Thompson, and the twins were due to arrive any minute. She'd be able to show her family their new home. She'd given Alex directions to Five Oaks over the phone the night before, thinking that afterwards they could all go together to the house at Hay Fever Farm. Cassie was dying to see the expression on Sophie and Jamie's faces when they first set eyes on it.

While waiting for the twins and Alex, she'd spent the last hour tending to Hot Lips. She'd brushed her and then bandaged her injured leg. Caleb had begun the laser therapy on it a few days earlier and seemed optimistic that the tendon would heal nicely. But besides helping her with Hot Lips, Caleb had maintained his distance from Cassie, checking on her progress with Orion, then quickly vanishing into the dark confines of one of the barns, Hank's office, or back to the animal hospital. And although she'd dutifully announced her schedule of morning runs, all so far had been solitary. Much to her annoyance, Cassie frequently caught herself scanning the road ahead for a glimpse of a tall, athletic figure, dark against the dawn-lit sky.

She told herself this polite distance between her and Caleb was for the best, exactly the thing she had counseled herself to do. She guessed she was simply surprised it was Caleb who had taken the initiative.

It wasn't as if she missed Caleb's teasing, his lazy charm, or his intoxicating kisses at all.

What did it matter what his reasons were? If one of her bosses preferred to avoid any contact with her, well, that was his business. She had plenty of her own work to do and was certainly old enough to go for a run without male protection. Never mind that on the morning Caleb had accompanied her, her feet had seemed light as air and the miles had flown past, hardly registering.

Cassie made her way to the box stalls where the twins' ponies, Pip and Topper, stood quietly munching their hay. Hank had been thoughtful enough to give them stalls next to each other, so that when the children groomed their ponies, she or Thompson could easily supervise them.

She led Topper out first, a twenty-year-old dapple grey, and hitched him up to the cross tie. Fondly, she scratched the pony behind the ears. She had so many memories associated with this old pony. The most recent one, though, caused Cassie to duck her head into Topper's warm neck, her cheeks aflame. Although two days had passed, Cassie's chagrin was uncomfortably fresh in her mind.

She'd been riding Topper bareback, trotting the pony over some low crossbars she'd arranged in the center of the ring. No big deal, just enough height to make sure the old guy didn't get rusty from lack of jumping. It was for fun, a lark. She was enjoying the sensation of riding bareback, something she did pretty infrequently riding highly strung jumpers. Caleb and Hank had walked into the ring, wanting to move some of the larger fences so that later on Hank could grade the ring with the tractor.

It was still unbelievable to her that it happened. Perhaps she'd been flustered or distracted by Caleb's presence, idly watching her exercise the large grey pony, but one minute her legs were wrapped firmly around Topper's barrel-like belly, and the next she found herself butt deep in a large, muddy puddle. Hank and Caleb's roars of laughter could have filled Madison Square Garden. Even Topper had looked astonished, and then mightily pleased with himself at having unseated her so effortlessly. Cassie had stood, too mortified to bother wiping the wet muck coating her backside, and had caught hold of the reins. With as much dignity as she could manage, Cassie had scrambled back on, feeling the cold mud spread against her skin as she resettled herself on the pony's back.

She supposed she should feel lucky that Caleb and Hank were so convulsed with laughter that they couldn't catch their breath enough to make any obnoxious comments, but later, the story had spread like wildfire around the barns. Even Melissa had ribbed her at being humbled by an old, retired show pony.

Cassie finished grooming the two ponies and gave them each fresh hay to munch on. Satisfied they were spotless for Jamie and Sophie, she walked slowly back toward the house, thinking of a cup of coffee and the chance to change her clothes before Alex, Thompson, and the twins arrived.

She'd resisted the temptation of moving into Caleb's parents' house, telling herself that she wanted the experience to be shared by her entire family. It was also an excellent precaution against succumbing to Caleb's seductive charms. Not that he'd been trying any seducing lately. But better safe than sorry. She wasn't sure she'd even try to resist him if they were alone and he chose to renew his interest in her.

The sound of crunching gravel and the tooting of a car horn brought Cassie's head whipping around. A smile of joy lit her features and she waved her arms wildly as her green Jeep came around the loop of the driveway and parked in front of her. An instant later came the noise of the twins fumbling with the door handles. Their high-pitched voices escaped the car's interior, the sound sweet to Cassie's ears.

The four doors opened simultaneously, with the twins tripping slightly in their race to reach Cassie first. She knelt, her arms stretched wide to embrace her children.

"Lord, I can't believe how much you two have grown in one week!" Cassie laughed, hugging them close, kissing their plump, soft cheeks. "What have Alex and Thompson been feeding you? Spinach and steroids?"

"Yuck! We hate spinach!" Sophie said indignantly. "Jamie and I got to have pizza *three* times. Soda, too! It was so good, Mom. Can we have pizza tonight, too? *Please?*" Sophie's bright blue eyes peered up into Cassie's face imploringly. Her heart melted at the sight of her daughter's face, so dear to her. Cassie hugged her once more.

"We'll see. I'm not sure there's even a place in town." At their shriek of horror, Cassie, sensing a scene of epic proportions, hurriedly qualified her statement. This was definitely not the time for the twins to suspect their new home town might be lacking such a basic necessity for happiness. "Of course, there must be a pizza parlor some-where. We'll just have to ask Mr. and Mrs. Sawyer where it is."

Cassie looked up and caught her brother's eye. She tried for a tone that conveyed adequate censure. "So, Alex. I leave them in your and Thompson's care for one week and they come back 'zah junkies. Whose influence is that, I wonder?"

Alex Miller shrugged his shoulder negligently, flashing his little sister a lazy smile. "Pizza fulfills the essential FDA food groups, Cass: bread, vegetable, and dairy. Food of champions."

"Yeah, what about the thousands of calories and count-less grams of fat?"

Cassie's brother gave her a look of comic disbelief. "With *these* two? I think we burned any extra calories in about half an hour. We were into some pretty heavy duty athletics, weren't we, Thompson?"

Alex turned to the older woman for support. The com-fortably plump older woman smiled but refrained from commenting. Thompson had nothing but affection and loy-alty for Alex Miller. In part this was due to the fierce love this man lavished on his niece and nephew. But also because he listened to her advice. Generally, that is. Even she had been amazed at the quantities of pizza the two five-year-olds had consumed.

Like a true diplomat, Thompson decided that the less said on the subject of pizza, the better. Instead, she offered, "They made the Olympics look like a couch potato fest. Soccer, running races, wrestling matches. I was exhausted just looking at them."

"Don't believe her, Cass. Thompson was in on it, too. Made a great fullback, and she *almost* beat Sophie and Jamie a couple of times in the running races. Actually, we probably all lost weight when you think about it. Even with the countless hot fudge sundaes we devoured."

Cassie gave a shudder of horror, only part pretend. "Well, I guess that makes it all right then. They'll just have to be weaned off the junk food slowly so they don't go into withdrawal."

"Please, Cass, can you wait until I'm safely on the plane for New York? I don't think I could stand to witness such torture."

Laughing, she stood on her tiptoes to kiss Alex on the cheek. "I missed you all so much." She turned and hugged Thompson next. "Come on into the house. I was just heading there to change my clothes. You can meet Hank and Melissa. Then we can head over to Caleb's place. You're going to love it, Thompson."

Cassie extended her arm so that it encircled Alex's back. Her brother smiled and brought his arm around her shoulders, pulling her close, so that they could walk side by side. Cassie's cheek rubbed the soft, chocolate brown of his suede jacket. The light, tangy citrus scent of his cologne reassuringly familiar.

Alex's tall, solid presence by her side was like a soothing balm. He and the twins were all that remained of her immediate family. Since the automobile accident, Cassie and her brother had grown extremely close, depending on each other, supporting each other. Doing their best to help each other survive the awful tragedy life had thrown at them.

Cassie, Alex, and Thompson walked together as the children ran ahead toward the house, Thompson and Alex continuing their narration of the week's events. Over the adults' softer voices, Cassie caught the words *chocolate chip cookie* floating in the air behind the racing figures.

Melissa was struck momentarily speechless at the extraordinary sight of Cassie, Alex, Jamie, and Sophie standing together in her kitchen. Genes certainly ran strong in the Miller family, she thought to herself. Alex looked like the male version of his sister, though she noted that his face was more harshly chiseled. And his hair was clipped short, close to his head, ruthlessly suppressing even a hint of a softening curl.

Melissa supposed he probably didn't *want* to look like a Renaissance angel. But there was little he could do to alter the astonishing perfection of his features. It was a shame his eyes were so hard, though. They made her think of ice blue glaciers, and she imagined they'd frozen more than one business adversary before. But those eyes might, however, have quite a different effect on the opposite sex. More than a few women would find them irresistible. Eternally hoping they'd be the one to turn the ice to a burning blue flame.

While Cassie excused herself to run upstairs and change, Melissa filled any moment of awkwardness by offering Thompson and Alex some iced tea, the twins some milk and cookies. Melissa liked the way Thompson handled the twins, reminding them every few minutes, in a quiet and gentle voice that brooked no nonsense, not to stuff three cookies in their mouths at the same time, and to say please and thank you. Alex and Thompson made small talk with Melissa, complimenting her on the beauty of the farm, asking her about Five Oaks's operation. Their interest in Cassie's new job revealed how much they cared for her.

Cassie rejoined them a few minutes later. "Melissa, I thought I'd take everyone to look at Orion. I'm sure Jamie and Sophie want to see their ponies, too. Right, kids?" At their enthusiastic cries of agreement, Cassie continued, "Then I thought we'd go over to Caleb's house. I can't wait for them to see it." She hesitated a moment before asking, "Do you know when Caleb will be getting back? I don't want him to think we're barging into his home."

Melissa laughed. "It's your home, too. You're going to be living there. And you should know how eager he is to

meet the rest of your family, especially Jamie and Sophie."
Melissa turned to Thompson and explained. "Caleb Wells
is my husband's partner. A vet, although sometimes I wonder why he didn't go into pediatrics. He's got a way with
children."

"Probably because he's still a lot like a kid himself.
Real immature," Hank Sawyer joked, coming into the
kitchen with Caleb at his side.

"Very funny, Hank." Caleb smiled, his eyes scanning
the room. Pretty easy to figure out who was who among
this lot. He walked immediately up to the older woman and
held out his hand. "Hello, you must be Mrs. Thompson.
I'm Caleb Wells." His smile was warm, his dark brown
eyes as inviting as a three-layer chocolate cake. "Cassie's
told me about you and the children. It'll be nice to have
company over at Hay Fever Farm."

"Please call me Thompson. Mrs. isn't necessary, Dr.
Wells," Thompson replied a bit breathlessly, smitten by his
looks.

"Thompson? Is that your given name?" Caleb's smile
and manner were so easy, it might have been as if he and
Thompson were alone in the room.

"Well, no, actually. It's Bessie. But I've never liked the
name. Just don't feel like a Bessie somehow."

"I knew a Bessie a few years back. A piano teacher. She
broke my heart when she married an accountant and
moved to California. You have similar eyes. And please call
me Caleb, Mrs. Thompson."

"Oh my." Thompson's cheeks were a rosy pink now.
"Thank you. And please call me Bessie." Cassie and Alex
stared at her in amazement.

Feeling their eyes upon her, Thompson returned their
stare, saying defensively, "A person's got a right to change
her mind, if she wants. But I'm still Thompson to the rest
of you."

A goddamn southern rake, Alex thought looking at

Caleb with disgust. All polished manners, he'd been clever, zeroing in on Thompson first and winning her over in a mere thirty seconds with that soft Virginia accent and effortless charm. Handsome son of a bitch, too, with his dark, slightly dangerous good looks.

He'd bet his last penny he'd been making the moves on Cassie, too. Alex had recognized the possessive light in Wells's eye when he'd looked at Cassie. And he'd noticed how Cassie had been surreptitiously glancing at Wells when she thought no one was looking. The longing he'd read in them told him his sister was already half in love.

His blood ran cold at the thought of Cassie being used by this Virginian Don Juan. Before he returned to New York on Sunday morning, he was going to set this asshole straight about messing with his sister. He'd let that jerk Brad hurt her badly. He wasn't going to let it happen a second time.

Now that Thompson was virtually putty in Caleb Wells's hands, Alex watched him turn his attention to the twins. Caleb squatted down on his haunches, bringing his tall frame almost down to their eye level.

"Hi. You must be Sophie and Jamie. I'm Caleb. I work with your mom and Hank. Your mom's a fine rider, and I've heard you two are pretty good, too. I've even seen your ponies, they're really special looking. Now, what are their names again?"

"Pip and Topper," Sophie and Jamie replied in unison, with Jamie adding, "Pip is short for Pipsqueak, 'cause he's so small. Topper comes from some movie Mommy watched when she was a kid. She's had him *forever*. He was her first pony. He's ours now."

A quick look at Cassie's pink-tinged face confirmed the accuracy of Jamie's assertion. Caleb chuckled softly. "Her first pony, huh? That I didn't know, but somehow it doesn't surprise me. Your mom cares about horses and ponies a lot.

Did she tell you what happened last week when she was riding her old friend Topper?"

Sophie and Jamie shook their heads vigorously.

"No? I can't believe it! Well, I'll tell you about it." Caleb proceeded to regale the children with a comic account of Cassie's tumble off Topper's back and into the wet, gooey mud. The children asked a dozen questions, wanting Caleb to repeat each second of Cassie's ignominious fall. Caleb patiently answered them, keeping the tale light and humorous.

Looks like conquest three and four, Alex Miller thought resentfully, taking in Sophie and Jamie's excited expressions, lapping up the story involving their mother and their pony the way kittens would a bowl of milk.

The only good thing he could say about Wells at this point was that at least he didn't try to win the twins over by talking baby talk, Alex conceded grudgingly. He'd always felt nothing but contempt for adults who started talking in high-pitched voices, bad grammar, and cutesy language whenever they addressed children. He figured any kid with half a brain could see through that kind of schmaltzy stuff as well. Sophie and Jamie might be only five, but they were sharp as tacks.

Caleb smiled at the small faces of Jamie and Sophie. They were adorable. And they looked so much like Cassie his gut ached. It didn't seem as if they were spoiled rotten, either. God knows, if they were his kids, he'd be tempted to give the pair anything their hearts desired. He wondered how much of the credit was due to Cassie and her brother, how much to Bessie Thompson.

He liked Bessie, too. She reminded him of a great-aunt on his mother's side, a woman who on first acquaintance appeared to be a no-nonsense kind of person, but whose sudden laughter could fill a room. Caleb had responded to the warmth and generosity he saw in Bessie Thompson's face. And she did sort of make him think of a piano teacher he'd dated years ago, never mind that her name had been Becky.

Ruffling the soft curls springing from the twins' heads, he straightened, rising to meet the last member of the Miller clan. Caleb's expression changed to one of bland speculation as he met the barely veiled hostility in Cassie's brother's eyes.

Ahha, Caleb thought. So big brother's territorial. Certainly suits the way he looks. A shark. A rich, success-ful shark, he added, taking in the suede jacket, the button-down shirt opened casually at the collar, and the charcoal grey flannel trousers. Even his shoes look fancy, Caleb thought, contemptuously.

He probably has women crawling all over him. Caleb wondered idly whether Stuart Ross would have been so successful with his wife Pamela if Alex Miller had been living in the neighborhood. If she had laid eyes on Alex Miller, how long would it have been before Pamela tried to crawl into his bed? He wondered, too, if Alex Miller was the kind of scumbag who poached on another man's pre-serves. He wouldn't want to lay odds on that one.

In the short space of time it had taken for that summary inspection, Caleb's dislike for Alex Miller was equal to Miller's for him. Had Caleb been alone, he doubted he would have bothered to shake Miller's hand. As it was, he was aware of the other's presence in the kitchen, above all Cassie's. He'd seen the way her face lit up when she talked about her family. The quickest way to alienate Cassie for-ever was to cut Alex Miller publicly.

He extended his hand. Alex mimicked the gesture. Neither man prolonged the contact unnecessarily.

"Good trip down?"

"Not too bad."

"Glad to hear it."

Satisfied that he'd been as polite as the situation war-ranted, Caleb nodded briefly and let the conversation die a natural death. He turned to Cassie, while Hank introduced himself to Thompson and Alex in turn.

"I guess you'll be taking everyone up to my parents' place in a bit."

She nodded. "We were just going to check on the ponies, and I wanted to show Alex and Thompson Orion."

"I've got some calls out at a few farms, so I won't be able to head over there now. I'll drop by later to make sure you're all settled." He shoved his hand into his front jeans pocket and fished out a set of keys.

"Here. I locked both the front and back doors, just in case you weren't planning on going there 'til dark. There are extra keys on the kitchen counter."

The keys were warm from his body, and Cassie clasped them firmly, savoring the heat.

She inclined her head in mute acknowledgment, the words she wished she could say locked in her throat. She wanted to ask him to stay with them, to be with her, to tease her as he had in the beginning, and then later to touch her with his wonderful, knowing hands and mouth. But out of the corner of her eye, she saw Jamie and Sophie talking excitedly with Hank and she remained silent. She was a mother, a horsewoman, not a lovesick fool. But involuntarily, her eyes followed Caleb as he said his good-byes and left.

11

"*O*h, my! What a pretty house."

Cassie grinned. Thompson's enthusiasm was a good deal warmer for Caleb's house than it had been for his horse. When Cassie had led Orion out of his stall, Cassie had heard her mutter something about a "big brute" and then back away to a safe distance. At least Alex had been appropriately impressed, taking in the stallion's proud, elegant carriage. Although Alex didn't ride, he'd picked up enough from watching Cassie's horses and those in the stables where she'd ridden to recognize a superb animal when he saw one.

"Come inside, everyone. The inside is as nice as the outside. No, kids, don't run ahead. Let's all go in together."

"Mom? Will Caleb be living with us? It's his house, right?" Sophie asked.

"No, Pumpkin. The house we'll be living in is that of his parents. Caleb has his own house that's in back of ours. It's very nice, too."

"Oh," Sophie paused as she digested that piece of information. "Well, that means Jamie and I can still play with

him. He's so *funny*." Her little five-year-old voice made it
sound as if she'd just spent the afternoon with Robin
Williams.

Cassie didn't try to dissuade Sophie from thinking of
Caleb as a source of fun and games. She realized that the
kids probably considered most of the grown-ups they
encountered potential playmates, as the friends Alex sometimes brought home were more than willing to take a break
from the stress of their jobs by romping around on the floor
and playing with Legos. Cassie figured that as the children
made new friends in the neighborhood and at school, their
interest in Caleb would wane.

They walked up the front porch steps as a group. Cassie
inserted the key in the lock and pushed the door wide open.

The warm water bubbled and lapped around her. She
wondered whether she'd died and this was paradise. It was
everything she'd thought it would be, and more. After
showing her family around the house and letting the twins
choose their bedrooms, Cassie had carried her bag to her
own room to unpack. She'd put her things away in the
drawers and closet and stepped into the bathroom with her
bag of toiletries. And stopped, immobilized with wonder
and delight.

Around the jacuzzi stood four vases bursting with lilacs,
peonies, and lilies. A sheet of white paper lay on the rim of
the tub with a single sentence written on it. "Honeysuckle
is still my favorite." At the end of the tub was a bottle
wrapped with a large satin bow. Cassie lifted the bottle and
read the label: Wild Honeysuckle Bath Foam.

As if in a trance, Cassie turned the tap on. Steaming
water cascaded out of the spigot, filling the silence with its
soft roar. Slowly she unscrewed the bottle and sniffed
appreciatively. The heady floral scent greeted her. Pouring
a small stream of the golden gel under the rush of water,
she watched as bubbles formed in white foamy masses.

Layer by layer, she stripped off her clothes, then stepped into the warm perfumed water swirling and lapping around her calves and knees. Slowly, she eased her body down.

Dear God, she thought dreamily, what woman could resist a man who transforms her bathroom into a summer bower? Who gives presents that dazzle the senses? It was so intimate to have these lushly perfumed flowers filling her bathroom. A secret garden. Caleb had to be a magician to know what would captivate her so thoroughly.

And did it mean that he, too, couldn't erase the memory of how they'd stood in this very room, sharing heated kisses, his hands touching her, learning the soft curves of her body? She longed to experience once again the wonder of his embrace and the passion of his kisses.

She gave herself up to the sensation of the wet warmth against her skin, wishing only it were Caleb's hands instead touching her so intimately. Closing her eyes, she allowed herself to dream.

Caleb saw the twins perched on the front porch steps as he walked up the path to the house. He was hot and tired, had been thinking of little else these last twenty minutes but the ice-cold six pack tucked away in the back of his refrigerator. The sight, though, of the two blond mops of hair bent over a big white bowl drew him like a magnet.

"Hi, what's up?"

Jamie and Sophie both looked up and flashed him huge smiles of welcome. Then dropped their heads back down, absorbed in their task.

Intrigued by their deep fascination in the bowl's contents, Caleb asked, "So what's in the bowl? Have you two caught yourselves some frogs?"

Jamie's head shot up at once, his face eager. Words rushed out, tumbling over each other. *"Frogs?* There are frogs here? Where? Can you show me, Caleb?"

"Well, sure. There's a little goldfish pond behind the

house where a lot of frogs like to come and swim. I'll take you and we'll see whether we can't catch one for you. But show me what you've got in that bowl of yours, first. Looks mighty interesting."

Sophie lifted her head and shoved the bowl toward Caleb.

"Grapes. Jamie only likes the red ones, and I just like green ones. Thompson sometimes gives us two bowls, one for Jamie and one for me, but she was busy unpacking stuff." Sophie paused and held the bowl out invitingly. "Want one? Which kind do you like best?"

"Oh, I like both."

Jamie and Sophie looked up at him, matching frowns marring their faces, clearly appalled by the idea that a person could like *both* red and green grapes. They watched in reluctant fascination as Caleb selected one of each and popped them into his mouth.

Caleb closed his eyes, allowing the juice of the grapes to fill his mouth. It wasn't exactly the cold brew he'd been wishing for, but what the hell. He gave an exaggerated sigh of pleasure. "Mmm . . . these are terrific. Got any more?" At the twins' enthusiastic nod, he suggested, "Let's take them with us. We can eat while we hunt for those frogs."

Sophie scrambled to her feet quickly and grabbed hold of Caleb's hand. Caleb felt the wet stickiness of grape juice coat his palm and fingers. He gave her hand a little squeeze and watched as Jamie stood up with the bowl of grapes cradled in his arms.

"Want help carrying that bowl, Jamie?"

"No, I got it," Jamie replied. Caleb watched with mixed dismay and delight as Jamie tried to tuck the bowl under one chubby arm while his free arm latched onto Caleb's. The bowl listed drunkenly, sprinkling grapes onto the grass. Laughter lacing his deep voice, Caleb addressed his small companions. "All right then, let's go catch some frogs!"

The threesome moved around the house passing by the

kitchen in the back. Caleb eyed the nearly empty bowl that was in imminent danger of following the same trajectory as the grapes.

"Uh, why don't we drop that bowl off in the kitchen on our way? Then we won't have to carry it on the way back."

Jamie released Caleb's hand and bolted for the kitchen door. Caleb heard his high-pitched voice through the storm door.

"Hiya, Thompson, Caleb's taking us to catch some frogs at the pond. Can mine sleep in my bed? See ya." He tore through the door with the speed of a small torpedo and grabbed Caleb's hand. "Okay, let's go."

Caleb reasoned that it must have been the weight of the bowl that had kept the five-year-old below light speed before. Now that it had been jettisoned, Jamie moved as if he had rocket boosters for shoes. Caleb felt as if his arm was being stretched like a rubber band, so impatient was Jamie to reach the pond. As they made their way, the twins kept up a steady stream of questions about the house and what Caleb had liked to do as a kid himself. They also supplied an encyclopedia's worth of information about themselves, their favorite foods, and any other subject that flitted across their minds. After a few minutes, Caleb realized his tongue was getting tired trying to answer all their questions and opted for companionable grunts and hmms instead. The twins' stream of conversation continued joyfully unabated.

"Gee, it would be neat if Uncle Alex were with us. He likes things like frogs. Mom doesn't."

"Yeah, I don't know why he had to take a nap. We waited, just like he told us, until it was light before we woke him up this morning. We only came in and asked him a couple of times if it was time."

Caleb grinned, feeling almost sorry for the poor bastard. He inquired instead, "What's your mom doing? She's resting, too?"

"No, she's taking a bubble bath. We heard the water running and went and peeked. She was in the bath with her hair all piled up and her eyes closed. Boy, were there lots of bubbles."

"And there were all these pretty flowers in there. She looked just like a princess, like *The Sleeping Beauty*," Sophie chimed in, remembering the movie her Uncle Alex had rented for her. Sophie had spent the following three days dressed in a princess costume, reenacting her favorite scenes.

Caleb groaned inwardly at the erotic image that sprang up in his mind. He'd bought the flowers and the bath gel on impulse, on a whim. He'd told himself that he'd purchased them as a gift, to thank Cassie for staying on at Five Oaks in spite of the problems Pamela represented, but he knew that was just a convenient excuse.

He wanted Cassie to remember his kisses, hoping that she'd realize what she was missing, what they could be sharing. Now he feared it would be he who would be haunted.

"Sleeping Beauty didn't sleep in a bathtub, silly. Anyway, I heard Mom humming, so she couldn't have been sleeping," Jamie retorted hotly, annoyed at his sister's interruption. "We were going to surprise her, but Thompson called us down to the kitchen. It would have been fun to take a bath with her. We used to do that, but Mommy says we're too big now. But I bet we could fit in that tub. It's *humongous!*"

Caleb didn't think he could take much more of the twins' chatter, innocently conjuring pictures that made his body tighten with need. He would have happily sold his soul to the devil to be the one to "surprise" Cassie in her bath. He'd have started with her toes, all soft and pink, and moved slowly up her ankle, molding his mouth against the delicate bone, then along her slender calf to the back of her knee. She had such endless, wonderful legs. Damn, he could devote an entire afternoon exclusively to her legs.

Oh, Christ, he was going to die from acute arousal.

Caleb almost shouted aloud with relief when the goldfish pond came into view. Nothing like trying to catch slimy frogs for two rambunctious five-year-olds to get the delectable Cassie Miller off his mind. As a matter of fact, this was probably the *only* activity in the world that might be able to shake loose the incredible fantasy unfolding in his mind.

The twins spotted the pond a few seconds later. Releasing their grip on his hands, they dashed toward it, their short legs pounding the ground like a herd of buffalo. Caleb smiled slightly at the series of plops coming from the edge of the pond: Frogs diving hurriedly for the safety of the water. At the excited cries of the twins, Caleb knew that they, too, had witnessed the mass exodus. Sophie came running back to him, arms waving wildly, her face flushed scarlet with dismay.

"Caleb, Caleb, the frogs all ran away!"

"Yup," Caleb nodded his head. "I've never seen frogs run so fast in all my life. They must have known right away that you two are super frog catchers."

"But how will we catch them if they've gone?" Sophie asked, deeply worried.

"Maybe we can trick them into thinking we've gone. That's going to be pretty tough, though." Well nigh impossible with these two chatterbugs, Caleb added silently.

After about fifteen minutes of explaining, cajoling, and outright bribing, Caleb managed to convince Sophie and Jamie that if they stood very still at a slight distance from the pond, he might be able to get close enough to grab a frog for each of them. The children reluctantly agreed, but Caleb could see skepticism in Jamie's face. Caleb had to admit that Jamie's own plan had sounded infinitely more exciting. Jamie had wanted to wade into the pond and chase the frogs so that they'd all jump back out. Then Caleb and Sophie could be waiting on the bank to catch them. More than a bit awed by the little boy's tenacity to his plan, Caleb prayed that this season's frogs were especially stupid and slow. He frankly didn't know how long he could keep Jamie from testing out his own frog-catching method. It was doubtful that the Miller clan would be too thrilled to see Jamie come back covered from head to toe in pond slime.

As the third frog dove to the safety of the pond's muddy bottom, Caleb began muttering curses under his breath, wondering what in hell had possessed him to suggest a frog hunt. He was slightly worried, too, that he'd gotten too tall for frog catching—he'd been about three feet shorter the last time he'd attempted to swoop down and grab one.

Out of the corner of his eye, he saw Jamie squirming impatiently, jumping from one foot to the other, and knew time was running out. Caleb edged his way around the water's edge, his gaze trained on a brownish green lump nestled in the weeds. He bent his long, muscular frame slowly, raising his arms sightly, so that his hands were in front of his waist, his fingers open and ready. He pounced, letting his body fall forward, his hands scooping up the brown blob before it could leap away. Cold, slimy, brown water oozed between his fingers. But he'd done it. The frog squirmed frantically in his hands. Caleb grinned in triumph, feeling like a conquering hero, as the twins started jumping up and down in excitement.

"You got one! You got one, Caleb!"

"*Please* can I hold him, Caleb?" Sophie looked up at him, and he imagined this was precisely the way Cassie would have looked at her age. He glanced down at her two small, open hands waiting to receive the frog. Kneeling, he brought himself and the treasure down to her level so that she and her brother could admire the catch. He kept his fingers pressed against each other, forming a miniature cage.

"This guy looks a little jumpy, Sophie," Caleb replied gently. "Why don't I stick him into my shirt pocket—see how it's big enough—then I can just button the flap while I catch another frog for Jamie. Then, when we get back to the house, you can both hold your frogs at the same time." Sudden inspiration struck and, convinced Einstein couldn't have done better, Caleb added, "That would make it more fair."

Sophie looked at the frog and then nodded at Caleb solemnly, her eyes blue as forget-me-nots. The twins watched as Caleb gingerly tucked the frog into his faded denim shirt's breast pocket and then turned to make his way once more to the edge of the pond. Caleb felt the frog's legs pumping frantically against the fabric. *God help me if I smush this sucker while I'm catching the other one,* his lips twitching at the thought.

Thompson heard the excited cries of Jamie and Sophie and moved to the kitchen window in order to witness their triumphant return. She smiled at the sight of the twins alternately hopping and skipping around Caleb's measured stride. They reminded her of cocker spaniel puppies she'd seen once at a fair: all golden bounce. Jamie and Sophie were bombarding Caleb with questions as they jumped in frenzied circles around him, unable to contain their excitement. Snippets of their conversation floated on the afternoon air.

"What can we put our frogs in, Caleb?"

"Let's take a look in the basement. I seem to remember having a couple of fish tanks when I was little. Maybe they're still around."

"Let's catch some goldfish tomorrow, 'kay, Caleb?"

"Do you like pizza, Caleb?"

Thompson opened the kitchen door and stood in the door frame, her arms crossed against her bosom as the trio approached. *A fine-looking young man,* she thought appreciatively. And good with children, too. Exactly what Cassie needed in her life. Thompson had been deeply concerned at the way Cassie had shut herself off after her breakup with Brad. Although she didn't know the full details, Thompson had seen how rarely Cassie accepted a date, how reserved she was.

It just wasn't right for a beautiful, young, unmarried woman to have no life outside the care of her children and her horses. Cassie needed a man to stir her juices, to make her feel giddy and foolish. Thompson figured that Caleb Wells had enough charm and charisma alone to stimulate the interest (as well as just about everything else) of the most reluctant of women.

Nevertheless, it might be wise to set the record straight with this southern charmer. If his intentions were less than honorable toward Cassie, then she'd sit out on that comfortable-looking rocking chair on the front porch, a shotgun warming her lap.

Thompson was ready for him before dawn the next morning. The night before, over dinner, Alex and Cassie had discussed plans to run together before Cassie set off for Five Oaks. Thompson thought that this would be the perfect time to invite Caleb Wells over for a cup of hot coffee and breakfast. After hearing the sound of the front door closing, she made her way downstairs. With any luck, the twins would sleep in this morning. Last night, they hadn't even complained at going to bed, the day's activity and excitement having finally caught up with them. She might have until about six-thirty for that private conversation with Caleb Wells. Luckily for Thompson, there wasn't a shy bone in her body—at her age, she considered that emotion an utter waste of time—and anyway, what she was doing concerned the welfare of her employer.

Caleb looked somewhat taken aback when he answered the knock on his front door and saw Thompson standing before him. It wasn't too often people called on him at five-thirty in the morning. His dark hair glistening with moisture, his jaw freshly shaven, it was obvious he'd just gotten out of the shower and was still in the middle of dressing. So far, he'd gotten on his jeans. His feet were bare and so was his chest.

Excellent pectorals, Thompson judged approvingly. She'd always liked men who didn't have rugs on their chests. With a nice bare chest like Caleb's you could see each of those lean muscles ripple and flex. A lovely flat stomach, too, with just a thin line of dark hair disappearing beneath the button of his jeans. Fleetingly, Thompson wished that she were thirty years younger. This young man looked like he had all the right stuff. She hoped Cassie would have the good sense to take what he offered and enjoy herself every step of the way.

"Good morning, Bessie. Anything up? Something broken at the house you need me to take a look at it?"

"No, no, everything's fine. I'm something of an early riser and I noticed you came back from a run about twenty minutes ago. I was wondering if I might interest you in some eggs and bacon and a cup of hot coffee."

The smile he gave her could have melted both polar ice-caps. "Bessie, you are one smart woman. Offer me food, and I'm yours. Give me five minutes."

Thompson looked pleased. "Just like my husband. That man could eat half a lamb in one sitting and still have room for dessert. Alex is that way, too. You all must have metabolisms to rival supersonic jets. How do you like your eggs, by the way?"

"Over easy," Caleb replied, a little annoyed to learn that he and Alex Miller shared anything at all in common. But hell, Miller would probably look like a fat slob in fifteen years, given his cushy desk job in some Manhattan skyscraper.

The thought pleased him immensely.

Whistling softly to himself, Caleb returned to his bedroom. He grabbed a white T-shirt and a black flannel button-down shirt from his closet. From the top of his bureau drawers, he retrieved his beeper and hooked it onto the waistband of his jeans. Shoving his keys into the front pocket of his jeans, he rummaged for a pair of socks from the top drawer and padded barefoot into the mudroom at the back of the house to don his work boots. A scant four minutes had elapsed since Thompson had appeared at his doorstep. Caleb shut the door behind him and strode toward his parents' house and the promise of a hearty breakfast.

12

"So what do you think of Cassie?"

His smile was obscured as he lifted the steaming mug of coffee to his lips. Definitely a no-nonsense kind of a woman, Bessie Thompson was. At least she'd had the patience to wait until Caleb had wolfed down his three eggs, buttered toast, and bacon before getting down to brass tacks. He took a slow sip of the deliciously brewed coffee and leaned back in his chair, his hands cradling the warm mug against the flat of his stomach.

"Nice girl. Excellent rider. She just might be our ticket to getting Orion the ribbons he needs," Caleb offered blandly, intentionally sounding as clichéd as a football coach interviewed on television.

"Piffle." Thompson waved her hand in the air dismissively. "You know I'm not asking about how good a rider she is. I assume that if you had the brains to hire her, it's because you recognize how good she is." Thompson locked eyes with Calebs, her expression as serious as a judge's. "What I want to know is what you think of her as a *woman.*"

Yep, she definitely knew how to grab the bull by the

horns, so to speak. Caleb pondered just how long he might be able to avoid the issue Thompson seemed so determined to discuss, but decided it probably wasn't worth the effort. The look on the older woman's face, her body language— arms folded across her chest, backside resting against the kitchen counter—told him that there was no way he was going to get out of that kitchen until he provided Thompson with the heart-to-heart talk women seemed to love to have.

Caleb expelled a slow breath. "Well, Bessie. What do you want me to say? Cassie's a beautiful woman. I'd be lying if I told you I wasn't attracted to her, because I am."

Thompson nodded her head, like an elementary school-teacher encouraging a reluctant child. "Well, then, what are you going to do about it?"

Caleb coughed, glad there wasn't coffee in his mouth or it would have splattered all over his shirt front. Sure was ballsy of her, discussing his intentions toward Cassie as calmly as if she were discussing the weather. Caleb would have given anything to see the look on Cassie's face if she knew just how seriously her housekeeper took the job of tending to Cassie's happiness.

Do about it? I know what I'd like to do about it, but right now that's pretty much in the realm of fantasy.

He sighed heavily. "Look, Bessie, I'm divorced, and my divorce left me pretty cynical about all this happily-ever-after stuff. From what I know of Cassie, she's just that sort of girl. Innocent and sweet." Caleb raised his eyes to Bessie's shrewd gaze. "I may want to make love with her, but there's no way I'm about to promise her all the rest. One marriage was definitely enough for me." Caleb figured that if Thompson wasn't going to be shy about sticking her nose into other peoples' private lives, then she shouldn't be shocked by what he said. If she didn't like the answers he gave her, too bad.

Thompson looked at him silently, her expression

inscrutable. Finally, she spoke, smiling wryly. "I suppose that's what I get for being nosy. But I won't apologize, because Cassie's exactly as you said: sheltered, sweet, and innocent. She's also a fine, caring person, and she's suffered a great deal. Not a lot of people could have taken on the responsibility for two infants like she did." She shook her head sadly, remembering the cloud of sorrow that had hung over the Miller house after the accident. Pushing away the memories, a glint of humor returned to her eyes as she spoke again. "I can tell you, though, that I like your honesty a whole lot more than that so-and-so of a fiancé's saccharine words and empty promises."

Caleb grinned, irrationally glad Thompson had disliked Cassie's ex-fiancé. "A real creep, huh?"

Thompson nodded. "Spoiled and selfish. He had so much given to him: money, looks, education, you name it. He seemed to think the world was his for the taking. But when the moment came for him to give of himself . . . Well, Cassie's better off without him. But he let her down when she needed his support the most." Thompson paused and gave him a wide smile. "That's why I think she needs a good-looking devil like you in her life."

"Uh, Bessie, exactly what are you implying?" Caleb had the embarrassing suspicion that he was being looked over like one of the studs at Five Oaks. He didn't like the feeling one bit.

"Cassie needs to be shaken up a bit, made to remember she's made of flesh and blood. She's been living in a cocoon these past five years. Time she should have spent loving and laughing with a man at her side. The way I see it, you're enticing enough to get her realizing she has *needs*."

"What makes you think that I might not hurt Cassie as badly as her fiancé did? What makes you think I won't leave her with a broken heart, too?"

A thoughtful look came over the older woman's face as

she chose her next words. She wondered how Caleb would react to the idea of Cassie belonging to another man. She hoped that Caleb's apparent indifference to commitment might be just a defensive reflex.

"Well, of course, if you're fool enough to let a woman like Cassie get away, that's your business. Even though she may lack experience, I'm betting that emotionally, Cassie's grown up a lot since her engagement to Brad Gibson. I think she'll be strong enough to understand that there are plenty of other men who don't consider commitment a four-letter word. You'd end up being just a very pleasant wake-up call for a fine woman."

"Damn, Bessie," Caleb exploded, insulted by Thompson's lethally frank description. The image of himself as some kind of sexual warmup so another man could step in and experience the delights of Cassie's body was repellent. Infuriating. "What kind of talk is this? You make Machiavelli seem like a really fuzzy, warm kind of guy. You could have probably given him lessons. And what makes you think I'm going to let myself get involved with Cassie in *any* way after this?"

Bessie concealed a smile at the frustrated edge to his voice. *Oh, Caleb,* she thought, *from what I observed in the Sawyers' kitchen yesterday, I don't think you're going to be able to help yourself. You've got the look of a man who's closing in on his woman, watching her every move.*

"You're right, of course, a man with your experience of women and commitment *should* stay away from a girl like Cassie, but unfortunately, I'm just a hopeless romantic. I see two young, handsome people, and I automatically want to try to get them together." She gave an innocent smile that didn't fool Caleb for a minute. "I guess it's the matchmaker instinct," she concluded with a dramatic sigh and then brightened, as if another thought had just occurred to her. "Of course now that Cassie's showing again, I'm sure she'll meet lots of nice men who'll want to take her out.

Then you can stick to women who aren't interested in commitment, in sharing."

Alex Miller was in a piss-poor mood. He and Cassie had returned from their morning run to find Caleb Wells comfortably ensconced at the kitchen table with Jamie and Sophie seated on either side of him. The twins happily spooning up fruit loops and chattering away, while Thompson hovered nearby, a pot of her delicious coffee at the ready.

Jealousy, stemming from an irrational fear that he would be displaced in the twins' hearts by a virtual stranger, swept over him and left him consumed with an intense need to plow his fist into Caleb Wells's face. He hated, too, the hungry look that had entered Wells's eye as he had taken in Cassie's clinging, sweaty T-shirt and the running shorts that showed off her sleekly muscled legs. Long legs, shiny now with the sweat that covered them.

Never mind that he, Alex, would have responded in precisely the same way if a woman as beautiful as Cassie had entered the room, dressed in clothes that revealed as much as they covered. But Cassie was his kid sister, damn it!

Alex doubted whether warning Wells away from Cassie would have any effect. He smiled grimly to himself, his mood improving fractionally as an alternative solution occurred to him. It would be infinitely more effective, as well as deeply, deeply satisfying, if he just went and pounded the daylights out of him.

Cassie entered Hot Lips's stall, and brought her out to the nearest cross ties. In the days since Caleb's diagnosis, he had diligently followed through with the laser therapy, and Cassie had restricted the mare to stall rest. It was clear, however, that the lack of exercise was making Hot Lips even more excitable and high-strung than ever. Cassie fretted about what would happen once Hot Lips finally healed and was taken out. Would she go into high gear, flip out, and reinjure her leg, perhaps hurting herself worse?

Crooning softly to the radio as she curried her mare's burnished chestnut coat, Cassie's mind raced as she checked off changes in diet that might help Hot Lips in her recovery—rationing her grain, increasing the amount of hay in her stall, and adding a nutritional feed supplement to make sure Hot Lips received an adequate supply of vitamins and minerals while she was healing. But her mind drew a frustrating blank when she tried to design a safe exercise program following Hot Lips's recovery. She hoped that Caleb and Hank might be able to help with a viable plan.

Cassie groomed her mare until her coat gleamed in the soft light of the barn's interior and then inspected each of her hooves, cleaning them with a hoof pick and examining each one for any cracking or sign of disease. Looking down at the hoof supported in the palm of her hand, Cassie wondered whether using magnetic pads on the soles of Hot Lips's hooves might help. Another question to ask Caleb when she saw him. Cassie shook her head, annoyed at how often thoughts of Caleb intruded.

She led Hot Lips back into the stall and fished out an apple treat from the pocket of her beige breeches, which she dropped into the feed bucket. The mare immediately brushed her head against Cassie's torso as she followed the scent of the treat. Impatient, she pushed her nose against the rubber bottom of the bucket and rooted delicately. A quiet chomping mingled with the other barn noises as Cassie gave the horse an affectionate pat and left the stall.

Cassie had arranged her schedule so that she'd ride Orion before lunch. She wanted to be fresh for the stallion and knew that working with him demanded her clearest thinking and quickest reactions. She'd been alternating workouts with the stallion, mixing in jumping with flat work, progressively asking more and more of Orion as he

came to know her better. Cassie was thrilled by the promise the stallion showed. He had great athletic ability,
courage, and intelligence. What remained to be seen was
whether he had *it*—the fierce competitive drive to be the
best. That's what made the champions, whether they were
racehorses such as Man o' War or Secretariat, or jumpers
such as Idle Dice, Abdullah, Galoubet, or Big Ben. If
Cassie could bring that quality out in Orion, what a time
they would have together! And Five Oaks would have a
stud whose get people would be eager to pay for.

"I brushed Orion off for you, Cassie. He'd gotten
muddy from his turn out in the field this morning. Now
he's all pretty for you."

"Thanks, Raff." Cassie smiled in gratitude as she neared
the barn manager. "With all my family here, and my
brother leaving tomorrow, it's great not to have to face an
enormous muddy stallion! I hope it didn't take too much of
your time."

"Oh, no, Cassie, no problem. You know, those other riders, they never groomed Orion or any of the horses they
worked with. Maybe that's why Orion likes you. You take
care of him, not just hop on his back and boss him around."

"Maybe so, Raffael." Cassie smiled, secretly pleased by
the idea that the stallion might recognize the time she took
in grooming him, rubbing him down, massaging him. But
even if he didn't appreciate it, Cassie thought, she herself
derived immense pleasure from the simple, repetitive acts
involved in caring for horses. She wouldn't trade her profession for any in the world.

Raffael moved past Cassie with Kenyon, Orion's sire,
leading the older horse outside to the stallion's pastures.
Cassie approached Orion's stall and peered in. Orion was
standing quietly with the donkey, Barney, dozing at his
side. The donkey's large ears were cocked to the side, a
wide, fuzzy V. The contrast between the shaggy, spindly

legged donkey and the sleek, massive stallion, was absurd, causing Cassie to laugh softly. Orion raised his head slightly at the sound and as Cassie moved to the metal bars of his upper stall door, he came over, his large, flared nostrils blowing warm against the knuckles of her hand.

"Hey, big guy, you ready for a little work? We're going to have to look extra good this morning because Alex will be watching. I want to show him what a great horse you are. And who knows," her voice dropped, whispering confidentially into the horse's ear, "maybe Caleb will be around, too."

Cassie turned away and went to the tack room to grab her saddle, saddle pad, and Orion's girth and bridle. She set them beside the cross ties and brought the stallion out. Raffael had done a fine job grooming Orion—not a speck of dust showed on his dark bay coat—but Cassie nevertheless took a soft brush and ran it over the satiny coat, wanting the stallion to sparkle in the spring sunshine.

Finally ready, she led the stallion out into the brilliant sun. It was a glorious day. For the first time the warmth of the air and the blue of the sky promised bright flowers, green grass, and T-shirts without sweaters. It was the kind of weather that made Cassie want to shout with happiness, swing her arms in the air, and do a jig, grateful to Mother Nature that the warm weather had finally arrived and winter was banished once more. Instead, she pulled the stallion walking beside her to a halt and turned her head to nuzzle his neck. Her arms wrapped around the front of his chest, she gave the horse a hug, squeezing him tight with happiness.

"Getting mighty familiar with my horse, aren't you Slim?" Caleb's voice came from behind her, laced with amusement at the sight of Cassie hugging the big stallion as if he were a cuddly kitten.

Embarrassed as she was, Cassie managed nonetheless to reply casually as if she hadn't been caught looking like a complete mush head, a sentimental dolt. "It's such a beautiful day. I always get excited when the warm weather comes." She shrugged her shoulders and added a bit defensively, "Spring fever. I just wanted to share it with Orion."

Damn, she was adorable. Caleb thought of telling her that any time she wanted to reach out and touch someone, to share her pleasure in the joys of spring, he'd be happy to stand in. She could be as effusive as she wished. But he decided he'd save this topic for when they could be guaranteed some privacy. He'd seen Alex Miller and the twins in the distance and knew they'd probably be showing up any minute.

Thinking of Alex Miller, Caleb's jaw tightened. The sooner he headed back to New York, the better. The guy really ticked him off. On account of him, he'd almost refused Bessie's suggestion that he, Hank, and Melissa join the Millers and her for a celebratory dinner that evening. The twins had gotten so excited at the prospect of guests at their new home that Caleb hadn't the heart to let them down. And perverse bastard that he was, the irritation in Alex Miller's icy blue eyes at Thompson's impromptu invitation had clinched the decision. Hell, he'd just eat Bessie's fine cooking and feast his eyes on Cassie . . . and let Alex Miller stew.

"So what have you got scheduled for Orion today, Slim?" Caleb inquired, steering his thoughts back to more professional ground.

"I was going to work on angled approaches and distances for jumps. Hank got a shipment of brand new fences that I thought I'd show him, too. We don't want him spooking at any of the wilder fences he'll be seeing at the shows."

Caleb nodded. Inexperienced horses often had enormous problems when they confronted some of the zanier concoctions course directors designed for jumping classes. Shying and refusing a jump were fairly common occurrences at shows where the sight of plastic pink flamingos clustered around the edge of a water jump scared the willies out of the greener horses. Even a smart horse like Orion might have second thoughts about certain types of fences.

"That should be fun."

Cassie grinned, her good spirits heightened by the beauty of the day, by the chance to stand near Caleb and drink in the sight of him. Just talking to him like this caused her heart to pound loudly in her ribcage, making her feel that much more alive. Would she ever get used to his effect on her?

"I'm sure he'll do fine with these jumps. You know, sometimes it's not even the jumps that rattle them, but something they see peripherally, like a plastic garbage bag flying through the air on a windy day or someone's umbrella opening suddenly."

"Well, if you want, I can root some stuff out from the back of my truck and start tossing it around. See whether that gets a rise out of him."

"Thanks, but no thanks," Cassie replied dryly.

"Chicken."

"You betcha." Cassie laughed, delighted to hear his teasing banter once more. "I don't want Orion to dump me because of a greasy paper plate you got at some delicatessen last month! If Orion's going to freak, I'd like to think it was over something a little less disgusting than what you've got in the back of that truck."

"That bad, huh?" His eyes crinkled at the corners as he grinned good-humoredly.

"*Definitely* needs a trip to Tidy Car."

"Haven't you heard that clean cars show a lack of character?"

"Well yours looks like something out of *Animal House*."

"One of my favorites. A classic." His smile spread, his white teeth even and strong.

God, Cassie thought, unnerved at how Caleb's smile made her insides melt and turned her knees to putty. Please don't let me fall in a boneless heap at his feet.

With a heroic effort, Cassie scrunched up her face, feigning disgust at his cinematic preferences. "Figures," she said, ending the conversation by leading the stallion away before she revealed just how easily Caleb affected her.

The little group stood watching Cassie school Orion in the large exercise ring. Hank looked at the different faces of Alex Miller, the twins, Melissa, and Caleb. *We should start putting announcements in the paper giving the hours Cassie's going to be riding and charge admission,* Hank thought to himself. That would bring in a tidy sum. She really was a treat to watch. It was also astounding how quiet the twins could be, one minute as chaotic as two force-ten gales, the next, standing still as stones, their eyes following their mother as she maneuvered the horse around the ring, concentrating on her riding with a seriousness that belied their young age. The breeder in him couldn't help wondering, was this a case of nature or nurture? Was Cassie's ability with horses a genetic trait shared by other members of her family? Or was it Cassie's intense love for horses that had transmitted itself to the twins, so that they, too, were little equine professionals at the ripe age of five?

Hank looked over at Caleb, who stood next to Melissa, his dark head occasionally nodding at some comment she made, unwilling to engage in any deeper conversation while he watched Cassie work his stallion. Caleb watched her with the intensity of a hawk, his eyes never leaving her slim, athletic form.

Poor guy, thought Hank sympathetically. Caleb had managed to surprise Hank and Melissa. It was clear as daylight Cassie and Caleb were attracted to each other but were equally hesitant to act on it. That Cassie should be wary came as no big surprise to him. For Caleb, however, it was a first in a long, long time. Hank couldn't even recall when last Caleb had bothered to wait once a woman revealed her interest in him. That meant Caleb must have recognized Cassie was different. If she'd been like the other women Caleb had known, she'd already be in his bed every night.

From the tension sizzling between the two of them that happy event had yet to take place. Hank wondered whether Caleb instinctively understood that getting involved with Cassie would require a level of commitment that he might not even have shared with Pamela. That was a lot for some-one like Caleb to come to terms with. Well, Hank sighed to himself, one thing was sure: It was going to be a heck of an interesting summer watching these two circle around each other.

13

Caleb left for the animal hospital shortly after Cassie's workout. These days, he was especially grateful that he'd formed a partnership with Derek Cole and Mark Winterer. It gave him the flexibility in his schedule to be able to stay longer at Five Oaks when he wished. It wasn't *just* the chance to see Cassie that had him spending more time standing around the exercise ring. After months of seeing Orion fall short of his potential, it was an incredible source of pleasure and pride to watch the stallion begin performing the way Caleb had instinctively known he could. Caleb had invested so much time and energy, charting bloodlines, working toward breeding a horse that epitomized strength, stamina, and elegance. Caleb wanted Orion to be the first star among many to bring Five Oaks to glory.

As he entered the hospital's front door, Caleb's eyes immediately swept the waiting room, scanning who was in the line up for immediate attention. Caleb was gratified to see just four patients: a small dog that looked like a terrier-spaniel mix, a black lab, and two cat carriers. Caleb never liked to have too many animals in the waiting room at once—the nerves and fears of the animals as well as the owners simply escalated with overcrowding. With Mark Winterer in the office this morning, they could reduce the number of animals waiting to be treated by fifty percent.

"Morning, Joyce. What's up?" Caleb smiled at his office manager/receptionist/lifesaver. Caleb considered hiring Joyce one of the most intelligent moves he'd ever made. She was efficient, tireless, dependable, and didn't pitch a fit when a dog peed on the waiting room floor. Caleb had gone through about four secretaries who seemed to think it was beneath their dignity to use a mop once in a while. Heaven knows what they thought working in a veterinarian's office was all about. It was a job where you needed compassion and a healthy sense of humor. Luckily for Caleb, Joyce had both in addition to her other qualities.

"Hi, Caleb," Joyce replied cheerfully. "Everything's going smoothly so far. There were a couple of cancellations for this afternoon, but they're sure to fill up in the next fifteen minutes or so. Mark did a neutering this morning—a ten-month-old Belgian sheepdog. He came out from under the anesthesia just fine. He's lying down in the back. Probably wondering what hit him."

"Poor guy. I can sympathize. Any calls?"

"Other than your ex-wife? Five. Nothing too urgent. Mrs. Schwartz would like you to come and check on her pregnant bitch. She's due any day. You know how she is about her dogs." Joyce smiled and raised her brows. "Now, if you want to know how many times dear old Pamela rang . . ."

Caleb raised his hand. "No, no. That's quite all right. If she tries to talk to me, or comes by, tell her I volunteered for NASA's next shuttle voyage." Caleb grinned. "And Joyce, be real careful not to let the 'dear old Pamela' line slip out if she's within hearing distance. She'd probably come after you with an Uzi. You're too important to me to lose to my ex-wife's vanity."

Joyce gave a comic shudder. "There's a scary thought.

But don't you forget about Mrs. Schwartz. She's almost as tenacious as Pamela."

Caleb laughed at Joyce's more than apt description. "I promise I'll call Mrs. Schwartz after I've seen to this batch of patients." Mrs. Schwartz was outrageous when it came to her flat coated retriever. Caleb had read about royalty whose lives weren't as pampered as her dogs. "Who's my first patient, by the way?"

"Marjory Pierson and her cat, Waldo."

"Right. What's Waldo in for?"

"Vomiting." Joyce handed Caleb a manila folder containing Waldo's records. "Mrs. Pierson doesn't know if it's hairballs or something more serious. He also needs his feline leukemia and rabies shots."

"Well, we may have to reschedule those shots depending on what's wrong. Have her bring him back to the examining room in a minute. I'm just going to hunt down Mark."

"He's in the office looking at the x-rays of that black lab in the waiting room. The dog's been limping badly recently."

Caleb had decided to economize on space in the animal hospital by having one large office that the three doctors shared. This resulted in three comfortably sized examining rooms and a spacious, well-equipped operating room. Caleb pushed open the door to the communal office to find his colleague staring at a backlit x-ray film attached to the wall. Mark Winterer paused in the act of bringing a steaming cup of coffee to his lips to greet Caleb.

"Hey, Caleb, how's it going?"

"No complaints, Mark." Caleb nodded his head in the direction of the illuminated x-ray. "What's the x-ray show?"

Mark Winterer sighed and shook his head. "Here, take a look for yourself. Maybe I'm just being pessimistic. The owner brought him in earlier this week for x-rays, the dog's been limping pretty badly for close to two weeks now."

Caleb stepped forward to examine the x-ray more closely. He was silent for a few minutes. Finally, he asked, "How old's the dog?"

"Not even a year."

"Looks to me like juvenile arthritis. Already afflicting the right elbow. The left one, though, seems to be still all right."

"*Damn.* I was hoping my eyes were fooling me. A really nice dog, so happy. I hope we can keep him as free from pain as possible. I don't think it's worth operating, do you, Caleb?"

"Not really. The studies show that this type of arthritis isn't helped all that much by surgery. The dog usually ends up needing Cosequin or Rimadyl, anyway. And if you've operated on the joint, well, then you've added the stress and the discomfort of recovering from a surgical intervention. Better to save the owner's money and keep the dog comfortable with the arthritis medicine. Do you want me to talk to the owner with you?"

Mark Winterer gave Caleb a smile. "No, thanks. I can handle it. I just hope Mrs. Gaffney doesn't cry. I hate it when they cry."

"Well," Caleb offered sympathetically, "make sure you've got a box of Kleenex in the room. You might also mention some of the homeopathic medicines people are trying these days. I think Joyce might have a catalog somewhere. Sometimes if you give the owners alternative options, it helps take their mind off the pain their animal is suffering."

"Gives them a sense of control, huh?"

"Something like that. Look, if you need me, I'm in the examining room. I don't want to keep this cat waiting any longer." Caleb turned toward the door.

"Thanks, Caleb. By the way, Joyce mentioned she met your new trainer. Said she was quite a looker. You going to introduce me?"

Caleb shot a grin at his partner. "*Forget it,* pal. I'll probably introduce you to her in about fifty years or so. Maybe by then your face won't be so piss ugly and you might have a fighting chance. You already scare far too many women," he joked.

Half the women in town were in love with Mark Winterer. Caleb had even overheard Joyce, their office manager, rhapsodize about Mark's uncanny resemblance to some male fashion model named Mark Vanderloo. Caleb didn't know who the hell that was, but the women sure seemed to. At times, Caleb suspected the reason why the animal hospital was so popular was because all the women, single and married, brought their pets to see "that charming" Dr. Winterer. Luckily, Winterer remained unfazed by the obvious interest he generated with female clients. He was a dedicated professional and, Caleb was pleased to note, animals seemed as drawn to Winterer as the women were.

Mark Winterer's laugh rang out in the quiet of the office. Chuckling to himself, Caleb proceeded down the hallway, ready to meet Waldo.

"Caleb, it's Mrs. Walters on line three. She's just gotten a new kitten and says it's urgent. Can you speak to her now, or shall I tell her you'll return her call?"

It was four-thirty in the afternoon, and the waiting room had finally emptied out. Caleb had worked steadily through the day, examining dogs, cats, even a ferret with a runny nose. He'd taken a fifteen-minute break to wolf down a submarine sandwich Joyce had picked up from the local deli and now was sitting at his desk, going over paperwork—a task he thoroughly loathed. Caleb swung his feet from off the top of his desk and dropped the sheaf of papers he'd been reading onto the large pile stacked next to his boots. He punched the intercom. "Sure I'll speak to her. Anything to save me from this paperwork. God, I hate invoices, Joyce!"

"Don't I know it. I've got another batch here waiting for you. And some insurance forms." Caleb gave a long-suffering groan to which Joyce replied with an unsympathetic chuckle, "Think of this as penance for your sins, Caleb. Here's Mrs. Walters."

Caleb picked up the receiver and pressed the lighted button on the telephone's console.

"Hello, Mrs. Walters, this is Caleb Wells. What can I do for you?"

"Oh, hello Dr. Wells. It's about our new kitten. Oh, she's just so adorable, this tiny little ball of grey fluff, really. We got her this morning, but I'm very worried."

Mrs. Walters's voice trailed off as a knock sounded on Caleb's door. Swiveling his office chair around so that it faced the window, Caleb placed a palm over the mouthpiece. Assuming it was Joyce with more blasted papers for him to read, he called out, "Come on in." His back to the door, Caleb returned to his telephone conversation.

"And what seems to be the matter with the kitten, Mrs. Walters?"

"Well, she's eating and drinking all right, but she won't go."

"Won't go?" Caleb inquired blankly. His dark eyebrows drew together in a puzzled frown.

"You know, she won't, well, er, use the kitty litter." Mrs. Walters's voice rose dramatically. "I'm afraid she's going to explode or something! I've put her in the litter box, but she just hops right out. Do you think there's something wrong with her?"

Caleb carefully suppressed his laughter. "No, no, Mrs. Walters, I'm sure the kitten is just fine. How old is it, by the way?"

"She's seven weeks."

"Well, that probably explains it." Caleb cleared his throat as he pictured in his mind the fastidious society matron. He grinned as he spoke into the receiver, making an effort to keep his tone brisk and professional. "She's still quite young. Now, Mrs. Walters, this is what you'll need to do. First, you should take an old washcloth and run warm water over it. Then wring it out, so it's just slightly damp. Next, take your kitten and the cloth over to the litter box, and hold your kitten's tail up as you wipe the warm wet cloth over her anus."

"You want me to *what?*"

"Really, Mrs. Walters, the wet cloth is as close as you'll get to a cat's tongue. That's what your kitten's mother would do to get her kittens to defecate. You're just being a mother cat for your new kitten."

"That's disgusting!" Mrs. Walters's voice trembled with outrage. "I thought only dogs had such repulsive habits. My son has a dog, and I swear, I've never seen such a revolting animal! Plopping down and licking itself whenever it gets a chance."

"Actually, Mrs. Walters, lots of animals behave this way. You know, if it worked as effectively with toilet-training babies, we humans would probably be doing it, too. Anyway," Caleb continued, ignoring the shocked gasp he heard, "it's the best method I know for avoiding cat stains all over your house."

"All right," Mrs. Walters replied doubtfully. It was clear that she had never dreamed cat ownership might involve something as sordid as wiping her kitten's rear. "I don't suppose you'd be willing to make a house call and, uh, take this matter into your own hands."

"I'm terribly sorry, but I'm afraid I can't, Mrs. Walters," Caleb replied smoothly. "I've still got patients to see, and from your description, it sounds as if your kitty might need to go rather pretty badly at this point. I'd go get that cloth right away, if I were you. Call me if you have any problems, and don't forget to bring the kitten in soon for a check-up and shots. Good-bye, and good luck." Caleb hung up cheerfully, imagining the beleaguered lady's expression as she wiped down her kitten's rear. Welcome to the animal kingdom, Mrs. Walters.

A short laugh erupted loudly from the opposite side of the room. Caleb spun his armchair around in the direction of the noise. There, standing by his office door, an annoying smirk on his face, was Alex Miller, flanked on either side by Jamie and Sophie.

What the hell are they doing here? Belatedly he remembered how Sophie had begged to be allowed to come and see a dog bathed, and that he'd told Bessie Thompson the kids might get their wish if they came around some time toward the end of the afternoon. He'd never imagined it would be their uncle who would accompany them, though now that he thought about it, he realized Alex Miller would want to spend as much time with the twins as possible before heading back to New York. Fucking great.

"What's a anus, Caleb?" Sophie asked by way of greeting.

Your uncle, thought Caleb. Aloud, he replied, "That's another way of saying bottom, Sophie. The lady on the phone needed help teaching her new kitten how to go to the bathroom."

The sneer on Alex Miller's face said it all. Caleb watched as Alex kneeled down so he was close to the twins' heads. His voice, though, carried as if he were speaking at a stockholder's meeting. "Yes, Sophie, that's why Caleb had to go to veterinary school for so many years. You have to know a lot of important things when you're a vet. Where would that poor lady be without someone as smart as Caleb?"

If the kids hadn't been in the room, Caleb would have been tempted to deck him.

"Hey, Jamie and Sophie, why don't you go to the front desk and see whether Joyce will give you some of those chocolate kisses she has stashed away in her drawer. Then you can help me give one of the dogs that's staying here a special bath."

The children made a dash for the door at the mention of chocolate. Caleb waited until the door banged shut, then shifted his gaze to Alex Miller. His body was deceptively relaxed as he leaned back in his chair, regarding his visitor. But his dark eyes narrowed slightly as he contemplated where he would land the first blow.

Alex's eyes flicked over Caleb's lean form, filled with contempt as he took in the other man's almost indolent posture.

As the two men eyed each other, Alex's clipped voice broke the hostile silence. "Okay, Wells. Listen and listen good. I hope what I say will get through your southern hick head. I'm going to keep it really simple for you, just in case. Stay away from my sister. Don't kid yourself for a second that your slick charm is going to get her in your bed." Placing his hands flat on Caleb's desk, he leaned forward. His voice dropped until it was a low growl of warning. "Cassie's not like the bimbos I imagine are your usual preference. You hurt her, and I'll break you. Physically. Financially. Professionally."

If anything, Caleb's body seemed to become even more relaxed. His dark, pupilless eyes locked onto Alex's bright blue glare. Caleb smiled. His smile had all the warmth of an arctic winter.

"You know, Miller," Caleb began, his drawl more pronounced than usual, "I've never taken threats too well. You probably should go on back to New York and practice a bit on those city boys in your office. Might have more success." With the speed of a striking snake, he sat forward suddenly, bracing his arms against the desk as he rose up, his face only inches away from Alex's.

"I don't give a goddamn how you feel about me and Cassie. Cassie's old enough to make her own decisions without her big, badass brother playing nursemaid. Now, why don't you get the hell out of my office before I beat the crap out of you?"

Alex Miller gave another short laugh. "Oh man, you've just made my day. I've been itching to take a piece out of you. Come on, Wells, take your best shot."

Caleb was around the large oak desk and facing Alex Miller in three seconds flat, more than happy to comply. The desire to smash Miller's face to a pulp was all consuming. Not even for Cassie's sake was he willing to curb his overwhelming need to plow his fist into the soft tissue of the man before him.

The two men squared off, their weight balanced on their toes, their bodies swaying slightly, poised to land the first punch. Grim anticipation mirrored their faces.

The quiet squeak of the office door opening had both Caleb and Alex starting, as if wakening abruptly from a trance, the outside world having been eclipsed in the blood lust that had enveloped the office. Guiltily, they dropped their clenched fists, relaxing them by their sides.

The twins swept into the room with their customary energy.

"We're ready now, Caleb," Jamie announced triumphantly. "We can help with the dog bath." But it wasn't just the dog who needed a bath, now. Telltale smears of dark brown covered the two five-year-old faces. Looking at them, Caleb calculated he probably owed Joyce an entire bag of chocolate kisses.

Slowly, the tension in the room dissipated. The two men eyed each other warily, both aware that for the children's sake, their mutual animosity had to be buried, momentarily at least. Little by little, Caleb's muscles relaxed. But he promised himself that, should a second opportunity arise to rearrange Alex Miller's face, he wouldn't deny himself the pleasure.

No doubt Miller was making himself the same promise. With a smile that bore a striking resemblance to a barracuda's, his icy blue eyes held Caleb's. "Remember what I said, Wells. Remember, too, I always keep my word."

Miller then swept first Sophie then Jamie in his arms, hugging them tightly. "Okay, squirts, here's the deal. Thompson gave me a huge list of things to buy for supper tonight. I'll go get them now while you watch the dog get a bath. I'll swing by and pick you up after I'm done. How does that grab you?"

He'd bet money this was now the cleanest border terrier in the history of the canine race, Caleb reflected ruefully. The owner had called yesterday, wanting to drop him off as soon as possible. The dog had apparently been let out to roam the woods. From the way he stank, Caleb figured he had probably run through a primeval swamp and then had an unlucky encounter with a skunk—more likely an army of skunks.

The dog reeked to high heaven.

Amazingly enough, Jamie and Sophie didn't even seem to notice the smell. Or perhaps not so amazing, after all. Caleb was coming to the conclusion that five-year-olds were about as predictable as little green men from Mars.

As soon as Caleb had placed the small, wiry-haired terrier in the tub the staff used for flea dips, shampoos, and medicated baths, the twins were eager to lend a hand, oblivious to the god-awful stench coming from the little dog's coat.

He'd been extra cautious in the beginning, instructing the children repeatedly to be quiet and to move slowly so as not to frighten the dog, but it soon became clear that the terrier was neither fazed by the prospect of a bath nor alarmed by the feel of two small children rubbing their lathered hands over his grimy body.

Caleb hadn't actually planned on being the one to administer the bath to the terrier himself—there was a high-school student who worked as an apprentice during the afternoons and on Saturdays who could have had the pleasure of dealing with this mini stink bomb, but for some reason, Caleb couldn't resist the sight of these kids' undiluted pleasure in scrubbing an animal clean.

14

*I*t was a cloudless evening, a perfect ending to the first truly beautiful spring day. The sun had set, but there were still jagged streaks of deep pink and peach coloring the darkening sky. The air was pleasantly crisp, lending a refreshing bite to the evening air. Virginia's weather was nothing if not bizarre. In the short space of a week people might very well need their air conditioners to sleep comfortably through the night.

In deference to the chill in the evening air, and also to the fact that he'd forgotten to pick up his laundry at the dry cleaners, Caleb had dragged from the far recesses of his closet shelf a light sweater his sister Emily had given him a few years back. It wasn't one of his favorites, even though his mother and sister had both oohed and aahed when he'd dutifully tried it on for them that Christmas morning. And he couldn't very well show up to dinner in a ten-year-old T-shirt or a dirty sweatshirt. All his other clothes were either still at the dry cleaners or crammed into the laundry hamper, waiting for the expert washing of his housekeeper, Mrs. Trapp.

The big house was brightly lit as Caleb made his way

through the deepening darkness. Seeing the house this way, Caleb acknowledged that Melissa Sawyer had been right. His parents' house did need people living in it. It was good to see it filled again, illuminated from within.

As he neared the front of the house he saw that in spite of the coolness of the evening, the porch was the predinner gathering place. Caleb heard the voices of Hank and Melissa, mixed with the higher tones of Jamie and Sophie. Coming closer, he saw that both Cassie and Alex Miller were present, too.

His steps ground to a halt as his eyes slid back to Cassie's seated form. He drank it in. She was seated on the wicker sofa, her long legs curled up underneath her. Her skirt flowed out from her waist, pooling in a circle around her. The golden shimmer of her hair picked up the lights of the porch's lanterns. Cassie had twisted it up into some kind of a knot, but, as usual, little wisps escaped and fell in curling tendrils down the slender column of her neck. Caleb's eyes traveled over the soft, delicate flesh. His blood began to pound just from the sight of her.

He saw her head turn in his direction, searching the darkness, as if aware of his presence. Their eyes collided and held. The night air changed. Heat flared, the atmosphere alive with a charged energy that pulsed between them. Both remained utterly still. Simply looking. Absorbing.

"Caleb! Caleb!"

The spell was broken.

Sophie had noticed Caleb's arrested figure in the deepening shadows and had jumped from her perch on Uncle Alex's lap to greet the newcomer.

"Caleb, Caleb," she repeated, barreling down the front porch steps. Her arms flapped at her side with every step she descended.

"How's Jake? Did he go home?" she inquired, referring

to the border terrier she and Jamie had helped bathe earlier in the afternoon.

"Hey, munchkin," Caleb replied affectionately, his hand reaching out to ruffle her curls. "Yeah, Jake's owner came by and picked him up. Boy, was he impressed with the fine job you and Jamie did. Said he'd never seen Jake so clean before." Caleb grinned at the sight of the little girl beaming with pride. He turned his attention to the others, his gaze finally coming once again to rest on Cassie. Closer now, Caleb could see the soft blush that colored her cheeks. The lip gloss she wore made her lips look wet and luscious, tempting him to wrap his arms around her and kiss her for a year, then move on to all the other body parts he'd been dreaming about.

His voice, low with desire, addressed her. "Good evening, Cassie, you look lovely tonight." His eyes still targeted hers with laserlike force, before reluctantly acknowledging the others seated around her. Turning to the older woman, he nodded, his expression losing its intensity as a friendly smile of greeting replaced it. "Melissa, you look nice, too."

Melissa laughed dryly. "Gee thanks, Caleb. That's the nicest compliment I've heard in a while."

"Now, Melissa, you know I have to watch what I say to you or Hank will deck me. I'm just protecting our partnership."

"Damn straight, Casanova. Can't have all the women in the county at your beck and call," Hank shot back good naturedly, momentarily forgetting Cassie's quiet presence. A sharp pain from his wife's elbow jabbing his rib cage had him muttering embarrassedly something about Caleb being such a "good vet and all."

Hank's careless statement stung like a slap in the face. Idiot! Why did she persist in living in this fantasy world? Of course someone like Caleb would have women falling over themselves, eager to feel the heat of that dark gaze on them and the sweet, drugging pleasure of his kisses. So what if she was susceptible to his intense, seductive power? It didn't matter that tremors still raced through her, just from the way he'd been looking at her moments ago. He probably wasn't even aware of his effect on her. That was just the way he was. She had to stop kidding herself that the way Caleb looked at her was special or unique, that the desire she read in his eyes was for her alone.

An uncomfortable silence settled like a wet blanket on the porch. Broodingly, Caleb watched Cassie, wishing he could read her thoughts. Her head was averted now, showing the clean lines of her delicate profile but hiding her expression from him. His gaze dropped to her hands. He frowned as he saw how tightly she clasped them together in her lap.

Suddenly Melissa stood, drawing everyone's attention. With determined cheerfulness, she announced that Thompson must need help getting dinner on the table.

"Cassie, dear, let's go see whether we can make ourselves useful. I'll bring out the cheese and crackers. Caleb, do you want a beer?"

"That'd be great. Thanks, Melissa."

The men remained silent as Cassie and Melissa opened the front door and disappeared into the house. Caleb shot Hank a glance that had the older man apologizing sheepishly.

"Geez, sorry, Caleb. Just shooting the bull. Forgot about Cassie sitting there."

Alex Miller spoke up for the first time since Caleb's arrival, his voice hard with cynicism. "Don't lose any sleep over it, Hank. You didn't say anything Cassie couldn't figure out for herself. She'd be foolish to think otherwise."

Caleb's jaw tightened, but he remained silent. No way he was going to justify his sex life to that hypocrite. From where he stood, Miller looked about as capable of monogamy and fidelity as a tomcat on the prowl. Ignoring

Miller completely, he moved from his position next to the porch's column to sit next to Jamie.

"Hey, Champ. How's it going?"

"Okay." Jamie looked at Caleb with slightly troubled eyes, his face screwed up. A study in five-year-old perplexity. Oh, no, thought Caleb to himself. He had a bad feeling about this. He braced himself for the unknown.

"Caleb," Jamie began, his voice as puzzled as his expression. "What are you wearing a purple sweater for?" He paused a minute as if considering and then continued, his voice now full of certainty. His small voice rang with authority. "Only *girls* wear purple . . . purple's yucky!"

Damn, this kid was sharp. That's exactly what he'd thought when he'd opened up his sister's gift.

Caleb blocked out the muffled snorts of laughter coming from Alex and Hank as he racked his brain for a satisfactory response to Jamie's question.

His mind drew a complete blank.

Finally, he decided to parrot his sister Emily's words of fashion wisdom. "Well, Jamie, it's kind of like this. You see, I can wear purple if I want because it means I'm in touch with my feminine side."

Damn, that sounded utterly bogus. Lame.

"What's a feminine side?" Jamie inquired, his voice puzzled once more.

Beats me. "Uh, women seem to understand what it means a bit better than men, Jamie. I think *Cosmo* must have invented it."

"Oh. Who's he?"

The snorts of laughter grew to guffaws.

Luckily, Caleb was rescued from having to answer Jamie's last question when Thompson's voice called Jamie inside to supper. Caleb breathed a prayer of thanks as the little boy scampered back into the house.

Quiet descended once more on the front porch.

"So, Wells, does that mean you like pastel-colored boxers, too?" Alex Miller's tone was calculatingly provoking.

Caleb looked at Cassie's brother and gave an amused shake of his dark head. Smiling broadly, he stretched his long, muscular legs in front of him. "Oh, I never wear shorts, Miller. I find it interferes with the action. Know what I mean?"

Alex's chair screeched loudly against the wooden planks of the porch as he shot out of it. His face taut with fury. However irrationally, since the moment he first laid eyes on Caleb, it seemed as if Alex was waiting for the slightest excuse, the tiniest provocation, to try to annihilate the man. Anticipating his response, Caleb bounded up, ready for him, just as eager to pound him into the ground.

Hank stared, astonished at the lightening quick reflexes of the two younger men. Realizing that he was about to witness the equivalent of a barroom brawl on the Wells's front porch, he rose a fraction more slowly to his feet, placing a restraining hand on each man's chest.

"Hey, come on guys, calm down. This is neither the time nor the place. Melissa and Cassie'll be back any minute."

"Just keep your goddamn fly zipped around my sister, Wells," Alex ground out through clenched teeth. Raw anger still stamped across his face, he left, slamming the screen door behind him.

Hank let his breath out in a slow whistle. "Jesus, Mary, and the Heavenly Host, Caleb, what's the matter with you two?"

"The guy really rubs me the wrong way," Caleb replied shortly. "Came to the hospital today and warned me to keep my hands off Cassie."

"So?"

"So, I told him I didn't like being threatened." Caleb flashed a feral smile at Hank. "Almost got to pound the shit out of him this afternoon, too, but the twins popped up. Guess I'll have to save it for later." He sounded as impatient as a kid waiting for Christmas.

Hank grinned at the younger man. "I wouldn't get too cocky, kid. Miller doesn't look exactly like a wuss to me." He paused and added more seriously, "Anyway, he's just doing the same as you'd do, too."

"What do you mean?"

"Well, let's imagine you in his shoes. Take Emily. Suppose that instead of her being twelve years older than you, she was your kid sister. Then imagine that she was basically all you had left in terms of family. I ask you, what would you do if someone like you was practically living in the same house, seeing her every day, giving her those long, hot looks . . . can't say I blame him. Especially with the way you look at Cassie, like a Texan in front of a steak, like a chocoholic in a confectionery, like a teenager in a mall, like a . . ."

"Yeah, yeah . . ." Caleb interrupted dryly. "I think I get the subtle simile you're trying to make here. A Texan with a steak? Jesus Christ, Hank!" Caleb grimaced in distaste.

"Melissa says I have a poet's way with words."

"Does she mean those little paperback things they sell at the checkout line, right next to the *National Enquirer,* the ones you stick in your back pocket and carry around for inspiration?"

"Yup." Hank rocked back and forth on the balls of his feet, his hands behind his back, his face choirboy innocent. A broad smile slowly covered his face. He felt inordinately pleased with himself. He loved getting digs into Caleb and jumped at every opportunity that presented itself.

"Well, I'm still looking forward to knocking that SOB's lights out."

"Hell, partner." Hank chuckled. "From what I've seen, my guess is that he's thinking precisely the same thing."

Cassie wasn't sure she'd survive dinner. By the time she'd helped the twins into their pajamas and come back downstairs, Melissa and Thompson had set all the food on

the table and everyone had gathered at their places.
Cassie's heart plummeted as she realized the only remaining seat was next to Caleb. He was holding the chair out
for her. Their eyes met, and Caleb's eyebrow lifted slightly,
sardonically. He was challenging her, as if he knew exactly
how reluctant she was to sit next to him.

His look dared her to back down.

Silently, she took her place and steeled herself to ignore
him. Her resolve lasted about five minutes. As the conversation began to flow about her, Cassie caught herself stealing
little peeks at the sleekly muscled forearm that rested so
casually next to her. How was it possible to feel such positively guilty pleasure shoot through her simply from the
sight afforded by her peripheral vision? Once they'd strayed,
her eyes traveled involuntarily, repeatedly, down the length
of his arm to his strong, well-shaped hands and then back up
again. She noted the shape, the strength, the colors. She
loved how the deep purple wool of his sweater contrasted
with the dark hairs sprinkling his lightly tanned skin. He was
all muscle and sinew. He took her breath away.

Had a woman bought him that sweater, knowing how it
would accentuate his dark, masculine good looks? Without
a doubt, she concluded glumly.

It only took a glance, first at Cassie's strained face, her
eyes seemingly fixed on the cotton weave of the tablecloth,
and then at the simmering anger emanating from her
brother, Alex, for Melissa to realize that unless someone
did something fast, the dinner had all the earmarks of a disaster. Melissa was hopeful, however, that if she could get
the ball rolling, Cassie might soon feel in her element.
While she didn't know what had sent Alex Miller into this
seething rage, that came a far second in Melissa's list of
priorities. What she really wanted was to give Cassie and
Caleb yet another nudge down the path to happily ever
after. But it wouldn't happen if Cassie continued to sit
there like a statue entitled, *Misery*.

Melissa began talking shoptalk.

Slowly, by imperceptible degrees, Cassie's body relaxed. She leaned forward, elbows braced against the table, listening to Melissa as the older woman rattled off questions for Hank about bloodlines and the selection of broodmares. Like a pro Melissa gently reeled Caleb into the conversation, encouraging him to recount some of the more outrageous escapades he and Hank had been involved in during their buying trips.

"And how's your mare Hot Lips doing, Cassie?" Melissa inquired, hoping she'd hit upon a topic that would draw both Cassie and Caleb into conversation.

"Well, Caleb's been using laser therapy on her tendon. And we've finished having to ice her," she paused, and her head tilted inquiringly at Caleb. "But I have to confess I'm not sure what you have in mind for her next."

"Yeah, I know. Sorry about that. Didn't get a chance to discuss it with you earlier today, but I decided to give a call to an old friend of mine who's a professor now at U. Penn. We were at vet school together."

"What's your idea, Caleb?" Hank asked, joining in.

"It's Cassie's decision. But if it's all right with you, I thought that once we finished the first phase of treatment on Hot Lips, after we've seen how she goes with hand walking, and after she's ready to begin some light exercise, we might send her up to Pennsylvania."

"What can they do for her there?" Cassie asked, anxiously hoping that surgery wouldn't be involved.

"They've got a tank. It occurred to me we can get her strong again working her in the water. The exercise in the water will help ensure that her recovery is stress free."

"It sounds wonderful," Cassie agreed, thinking of how Hot Lips's crow hops and bucks would be avoided with Caleb's solution. "But isn't there an aqua tank that's closer? Do you think it would even be possible to arrange?" Her mind was already awhirl with the details involved: how to transport Hot Lips, the probable cost of treating her at a place like U. Penn . . .

Caleb shook his head and lifted his hand to rub the line of his jaw. "I wish we had a tank here ourselves, but at this point, we don't have the money or the necessary facilities. U. Penn is the closest and has the best school around, and I have a friend on the staff who owes me a favor. He'll take on Hot Lips pro bono."

"Wow. That's some favor he must owe you," Hank commented.

"I can't tell you how much I appreciate all the time and effort you've given to Hot Lips."

"I'm happy to. She's a horse with lots of potential. I'm curious to see what you make of her. Besides, Tod loves doing me favors." He smiled roguishly. "I helped him find true love." Those had been the good old days, back at vet school. His best friend at school, Tod Harper, a dedicated womanizer, had been bent on seducing the daughter of the dean of the veterinary school. It had been Caleb who'd consented, after hours of pleading on Tod's part, to sit up half the night, drinking brandy with the dean and racking his sodden brain for one medical question after another.

Meanwhile Tod, having snuck upstairs, spent the evening much more pleasantly entertained: wrapped in the delicious body of Miss Delia Baxter. Luckily for Tod, Caleb had managed to drink Dean Baxter under the table, so the gently snoring man never witnessed one of his best third-year students sneaking down the stairs of the Baxter home at four-thirty the following morning.

A good thing, too, or Tod wouldn't have had a snowball's chance in hell when three months later he asked for the entrancing Delia's hand in marriage. Caleb was best man at their wedding. Ten months later, Tod and Delia asked Caleb to be the godfather for their first child. They were expecting their third this August.

From across the table Melissa watched Caleb and

Cassie talking. A satisfied smile lit her features as she studied them. What a gorgeous couple they made: Caleb's dark coloring complementing Cassie's riotous blond hair and bright blue eyes as night complements day.

She sat back, pleased with her effort and oh so grateful that she was no longer in her twenties, struggling with the tempestuous emotions of love. Not that she still didn't love Hank desperately. Completely. She did. But they had something more—they had trust, and they had a true friendship that made the rough spots in a marriage that much easier to weather. She hoped Cassie and Caleb would be able to find that together.

15

She never realized how much it would hurt. How her heart would feel as if it were being torn into tiny pieces. With a cry, she threw her arms around her brother's neck. "Alex, it's killing me to say good-bye. What will we do without you?"

Alex enveloped his sister in a fierce hug, squeezing her hard. His own voice was tight, trying to mask his own pain. "Remember, there's still that position with Sam Waters if you want to change your mind. You know how happy I'd be if you wanted to come back to New York."

"Oh, Alex. Thank you, but you know I can't. I've said yes to Caleb and Hank's offer, and I'll see it through. For however long it lasts," she finished with a small smile.

"However long it lasts?" Alex repeated, zeroing in on the qualifier. "What's up, Cass? You signed a contract, didn't you? They're not jerking you around . . ."

"No, no, it's not that at all." Cassie shook her head reassuringly. "It's just that I found out last week Orion legally belongs to Caleb's ex-wife, who is definitely *not* all sweetness and light. Caleb's buying him back on a monthly payment plan, and you know how much a horse like Orion goes for. But until then, Orion's not actually Caleb's horse."

Alex digested this startling piece of information without commenting, his mind shifting into high gear. Yeah, he knew exactly what a horse of Orion's quality would go for—about the equivalent of a luxury apartment on Park Avenue. So Wells was locked into a payment schedule for the stallion. Interesting.

"The ex-wife owns Orion? What did you say her name was?"

"Pamela something. I didn't catch her last name."

"Doesn't matter." It would be easy to track down. "But Cass, that places you in a really tenuous position, right?"

"Yeah, a bit. But that's how it is in the horse world, easy come, easy go . . ."

"Cassie, listen," Alex interrupted urgently. "Think about this carefully." His arms reached out to clasp her shoulders as blue eyes akin, yet markedly different, met. "Look, you know I've got enough money just from interest on my investments to back you if you want to buy a farm of your own. I'd like to give it to you. Sure, I might have to commit the cardinal sin and dip into capital to get you some of the horses you'd need, but you could start out small and you'd be the boss. Complete control, Cassie. And I'd have the fun of earning the money back. It'd be great. You don't need to stay here." *And then I wouldn't feel like I'm losing you and the twins, and losing my sense of self when I go.*

With a shaky smile, Cassie stepped forward, slipping her arms about her brother's waist, hugging him convulsively. Cassie knew Alex would do anything for her, whatever the cost personally or financially. He was the best brother, the best friend she could have. But no matter how tempting his offer was, she couldn't accept it.

With a small shake of her head, Cassie stepped back, breaking the link of his arms. Alex dropped his hands to his sides, his handsome face registering defeat.

Cassie bit her lip. "I'm sorry, Alex, but I just can't accept your offer. I'll ride at Five Oaks for however long it lasts. You've done so much already for me and the twins. But I've got to prove to myself that I can succeed on my own. I *need* to stand on my own two feet."

"Aw, Cass, anyone who knows you recognizes how competent you are. You don't need to prove anything."

"But I *do*," she replied urgently. "Since the accident, since Brad and I broke up, you've been taking care of us, protecting us, keeping us safe. But now I've got to take some chances, show myself I've got what it takes to succeed. I've got to grow up."

It pained him that Cassie couldn't see just how much she had grown since Tom and Lisa's deaths. Sure, he'd arranged things financially. But it was Cassie who'd had the courage to become a mother, to put her life on hold when the twins were still babies. He knew few people who would have surrendered their independence so graciously, without complaint. For that reason alone he would let her try her wings at Five Oaks.

But as he looked at his sister standing before him and heard the animated shrieks of the twins playing noisily in the backyard, despair rocked him. *How in the world will I survive without the twins and you?* he thought to himself. He wasn't certain he could, but for his sister's sake, he wouldn't reveal just how lost, how empty he felt at the prospect of returning to New York without them.

"Cass, promise me something. If this job here doesn't work out for any reason whatsoever, come back. I don't want to torture myself worrying that you and the twins are unhappy."

Cassie nodded tremulously, her eyes bright with unshed tears.

"And you'll send the kids back with Thompson for visits often, like for Memorial Day and for part of their summer vacation?"

Again, Cassie nodded her head. "Of course, you silly," she teased, a catch in her voice. She wanted the conversation to end on a cheerful note. "You don't imagine that Sophie and Jamie aren't going to need frequent visits with their Uncle Alex? My guess is you'll be making so many trips back here that your latest flame . . ." She paused, pretending to search for an elusive detail. "Uh, Diana, right?"

At Alex's amused nod, she continued. "Diana will doubtless think you've got another woman tucked away down in Virginia." She gave a mock shudder. "Boy, I'd hate to see her jealous. 'Hell hath no fury,' and all that."

Alex laughed, drawing her head back to rest against his collarbone. "Can it, Sis. I can handle Diana. Just make sure I get lots of avuncular time."

"Is that like quality time?"

"No, a whole lot more fun. Pizzas by the carton, daily pilgrimages to FAO's, movies, you name it. Serious spoiling sessions."

"Lord help us."

Alex checked the time on his steel-linked Swiss watch. The taxi he'd arranged to pick him up was due any minute. He'd refused Cassie's offer to drive him herself, unwilling to have his sister make the long return trip alone. He also needed time to himself, time to accustom himself to the icy numbness that was invading his heart. The impersonal anonymity of a taxi ride suited him perfectly.

The sound of car tires rolling over the gravel momentarily disrupted the chickadees' song as they flitted from branch to branch in the bushes next to the house. Cassie and Alex watched from the porch as a blue and silver sedan marked Dan's Taxi pulled alongside them. The driver leaned out his car window.

"You called for a cab?"

"Yes. Be with you in five minutes." The cabdriver folded himself back into the front seat of his car and cut the engine while Alex turned back to face his sister.

So little time left and now he had to bring up the thing that had been weighing on his mind since he'd first arrived. "Cass, there's one last thing I wanted to say. Be careful with Caleb Wells."

"What do you mean?" Her tone was cautious.

"Cass, there's not enough time now to be subtle. I should have talked to you about this earlier, but the weekend flew by faster than I expected. Look, it's clear the guy has the hots for you. Real bad. A blind man could see it. I don't want you to end up getting hurt."

Cassie stiffened. "I guess you think I'm pretty hopeless where men are concerned. I know I'm not as sophisticated as you, but I think I can tell when a man just wants sex with no strings. After all, I spent so many years watching you go through girls like you were sampling the flavor of the week."

Ouch. He'd deserved that one. "That's not what I mean. It's just that after Brad . . ."

"I'm over Brad," Cassie interrupted firmly. Determined to avoid a fight with her brother, Cassie summoned a smile. "Come on, Alex, you know how busy we're going to be with the show season around the corner. I don't think you have to worry about Caleb trying to hustle me into his bed."

Yeah, right. But Alex realized it was useless to continue. He'd keep as close tabs as possible on the situation. If he found out Wells had caused even one tear to fall from Cassie's eyes, he'd destroy him. Thanks to Cassie, she'd provided him with a way of doing that quite neatly.

"All right, Cass, I won't pester you. But remember what I said. I've got to grab my bag. Can you tell Thompson and the twins I'm leaving?"

They were all assembled and waiting when he came down the staircase, the broad strap of his leather-trimmed weekend bag resting on his shoulder, his hand gripping the small, black case with his laptop. Setting both down, he knelt, his arms spread open wide. Jamie and Sophie flew into their uncle's arms. He clasped them to him and breathed in the sweet, distinctly childlike fragrance of their hair.

He swallowed hard, struggling to find his voice. "You two be good, okay? Don't give your mom and Thompson too much trouble."

"We won't, Uncle Alex," they promised solemnly.

"I'll be seeing you very soon. At the end of May you'll have a holiday. Thompson and you can come visit me in New York."

"Goody. When's May?" Sophie asked.

"In just two months."

"Oh. Okay."

Alex smiled, an uncomfortable ache lodged in his chest. The five-year-olds hadn't a clue as to how long a month was, let alone a week. He envied them. He wished his conception of time were as fluid. For him, the months stretched ahead interminably. "Take care, Thompson."

Thompson nodded. "We'll take good care of them, don't you worry, Alex. And you remember not to work so hard. We expect a visit from you *before* Memorial Day."

"Sure thing. Cassie, let me know how things are going with the kids and school. . . . I love you."

"We love you, Alex. Have a safe trip back. And don't forget what Thompson said. We want you back here soon." Cassie kissed Alex's cheeks, willing herself once more not to cry. Especially not in front of the twins.

Alex turned and hurried down the steps. Pausing briefly, he lifted his hand in a final farewell to Jamie and Sophie before disappearing into the taxi. His family stood watching until the taxi was lost from sight.

He heard the sniffle and the muffled hiccup in that brief millisecond of dead air on the radio, as one song fades and another has yet to begin. Following the noise, he found her in one of the pony's stalls. Topper, he remembered. She was standing with her back to the stall door, her arms wrapped around the old grey pony's neck, her head bowed, resting on the crest of its mane.

Sobbing her heart out.

He was at a complete loss. What should he do, slip quietly away, leaving her to cry until no more tears could fall? Or risk embarrassing her by intruding and forcing her to share this overwhelming sorrow?

It was the second hiccup combined with her anguished cry of "Oh, God, help me!" that decided him. Moving swiftly to her side, laying his broad hand gently on her rounded shoulder so as not to startle her. Surprised nonetheless, she jumped and turned to face him—her breath whooshing out in a shaky "oh"—to find him standing so close, his face etched with concern as he looked down at her.

Cassie's blue eyes, normally so clear and bright, like sapphires set against a snow-white satin, now swam in a red, salty sea. Red blotches stood in isolated patches across her forehead and cheeks. Her nose was raw from blowing and sniffling.

She had been crying long and hard. Not the pretty, barely-run-your-mascara kind of crying some women excelled at, but a gut-twisting crying that tore one apart with its intensity.

He looked into her shiny, tear-soaked face and was lost. Gently, he gathered her into his arms. His hands rubbed up and down the length of her slim back in long, slow, soothing strokes as he murmured, his voice low and quiet, "Come on, Slim, don't cry. Please don't cry. It will be all right. Shhh, everything's going to be fine."

Cassie's arms were folded tightly at the elbows, both hands clutching fistfuls of Caleb's shirt front in much the same way she had grabbed the pony's mane earlier for comfort. Her sobs were now mixed with broken, jumbled words of explanation. Caleb, his head bent, strained to catch them.

"I'm sorry. I was doing fine. I was *not* crying. I didn't cry when he left. I didn't even cry when he kissed Jamie and Sophie good-bye. I came here to let Topper and Pip out in the pasture before the twins come to ride this afternoon." Her voice rose on a soft wail of despair. "But then that song by Eric Clapton came on, 'Tears in Heaven.' I can't bear that song. I always think of Tom and Lisa, of how much Sophie and Jamie have lost . . . and now Alex is gone. What am I going to *do?*" she wailed, her head rubbing from side to side against Caleb's damp shirt front as a new wave of tears spilled forth.

He absorbed the spasms racking her shoulders and back. His arms tightened, offering his strength and silent comfort, for words failed him. Hoping that his physical presence would suffice, he began to rock slowly back and forth, bringing her body with him, an unconscious gesture to soothe, as one might a small infant.

Long aching minutes passed.

Slowly, slowly she began to settle.

With some semblance of calm came complete and utter embarrassment. Cassie's immediate reaction was to step out of the circle of his arms, but Caleb simply drew her right back against the solid frame of his body, his hand cupping the back of her head to cradle it near his heart.

Yielding to his strength, she stood quietly in his arms, listening to the steady thud of his heart against the shell of her ear. A small, but audible sigh escaped her.

"What? What are you thinking?" Caleb's deep voice whispered above her.

She gave a tiny, broken laugh, her voice small when she spoke. "Well, I was thinking that I certainly won't have to worry now about embarrassing myself in front of you. This episode should hold me for quite some time."

"Nonsense, Cassie, you didn't embarrass yourself at all. You . . . you're . . ."

Cassie raised her head, lifting her eyes as she waited for him to finish his sentence. Caleb's gaze traveled slowly over her tear stained features.

His insides churned with an unnamed emotion as his eyes caught and held hers. Her eyes still reddened from crying, her lashes still damp from tears. His head dipped, coming closer until his lips were a whisper away.

"You're wonderful," his lips breathed as his mouth finally claimed hers.

The kiss started slow. Lips tentative, brushing, caressing with the delicacy of a butterfly alighting on a rosebud. Their mouths shifted, retreated, and came together again lingeringly, each time tarrying longer.

Caleb tasted the salty remains of Cassie's tears on her upper lip as his tongue traced its lush outline. Feeling the breathy sigh of pleasure at his sensuous exploration, his tongue slipped inside, slowly savoring the honeyed sweetness he found there.

This kiss was different, thought Cassie dreamily. Before, Caleb's clever, devastating kisses had seduced, delighted, and overwhelmed, Caleb making his hunger for her thrillingly apparent. But this time, Cassie detected something new. Caleb was giving more than he was taking. Though she was still raw and bruised from anguish, from the force of her tears, Caleb's kisses were like a salve, gently easing Cassie's hurt.

She never wanted him to stop.

She molded her body closer to his, pressing the fullness of her breasts against the muscular wall of his chest. She felt the intense heat of his body through the cotton fabric of her blouse. She wanted to be closer. Stepping forward, her legs aligned themselves, toe to toe, hip to hip, with Caleb's. She gloried in the rush of sheer feminine power as she felt Caleb's arms slide from the top of her shoulders to her waist, drawing her convulsively against his lean length. Hard against her belly, the rigid length of his erection strained the fabric of his jeans. Just the feel of his arousal turned her limbs to liquid, as a fiery heat pooled at her core.

She wanted him.

She returned his kiss, her mouth hungry, frantic with passion. With increasing desperation his lips responded, giving, taking, and then giving some more. His usually clever fingers moved to the front of her blouse to fumble awkwardly with the buttons. Inch by inch, he spread the edges of her shirt wide, revealing skin that rivaled the silky smoothness of her peach colored satin bra.

Panting, he tore his mouth from hers. His voice rough with desire. "Wait. I have to see you." Head bent so that his forehead could rest lightly against hers, Caleb opened his fingers, slowly pushing the fabric up and off Cassie's shoulders, until the material hung loosely off her elbows, draped at the small of her back. Reverently, his hands cupped the gentle swell of her breasts. Cassie's nipples tightened into sensitive buds, small pebbles hard against the palms of his hands. Her knees buckled as Caleb's beautiful mouth blazed a fiery trail down to the lace-trimmed edge of her bra.

Suddenly, without warning, uncomfortably moist, warm breath blew against the middle of her back, as startling as a foghorn, blaring loudly in the dark. Stiffening in alarm, she stilled, her eyes widening at the bizarre sensation. She gasped, freezing in alarm.

At Cassie's abrupt reaction, Caleb reluctantly lifted his head. His cheekbones were stained with bright red flags of color, his brain muddled, his thoughts disjointed.

Chest heaving, his eyes slowly focused, registering their surroundings. The thick bed of straw at their feet, the wide, blackish, kerosened planks of wood of the stall's interior. Then finally, he met the patient, dark stare of Topper, now nuzzling inquisitively at the nape of Cassie's neck.

No, God, please no. Caleb dropped his head back, his eyes squeezed tight, willing the vision away. Gritting his teeth in frustration, Caleb groaned loudly.

Neither spoke a word as Cassie readjusted her bra and hurriedly tugged the shirt back over her shoulders, wrestling the buttons back into place. Caleb, struggling to tamp down the force of his need, clenched his teeth until his molars started to ache. He kept his eyes averted, trained on the cobwebs in the corner of the stall, not daring to look at Cassie just yet.

"Hell, Cassie," he said finally, when his body was no longer threatening to explode. "I'm sorry. Definitely didn't intend for that to happen. I'd told myself I was going to keep my hands off you. That I wouldn't even kiss you again." *That I'd wait for you to kiss* me. *In any event not try to jump your bones in a box stall, for Christ's sake,* Caleb finished silently, his head shaking in self-disgust. He'd never been with a women before where he kept wanting to make love in the damnedest of places. Rotten timing. Cassie was turning his brain to mush, no doubt about it.

Her eyes gazed at the stall bedding to hide the hurt his words had inflicted. He didn't *want* to make love with her? Why not?

"Yeah," she replied, feigning a nonchalance that was utterly foreign to her. "A stall's pretty much of a cliché, isn't it?" She turned her back on Caleb and busied her hands adjusting Topper's halter. Grabbing the cheek strap, she glanced quickly over her shoulder in Caleb's general direction, refusing to make eye contact.

"I've got to get this guy out for a bit before the twins show up." She gave a small, strained smile. "Thanks for the sympathy, Caleb. I was a real mess." With that she led the pony out, leaving Caleb alone in the gloomy box stall.

"Cassie, wait . . ." Caleb's arm stretched out to stop her, but she was already beyond his reach.

*   *   *

She was becoming completely obsessed, she thought, disgusted with herself. What did she care if he wanted to kiss her or not? So what? Just two hours ago she'd assured her brother that she'd be far too busy to bother with the likes of Caleb Wells, and here she was, playing Caleb's words over and over in her mind. It was past time she remembered that her life had far more serious worries than wondering why Caleb Wells had decided on a kissing moratorium.

Was it with women in general, or just her? she wondered glumly.

Darn it. Okay, that was it. She refused to waste any more time even thinking about him. So far, he was proving to be one big sexual headache. She'd done just fine without a man in her life after her breakup with Brad. These past few weeks should have been one enormous caution sign, with blinking lights set all around it: Men were definitely more trouble than they were worth. And Caleb Wells took the prize.

She felt as if she'd been on an emotional roller coaster since she first laid eyes on him. Enough was enough. She had better things to do.

With that pep talk blaring like a PA system through her head, Cassie got through her exercise schedule, concentrating with fierce determination on the horses. By the time the twins arrived with Thompson to ride Pip and Topper, a gargantuan headache was pounding away at her brain. Cassie had about as much energy left in her as a sea turtle did after laying two hundred and fifty eggs.

She was in the tack room, wiping off her saddle with a cake of glycerin soap and a damp sponge when the twins and Thompson found her. Both children were dressed in matching jodhpurs and paddock boots with hunt caps securely buckled onto their small heads. Their eyes were shining bright.

For about half a second, Cassie hesitated, tempted to

say that she was too exhausted to teach Jamie and Sophie this afternoon. Then she thought of their certain disappointment. This was their first afternoon together starting their new lives in Virginia. She couldn't let them down.

She mustered a tired smile. "Hi, kids. You're right on time. Did you give Thompson a hand with your riding gear, or did you make her do all the work?"

"Oh, they were so excited to ride, they got dressed an hour early. I only had to help them with the laces on their boots." Thompson paused, concern lacing her voice. "Cassie, dear, you look done in. Are you feeling all right?"

Cassie nodded. "I'm okay, thanks, Thompson. Just a little tired, that's all." She hefted her saddle onto the rack and wiped her damp hands on the legs of her breeches before extending them for Jamie and Sophie to grab hold of. She took a deep breath, shaking off her fatigue, blocking out her headache. "Well, then, kids, let's go out to the paddock and get Topper and Pip. We'll brush them off, tack them, and then you can hop on."

As they headed outside, Cassie turned to the older woman.

"Thompson, if you want to head back home early, I can bring Sophie and Jamie home with me. I only have a few things left to do. They can keep me company."

"All right, that'll give me time to get a head start on dinner. I think we could all use an early night."

Cassie smiled wanly. "You can say that again."

She was glad she'd kept her promise. Sophie and Jamie looked so adorable astride their ponies, their thin legs struggling to grip the sides of their saddles, their bodies bouncing like large, multicolored Ping-Pong balls as they trotted around the perimeter of the ring. What little troopers they were. Cassie supposed she'd looked just as comical at their age, but fortunately the memories of her early riding years were far too blurry. All she remembered was intense happiness combined with a sense of awe that these majestic creatures would tolerate her presence on their backs. It was a feeling she'd never outgrown.

"Okay, Sophie and Jamie, come on into the center of the ring and you can switch ponies now." Cassie had devised a method for avoiding squabbles between the twins by strictly enforcing the fifty-fifty rule with the ponies. Each one got to ride both ponies for half the lesson. Anyone who complained forfeited the privilege of a lesson. So far, only Sophie had had the temerity to defy Cassie's rules. Once. She hadn't liked it at all when she'd been forced to watch her brother benefit from her tantrum by having a session all to himself.

It had been an important lesson for both children. If there was one thing Cassie couldn't abide, it was seeing kids act like spoiled brats around horses. Horses were a gift, a responsibility, and it literally made Cassie's stomach turn when she saw the careless manner with which so many kids and adults treated their horses. So she'd laid the law down from the first and intended to stick by it.

But at other times, on other issues, Cassie wondered whether she was too draconian. Whenever she stopped to consider the importance of her role in raising Jamie and Sophie, Cassie felt paralyzed with apprehension. She knew she would always come up short, in her own mind at least, compared to the kind of guidance and parenting Tom and Lisa would have provided. But she loved the twins as fiercely as if they were her own and was determined to instill in them a sense of right and wrong. Tom and Lisa would have wanted that.

Cassie watched as both children steered their ponies to the center of the ring and came to a halt in front of her. They had graduated from the longe line about two months before, but Cassie still watched their every move with an eagle eye, unwilling to risk an accident. Although she knew her children were as strong and nimble as monkeys, the thought of teaching them to canter had her heart in her mouth. Luckily, they had a way to go before they were ready to progress to that stage.

Cassie lightly grasped the ponies' snaffle bits as Jamie and Sophie swung their legs over the saddles and plopped down to the ground with audible thuds. Following the routine with a familiarity that would have made an army sergeant proud, the twins circled around the front of Topper and Pip and exchanged places. Cassie gave them each a leg up and adjusted the stirrups, Jamie's legs being a tad longer than Sophie's.

"Mommy, can we do around the world, today?"

"Would you like that, Pumpkin?"

"Yeah!"

"Do you want to do it now, or after you've done some trotting?"

"Now, now!" they cried in unison.

"Okay," Cassie agreed with a smile. "Go out on the rail and we can get started."

Sophie and Jamie nudged the ponies with their heels and steered them back out to the periphery of the riding ring. Cassie checked to make sure they both were sitting balanced in their saddles and that Pip and Topper were walking placidly along, in the semisomnambulant state the two old ponies slipped into whenever they knew it was lesson time. Cassie shook her head in wonder, recalling how Topper had managed to dump her a few days ago. He must have really been feeling peppy that afternoon, acting like a rowdy teenager instead of the plodding old geezer he'd become.

"All right, Jamie and Sophie, drop your stirrups."

The two children began the drill. As the ponies ambled lazily around the ring, Sophie and Jamie first swung their right legs over the pommel of the saddle, and next their left legs over the cantle. They always paused a minute in this position, the daring and excitement of being seated backwards in the saddle too heady to resist. Finally, their right legs joined the left, so that they were now seated sideways, their legs dangling on the righthand side of the saddle. The revolution was complete when at last their left legs swung over the pommel and the children found their stirrups.

"Excellent job, kids! Now let's see you move your ponies into a posting trot. Remember to check those diagonals. Up, down, up, down . . . that's the way, Jamie."

Cassie allowed them to trot and walk for a final fifteen minutes before she directed them once more into the center of the ring. After the twins had dismounted and brought the reins over their ponies' heads, the group walked back to the barn.

"After we've untacked Pip and Topper, we've got a couple more jobs to do before we go on home, okay kids?"

"Okay, Mommy."

Cassie helped the twins undo the girths and lift the saddles off the ponies' backs. After they'd gotten the bridles off and placed the halters on Pip and Topper's heads, Cassie stood back and observed while Sophie and Jamie went over their coats with soft brushes, letting the children do as much of the grooming as they physically could. A short time later they'd finished, and the ponies were back in their stalls, chomping on the treats the twins had dropped in their feed buckets. Taking a quick look to ensure the aisle was neat, with no brushes lying about, Cassie hefted the two saddles in each arm while Sophie and Jamie followed, carrying the bridles.

"We'll put this tack away and then go to Hot Lips's stall. I need to groom her and then walk her for a bit." Cassie paused as she saw Melissa approaching them from the other side of the barn. She smiled a greeting at the older woman.

"Hi guys. I ran into Thompson as she was leaving. She told me you were having a lesson. How'd it go?" she inquired cheerfully.

"It was fun. We got to do around the world," Jamie pronounced world as if it were spelled with an *i*.

"Wow. I loved that when I was your age. I just came by to see whether you might be interested in a snack after all that hard riding. By the way, Cassie, Hank was wondering if you could drop by the office after you're done for the day."

The twins reacted with their usual enthusiasm. Now that they'd ridden, the twins were just as happy to move onto life's next great pleasure: food. Cassie gave a small smile of thanks to the older woman. She'd get the last chores done a lot quicker on her own.

"Here, let me take those bridles from you. That's right, just slip the leather straps over my fingers. Jamie, Sophie, I want both of you to remember not to eat so much you spoil your dinner."

The children deserted her cheerfully. Laden down with tack, Cassie stood, watching them go, struggling not to laugh at the spectacle they made. Her little Jamie was doing his level best to match the longer strides of Melissa. Stretching his legs wide with each step, his body bobbing up and down, all the while talking a blue streak, in his high child's voice. For her part, Sophie was trying to introduce a skip into her step every few feet. The movement had her lurching from side to side. With typical good will, Melissa ignored the diminutive hip check she kept receiving from Sophie as she led the children back to her house.

"I've received the entry forms for all the shows on our list. I thought while we're at it, we might enter Limelight in some jumper classes, too. And we can take along Silverspoon and Arrow and put them in some prejumper classes, depending on how they're coming along. Just to make sure you have a full dance card."

Silverspoon and Arrow were the four-year-olds she'd been working with. Limelight was another horse Caleb and Hank had high hopes for. A six-year-old dapple-grey gelding, he was one of Gaspar's get. Smaller than Orion,

Limelight favored the thoroughbred in his bloodlines. But he had a wiry agility and jumping ability that was exciting to watch. Hank had already received some offers for the gelding.

"Sounds good," Cassie replied equably. "We can fill some of the early ones out this week if you want."

"Yeah, I'd just as soon wait 'til Caleb can join us. He lit out of here an hour ago like a bat out of hell—pardon the expression, Cassie—got a call that a dog was hit by a car. One of his patients."

"How terrible. Did he tell you how it happened?"

"No, he was in too much of a rush. I feel bad for Caleb, though. He's had the practice for just over five years now, and he's really attached to the animals in his care. Treats them as if they were his own."

Cassie nodded in sympathy. When one of her horses was sick, she was always beside herself with worry. But at least she had the comfort of knowing that there were professionals who could be relied on to help the animals as best they could. But Caleb *was* one of those people, and the owners' hopes would be pinned on him.

16

When they returned to Hay Fever Farm, Cassie waited until the children had bathed and were playing upstairs together in Jamie's room to tell Thompson about Caleb's patient.

"I'm so sorry. I'd noticed the lights weren't on in his house when you were upstairs with the children. He must be still working on the dog."

"I suppose it could take hours, depending on how badly hurt it is."

"Well, he's going to be utterly wiped out when he comes home," Thompson stated matter of factly, "I think we should have a hot meal ready for him when he returns. He'll probably be too exhausted to fix one himself."

She turned to face the stove, opening the oven door to check the roast chicken she was preparing. "Why don't you write a note, telling him we've saved some supper for him, and tack it on his front door?" she suggested, her head still deep in the oven's interior.

Cassie frowned at Thompson's bent form, torn between amusement and exasperation at the older woman. While she knew Thompson was simply acting in a concerned, neighborly fashion, she also knew that Caleb was perfectly capable of fixing a sandwich for himself and might not appreciate Thompson's well-meaning mothering. Realizing, too, that it was useless to argue with Thompson once she'd made up her mind, Cassie went silently to the counter where the telephone was placed and ripped a sheet of paper from the notepad. She jotted down a quick note, inviting Caleb to come and grab a bite, should he wish.

By the time Cassie had read the twins a story, tucked them into their beds, and given them their good night kisses, she was weaving on her feet, wiped out by the day's events.

There was still no sign of Caleb.

She hoped that simply meant Caleb had finished working on the dog and decided to go out to dinner. She didn't even want to contemplate how badly the dog might be hurt if it required this many hours of medical attention.

She slipped downstairs to bid Thompson good night, not terribly surprised to find the older woman seated at the kitchen table, a cup of steaming hot tea and a stack of magazines at her elbow. It looked as if she were preparing herself for a long night's vigil.

"'Night, Thompson. I'm sorry I can't wait up any more, but I'm exhausted. Tell Caleb if he comes that I hope the dog's all right."

Thompson nodded agreeably. "I'll just stay up for a bit longer, myself. You go off to bed now, you look wiped out."

Cassie turned and headed back up to her room, leaving the older woman reading in the kitchen's soft, golden light.

When the alarm went off at five-thirty the next morning, Cassie groaned with effort as she flung her arm out to silence its shrill ring. Groggily, she lifted her head and peered with half-opened eyes in the direction of the curtained window and saw only unrelieved darkness. The sound of rain hitting the windowpane slowly registered.

No way was she going running on a cold, rainy, miserable morning. With a deep sigh, she rolled over and buried her head in the soft pillow.

"Well," Thompson began as she sat down at the kitchen table with a plate of sliced fruit and toast. "I can drive them around town a bit so we all get used to our new home. Then there's Legos, blocks, and that finger paint set they got from Alex. That'll occupy them for a bit. Then after lunch they can play some more, perhaps bake a batch of cookies, and go over to the stable in the afternoon."

"This weather makes it hard, doesn't it? Maybe we could call and ask whether they might not be able to start kindergarten today," Cassie said, jokingly.

"No, everything will be fine, I just want to make sure they have fun today. If worse comes to worst, I'll dress them up from head to foot in their rain gear and they can jump around in the puddles. They love that."

It was seven o'clock and the rain was pouring down in hard, heavy sheets. Cassie and Thompson were taking advantage of a quiet breakfast to discuss the day's plans for the kids. Jamie and Sophie were to start their new school in the middle of the week, so Thompson had two full days to keep them entertained and out of mischief until it was time to bring them over to the barn for their afternoon lesson. Then Cassie would go on duty. At times like these, Cassie felt like a four-star general, discussing a battle campaign, but experience had taught Thompson and Cassie to be ready for anything when it came to dealing with these two youngsters. Especially in bad weather, when it was difficult to let off steam.

A knock on the kitchen door interrupted them. Cassie recognized Caleb's dark head through the rain streaked glass and rose quickly to let him into the dry warmth of the kitchen.

"Hi. Thanks," Caleb offered as he brushed by her. Large drops of water glistened in his hair as he moved, his shoulders had wet patches where the denim had absorbed the rain. Caleb stopped a few feet short of the table and ran his hand through his thick hair, splattering drops across the tiled floor. As he turned to face them, Cassie's heart lurched. His eyes were smudged with deep shadows of fatigue. Heavy, dark stubble covered his face, marking the strong lines of his cheekbones and jaw.

"Lousy day. I just dropped by to thank you for your note. What I could read of it, that is. The rain kind of smeared the ink."

"When did you get back? How's the dog?"

"Only about five minutes ago. I think he's going to make it, but it was touch and go all night. I stayed at the hospital so I could check on his vital signs through the night. One of my partners, Derek Cole, took over for me this morning."

"Would you like some breakfast?" Thompson made a gesture toward the kitchen table.

"No thanks. I just came back to shower and pour some more coffee down my throat before I head back. Finnegan seems stabilized, so I thought this would be a good time to clean myself up a bit. But I want to be back at the hospital when his owner comes by."

"Finnegan? You mean that lovely boxer? The one owned by that nice gentleman?" Cassie's voice rose with concern as she remembered the beautiful tawny boxer in Caleb's hospital.

"Yeah," Caleb confirmed sadly. "I'd forgotten you saw him the other day. Mr. O'Mally was in pretty bad shape, too, when he brought Finnegan in. The dog's really important to him."

Before he could continue, Thompson interrupted. "Here, Caleb, sit down for a minute and drink this." She brought over a steaming mug of coffee and placed it in front of him. "I'll just make some toast you can eat quickly before you shower and change. You can tell us what happened while you eat."

Taking a deep sip of the hot liquid, Caleb closed his eyes briefly. They felt gritty, as if a fine layer of sand was stuck between them and his lids. God, he was so tired. Well, the coffee and shower would have to do the trick. He could sleep later. With what seemed like a superhuman effort, he opened his eyes to find Cassie studying him, a look of worry marring her beautiful features. He gave her a small, tired smile. She smiled back, but the fine lines across her brow remained.

As the smell of toasting bread filled the air, Caleb recounted the previous afternoon's events. Francis O'Mally had been taking Finnegan for his afternoon walk when suddenly, the machine-gun sound of firecrackers erupted. Finnegan had freaked, terrified by the noise, and bolted, yanking the leash out of Mr. O'Mally's hand. The dog had run straight into the path of an oncoming car.

Fortunately, the driver of the car was fine, just terribly shaken at having struck an animal.

But Finnegan had been severely injured. Mr. O'Mally and the police officer who arrived on the scene telephoned the Animal Hospital immediately. Since it was a Sunday, Caleb had been paged on his beeper and had straight away called Matt Dupre, his veterinary assistant, telling him to get over to the hospital on the double, Caleb rushing over to meet them.

"Poor Mr. O'Mally, how terrible for him," Cassie interjected, shaking her head in sympathy.

Caleb nodded, bleakly recalling the look on the elderly gentleman's face after the injured dog had been examined. He had ushered Mr. O'Mally into his office so that he wouldn't be made even more upset by the sight of his injured dog lying with thick, plastic tubes sticking into him.

"I'm afraid Finnegan's been hurt pretty badly, Mr. O'Mally. The impact of the collision has collapsed his lung. For the moment, we've inserted a tube in his nose to help him breathe. And we've got an IV going, to help his body deal with the shock. We'll set about trying to reinflate the lung as soon as you and I finish talking."

Caleb paused for a minute, giving Mr. O'Mally a chance to come to terms with the severity of Finnegan's injuries. "So far, reinflating the lung's our immediate concern. Unfortunately, Finnegan's hip is also fractured. Because of the area of the break, he'll have to undergo surgery for that. But first I want to make sure that his lung is attended to and that there's no other internal damage. I don't want to risk operating on him until I'm sure his vital organs can withstand additional trauma."

Francis O'Mally pressed a fist to his trembling mouth. Unchecked tears streaked his cheeks. He kept his hand over his mouth as he spoke in a broken voice. "If only I'd been able to hang onto that leash. I feel so dreadful, so guilty. It all happened so quickly, too quickly to stop it. One minute we were walking along calmly, the next, that unholy racket, Finnegan crying in terror and bolting before I even knew what was going on. And then that awful noise. Of the car hitting his body . . ." A sob shook his shoulders. Caleb was silent as Mr. O'Mally tried valiantly to get his emotions under control once more.

At last the elderly man was able to continue. "Dr. Wells, I love Finnegan. I feel like he's part of me sometimes. But you've got to tell me honestly. Do you think you can save him, are we simply asking too much of him? Will he live the rest of his life in pain? I couldn't stand to see him suffer just for me. So if we are asking too much of his body, I'd like to end his suffering as quickly as possible."

Caleb nodded his dark head in sympathy. "I understand, Mr. O'Mally. But first, I want you to stop feeling guilty about the accident. I doubt anyone would have been able to keep a hold of Finnegan's leash. Firecrackers drive animals mad with terror. There's no way you could have prevented this accident."

The older man gave Caleb a weak smile, but continued to shake his head, unable to let go of his feeling of responsibility.

Not wishing to press the issue right now, Caleb continued. "With respect to Finnegan, Mr. O'Mally, we've got three important factors in our favor. First, he's young—barely four years. Second, he's strong and in tip-top shape. You've taken excellent care of him. Finally, he's got your love. No, no, I'm serious. The bond between the two of you will make the pain of his convalescence that much more tolerable as he recuperates."

"But will he be in pain for the rest of his life?" Mr. O'Mally persisted anxiously.

"Mr. O'Mally, I obviously can't give you an absolute guarantee. Finnegan's been badly hurt. I think we can successfully treat his injuries. And we have to remember and have faith in the incredible recuperative powers of animals. So I guess what I'm saying is that you've got every reason to be hopeful."

"Thank you, Dr. Wells." O'Mally stood and stretched out his hand. "I'm sure you'll do everything you can for him. Will you be repairing the lung and performing the hip surgery as well?"

"I'll reinflate his lung right now, that's our first priority. But I think Mark Winterer should do the hip operation. He's an incredibly gifted surgeon. We'll set a time tomorrow so you can meet him and we can go over the procedure with you."

"This is going to be quite expensive, isn't it?" Worry once more creeping into the older man's voice.

Caleb didn't hesitate a second. He quoted a figure that was roughly a quarter of what he thought the actual price would be. The animal hospital was doing well enough to absorb some of the cost, and he knew that his partners would be equally reluctant to charge an elderly man the full cost of such incredibly expensive procedures.

Luckily, Mr. O'Mally was blessedly ignorant of the actual amount of money that would be involved in saving his dog's life. The older man let out a sigh of relief at the fee Caleb quoted and allowed himself to be led out of the office. Caleb instructed him to call him later in the evening for an update, and then to return to the hospital in the morning. Then Caleb had immediately turned his attention to his patient.

That was that. After a night of worry over Finnegan's lungs and low body temperature, the dog seemed to be stabilizing. No one could say he was out of the woods yet, but Caleb was hopeful, even as he kept his fingers crossed.

Omitting from his account the conversation between Mr. O'Mally and him concerning the expense of the procedures, Caleb listed Finnegan's injuries for the two women as he alternately drank his coffee and consumed the toast Thompson had prepared, welcoming the calories and the jolt of caffeine that energized his exhausted system. Cassie's eyes were wide with anxiety as she pondered the extent of the dog's injuries, but she remained silent, not wanting to delay the story with lengthy questions.

Draining the last drop from his cup, Caleb stood, ready now for a quick shower before returning to the hospital.

"Sorry to eat and run, but I need to head back," he said apologetically as he moved toward the kitchen door. Cassie rose, too, and held the door open. He paused on the threshold, letting the persistent rhythm of pouring rain enter the bright kitchen.

"Don't worry, Caleb. As Thompson loves to say, you've

got enough on your plate right now. Just let us know if there's anything we can do to help."

"Yes," chimed in Thompson. "And don't even think about cooking a meal for yourself when you get home. You come on over and let me fix you something."

"Thanks. I appreciate it. Let's hope old Finnegan pulls through." He looked at Cassie, wishing he could take her into his arms and kiss her. Hating that he had to settle for a quick smile instead.

"See you, Slim." And he was gone.

The week rushed by with the speed of a locomotive. Jamie and Sophie went off to school with hardly any of the fear or anxiety Cassie had secretly worried over. Perhaps being a twin was a huge help in situations like this. Sophie and Jamie were there for each other, so neither felt completely alone in the new school without a single familiar face in sight. After only two days, they were already bringing home stories, telling about the other kids in their class, the day's events, and what their teacher, Miss Springer, had taught them.

Cassie continued working with the horses in her charge at Five Oaks, excited by the challenge each one represented. Every morning, she reviewed their schedules with Hank, trading ideas about how best to work with the animals. The first shows were coming up in a little over a month. The horses that would be competing needed to be up to snuff by then. Caleb was too busy these days at the animal hospital to do more than drop by for a few minutes now and then. Cassie didn't even see him on those brief visits, hearing only through the grapevine—operated by Hank and Melissa—that Finnegan's recovery, though slow, was progressing.

But on Friday night, Caleb at last made an appearance, knocking once more on the kitchen door. Cassie had been helping Thompson prepare dinner, and, hoping that the knock was Caleb's, hurried to answer it. The older woman saw the flush of anticipation on her face. Smiling, she turned back to the sink to busy herself with the fish fillets.

They stood staring at each other, neither of them speaking. She couldn't believe how much she'd missed him this past week, all the conflicting emotions she'd felt for Caleb since that day in Topper's stall suddenly evaporating now that he was standing there in front of her. A giddy excitement rose deliciously up inside her, like the finest of champagnes.

He couldn't stop the grin from spreading over his face. How was it possible, he wondered, that she looked better every time he saw her? Wasn't he supposed to get desensitized to that mass of golden hair, those sparkling eyes, and that so very kissable mouth? But there she stood, extraordinarily beautiful, looking up at him as if he were the greatest thing since sliced bread.

It occurred to him with a staggering clarity that he wanted nothing more than to be able to come home and see Cassie smile at him like this every night, with that happy, wondrous look on her face. Rushing after this thought was the realization that he'd happily devote himself to keeping that look on her face there forever.

The idea left him reeling. Ruthlessly, he reined his thoughts in. Whoa there, Caleb, he cautioned himself. Remember life's little lessons. You've already done the happily ever after. It lasted about nine months. Don't confuse lust for a gorgeous woman with what you know can't happen. Just stick with good old-fashioned lust. It's never steered you wrong.

Obeying his inner voice with lightning speed, Caleb grabbed hold of Cassie's hand. He flashed a wide smile at Thompson. "Back in a bit, Bessie. Got to show Cassie something. Mind if I invite myself to dinner?"

Without waiting for an answer, he tugged Cassie after him into the dark of the evening. Caleb broke into a lope, still holding Cassie's hand. Chuckling at her breathless protests, he didn't stop until they reached the small grove of trees by the edge of the pond. Once there, he turned toward her, allowing the momentum of her moving body to propel her into his arms. He smiled into the dark night at the impact, her body colliding softly with his. His arms tightened, drawing her even closer.

"Hi Slim," he whispered softly, his warm breath fanning her face, his mouth inches from hers. "Long time no see." He felt as much as saw her lips form Hello in reply as he lowered his head to capture the words. Sweet. He plundered her mouth again and again, desire and hunger coursing through him with a force that left him shaking.

Cassie could only moan and hang onto his broad shoulders for dear life as his sensual assault continued. He was so clever, intuitively touching, kissing her in places she never dreamed would elicit such wild responses. She felt him strain against her, his body thrillingly aroused. Suddenly frantic, her hands traveled down the length of his shirt, tugging the hem out of his jeans. So desperate to feel his flesh.

She touched him.

Her hands sought him like a blind person learning the contours of a sculpture, her fingers skimming along the waistband of his jeans. Her fingers moved to the top button of his jeans.

He thought he might explode.

His tortured groan was music to her ears. Her fingers responded accordingly, quickly freeing the flat metal button, sliding down along the worn fabric to search out the next.

Desperately, Caleb's hands shot out and circled her wrists like steel manacles, forcing her hands to a halt.

"Cassie, love," his voice was rough, strangled with passion. "If your hands go any further here, we're going to have a major meltdown. One more centimeter south, and nothing on earth's going to stop me from taking you." Just saying it had him instinctively flexing his hips, pressing against the juncture of her thighs, giving them both a preview of the pleasure that awaited. His body shuddered in reaction even as he forced himself to draw away.

Incapable of coherent speech, Cassie stood mute. As Caleb stepped back, and the cool night air invaded the few inches that separated their aching bodies, Cassie felt the loss as keenly as a razor's edge. Long seconds passed before her body was hers to control once more. She raised her eyes to Caleb's.

A wry smile of understanding lifted the corners of his mouth. "Holy Moses, what you do to me, Slim."

"I think it's more like what we do to each other," she replied shakily, still too close to combustion to try to pretend otherwise.

Caleb's strong white teeth flashed in the night as he laughed, grateful for her attempt at humor. Now that the moment had passed, he could only marvel at the instantaneous and uncontrollable effect she had on him. When he was with Cassie, it was like striking a match to a bonfire, flames quickly turning to a conflagration.

Well, at least he could forsake his absurd vow of self-restraint, he thought happily.

He looped an arm about her shoulder, squeezing it affectionately as they turned back toward the lights of the house. "Come on, Slim, let's go back inside. You know, there's only one thing in the world right now that could keep me from making love to you, right here under this tree for the rest of the night, and that's Thompson's cooking. I swear I haven't eaten a decent meal since last Saturday."

One didn't have to be a rocket scientist to be able to figure out exactly what Caleb had been "showing" Cassie for the past fifteen minutes. A single glance at Cassie's flushed features and swollen lips told the tale. Excellent for the appetite, Thompson reflected, pleased to see Caleb and Cassie's mutual attraction humming along nicely. Pretending not to notice Cassie's somewhat distracted state, Thompson ushered the two of them to the table and called for Sophie and Jamie to join them.

Over dinner Cassie and Thompson urged Caleb to fill them in on Finnegan's progress.

"It's been a long five days the boxer," Caleb began. "That first night, we managed to reinflate the lungs, but then discovered there was still some air trapped in his stomach. So we had to perform a tap to draw out the air. Otherwise his lungs wouldn't be able to reexpand to their normal size. To complicate matters, after we succeeded in removing the air, the poor guy developed arrhythmia."

"Arrhythmia, what's that?"

"Irregular beating of the heart. You see, the x-rays can't show contusions to the heart. That car must have really nailed him. It's just a miracle he didn't suffer even more internal damage."

"A contusion's a bruise, right?"

Caleb nodded. "Right. Well, that became our top priority, getting his heartbeat back to normal. No way could we put him under sedation and operate on his hip unless his heart could stand the strain. It took another seventy-two hours of continual ECG monitoring, medication, and painkillers for him. As soon as we thought he'd be able to handle the stress, we operated on his hip. The problem was, we couldn't wait *too* long to operate, or else the broken bones would start to set crookedly, opening up a whole new can of worms."

Caleb flashed a broad smile. "But hot damn, he pulled through! Yesterday, I assisted Mark Winterer in putting Finnegan's fractured hip back together with a plate and screws. He came out of the anesthesia just fine. That dog is something else."

"Amazing." Thompson shook her head in wonder.

"Why, I'd never have imagined that a dog could survive that much damage. Or that procedures like that existed."

"He was really lucky. If he'd ruptured a vital organ, we might not have been able to save him. Now all he has to do is rest. This brings up a huge favor I wanted to ask of you." Caleb finished hesitantly, lifting his eyes momentarily before dropping them to stare fixedly at the delicate wineglass stem his long fingers were toying with.

Cassie watched, surprised at his sudden show of uncertainty. She'd become so used to the supreme self-confidence and arrogance he usually displayed. A combination she found alternately exasperating and inexplicably compelling. What could possibly make the proud and assured Caleb falter?

"Go on, ask away," she encouraged.

Caleb's dark eyes held hers briefly. They flickered with conflicting emotion, debating with himself. At last he appeared to come to a decision. "I spoke with Mr. O'Mally yesterday, told him Finnegan would be ready to go home tomorrow afternoon. The trouble is, when I discussed Finnegan's physical limitations for the next six weeks, I wasn't aware that Mr. O'Mally lives in a walk-up apartment. It would be impossible for him to carry Finnegan up and down a flight of stairs every time the dog needs to relieve himself. Even with the weight Finnegan's lost since the accident, he weighs an easy seventy pounds." Caleb paused, shaking his head in disgust. "I can't tell you what a fool I felt like, saving this man's dog, feeling on top of the world, only to find out that it will be utterly impossible physically for him to take over the rest of Finnegan's recuperative care."

He grimaced, recalling the crushing look of dismay that had crossed Mr. O'Mally's face when Caleb breezily announced that Finnegan should avoid stairs, jumping, and running for the next six weeks.

Cassie's mind raced. "So Finnegan needs to be in a

place where he can get outside to relieve himself without having to deal with stairs."

Caleb nodded, sighing with frustration. "I don't want to keep him at the hospital for much longer. It wouldn't be good for Finnegan, exposing him to the germs and everything. And frankly, we're just too busy to care for him now that he's out of danger. We've got other sick animals to tend. And I want him in a place where he'll have company during the day, so that rules out my place. Hank and Melissa have steps out in front and in back, and Melissa's stubborn enough to try to lift the dog herself . . ."

"Our kitchen door leads directly out back, with just the shallow stoop," Cassie supplied. "Will he be able to go up that okay?"

"That would be no problem but . . ."

"Well, of course he can stay with us," Thompson interjected, knowing full well that Cassie, out of politeness, would leave the decision to her. "I figured I should put in my two cents' worth," she said, shrugging, "seeing as I'll be with the dog during the daytime."

Cassie suppressed a laugh. She loved Thompson's take-charge attitude. She'd been like this ever since Tom and Lisa's death, no-nonsense and immeasurably helpful. So much easier to live with than a mock show of deference.

"Well, if it's all right with Thompson, it's fine with me, Caleb. You managed to save the dog, and we'd love to help any way we can, but . . ." She turned to look at Sophie and Jamie's excited expressions. "You two are going to have to do *exactly* what Caleb says. This dog was very badly hurt. No rough-housing, or even playing with him until Caleb says it's okay. You've got to be very gentle, all the time. Do you two think you can do that?"

The twins nodded their heads slowly, eyes round as saucers. "We'll be very good, Mommy. That dog will love being with us, you'll see."

"I know you kids will be great with Finnegan, but what

your mom said was true. Finnegan's going to be feeling poorly for quite some time."

Jamie slipped out of his seat to come stand by Caleb's chair. He laid his small hand on Caleb's forearm. "Don't worry, Caleb," he said, his voice and manner solemn as he reassured the adult. "We'll take good care of him."

Caleb grinned. Wrapping his arm around the five year-old's tiny shoulders, he squeezed gently. "Thanks, champ." He breathed a sigh of thanks. Although he'd hoped Cassie and Bessie would be this generous, a part of him had feared rejection. Sure as hell was hot, Caleb knew that if he'd ever asked Pamela to shelter an injured animal she'd have laughed in his face. Either that, or she'd have insisted O'Mally pay for the trouble and inconvenience.

A brief silence settled around the table until at last Cassie spoke, suddenly aware of the lateness of the hour. "Okay, kiddos, time to get ready for bed."

"Can Caleb come and read us a story? Please?" Sophie pleaded, turning expectantly in her chair to Caleb. Caleb looked at her adorable face with its mop of golden hair and knew he'd be willing to read aloud *War and Peace* from cover to cover if asked. Crazy how a little five-year-old's acceptance could mean so much.

"Be happy to, Sophie-sweet. I'll be up in a second. You and Jamie choose the book you want."

With a cry that was as close to a war whoop as he'd heard in a long time, the twins tore up the stairs, their feet thundering loudly on the steps. Over the reverberation, the grownups heard their high voices raised excitedly arguing over what book to read.

"Thanks. They love it when someone else reads to them. Thompson and I are a bit old hat."

"No problem. Hope I'm not too rusty."

Cassie laughed. "Remember, they're only five. A lot more forgiving than your high-school English teacher."

Caleb gave a mock shudder as he rose from his chair.

"Thank God. That woman was a terror. I realized she was a direct descendant of one of Macbeth's witches as soon as I saw what she ate for lunch." A quick grin lit his face. "By the way, thanks for the dinner, Bessie. You've got a golden touch. I haven't eaten so well since Mom lived here."

Thompson flushed with pride. "It's nice to have someone who appreciates home cooking." She directed a reproachful glance at Cassie, who never had room for the additional helpings Thompson tried to ply her with. Thompson shook her head and made a tsking noise to emphasize her disapproval.

Cassie determinedly ignored her. If she ate as much as Thompson tried to feed her, she'd be too fat to even lift her foot into the stirrup, let alone haul herself into the saddle.

Caleb grinned. Both women's expressions made it clear this battle of wills was long standing. A wise man avoided quicksand.

"Well, I'd better go on up and see what Jamie and Sophie have chosen."

As Caleb closed the cover of the book, Sophie leaned back with a sigh of happiness. Caleb felt her springy curls brush the underside of his chin as she looked up from her perch in his lap. "Caleb, is there really such a thing as a pushmi-pullyu?" she asked, her voice hopeful.

Caleb hesitated, his mouth caught open like a fish out of water, but before he could fashion an acceptable answer, Jamie scornfully replied, "Of course not, silly."

Sophie sat forward as she turned to glare at her brother, sitting close by Caleb's side. "How do *you* know?"

"'Cause they don't *exist.*"

That seemed to settle the question definitively, but precisely how Caleb would have been hard put to explain. He felt Sophie collapse into his chest, her hope deflated, like a balloon pricked by a sharp pin. Caleb thanked his lucky stars that Jamie had intercepted Sophie's question. Caleb wasn't certain, but he suspected that debunking the pushmi-pullyu was right up there with claiming that Santa was a hoax and the Great Pumpkin just a cartoon. It was much better that her worldly-wise twin brother delivered the depressing news. Nevertheless, Caleb felt compelled to defend the wonders of the animal kingdom.

"Unfortunately, what Jamie said may be true, sweetheart. But I've got a great book in my office I'll show you next time you come visit. It's an illustrated encyclopedia of all the animals in the world. I bet you'll find some pictures of animals in there just as neat as the pushmi-pullyu."

Cassie stood in the doorjamb of Jamie's room listening to the bedtime conversation. Her heart constricted into a tight ball at the sight of the threesome seated on Jamie's bed. Sophie so small inside the shelter of Caleb's arms, and Jamie squished next to Caleb as close as he could get, making it difficult to see where one body began and another ended.

The three heads, the two blond ones framing Caleb's darker head, were bent, studying the cover illustration of Sophie's favorite story, *Doctor Dolittle.*

"He was a pretty good animal doctor," Jamie said thoughtfully. "But I think you're better. You've got frogs in your pond, not scary alligators. But he's got hedgehogs, and you don't." He finished somewhat sadly, no longer quite so certain Caleb could compare with Doctor Dolittle.

"Yeah, but Caleb's got goldfish, and Doctor Dolittle doesn't. Right, Caleb?"

"That's true, but hedgehogs are pretty great. Hard to beat hedgehogs."

"Well, I like you better. You let us help give Jake a bath."

"Munchkin, any time you want to give dirty old Jake a bath, I'm sure his owner would be thrilled."

"And you're gonna let us help take care of that hurt dog, Figgenan."

Caleb choked on a laugh at Sophie's mangling of Finnegan's name and glancing up, saw Cassie's slim figure leaning against the door frame. The look that passed between them rekindled the sensation of each touch, each kiss, each caress they had shared.

Even Caleb's words, his heated promise came back to her now: *But just to make everything crystal clear for you, Cassie, we are going to make love. You want to and I'm damn near dying to. And when we do, it won't have anything to do with where you live, your kids, your job, or the fact that I'm your boss. It'll just be the two of us. You and me. Alone. Together.*

It jolted her, the memory of his passionate words. Because he was so right and so wrong. Yes, she wanted him, and that desire transcended her children, her job, and the fact that she worked for him.

But she also realized, as she stood and watched this incredible man cradling her daughter in his arms as he read a bedtime story, that she could only really desire him *because* of this other side to him.

A ruthless Don Juan she could have resisted.

This caring, funny, sexy man she could not.

A bittersweet smile played upon her lips, for she suspected that if Caleb had any inkling of her thoughts, he'd run as if the hounds of hell were chasing him. Caleb cared for her a bit. Of that she was sure. But he wouldn't let his emotions be involved any deeper. His first wife, Pamela, had seen to that.

She supposed the sixty-four-thousand-dollar question was: Did she, Cassie, have the courage to continue, to give in to her desire when her heart told her she was teetering on the brink? Opening herself to love would mean toppling over the edge and finding herself falling into its fathomless pool. Because, when they made love, it wouldn't be just the two of them alone as Caleb had said.

Her heart would be there, too. A presence she feared would be rejected.

Keep it light, Cassie, she instructed herself. There was no point in rushing her fences, a metaphor she understood all too well. She wanted him. It was ridiculous to deny it any longer. The feeling had been building inside her since she first laid eyes on him, and it had grown with each infuriating and exciting minute she spent with him. She reassured herself with the thought that she'd recognized the dangers and potential for heartbreak.

She wouldn't be blindsided as she'd been with Brad. This time she'd let herself enjoy what Caleb so seductively offered and try to protect her heart as much as possible. It was a risk, but Cassie knew she'd regret it forever if she didn't take it.

For the moment, she pushed her turbulent thoughts aside. It was one thing to plot the course of her heart, another thing entirely when two rambunctious five-year-olds were seated a mere six feet away. She cleared her throat, alerting the twins of her presence.

"Come on, Sophie and Jamie, it's off to bed with you."

"Aw, Mom! Can't Caleb read us another story? I want to choose this one."

"Sorry, Jamie. It's late. Next time, you get to pick the book," Cassie replied firmly. "Got a big day ahead of us with Finnegan coming to stay. Both of you say good night to Caleb now. Thompson will be up in a moment to kiss you."

Cassie watched with amusement as Sophie twisted around in Caleb's lap, threw her arms around his neck and planted a wet, sloppy kiss on his cheek. Of course, most of the women Caleb associated with probably didn't then scramble off his lap with a happy, "Sleep tight, Caleb." Thank heaven for five-year-olds, Cassie thought as she hugged Sophie and hefted her up into her arms.

"Oof, you're getting heavy! Back in a sec, Jamie. I'm just going to tuck Sophie in." With Sophie still clutched in her arms, Cassie carried her into the adjacent room and lowered her onto the brightly colored comforter.

"Under the covers you go, Pumpkin. That's a girl. Did you have a good time listening to the story?"

Sophie smiled and rubbed her head enthusiastically against the pillow case.

"I'm glad, sweetheart." She knelt by the bed and brought her face close to Sophie's. She rubbed her nose against her daughter's. "'Night, Sophie. Sweet dreams. See you in the morning." She laid a kiss on the soft down of her daughter's cheek.

Ordinarily, Sophie might have held out for at least a half-dozen more kisses and a lullaby or two, but she was obviously so tired from the lateness of the hour and the excitement of her first week of school that she snuggled her head deeper against the pillow without a single word of protest.

"'Night, Mommy. Love you."

"I love you, too, Sophie."

Caleb stood on the landing outside Jamie's door as Cassie performed the same bedtime ritual with her son. A few minutes later Cassie quietly slipped out, closing the door behind her until only a small wedge of light from the upstairs hallway entered the bedroom.

They looked at each other, feeling the silence of the house settle around them.

Cassie offered a shy smile. "Asleep at last. Thanks for reading to them. I think you've just added two new members to your fan club."

"Always happy to have new members," he quipped lightly. "Question is, would you be willing to be in my fan club, too, Slim?"

Cassie's mind instantly conjured images of hundreds of

women who would probably give their eyeteeth to be president of a Caleb Wells fan club. "In your dreams, Wells," she replied lightly, determined not to succumb to the green-eyed monster threatening to consume her at the idea of countless women fawning over Caleb.

Caleb took a step nearer, his voice dropping to a husky whisper that sent thrills racing down her spine. "Ahh, but, Slim, you are in my dreams. Every night. I've been having some pretty, uh, exciting dreams. Shall I describe them to you?" *A demonstration would be even better,* he added silently.

She refused to laugh. "No thank you." Her voice was as prim as a young schoolgirl's. "I'm sure a lot is lost in the retelling."

"Oh, I promise I'd be real precise, right down to the last detail." He grinned, raising his eyebrows suggestively. "Now, let me see . . . should I begin with the one where we're marooned on a desert island? There's this cave we discover, and . . ."

"Who's marooned on a desert island? What's this about a cave?" Thompson interrupted, her ascent up the stairs unremarked by Cassie and Caleb until she was all of two feet away from them.

Cassie's lips split into a wide grin at the flush that stole over Caleb's cheeks. "Yes, Caleb, do tell Thompson all about your very interesting dream. Remember, don't leave out *any* details."

Caleb's eyes narrowed as he shook his head good-humoredly, silently promising her retribution.

"Well, you see, Bessie, it's a very *involved* dream. I'm sure you'd find it a real bore."

"Somehow I doubt that," Thompson returned dryly. "But right now I want to kiss my babies goodnight and then get to sleep myself. Make sure you tell Cassie what we need to do to get ready for that dog." She placed her hand on the doorknob, adding before she disappeared inside, "There's coffee on the stove. And some more of that cake you liked so much."

Caleb's voice dropped to a fierce whisper as they made their way down to the kitchen. "Nice going, Slim. Trying to get me in trouble with the best cook in the county. Have you no pity?"

"What baloney! You know perfectly well that if you do one more good deed, Thompson's going to swear you walk on water." She thumped her thumb against her chest as they neared the bottom step. "But I'm far more discerning. I see you for the scoundrel you really are. You'll do just about anything for a hot meal. I can't believe you had *thirds* and then two slices of that chocolate cake. Your system's probably reeling from calorie-overload."

Caleb was unrepentant. "What can I say, I'm a growing boy."

"The only thing I can think of that's growing is your head. That ego of yours is huge. Monstrous."

His grin was wicked. "Cassie, there's a whole lot more that's growing when you're around. Want me to show you?"

Well, she'd walked straight into that one, she thought ruefully. Men and their big-things-growing jokes. Tom and Alex used to laugh like hyenas, trying to outdo each other's outrageous one-liners. Her blond head shaking in exasperation, Cassie turned her back on Caleb as she led him once more to the kitchen, the sound of his pleased chuckle floating in the air behind her.

The days and weeks flew by, stunning Cassie one bright morning with the discovery that the trees, tipped with tightly closed brown nubs at her arrival, suddenly sported perfect, miniature, bright green leaves. Vivid yellow forsythia decorated the landscape, followed shortly by purple and white lilacs, their perfume scenting the air. Her first horse show with Orion was only eight days away.

Who would have guessed that life at Five Oaks could move as swiftly as a New York City minute?

But somehow, between Jamie and Sophie's school, Cassie's work at Five Oaks, along with the extra time allotted to things such as caring for Hot Lips's tendon, and squeezing in time for the twins' riding lessons, the days seemed filled to bursting. And that was without factoring in the added excitement that went along with having Finnegan in their lives. It was stunning how one badly injured, seventy-five-pound boxer could become the center of a family's life.

Three weeks had passed since Caleb had carried Finnegan into the kitchen and laid him gently down on the circular dog bed Mr. O'Mally had provided. Gone was the energetic, frisky dog she'd patted and stroked in Caleb's reception area. What she saw now was literally a shadow of the former dog. Finnegan looked like he'd lost about ten pounds. His body was a bag of bones without the muscles that before had rippled under his shiny coat. Even his coat was different. In order to reinflate his lungs, Caleb had had to shave patches of fur along his rib cage as well as his hind leg where his hip was fractured. Poor Finnegan looked like the helpless victim of an electric clipper run amuck. The crowning touch was the unsightly white adhesive bandage stuck between his shoulder blades. Cassie had dreaded to ask what *that* was for.

The poor dog had looked so pathetic and sorry for himself that Cassie'd wanted to cry. Somehow, although she knew how seriously he'd been injured, she hadn't visualized just how badly damaged he would look. Fortunately, the children hadn't met Finnegan before. Otherwise, it would have been awfully hard to convince them that the dog would indeed recover and be anything like his former self again. Cassie had been careful to hide her own reaction to Finnegan, especially when Mr. O'Mally had entered the kitchen right on Caleb's heels. If Finnegan's sorry state disturbed her, she could just imagine what his owner was feeling. Caleb had taken charge immediately. "Here we go, Finnegan," he began in an easy, soothing tone. "This is where you'll be staying for a while." His leg muscles bunched together under the faded blue of his Levi's as he slowly lowered the dog onto the padded bed.

Swiveling his dark head in the direction of Mr. O'Mally, he addressed the older man. "Mr. O'Mally, can you come here and just hold his collar while I bring Sophie and Jamie to meet him? I want to be sure he understands they won't hurt him."

Cassie and Thompson had stood quietly by the kitchen

table as Caleb had turned to the kids. He motioned with his arm as he remained in a crouching position, next to the injured dog. "Jamie, why don't you come first. That's right, nice and slowly. If you run around Finnegan right now, he's going to get scared. Wouldn't want that, right? Okay, now let him sniff your hand. See that big, white bandage on the top of his shoulders . . . yeah, that one. That's called a pain patch. There's medicine in it so he won't feel too bad, but it also makes him sleepy. That's why he's lying here so quietly. He'll be like this for a few more days. Then we'll take it off."

"What if he's still hurting?" Jamie asked, his eyes wide.

"Oh, I've got some other medicine in case he needs it, don't you worry."

Cassie remembered the collective sigh of relief that began to filled the kitchen when Finnegan's pink tongue came out to lick her son's small hand. Even in his pained and drugged state, the dog's first instinct had been to please.

"Can I pat him?" Jamie's voice was hushed. Caleb was silent, letting Mr. O'Mally decide.

"I'm sure he'd like that. Why don't you rub him behind his ear. That's his favorite spot."

Jamie's small hand gently rubbed the fold behind Finnegan's ear and the dog's eyes began to close. Jamie lifted his own eyes to Caleb's and Caleb gave him a smile, his head nodding in wordless approval. "Let's have your sister meet him now."

Sophie, squatting down on her short legs next to her brother, followed the same routine as her brother, but chose instead to stroke the silky fur on top of Finnegan's head. Both children sat quietly, patting the dog until Caleb was satisfied that Finnegan didn't feel threatened by their presence.

"Let's let Finnegan rest now. He's tired from all this

excitement. Why don't you two come out to the car and help me carry the rest of his stuff into the kitchen?"

When Caleb and the twins had left the kitchen, Mr. O'Mally looked up at Cassie and Thompson from his spot by Finnegan's head. Slowly he rose to his feet. He inclined his silver head in their direction.

"I want to thank you ladies for helping Finnegan and me. I can't tell you how much this means to me." His southern accent was softened further by the quiet sincerity of his tone.

"We're glad to help, Mr. O'Mally," Cassie reassured him. "We'll take good care of him, but I do hope you'll come by whenever and as often as you like. I know how attached you are to him."

Mr. O'Mally gave them both a warm smile. Thompson had responded, a hint of breathlessness threading her voice, by inviting him to stay for lunch.

From that weekend on, Finnegan's recuperation became the main preoccupation of their home life. Sophie and Jamie took on the role of surrogate mother and father to the dog, tending to him with a thoroughness that Cassie found exceptional.

Now, with three weeks passed, Finnegan's condition was vastly improved: he was walking with only a slight limp, willing to place more and more weight on the side of his injured hip with each passing day. A week earlier, Caleb had removed Finnegan's stitches. He was enormously pleased with the dog's progress. The twins beamed with pride each time Caleb praised them for the fine job they were doing, tending to Finnegan.

What Cassie thought was the best sign, however, was Finnegan's renewed good cheer. Although he wasn't doing anything more taxing than getting up from his dog bed to drink from his water dish, or walking outside to relieve himself, he seemed thrilled to do so, wagging his bottom

energetically whenever one of the twins entered the kitchen
to see him. And Jamie and Sophie were acting like utter
angels—at least, when they were in the vicinity of the
kitchen!

An unforeseen benefit of Finnegan's presence, was the
virtual guarantee that Cassie and Thompson would enjoy
the company of at least one man, if not two, at dinner each
night.

Caleb had taken to dropping in after work to check on
Finnegan's progress and to take him out after the dog's
supper, wanting to shoulder some of the burden of caring
for the injured dog as much as possible. More often than
not, he wound up joining them for dinner, entertaining the
kids with stories of his animal patients, discussing Hot
Lips's progress, or how Cassie's training with Orion and
the other horses was coming.

Certain evenings, Mr. O'Mally would stay for dinner,
too. Precisely when in the afternoon he arrived at the
house, Cassie hadn't a clue, and was too discreet to ask.
More often than not, though, he was in the kitchen with
Thompson and Finnegan when she came home from work.
One thing, however, was becoming crystal clear to Cassie:
Mr. O'Mally's devotion to his dog was just part of the reason for his prolonged visits to their house. The other reason
could be deduced from the openly admiring glances that
passed between him and Thompson.

Go figure, Cassie had thought to herself. If anyone'd
asked her, Cassie would have declared Thompson constitu-
tionally incapable of a girlish blush. But to her everlasting
amazement she'd seen the grey-haired matron turn a pleas-
ing shade of pink after a particularly warm compliment
given by Mr. O'Mally over dinner one night. Caleb had
caught it, too. And when his glance immediately sought
Cassie's across the dinner table, Caleb's eyes were filled
with an unholy glee.

Later that same evening, after Mr. O'Mally had left, and Thompson was upstairs kissing the children goodnight, Cassie returned to the kitchen to finish up the remaining dishes. The sound of the water and the clanking of the steel pans drowned the noise of Caleb's approach until he stood inches away, his warm, male scent tantalizing. She pretended to ignore him, to ignore the pull of attraction she felt. From the corner of her eye, she saw him angle his head to whisper in her ear.

"Guess it's not just a young man's heart that turns to thoughts of love." As his warm breath drifted over her cheek he let out a soft laugh. "Bessie and Mr. O'Mally. Who'd have thought it?"

"Thompson's an extremely attractive woman," Cassie replied loyally. The space separating their bodies seemed charged, atoms of desire zinging back and forth.

"You betcha. Matter of fact, I don't see how you can bear to be in the same room as her. Jealousy must eat you up. . . . *Oof!*" he grunted as Cassie jabbed him in the side with her elbow. "No, really. I think Bessie's a real looker. If I were a couple decades older I'd be tempted to give O'Mally a run for his money. I'd eat my way into dotage."

"You don't have to eat your way, you're already there." She shook her head as if in despair over such idiocy.

Caleb grinned as Cassie's hair swished back and forth across his mouth. He breathed the light, flowery scent of her shampoo, and treated his lips to the soft, smooth flesh as he nuzzled his way down the slender column of her throat. "Must be why I'm such a fool for you," he breathed.

She swallowed convulsively against the press of his lips, his words causing her heart to flip-flop. "Caleb," she began, then cleared her throat, trying for a less breathless voice. More firmly, "Thompson'll be back any second."

Damn. He stepped back, increasing the space between them so the air could cool his fevered body. Seconds passed as he tried to gather his wits and remember what the hell they'd been talking about. Oh, yeah. Reluctantly, he returned to the topic of Thompson's object of affection.

"So . . . you think I should have a talk with O'Mally, keep him on the straight and narrow?"

Cassie pressed her lips tightly together, fighting a smile at the idea Caleb and the perfectly respectable Mr. O'Mally sitting down for a heart-to-heart talk.

"I hardly think that will be necessary. Thompson's more than capable of dealing with anything that comes to hand."

"It might not be her hand Mr. O'Mally's after, Slim." Caleb trailed his own hand along her forearm until it reached Cassie's, resting on the edge of the sink, damp and pink with soap bubbles still clinging.

"'Course, hands are a great place to start. I love your hands on me, Slim . . . but I burn when your mouth touches me. These days, all I can think of is what it'd be like if I could have all of you. Touching me." He paused letting the heady words sink, to be absorbed like a rich, exotic perfume. "If Mr. O'Mally is feeling even a tenth of what I feel when I'm around you, we've got the makings of a real volatile situation."

Unnerved at how effortlessly Caleb could arouse her with just the stroke of a finger and a dash of his erotically charged words, Cassie tried to steer the conversation to safer ground, replying dampeningly. "Yes, well, poor Mr. O'Mally would probably have a heart attack if you started one of your sex spiels. You could give Mephistopheles himself ideas when you're on a roll."

"You think so?" Caleb's voice sounded far too pleased.

"That wasn't a compliment, so don't look so happy." Cassie thrust down the lever of the faucet, turning off the rush of hot water. "Excuse me," she said, giving an unlady-like shove against his too near form.

"You know, Slim, that's what I like best about you," he said, stepping back just enough to allow her to brush past him as she reached for the dishtowel. "Your incredible work ethic. Never an idle moment. My angel-eyed Puritan."

"Lutheran, actually."

"Yeah?"

"Old German stock. We were Müller first. Changed to Miller sometime in the nineteenth century. But you're probably right. Lutherans didn't go in for frivolity too much, either. Which explains why your shameless efforts at seduction are completely wasted on me."

"That so?" Caleb grinned widely.

"You betcha." Her tone mimicked his as she shoved a dishtowel at him. "And because I can't stand sluggards, you can do the drying."

"Yes, ma'am."

They worked in companionable silence for a few minutes, the dishwasher humming quietly in the background, Caleb drying and Cassie storing the pots and pans back in the cabinets. When the last pot was back in its proper place, Caleb spoke.

"By the way, I called my friend at U. Penn, Tod Harper, again this afternoon. Told him Hot Lips would probably be ready to head up to the facilities at U. Penn in a week or so. Thought you might want to come along, check it out. I was planning on driving there and then coming back the next day. How about it?"

Cassie's mind raced. Oh, God. Alone with Caleb? Without the protective buffer of Thompson and the twins constantly running interference? Was she brave enough? Was she ready to take the plunge? "Well, I'll have to see," she hedged, already formulating plausible excuses. "Orion's first show's coming up next week. I'll be pretty busy, ironing out all the glitches, getting ready for the following weekend's show. Then there's the kids. Everything's still so new . . ."

"I see." He began to laugh.

"What?" She rolled her eyes as his laughter continued. "What are you laughing at? Will you stop? You look like a hyena."

"Come on, admit it. You're scared I'm going to jump your bones."

"God that's funny! What a sense of humor."

"If that's not what's worrying you, then what's the problem? We can leave midday, so you'll have time to ride Orion in the morning. The following day can be his day off. I'm sure Thompson can handle the twins for one night. She is experienced, after all. I forget, how many grandchildren did she say she has?"

No way was she going to be a pushover. So what if using Thompson was a pathetically flimsy excuse? "I still have to talk it over with her," she repeated stubbornly. "It's only fair. I'll let you know after the horse show." That's what I should be concentrating on now, anyway, she reminded herself sternly.

"Sure thing, Slim."

"Raff and Tony will be riding in the van. I haven't decided whether or not to stick Tony in the back with Orion to keep an eye on him. It's only an hour-and-a-half drive to the show. I don't know if it's worth the risk of being pulled over by a state trooper. What do you think?"

"Either way sounds fine. You know how he trailers better than I do."

It was two days before Cassie's first show with Orion. Hank had called her into his office to iron out the final details. Cassie had found him and Caleb checking the entry form together. Cassie'd already memorized the events she was entered in. Not too big a deal, considering they were only bringing Orion to this first show. Later on, they'd be taking the gelding, Limelight, putting him in some jumper classes as well as the four-year-olds Cassie was riding. That's when things would get a little dicier—Cassie hopping from one mount to the next, then trotting over to a different competition ring for the younger horses. She couldn't wait. It was just too bad that Hot Lips might have to sit out the summer season. She'd been looking forward to trying her out at a couple of shows. But if her tendon wasn't a hundred percent, there was no way she was going to risk reinjuring her mare.

She sat back in the chair opposite Hank's desk and stretched her legs in front of her, surreptitiously tapping her field boots against each other, trying to dislodge the caked-on mud that covered them. It had poured buckets the past few days and the ground around the barns was boglike. Luckily, the sky had cleared this morning. If it stayed dry, the footing at the show wouldn't be too treacherous. Cassie was keeping her fingers crossed. She wanted her first outing with Orion to go as smoothly as possible. Even though she felt confident she and Hank had prepped Orion for these first shows, the stallion was still young and relatively inexperienced. Cassie didn't want to have to contend with lousy footing on top of everything else.

A large clump of dried mud fell onto the brown-speckled floor. Wow, that was a big one, she thought, somewhat impressed that she'd managed to dislodge it intact. Cassie looked up to find Caleb watching her. She blushed, feeling like a naughty schoolboy caught in the midst of a prank.

"Here, Slim. Try this." He handed her the wastepaper basket standing next to Hank's desk. Wordlessly, she took the black metal canister from him and bent down to retrieve the clump of dirt. It landed with a hollow thud.

Curious about the source of the sound, Hank glanced up. Her expression bland, Cassie surreptitiously tucked her feet underneath the wooden chair.

"Don't bother about picking me up, Hank, I'll take my Jeep. Thompson and the kids may or may not come, depending on the weather."

"Mind if I hitch a ride?"

Cassie glanced at Caleb, surprised. "You're coming, too?"

"I'm not about to miss Orion's first show. Mark's covering for me on the weekends during the season. I told him he could take off two weeks extra in the winter."

"Sweet deal." Hank grinned.

Caleb shrugged, explaining, "Mark likes to go on trips. Extreme adventuring, that sort of thing. Last time, he took off hiking in Nepal."

"That must be fascinating. He must have terrific stories to tell about it."

Caleb grunted noncommittally at the enthusiastic look on Cassie's face. He knew bloody well that if Mark Winterer were to see that excited look on Cassie's face, he'd have her back at his apartment, showing her his photo album in five minutes flat.

"Yeah, well, Mark's not real social, Cassie," Caleb fibbed smoothly. "He's kind of awkward around women. Probably why he enjoys going to the ends of the earth. So he won't have to talk to anyone."

Hank fished a crumpled handkerchief from the front pocket of his baggy khakis, blowing noisily to cover his laughter. Man, Caleb had it bad if he was this reluctant for Cassie to meet Mark. Especially seeing that Caleb was sitting pretty, if Hank was any judge. Over the past couple of weeks, something had definitely changed between Cassie and Caleb. They actually seemed to *like* each other. As far as Hank could remember, since the divorce, Caleb hadn't even bothered to feel anything deeper than arousal for a woman. And that never lasted long enough for Caleb to find out if the woman *was* likeable. Nope, all she had to be was, well, beddable. On the other hand, perhaps that was part of the reason for Caleb's possessiveness. As sure as God made little green apples, Caleb and Cassie had yet to get naked together. Poor kids.

It was almost embarrassing when Hank caught one of them looking at the other. The longing, the hunger. He felt as if he were peeking through their bedroom curtains.

One night, he'd talked it over with Melissa, when they were preparing for bed. Melissa had assured him that this was perfect. Sure, Caleb was probably taking cold showers in the middle of the night and Cassie probably felt like a walking, bundle of live wires, exposed, sizzling in the air for all the world to see.

But it was far better this way. If Caleb had succeeded in hustling Cassie into his bed too soon, he would have probably distanced himself from her, out of sheer force of habit. A reflex now as natural to him as breathing. That's why this relationship might actually stand a chance. Cassie was becoming a part of Caleb's life.

Melissa, too, had seen the way Caleb teased Cassie, making her alternately blush or laugh depending on his whispered words. And from her frequent chats on the telephone with Thompson, Melissa knew just how often Caleb had supper at Cassie's, and just how much time he spent helping out with Sophie and Jamie.

Not that she was surprised. Caleb had always been a wonderful boy.

In Melissa's opinion, history was full of good people doing really stupid things in the pursuit of love. It wasn't Caleb's fault that his younger self had mistaken love for the response of his wild, raging hormones when he encountered that cold-hearted sexpot, Pamela.

People deserved a second chance.

She just hoped Caleb would be smart enough to grab his with both hands.

For his part, Hank hoped his wife's instincts were on the money. With a small sigh, he shook off the niggling worry that these two might be speeding toward heartbreak and sorrow.

He forced his attention back to the conversation. "So

that's settled. I'll follow the van, you and Cassie come in the Jeep. Actually, this works out great. Caleb can show you the quickest route. Hate for you to get lost on one of those country roads."

"Oh, ye of little faith."

Hank grinned and stretched back in his chair. "Heck, Cassie, if you want to get lost *on the way back,* be my guest. I just want to make sure you show up in time for your class." Swiftly changing the subject, he inquired, "So tomorrow Orion's just getting a light workout?"

"Yes. Then we'll let him out, give him time to roll about in the mud around midday. Raff and I'll probably spend most of the afternoon cleaning him up."

Hank nodded. "Caleb, can you check all the first aid? I'll get Raff to pack the tack box afterwards. That about covers it, I think." He directed an inquiring glance at his partner. "I'm heading over to the breeding shed. Gaspar's going to tease Midnight. She should be coming into heat any day now. Want to come?" Caleb nodded and Hank turned to Cassie. "How about you, Cassie?"

"Uh, no thanks. I'm going to take care of Hot Lips before Sophie and Jamie show up." Cassie begged off hurriedly. *Teasing* was a standard breeding procedure. In order to determine whether a mare was ready for breeding, in estrus, the mare was led into a narrow enclosure and held there as the stallion was presented to her. The handlers would bring both horses close enough to smell the other. If the mare was in heat, or about to enter her cycle, she would, as Cassie often thought of it, assume the position, by lifting her tail up and to the side.

Standing next to Caleb and watching as one of the stallions was used to tease a mare was simply more than Cassie thought her nerves could bear. It was way too erotically charged. She knew right down to the marrow of her bones that she'd feel much too much empathy for the poor, aroused mare. And she could just imagine how hard Hank and Caleb would laugh if suddenly Cassie's knees buckled and she collapsed, overcome. A situation she most definitely wanted to avoid.

Cassie made her way to her own mare's stall, congratulating herself on escaping certain embarrassment. Never mind that the message in Caleb's eyes as she'd left Hank's office couldn't have been clearer if he'd written it in indelible ink on the wall: Cassie the Coward!

18

*S*he'd poured herself an extra glass of wine at dinner the night before, but it hadn't helped. She'd still tossed and turned for most of the night and had sprung out of bed at four-thirty, awake and ready to go. Her internal clock didn't seem to care that her first event with Orion wasn't for another seven hours.

Swinging her legs over the side of her bed, the cold of the wooden floorboards made her toes curl. Outside her window, the sky was black, but it would be pointless returning to bed. She was up, she was ready. And she couldn't wait for the moment when she and Orion would enter the show ring. Rubbing her face with her hands, she wiped away the last vestiges of sleep. Her fingers spread, raking through her tangled hair, pushing it back so it fell in a tumble down the length of her back. She padded into the bathroom.

After indulging herself in a long, hot shower, she emerged to clouds of steam wafting about her. The air cleared as she reentered her bedroom. From the dresser beside her bed, she pulled out an old pair of grey sweatpants, a T-shirt, and a cardigan and went downstairs to fix coffee and breakfast.

*   *   *

Caleb found her on the porch some forty-five minutes later, a large, brightly painted ceramic cereal bowl sitting empty beside her bare feet and a cup of coffee cradled in her lap.

"'Morning. Any coffee left?"

"I think so. This is my second cup, but there should still be enough. Put some more on, in any case. Thompson should be down soon."

Caleb bent down to grab the empty bowl and caught a hint of the floral scent that was Cassie's. Straightening slowly, he angled his head close to the delicate shell of her ear. Strands of still damp curls tickled his nose.

He inhaled slowly. "Mmm, I love the way you smell, Slim . . . Come to think of it," he added, as his lips nibbled the curve of her lobe, "I love the way you taste, too. All in all, you're not too bad to look at, either."

She suppressed the shudder of pleasure at the sensation laying siege to the delicate skin of her ear, allowing him to continue a second more, as frissons of delight ran up and down her spine. Then, worried that her brain would start to sizzle, too, Cassie drew her neck back against the rocker, breaking the contact.

"Gee, thanks, Romeo." She rubbed her arms briskly in an attempt to control her shivers. Far better to pretend that her trembling came from the cool morning air rather than the helpless and immediate reaction her body had to his presence. She hoped Caleb wouldn't glance down and see that her nipples had turned pebble hard against the wool of her sweater.

He did. His smile widened. "My pleasure, Slim." Still smiling, he straightened, male satisfaction written plainly across his features as he pulled the screen door open and headed into the house.

Only seconds passed before the bright chirruping of the birds was interrupted by Finnegan's excited yelps, indicating Caleb had entered the kitchen. As the noise didn't last long, Cassie assumed Caleb had dug out one of the many rawhide bones from the huge container Mr. O'Mally had brought over to the house to keep the dog happily occupied. Of course, given the speed at which Finnegan devoured them, the distraction only lasted about fifteen minutes.

Life certainly would be different when Finnegan went back home with Mr. O'Mally. The twins would be despondent without him. Finnegan had become like one of the family. And Cassie knew that Mr. O'Mally would really miss his visits here.

She wondered what excuse he would come up with to continue seeing Thompson—as if he needed one. Cassie was more than delighted that Thompson had found someone to spark her interest.

The screen door banged again behind her and Caleb hunkered down to sit on the step near her rocking chair, a mug of black coffee in one hand and a slice of Thompson's banana bread in the other. Cassie watched the top of his head as he alternately munched and sipped. The dark, tousled waves in his hair were temptingly glossy. She imagined their silky thickness sliding between her fingers. A pleasurable warmth spread through the pit of her stomach as she continued her silent perusal. Everything about Caleb's body seemed made to order. If she'd been asked to describe her fantasy man, Caleb would fit the bill perfectly—from the strong column of his neck; his long and dexterous hands; his broad muscular shoulders; his deep, melting brown eyes; to his utterly wicked smile. And that was just part of the dazzling inventory.

"So . . . you ready for it, Slim?"

"Uh, sure. Guess so." Startled out of her reverie, Cassie stammered, a blush creeping upwards from the base of her neck, unsure at first what Caleb was referring to. Could Caleb have read her thoughts, he would have been deeply gratified to know just how *ready* Cassie was. There were moments these past few days, when Cassie had been sorely tempted to throw herself at Caleb, to beg him to finish what he had been promising all these weeks. Sheer force of will, mixed in with a dose of innate shyness, had held her back.

Oblivious to the true nature of Cassie's thoughts, Caleb nodded, popping the last bite of banana bread into his mouth. Pivoting so his long legs stretched across the wood step, his gaze lifted, meeting hers.

"We should hit the road in about a half an hour. Might be some weekend traffic on the interstate. You going to the show like that?" His eyes dropped to take in her bare feet and sweatpants.

Cassie wiggled her toes. "Seems a shame to stick them in a pair of boots on such a nice day. Perhaps I'll create a new riding trend and jump on Orion bareback and barefooted."

Caleb grinned. "No doubt the judges would love that. Of course, Hank might have a heart attack. He's such a stickler for these kinds of things. You know, he even had Raff braid Orion."

She gave a small but dramatic sigh. "Well, if Orion's in formal attire, I suppose I shouldn't upset Hank. Boots it'll have to be."

Both Cassie and Caleb turned at the squeak of the screen door opening behind them. Thompson emerged, already dressed for the day in a knee-length denim skirt, white canvas sneakers, and a buttercup yellow knit sweater. Caleb rose to his feet. He probably didn't even realize how rare it was these days to see such unconscious chivalry, Cassie thought, a smile hovering on her lips. Better not to point it out though, otherwise he might try to stop being so uncommonly gallant.

"I can just tell it's going to be a beautiful day! When did you wake up, Cassie? I didn't even hear you go down.

Good morning, Caleb. What's the matter, don't you two believe in sleeping?"

"I always wake up early on the mornings of shows, Thompson. You should have seen me when I was little. You'd have thought it was Christmas every weekend I had a show with Topper. Hardly slept a wink. Mom and Dad gave up trying to convince me of the benefits of a good night's sleep on show days. I just can't do it."

"And what's your excuse?" Thompson directed an inquiring glance at Caleb, who had sunk back down to his spot on the porch step.

He flashed an easy grin, opting against telling them just how much he liked being in bed, although not necessarily for sleep.

"Just wanted to get a run in before we set off. No fair Cassie being the only one to get any exercise around here."

"Don't go blaming me. You could have chosen to drive to the show later."

"Hey, I'm not complaining. I like getting up." And it's beginning to seem like I'm always "up" when I'm around you, Slim, Caleb added silently.

"I'd better go check my gear bag one last time. Thompson, you sure you'll be all right on your own? Also please don't feel the three of you have to drive all the way to the show if you get busy with other things. Some of the other shows will be closer to home." She glanced at Caleb, who nodded his head in confirmation. "You, Sophie, and Jamie can come to one of those."

"We'll see how determined the twins are to see you," Thompson replied equably. "It's not that long a drive if they fall asleep on the way back."

"That's a pretty big if," Cassie replied laughing as she rose from the rocker. "I'll be ready in a bit."

"Okay. I'm going to take Finnegan out so Bessie doesn't have to deal with him, too."

"Thank you, Caleb. That's very thoughtful of you, but

I'm sure it's not necessary." Thompson's face colored faintly. "Francis mentioned he'd drop by sometime this morning, it being the weekend and all."

Caleb nodded, his eyes twinkling. "Now, Bessie, why doesn't that surprise me. Cassie, you think Bessie might be putting something special in Mr. O'Mally's food? The man acts like he's bewitched."

Cassie laughed as she pulled open the door. "Shame on you, Caleb. Thompson doesn't need any magic potions. With her looks and her cooking, I'm surprised there aren't more men knocking on our door."

"You've got a point there."

"Oh, stop it, you two. You're being ridiculous." But the rosy blush upon her cheeks was a fair indication of just how tickled Thompson was.

Laughing silently, Caleb followed Thompson back into the kitchen. Finnegan rose from his dog bed to greet them, his stubbed tail thumping back and forth like a crazed metronome. Caleb opened the back door, and the dog brushed past him to reach the backyard.

Hard to believe he was almost road kill a few weeks ago, Caleb thought to himself. If it weren't for the shaved areas that had yet to grow back completely and the fact that he was still moving somewhat gingerly, it would be difficult to guess that the boxer had suffered anything so traumatic as being hit by a car. Caleb followed the dog outside, reflecting happily that in a few more weeks Finnegan would be as good as new.

He waited patiently as Finnegan performed his dog chores: sniffing every bush on the property thoroughly, carefully, as if it held the secret to the meaning of life, then covering a particular twig or leaf with his own mark, delineating his territory and adding to the complex bouquet for the next animal to decipher. A job Finnegan performed with heart and soul.

Caleb gave a sharp whistle, followed by, "Here,

Finnegan," and the dog obediently followed him into the house.

Thompson was busy setting the table for breakfast. Small plates, cereal bowls, and glasses for milk and juice. It was just past six, so the twins would be coming down any time now. Caleb walked over to the coffeemaker for a refill. Cup in hand, he pulled a chair out from the kitchen table. A mischievous smile hovered about his lips as he lifted the rim to his lips.

He drank deeply, then spoke. "Uh, Bessie, I've been meaning to talk with you for some time now, but we've all been rushing around so. How are things going?"

"Oh, just fine, thank you, Caleb." Thompson gave a puzzled smile.

"You're feeling comfortable here, not too lonely?"

"Why, of course not. There's Cassie and Jamie and Sophie . . ."

"And of course, Mr. O'Mally," Caleb interrupted with a roguish grin. "He's been keeping you company an awful lot lately."

Thompson stopped in midstride from table to counter and spun around toward Caleb, her hands on her hips, arms akimbo, her face indignant.

"Caleb Wells, just what are you implying? Let's remember whose patient is boarding at this house. It's hardly my fault the man wants to come and visit his sick dog."

Man, he'd ruffled her feathers pretty fast. Bessie must really like him. Grinning widely, he rocked the chair back on its hind legs, then lowered it to rest on all four once again. He held up his hands in a gesture of surrender. "Whoa, there. I simply wanted to find out your feelings toward Mr. O'Mally. He's been a good client and I'd hate for him to have his heart broken."

"Go on with you. Francis is in no danger of falling in love with me. He's a charming man."

"Yeah, he is a nice man. Like I said, one of my best clients. You know, Thompson, there's something about him, he kind of reminds me of someone, know what I mean?"

"Henry Fonda. Especially when he smiles," Thompson replied with such alacrity that Caleb almost burst out laughing. *Henry Fonda?* Yup, when a woman started comparing a man to a movie star, it was fair to say she was a goner.

"Right. I don't know how I missed it. Well, he certainly seems to be smiling a whole lot more these days, Bessie. And I think it has more to do with your pretty face than with your pineapple upside-down cake."

Thompson blushed furiously. Before she could formulate a reply, however, Caleb was on his feet, moving to the door. "Gotta run now, Bessie. But remember, don't do anything I wouldn't do."

"Well, that doesn't close too many doors, now does it?" she shot back loudly at his retreating form. Exasperating young man.

Caleb didn't bother checking his answering machine. The odds were pretty slim that anyone would be calling him at this hour of the morning. But out of habit, he clipped his beeper to his belt on the off chance Mark Winterer or someone from the hospital needed to contact him. Even though he'd worked out this arrangement with Mark covering for him during the weekends he was at shows, Caleb nonetheless felt responsible as the senior and founding partner of the hospital.

He couldn't just disconnect.

He and Cassie met in front of the Jeep.

"Hi. Got all your stuff?"

Cassie nodded. His eyes swept over her. Still in her grey sweatpants, she'd put on paddock boots, a T-shirt that looked about a thousand years old, and a frayed, faded

Yankees' cap. Going for the relaxed look, he guessed. Wisely, he made no comment other than, "Gotta do something about that cap, Slim. You could get into some serious trouble wearing a Yankees' cap around here."

She shook her head vehemently. "Never in this lifetime. This hat is precious, it was my brother Tom's. He gave it to me for my seventeenth birthday after I bugged him for it for months."

"All right then, we'll just make you an honorary Orioles' fan. That means you get special dispensation."

"Whew," Cassie exclaimed. "Now I'll be able to sleep at night. Before we go, I want to run back and give the kids a kiss good-bye. They just woke up."

Caleb fell into step beside her. "Good. I'm ready for a couple more slices of that banana bread."

Ten minutes later they were on the road, Cassie having insisted on driving, claiming she was too wired to sit idly in the passenger seat, promising Caleb he could drive on the way home, when adrenaline was no longer making her feel like an overwound wristwatch.

After they'd left the town limits, Caleb directed her to the interstate. "We'll be on this for the next fifty miles, so you can open her up a bit, if you want. The show grounds are about fifteen miles from the interstate."

Cassie glanced over at him and smiled. Her eyes sparkled under the navy brim of the cap. She eased her foot down on the gas pedal, and the Jeep shot forward in response.

She drove fast, and competently. Caleb had been pretty sure she'd be a good driver, given her quick reflexes. Reaching forward, he turned on the radio and found the college station they always played in the barn, letting the music fill the interior of the car.

He waited.

It took only a few minutes before Cassie overcame her self-consciousness and began singing. Leaning back into the bucket seat with a small smile on his face, Caleb let himself enjoy the sensation of being taken for a ride by Cassie.

A little over an hour and a quarter later, they pulled into the showgrounds. Rows of horse vans were parked in bright green fields. Horses were being schooled in small circles on longe lines. Wooden-fenced riding rings were filled with the fluid movement of riders exercising their mounts, some on the flat, others over jumps of varying heights. The tinny blare of the PA system was a background accompaniment, announcing classes and results. In the far distance, they could see little ponies filing into one of the show rings, signaling the start of a children's class. Beginners' and children's classes were generally held in the early morning, with the jumper classes later in the day.

Cassie slowed the Jeep to a crawl as she negotiated the ruts and bumps made by the heavy vans over the soft spring ground.

"You see the van anywhere?" Her eyes scanned the rows of trailers and larger horse vans.

"Yeah. Way over on the end there. You might as well park here and save your suspension. By the end of the afternoon, these bumps are going to look like war trenches."

Cassie found a spot near the base of a large elm. She and Caleb climbed out. Caleb took the opportunity to stretch his long frame as he waited while Cassie opened the trunk door to grab her gear bag.

"Need a hand carrying that?" He nodded at the large duffel bag Cassie had hefted over her shoulder.

"No thanks. I've got it."

Caleb eyed the bulk of the bag and reached out, tugging the strap from her shoulder. Cassie scowled at him as she felt it slip down her arm. "Really, I'm fine." She stepped to the side in an effort to keep hold of the bag.

"Sorry, Slim. Employer's privileges. You get to ride my

horse, I get to boss you around." He gave a slight tug. "Now give it over."

Cassie let the bag drop to the ground with a thud. Smiling sweetly, she watched as Caleb lifted the bag over his shoulder and his expression turning to disbelief.

"Christ, what have you got in this thing? Cinder blocks?"

"Just a few essentials. Let me know if it gets too heavy for you."

"If I'd known you were bringing *The Encyclopaedia Britannica* with you, I'd have let you park within spitting distance of the van."

"What a whiner. You're the one who wanted to be macho and carry the bag."

"You've got to be kidding. Hercules himself would think twice about hauling this sack around. You going to let me see what you mean by essentials when we reach the van?"

"Not on your life."

"Hah! I thought not." Caleb's good-natured grumbling continued as they crossed a field that had been transformed into a trailer parking lot and came within sight of the dark blue horse van with the name Five Oaks emblazoned on its side.

Raffael, Five Oaks's stable manager, and Tony, the groom, were busying themselves with Orion when Cassie and Caleb approached. Tony was unbuckling the light blanket from Orion's back while Raffael was kneeling beside the stallion's forelegs, his quick hands unwrapping the thick cotton bandages protecting them.

"Morning, Tony, Raff." Caleb greeted the two men as he and Cassie came within hearing distance.

"Hi. You just missed Hank. He went over to the officials' tent to pick up Cassie's number."

"How'd Orion do in the van?"

"Settled down pretty well. Doesn't seem too excited by

the commotion." His glance swept toward Caleb. "That eucalyptus stuff you gave us is working real well."

"What eucalyptus stuff?" Cassie inquired.

Caleb shrugged. "It's a salve I found to rub on the inside of his nostrils. So he won't be bombarded by all these distracting scents."

Cassie walked over to the stallion and stroked his sleek neck. Her fingers stole up to the row of neat braids along his neck and she scraped her fingernails lightly around them. Orion flexed his muscles against her, encouraging her to scratch around the braids some more.

Raffael laughed. "He's like a cat rubbing against your pants legs. Doesn't have a clue he weighs about a thousand pounds more. Careful, Cassie, Hank'll kill you if you mess up those braids."

"They must be so itchy, but I suppose even horses have to suffer to look beautiful. You did a great job, Raff. I always love it when a jumper's braided, it's so elegant." In the jumper division, braids on a horse were optional, but Cassie personally thought it made everything that much more special.

"Oh, Tony, he looks just spectacular," Cassie exclaimed. She was right. Tony had pulled off the blanket, and Orion's coat gleamed in the morning sunshine like dark satin, the white markings on his legs spotless.

"Yeah, he's really going to stand out. What a looker you are, big guy." Caleb patted the horse's neck affectionately. "Why don't you put Cassie's saddle on him while I go hunt for Hank. The farthest practice ring over there doesn't seem too crowded. That okay with you, Slim?"

"Sure. I'll pull on my breeches and boots and we'll meet you over there."

19

Cassie didn't hurry Orion as she and Raffael led him to the exercise ring, allowing the horse time to take in the unfamiliar surroundings. She could tell by his gait and posture that he was excited. There was a coiled energy in the spring of each step, in the carriage of his head, and in the busy twitching of his ears. So Cassie allowed her pace to be casual, almost lazy, as if the three of them were out for nothing more exciting than a weekend stroll.

Hank had chosen the first couple of shows as a warmup for Orion. These first few shows were held on Saturdays rather than Sundays, meaning that the Grand Prix courses were slightly less challenging and the prize money significantly more modest: ranging anywhere from five to fifteen thousand as opposed to the really large purses of twenty-five to over seventy-five thousand. Those were reserved for the Sunday Grand Prix events, shows Cassie would start competing in toward early summer.

Sam Waters, Cassie's old trainer back in New York, always referred to these smaller horse shows as leaky-roof shows. Not classy, big, or rich enough to attract the elite riders and horses, but an excellent place for a young or inexperienced horse or for riders who wanted to build their horses' confidence and, perhaps, give them a shot at some prize money.

Cassie found herself scanning the crowd to see whether she knew any of the other riders. Although she thought she recognized one or two faces as vaguely familiar, she wasn't inclined to move any closer and verify their identities. She'd find out later who was who as the PA system announced each rider. Caleb had been right, though. Without a doubt, Orion was the classiest looker in the place. He'd already turned quite a few heads as they passed by, riders and grooms alike flicking their professional eyes over his powerful build.

A number of the male riders also let their eyes linger over Cassie, taking in her long legs, her slender waist encased in the snow-white breeches. She ignored them, indifferent to the appreciative glances she was generating.

"She's moving well out there. Orion's settled down pretty quickly."

"Yeah," Caleb agreed, standing by the railing of the practice ring, watching Cassie warm up the stallion. "He's nice and collected. That flat work she's been doing with him seems to be really paying off."

"His jumping's been looking real sharp, too." Hank grinned. "God, I can't wait to see them in the show ring."

"Slow down there, partner." The corner of his mouth lifted at his friend's impatience. "Let her school him over a couple of fences first." He glanced at his watch. "Her class is scheduled to start in about an hour." Caleb bent to duck between the railings of the fence. "I'm going to see whether she needs any of the jumps adjusted. Come on and give me a hand. It'll keep you from getting antsy."

"Antsy my foot. I can tell by that gleam in your eye that you're just as excited as I am."

Caleb grunted but didn't bother to deny it.

* * * *

"How's he feel, Slim?"

Cassie had spotted Caleb and Hank and trotted over Orion to the center of the ring where they stood. A few other trainers and riders stood near, talking among themselves.

She shrugged. "Stronger on the bit than usual, but that's to be expected. He's listening, even with all this commotion about, so that's a good sign."

Hank spoke. "Caleb and I were wondering whether you wanted anything done with the jumps."

Cassie considered the fences that had been set up to warm up the horses. "No thanks, they'll do. But after I've finished, I want to walk the course." She paused, hesitating. "Would either of you mind coming with me? I find it really helpful to talk to someone as I'm walking. It's one of my show rituals . . ." her voice trailed off, feeling somewhat self-conscious at having to explain.

Hank clamped his back molars tight to keep from volunteering. Strategy. He loved it. Going into the ring to count out the strides, checking the shallowness of the cups, discussing angles of approach.

Instead, he turned to Caleb. "Uh, why don't you go over the field with Cassie. I'll take Orion back and give him a bit of water and check his boots and all."

"You sure about that, Hank?"

Hank thought of his wife, Melissa, and nodded. Man, she was going to be so proud of him, he just knew it. She'd sit on the edge of their bed in her pretty flowered cotton nightgown and tell him how clever he was to have let Cassie and Caleb have this time together, to pull them closer together, to . . . what was that word she liked so much? Oh, yeah, to bond. And then he'd lean back against the headboard and watch while she slowly took off her nightgown so that they could do a little bonding of their own.

Yeah, he thought as he caught the look that passed between Caleb and Cassie. Bonding was a good thing.

She was up next and Caleb's gut was suddenly knotted in a twisted snarl of anxiety. Christ, he hadn't felt this nervous since he'd had the lead role in the eighth-grade play. He'd certainly never been this anxious when he'd competed in shows himself.

He concentrated on keeping his features relaxed as he swallowed the panic threatening to overwhelm him. Damn it, if he was feeling this way now, he was going to be a basket case by the end of the afternoon.

Eight riders had gone around the course already. Three of them had knocked down poles and another rider's horse had balked at a neon striped double oxer. But that left four riders with clean rounds already, so a jump-off was inevitable. Caleb glanced up at Cassie astride Orion and swallowed once again, amazed at how composed she looked. Since the beginning of the jumper class, she'd sat still as a statue, her gaze focused with intense concentration as she followed the progress of each rider.

He guessed he'd underestimated her. Or perhaps he'd just never glimpsed this facet to her personality. He'd recognized that she was an incredibly gifted rider, but he hadn't foreseen just what a ferocious and intense competitor she would be.

Cassie gathered up her reins a slight notch as the rider before her approached the second to last fence. She walked Orion in a circle and then began making her way toward the gate. Hank and Caleb fell in step beside her and Hank spoke quietly to her as they approached the entrance to the ring. Caleb's terrified heart was pounding too loud for him to make out the words, but he saw Cassie nod her head in agreement and smile.

This was it. The previous rider trotted out of the ring, his face reflecting the disappointment of the seven faults he'd accumulated. Cassie nudged Orion gently behind the girth. They moved toward the in-gate.

Clearing his throat forcefully, he got his tongue working well enough to blurt out, "Cassie."

Turning her head, her eyes a deep blue under the rim of her velvet hunt cap, she stilled the horse. "Yeah?"

"Break a leg." His lips felt wiggly as he formed the words, like pudding that hadn't quite set.

She laughed, the sound full of confidence and daring. "Thanks."

She was gone. Caleb gripped the fence boards tight, the grain of the wood imprinting itself like tracks upon his flesh.

"Looks pretty as a picture out there, doesn't she?"

They were watching as Cassie trotted Orion toward the judges stand and drew him to a halt. They paused a moment, in that brief instant taking on the grandeur of a magnificent Renaissance equestrian statue. Then Cassie dipped her head toward the judges' stand in salutation and moved Orion into a controlled canter at the far end of the ring.

Caleb dropped his head and muttered a mangled prayer. "Hank?" The older man's eyes remained fixed on Cassie's form. "Yeah?"

"You nervous?"

"Yup. My knees are shaking, and my hands are trembling so bad you'd think I'd come off a three-day binge. How about you?"

"I think I might puke."

Hank let out a chuckle and glanced at him out of the corner of his eye, then returned to Cassie's distant form. "Now that you mention it, you do look a little green around the gills." He fell silent at the sight of Orion moving into an elegant, rolling canter, the horse's tail fluttering behind in the light breeze. "Funny, isn't it, here we are, nervous as two old grannys, and there she is, cool as a cucumber. It's not as if we haven't been in the business for some time now. Longer than her, come to think of it."

"It's different now. There's Orion and there's . . ."

"Yeah, I know. She's kinda special."

"Yeah."

Hank smiled to himself, not needing to reply, and the two men fell silent as Cassie approached the first row of jumps.

God, she loved this! She'd missed the excitement of competing, the hours of hard work and training finally coming together for this one moment, the feeling of power and glory as she and the one-ton animal beneath her flew over the ground and into the air.

She kept Orion balanced in his canter, her thigh muscles gripping the saddle beneath her as she rode him around in a circle. Fluidly she moved into a two-point position, inclining her body forward slightly, bringing her hands forward a mere fraction on Orion's neck, increasing the tempo of his canter with a light pressure from her legs, readying him for the first set of jumps.

Orion felt good. His canter was strong yet controlled, his enormous strength waiting to be tapped, like a rich vein in a gold mine. She kneed him forward as they rounded the curve and then straightened into the first line of jumps.

She felt the surge of energy beneath her as Orion sighted the first fence. Ears pricked forward, his gallop ate up the ground. Cassie checked him slightly, bringing his pace under more control. Orion snorted impatiently, and Cassie pictured the massive muscles underneath her bunching and flexing in anticipation. But she maintained the tempo, determined not to rush her fences.

"Steady Orion . . . okay, here we go."

She let her fingers open fractionally, relaxing on the reins, and squeezed, supporting him from behind with her legs. She counted off the strides as the first jump came nearer and nearer, her heart pounding to the rhythm of Orion's hooves, her entire being focused on his every move.

They flew, they landed, they moved on, Orion negotiating each fence with the ease that his strong body promised. Jump by jump passed underneath his hooves, Cassie bending and rising, shifting her weight to follow the rhythm of his takeoffs and landings. Jumbled words and thoughts raced in and out of her head now as fence after fence loomed ahead.

"Here comes the triple combination. Don't cut your corners. Let him see the full line straight as an arrow. Here's where you pick up the pace. That's right. Great, not even a nick. Now we've got that double-oxer and then the rollback. Uh-oh. I take it you don't like the look of this oxer, either. Come on, you can do it, Orion. No, don't back off. The only way to get around this fence is over it. No detours allowed. Squeeze, Cassie, give him some extra leg . . . Holy smokes! That was a big jump. Lost my stirrup on that one, and you almost left me back there in the dirt, didn't you? Now for the rollback, the stone wall, and then that last vertical, and we're home free."

When Orion's four hooves landed clear of the last fence Cassie's face broke into a grin. As she slowed Orion back down to a trot, she leaned forward in the saddle, thumping her open hand on his muscled shoulder, proud of his fine job.

The smiles on Hank and Caleb's faces mirrored her own as she exited the ring.

"Good ride out there. Clean round. You'll be in the jump-off. You looked great except for . . ."

She interrupted Hank with a laugh. "Except for that oxer. I know. That must have been one ugly sight. I thought I was going to end up in a heap on that one. We'll have to order up some day-glo poles, or have Jamie and Sophie do some painting." Cassie laughed, imagining the twins running around with paint buckets and dripping brushes. Shaking her head at the two men standing beside her, Cassie gave a happy grin. "Wow! Your horse sure can jump big."

"From back here it looked like he'd decided he didn't want to be in the same zip code as that fence. Jumped about half its height again in order not to touch it," Hank offered.

"Take off was a bit early, too," Caleb said, thinking that was the understatement of the century. His heart had been in his throat when he'd seen Orion hurl himself into the air like that. His heartbeat only now returning to normal.

Cassie shook her head at the memory. Orion had simply jumped out of her hands, leaving her scrambling to keep up with him. She'd lost one of her stirrups when they landed, but luckily she'd caught up with the flow of Orion's momentum as his front and then back hooves hit the ground and he galloped on. If she hadn't regained her balance and body position, there wouldn't have been any chance staying on his back.

Lifting her hand to her hunt cap, she pulled it off, letting the breeze cool her sweat-matted hair. "That's about what it felt like. Like I was riding a thousand-pound jumping frog. Had me fooled. Totally out of the blue and I was slow to anticipate him . . . Sorry. Well, at least he didn't refuse it. I just hope he feels better about it in the jump-off."

"Don't worry about it, Slim. Another rider would have been on the ground eating dirt. Hop off his back, and Raff will walk him around. There are about fifteen more riders to go, so you've got some time still."

"Okay. Thanks, Raff," Cassie said as she slipped from the saddle and lifted the reins over the stallion's head. She dropped her head to place a kiss on his warm velvety muzzle. "I'm proud of you. You did super out there. We'll nail 'em on the next round."

She closed her hand and rubbed her knuckles against Orion's jaw, then stretched her fingers, searching out the itchy spots she knew he loved to have scratched. When she found one, the horse responded by rubbing his massive head against the front of her riding jacket, leaving dark bay hairs all over the navy blue fabric. Finally, she stepped back, laughing as she looked down her front and saw hundreds of tiny hairs stuck to her. She brushed at them with her hands, sending dark hairs floating to the ground. Slightly more presentable, she looked up to discover Caleb watching her, his dark brown eyes intense.

He was drawn like a lodestone by the wonderful contradictions she possessed: One minute a consummate professional with the talent and skill to compete at the highest level, and the next looking for all the world like an overgrown pony camper, cuddling a seventeen-hand stallion as if he were the family pet.

In either guise, she was incredible. Irresistible.

Shaking his head, an enigmatic smile playing about his lips, he held out a cold bottle of water. "Here, I got Raff to pick this up at the concession stand."

"Oh, thanks. My throat's parched from the dust in the ring." Cassie unscrewed the top and drank deeply. "They serving lunch yet?"

At Caleb's nod, Cassie continued. "Great. After the jump off, I'm going to go grab a couple of hot dogs before my next event. Want to come?"

"You sure you want to eat hot dogs and then ride?"

"You bet." She flashed a cheerful smile. "I should confess right now to my terrible, guilty secret. Whenever I'm at horse shows I'm the biggest junk-food junkie around. I can't resist the stuff. The rest of the time I try to eat properly, but somehow, the smell of all those hot dogs and hamburgers sizzling on the grill . . ."

Caleb held up his hand, halting her flow of words. "Right. I get the picture. We'll head on over after you ride."

His stomach was still fluttery enough from watching Cassie ride that he didn't think he could take any more descriptions of frying grease.

Caleb and Cassie joined Hank by the railing and watched the final riders in the class. Silent observers at first, they soon succumbed to the age-old habit horse people have of analyzing each rider's style and horse's conformation that entered the show ring. By the time every rider had finished, there were ten clear rounds, including Cassie's.

Cassie had drawn third in the jumping order so she'd remounted Orion and was warming him up, her mind gearing up for the demands of the jump-off. The timed jump-off consisted of eight fences, including that double-oxer Orion had disliked so much. The first rider of the jump-off had just had a clean round, so Cassie knew that she would have to push the pace a little more this time round in order to beat that rider's time. With Orion's big strides that shouldn't be too difficult.

What she didn't want, however, was to get him racing around the course like some whirling dervish. They'd doubtless beat other rider's times, but they might also end up racking up points on knocked down poles. At this stage, it'd be better to go for a fast but conservative ride with Orion. They could go hell-for-leather later on in the season.

She was up. For the second time, she trotted Orion into the show ring, urging him to a canter as she headed for the far end of the ring. She wanted Orion up to speed by the time she passed the starting timers. With each stride, the stallion's pace increased, effortlessly consuming the distance as they rode into the first fence.

In the jump-off, the altered, shortened course made for sharp turns. As Cassie and Orion cleared the first fence, she was already cutting the corner, saving time, relying on Orion's natural balance to see them cleanly over the next set of jumps. He responded willingly, seeming to understand the new urgency in their pace. At the triple combination, Cassie saw the chance to cut out a stride, and the horse took it gamely, jumping wide on the second fence and recovering quickly, ready for the third obstacle.

Only four jumps remained. Heading now for the double-oxer that had troubled Orion before, Cassie kept his gallop strong, her body poised and ready should Orion decide to go for a second trip to the moon. She felt his body shift, tensing, as he, too, recognized the despised fence. Bracing herself for any unpleasant surprise, she urged him forward with her legs and seat as they came closer and closer.

Then she felt it. That split second of hesitation in his stride. Would it be a refusal this time? Instinctively, Cassie dug in her heels, urged him on with her seat, and gave a cluck loud enough to be heard back at the trailer.

Orion jumped.

They were over the fence, but then, as if he'd measured the distance with a calculator, Cassie felt Orion's back hooves lash out and strike the top pole. The crash of the fence as poles clattered to the ground resounded in her ears as she and Orion landed and thundered onto the next jump.

Oh, damn. So close. Well, she thought, let's pick the pace up, there's bound to be a few other rides with four faults. At least we can beat their times.

Surprisingly, unlike some horses she'd ridden, Orion didn't seem in the least bit rattled by the knockdown of the double-oxer. They cleared the last three jumps without a hitch, galloping round the last corner to stop the time clock.

She made a beeline for Hank and Caleb, jumping off Orion's back before he'd even come to a halt. "Check his hind legs, will you, Caleb? I'm worried he hit them against that pole on the oxer." Her arm slipped through the reins as she knelt, fumbling with the buckles on Orion's ankle boots.

A warm hand squeezed her shoulder. "Easy, Slim. It's all right. We saw him hit the oxer. In fact, we were standing right behind it. He shot his legs out and nailed it. Only his hooves struck it. I'll take a look at his legs, but I'm sure he's fine. Probably practices that kick on the walls of his stall every day."

Cassie sat back on her boot heels and forced herself to breathe in and out in slow, measured breaths. "Damn. When I finally cleared the course and got a look at that oxer—he'd demolished the entire jump. The whole thing's lying there, scattered like match sticks. All I could think was that he must have injured something." Disbelief crept into her voice as she repeated in stunned amazement, "He knocked down the whole thing!"

"Yup. Perfect strike. Like bowling for dollars. A pretty neat trick for a double-oxer," Hank offered.

Caleb knelt beside her and finished removing the stallion's boots. His long fingers moved carefully down the fetlock, probing gently around the pastern for any sign of tenderness or pain. Quietly, he moved around the stallion and repeated the same procedure with the other leg. Still anxious, Cassie watched in silence.

"Orion must have some sort of radar tucked away in that big head of his. Most other horses would need a rearview mirror to be able to wipe out an entire fence like that."

Hank nodded, his eyes twinkling. "I told you we had a smart horse here, Cassie. Take a look at the ring. The ground crew's only just finished putting the fence back up."

"You're sure he's okay, Caleb?"

"He's fine. We'll poultice him when we get home. He's a strong horse . . ."

A saccharine voice interrupted him. "He'd better be a strong horse if you're going to let such an incompetent rider on his back. Really, Caleb, I'm more than a bit shocked to discover you intend this girl to ride Orion. You were too embarrassed, perhaps, to mention it the other day?"

He didn't need to look up to recognize the speaker.

As he crouched beside Orion's hocks, Caleb's eyes lifted and met Hank's, who shrugged helplessly. Caleb didn't need to look at Cassie to know she'd frozen. Pamela's brand of poison often had that effect, something akin to arsenic. Rising to his feet, Caleb patted the stallion on the hindquarters. Only then did his gaze finally rest on his ex-wife, standing there, one hip cocked provocatively.

It was incredible, the contrast between Pamela and their small group. She was dressed in shimmery blue silk go-go pants, the kind that hugged the hips and legs, so that even the slightest bulge or flaw in the figure was magnified. Of course, with Pamela there were no flaws, as she well knew. The cropped jacket she wore was made from a matching fabric, with lots of gold necklaces hanging over it. Her feet were encased in what looked like alligator-skin shoes, sporting three-inch heels. Truly amazing. He'd seen women dressed more casually for a power lunch at the Ritz. He told himself that if he'd ever caught Pamela in a similar outfit before their marriage, he would have been wise enough to avoid her like the plague.

Deliberately, he wiped his hands on the legs of his jeans. With a cynical smile, he finally acknowledged her presence.

"Hello, Pamela. Fancy running into you here." Then, ignoring her before she'd even had time to reply, he turned to Raffael. "Raff, could you throw his cooler on, then walk him around for a while. You can untack him after the jump-off's over. Cassie's not riding again until the afternoon. We'll come by and spell you after we grab some lunch."

"Sure, Caleb." Raffael nodded, leading the stallion away. Cassie's first instinct was to go and help with the stallion's cooler, but Pamela's voice stopped her in her tracks.

"You know, Caleb, while I can imagine what you actually hired her for, surely competitive jumping wasn't part of the job description. It makes me wonder, too, if perhaps you've forgotten the terms of our agreement. I have your signature promising to keep me informed of *all* training decisions involving Orion."

"Come off it, Pamela. You know you don't care about anything to do with Orion except the money I give you every month. What does it matter to you if we hired Cassie? The riders you forced us to hire were morons. They couldn't get a merry-go-round horse to canter in a circle."

"Well, I certainly don't remember any of them injuring my horse, *my property*. And when they rode, they didn't demolish fences, either. If Orion hasn't injured himself, it's not through lack of your rider's trying, is it?"

Not that Pamela really cared, Caleb was right about that. Actually, the possibility of Orion seriously injured delighted her. It would suit her just fine if Caleb got stuck with a lame horse. If his precious stallion were out of commission, then that would be the end of this Cassie's so-called job.

What did Caleb see in her, anyway? Pamela wondered with a contemptuous glance in Cassie's direction. She certainly didn't come close to rivaling her own looks.

Bolstered by the thought, Pamela smiled confidently at Caleb. She toyed with the gold chains against her chest. "It really surprises me that you would hire such a . . . shall we say, mediocrity. Surely you realize that I need to protect my investment. This being the case, I'll expect regular reports on your new, uh, rider's progress with Orion. Otherwise, you'll hear from my lawyer. You remember him, don't you, Caleb? Such a smart man."

As a matter of fact, her lawyer would be getting a call

from her that very day, thought Pamela triumphantly. She was sure he'd be more than happy to hear from her. With his hourly fees, he was always delighted to hear from clients. It occurred to her it might be a good idea if they reviewed the terms of the contract he'd written for Orion's sale. She seemed to remember this one nifty section about null and void.

Her lips parted in a wide smile at the mental image of Caleb at her mercy. Leisurely, she let her eyes travel over, lingering beneath his belt buckle just long enough to make him feel the heat of her stare. Slowly, tauntingly, she lifted her eyes to his, blew him a kiss, and sauntered off to rejoin her friends, pleased with the morning's accomplishments.

It was Hank who finally broke the awkward silence that had descended on the group after Pamela's departure. "I wish she'd go suck a rotten egg," he muttered under his breath.

"I'm with you there, buddy. That, or step in a huge dump. What the hell, Hank, I thought you'd planned this perfectly, that this show would be too puny for Pamela to bother with."

"What can I tell you, that ex-wife of yours is perverse as the day is long. Actually, I spotted some of those socialites she hangs out with. Somebody must have had the bad taste to bring her along," Hank replied, an expression of disgust on his face. He couldn't believe the stuff Pamela pulled. Made his stomach turn, the way she treated Caleb. Couldn't have been too pleasant for Cassie to witness, either. Turning to her, he asked, "Cassie, honey, you okay?"

"Yeah. Thanks." She nodded vigorously, aware of Caleb's eyes on her. She was darned if she was going to let the likes of Pamela ruin the day. Resolutely, she blocked from her mind the image of his ex-wife staring at Caleb's crotch like a kid in a candy store. "Owners can be a real bitch," she quipped lightly, startling a laugh out of both Caleb and Hank. "Of course," she continued, "if Orion had gotten injured, that would have been a different story. But if Caleb thinks he's fine, then . . ."

"Slim, Orion's legs are made of iron. Like I said before, he probably practices those kicks on the walls of his stall. Come on, let's take a look at the other rounds. What with one thing and another, I've lost track of the standings."

The altered course for the jump-off had taken its toll. Several riders had their share of mishaps. Some had poles down, one rider's mount refused a fence, and then was given additional penalty points for exceeding the time limit. But none of the faults were nearly as spectacular as Cassie and Orion's knockdown.

The quirky thing about show-jumping rules, however, was that a rider received four faults regardless of whether just a single pole fell, or the entire fence came down, which after this morning's ride Cassie came to appreciate in a whole new way. If they'd counted faults per pole against her, she'd have been in the double digits! Other mistakes could be costly, too. For instance, a refusal was three points, but as it generally took the rider precious seconds to get his horse over the refused fence, a time fault of four points could be expected.

Cassie knew, after watching the remaining riders' rounds and the points they racked up, that her ride with four points and a decent time would place Orion and her ahead of a number of them. While she would have loved to go clean on both rounds, all in all, she realized Orion had responded beautifully.

She'd just have to work hard on getting him to accept jumps that looked like a designer's nightmare!

The last rider off the jump-off managed a clean round, dropping Cassie's standing to fourth place. She was pleased that she'd had the right instinct in pushing Orion a little harder at the end of the jump course. Cassie and Orion had beat out the next rider with four points by a mere three tenths of a second.

With a whoop of joy, Hank enveloped Cassie in an enthusiastic bear hug, thrilled that they'd placed so well their first time out. Cassie stepped back from his embrace breathless, half-worried she might have fractured a rib.

Her eyes instinctively sought out Caleb, standing to the side, a smile lighting up his handsome features. How incredibly beautiful he is, she thought for the hundredth time, wanting to preserve the memory of his smile forever in her heart.

Caleb stepped toward her and lifted her chin with his finger, a smile still curving his lips. Lowering his head, his eyes, dark and compelling locked with hers, now shaded to a deep blue underneath the brim of her hard hat. "Not too shabby, Slim," he murmured before his lips claimed hers.

The kiss was brief, both of them too aware of their surroundings. Cassie could just imagine what might happen if Pamela were still lurking around, like some dreaded ghoul. Nevertheless, Cassie's pulse was racing as she stepped back, a hint of breathlessness in her voice.

"Orion was the one who did all the work. Speaking of which, I've got to get him so we can collect our ribbon." She paused as a thought occurred to her. "You know, I think we may have even won some prize money, so I'm buying lunch."

"Hear that, Caleb? Got ourselves a sweet deal. A great rider and a big spender, too."

"Who could resist? How many burgers are you worth, Slim?"

She laughed, scanning the crowd for a glimpse of Raffael and Orion. Spotting them at last, she moved off in their direction, calling over her shoulder as she went. "Just let me grab our earnings, first. Then we'll eat 'til you're crying for mercy."

A blue ribbon would have been infinitely more becoming on Orion, Cassie decided, and the four hundred and forty dollars they won didn't even begin to cover the expenses involved in bringing him to the show in the first place, but, hey, it was a start.

Leading Orion back to the spot where she'd left Caleb and Hank, she found them in conversation with another man. Moving nearer, she recognized him as the winning rider of the jumper class.

The conversation broke off as the men became aware of Cassie and the stallion's approach. Caleb stepped forward to hold Orion's bridle as Cassie dismounted, while Hank and the rider stood back a bit, their eyes traveling over the dark bay.

Hank spoke first. "Rob, I'd like you to meet Five Oaks's new rider and trainer, Cassie Miller. Cassie, this is Rob Buchanan. Rob has a farm south of here. Sold him a few horses over the years."

Rob Buchanan stepped forward as Cassie extended her hand. He smiled and shook it. Cassie placed him at about forty. Tanned face, hazel eyes, and dark blond hair that curled under the rim of his hat. He had the wiry build of an equestrian.

Cassie smiled back politely. "Hello. That was a nice ride you had. Your horse made some impressive distances on those jumps."

"Thanks. Otto's a real trooper. I was just telling Hank and Caleb how much I liked Orion here. That was some show he put on for the crowd. Really dramatic."

"Yeah, well this is his first show of the season. We're just getting some mileage under our belts."

Buchanan nodded. His smile went up a notch. "Now, tell me about a bit about yourself. Why is it that this is the first time I've seen your face? Where have they been hiding you?"

"Oh, I've been up north mostly. Except for Florida, I've never made it this far south before."

"It's a real treat to have a new face to look at. The old crowd's getting pretty dull around here. I hope we'll be seeing a lot of you."

"Thanks," Cassie replied, before turning to Caleb. "Caleb, I'm starving. Do you mind heading over to the concession stand now?" She gave a friendly nod to Rob Buchanan. "Good to meet you, Rob. Hank, come find us when you're ready. Remember, I'm buying."

Caleb was sure he used to like Rob Buchanan. Good horseman and honest, to boot, which was fairly rare in the horse world. Now, after having seen the way he tried to ooze charm all over Cassie he wouldn't be terribly sorry if the guy came down with a sudden attack of flesh-eating disease.

He wondered whether Cassie had even noticed.

He gave her a quick sideways glance. They were walking side by side, heading in the direction of the trailer. She was leading Orion by the reins, her face calm and composed. She had such unbelievable cheekbones. The faint freckles on the bridge of her nose were pretty irresistible, too. He cleared his throat. "So, what do you think of Rob Buchanan?"

"Seems nice. Had a good ride, that's for sure."

She was obviously clueless. A hint of asperity entered his voice. "He seemed to like you an awful lot."

Cassie shrugged her shoulders, the dark blue fabric suddenly hot in the midday sun. She hadn't realized how warm it had become. She'd take it off when they got to the trailer.

"Sorry, what'd you say, Caleb? I was thinking of something."

He blew out a loud breath, exasperated with the way the

conversation was going. He stopped abruptly so he'd have her full attention. "I said, he certainly seemed to like you." He enunciated his words carefully, as if he were speaking to a not terribly bright child.

Cassie giggled. "Oh, *that*. Funny isn't it? Well, to tell you the truth, most of the guys on the circuit talk to me that way. That is, until I start beating them consistently. That usually does the trick in stopping the 'Me, macho rider, you, show bunny' routine." She started walking again, her mouth watering in anticipation of those hot dogs. "Just wait and see how much he likes me when Orion and I beat him in the Grand Prix class this afternoon."

Relief flooded Caleb. Thank God, was all he could think.

"Damn, Slim, you're a regular Amazon."

"You betcha. Hey, you think you could walk a little faster?"

20

Thompson and the twins arrived in time to watch Cassie compete in the Grand Prix. To Caleb's relief, he found that this time around he wasn't nearly as nervous for her, probably because he was too busy answering the thousand-and-one questions Sophie and Jamie were peppering him with.

When Cassie's number was called, Caleb hoisted Jamie up onto his shoulders so that he was high enough to see his mother ride, Hank good naturedly doing the same for Sophie. The two men had both promised that if there was a jump-off, the twins could switch shoulders.

Grand Prix classes were designed to up the ante in terms of challenging horse and rider. The courses consisted of two parts, the first part emphasizing puissance, or strength, and the second half testing the horses' speed. In addition, the time limit set for finishing the course was often shorter than the times for jumping classes, so that the pace for the course had to be ridden much faster. What it boiled down to was: higher, harder, faster.

Caleb knew that Cassie and Orion could handle the difficult twists and turns that the course designer had created for this class. He and Hank had both walked the course with her this time; although there were definitely some tricky spots, no one had stopped and uttered the big "uh-oh." The only jump Caleb remained concerned about was that double-oxer. It had been raised about a foot higher. That much more sheer ugliness for Orion to get worked up about.

His eyes were glued to her as she trotted into the ring. Above him, Jamie squeezed his legs together in excitement and Caleb raised his hands to the little boy's knees to keep from being strangled.

Cassie and Orion looked as fresh as they had this morning. Caleb still had trouble believing that all the ketchup and relish she'd slathered on her *three* hot dogs hadn't ended up on the snow-white breeches she wore, but miraculously they'd escaped a single drop of condiment. Almost as amazing a feat as watching her eat three hot dogs in a stunningly short period of time.

He hoped she wasn't feeling the effects of her lunch out there.

Cassie's world had narrowed to three things: her horse, the course, and the clock. She'd drawn second in the jumping order, so she knew she was setting a ride for everyone to chase down and beat. The first rider had blown it from the start. She'd watched him sawing away at his horse's mouth, jerking his poor mount's head so high there was no physical way it could have jumped the fence cleanly. It hadn't. Rattled, the horse had had a devil of a time just finishing the course. Cassie hadn't even wanted to watch.

Earlier on, when they'd been walking the course, Hank had suggested a strategy. Go for the shortest distances she dared on the first six jumps, the big nasty fences that would suck the energy out of most of the other horses' legs, and then put on the gas for the final six, relying on Orion's incredible stamina to bring them home faster than anyone else.

Cassie knew a second's panic as the first fence, a huge brightly striped vertical, loomed up at her. It looked enormous, even from her vantage point astride Orion. But then she felt the stallion go into gear, his galloping legs pumping underneath her, and she knew he had the heart to take on anything if she just played it right.

Cassie rode him brilliantly.

From the side of the show ring, it seemed as though Orion didn't even bat an eye this time at the double-oxer, simply sailed over it, his knees tucked tightly under him. The spectators became increasingly enthusiastic with each fence they cleared. When Cassie landed the final jump, her torso bent low over Orion's neck racing to cross the line and stop the electronic timer, the small crowd applauded loudly at the first clean round.

"I can't believe it! I can't believe it!" Her first Grand Prix with Orion and they'd gone clear! Cassie was ecstatic, grinning from ear to ear as she patted Orion's lathered neck.

"Mommy, Mommy, you were going so fast."

"I sure hope so, Jamie. It certainly felt that way to me."

"And nothing fell down!"

"I know. Maybe Orion was satisfied he'd had his revenge on that oxer," Cassie offered, still marveling. She dismounted, her legs more than a little wobbly as she hit the ground. "I think you and Jamie should cross your fingers and hope very hard that Orion's the only one to pull off a clear round."

Raffael stepped up with the cooler in his hands. "Nice ride, Cassie. You two looked real tough to beat out there."

"Thanks." Gratefully, she handed over the reins for him to walk Orion in the shade of some trees.

Jamie scrambled down from Caleb's shoulders with the agility of a baby chimpanzee and sped to his mother's outstretched arms. Sophie took her cue from Jamie and in a moment she, too, was being embraced.

"Thank you, Pumpkin. Yes, Orion is a really good horse. Why don't we watch the others now and see whether they can do as well. By the way, what have you two rascals done with Thompson?"

"Uh, Slim, Thompson had to take a walk. I think she needed some air, expand her lungs a bit." A euphemism if there ever was one. When Bessie had seen the size of the first fence, she'd almost started hyperventilating.

"Oh, right. Air. I'd forgotten." Thompson wasn't a big fan of horses in the first place, always fretting that Cassie was going to break her neck. Cassie considered it a true sign of loyalty that Thompson willingly accompanied the twins to see her compete.

The fates must have been smiling down on Cassie that day, or maybe it was the twins' fingers crossed tightly together that did the trick. In any case, none of the other riders got a clean round. Although a few came agonizingly close, Rob Buchanan among them.

Caleb almost laughed out loud when he saw the look Buchanan shot Cassie as she accepted the winner's trophy and prize money and then led Orion away, with the long blue ribbon fluttering against the cheek piece of his bridle.

The twins insisted on driving back with Cassie and Caleb in the Jeep, even though Cassie explained to them that they wouldn't be driving home directly. First, they had to stop off at Five Oaks and poultice Orion's legs. And Hot Lips had to be hand walked before they could head on home. The twins had promised to be on their best behavior as they were unloading the stallion. Even those stringent conditions didn't dampen their five-year-old enthusiasm. Thompson said the twins' abandonment was fine with her, she'd be able to get dinner ready in peace. She called out to Caleb as she was driving off that she'd be expecting him, too. Caleb accepted the invitation gratefully. He was almost positive that once there'd been a can of tuna fish in the back of the refrigerator, but he couldn't remember whether he'd eaten it or not. Truth be told, he'd gotten so used to the bounty of Thompson's cooking that his grocery shopping skills, shaky at best, had fallen by the wayside.

Cassie dropped her car keys into his outstretched palm and opened the rear door for the twins to climb in. She fastened their seat belts, giving them each a kiss before shutting the door. Caleb waited until she pulled off her field boots and socks, tossed them in her bag in exchange for a pair of beat up tennis shoes, and settled herself in the passenger seat before turning the key in the ignition.

The twins amused themselves for the first few minutes by groaning loudly, extravagantly as the Jeep heaved and rolled over the rutted field and then onto the pothole-riddled dirt drive.

After an especially loud groan from the back seat, Cassie observed, "Good thing you told me to park close to the exit, Caleb."

"Yeah," he replied dryly.

Once they'd reached the tarmacadam, the shrill groans and moans died down. There were a few moments of animated whispers. Then, "Mommy, are we there yet?"

"No, Sophie, honey. We've got a long way to go. Why don't you look out the window?"

About a minute and a half of silence. "Mommy, tell Jamie to quit it. He's bothering me."

"I am *not*," Jamie's voice erupted, indignant at the accusation.

"Are so. You kicked my leg!"

Cassie shot Caleb a look of apology. "They're wiped out." Turning around to address her children, she spoke firmly. "Kids, there's plenty of room back there. Please don't fight. No, Sophie, don't stick your tongue out at Jamie. It's not nice and you know you'll get upset when he

does it back at you. Look," she said a bit desperately, seeing the mutinous set to their faces, "would you like to listen to a tape? Let me see what's in the glove compart-
ment." She reached forward and fumbled inside, drawing
out three cassettes.

"Okay, we've got *Winnie the Pooh;* Peter, Paul, and
Mary singing 'Puff, the Magic Dragon,' . . . remember how
you love that song? And there's Dr. Seuss's *Green Eggs &
Ham* and *The Cat in the Hat.*"

"I want to hear *Where the Wild Things Are!*"

"Sorry, Jamie. That tape must be in Thompson's car. We
only have these three."

Jamie and Sophie spent the next five minutes arguing
fiercely over what tape they wanted. Cassie's head began to
pound, exhaustion after the long day fraying what patience
remained.

She sighed wearily. She supposed it was time to read
them the riot act.

"You know, Cassie," Caleb speaking loudly enough to
be heard over the din. "I'm not sure I remember how *The
Cat in the Hat* goes. Is that the one where the Christmas
presents get taken?"

Sophie and Jamie giggled. "No, Caleb. That's the one
with the Grinch."

"You sure about that? I remember that story pretty well.
My mom read it to me about twenty-five years ago, so I
guess I'd remember a thing like that."

"Mommy, let's listen to that one. Caleb's forgotten the
whole thing!"

Cassie shoved the cassette inside the tape player. She
mouthed the word *thanks* to Caleb and he shrugged his
shoulders, grinning. She simply hadn't had the energy to
figure out how to distract them out of their quarrelsome
mood.

Blessed peace was restored to the back seat as the zany,
magical words of Dr. Seuss filled the air. Caleb turned his

attention back to the road, negotiating the weekend traffic, and Cassie slowly allowed herself to relax.

"Cassie, I, uh, just wanted to tell you what a fantastic job you did today. Don't worry about Pamela. The way you rode Orion was awesome, you two are a dynamite team."

Silence.

Caleb glanced over, chagrined to find Cassie fast asleep, her hands fisted under her chin, her head pressed against the car window. At this moment, she looked barely older than Sophie. Well, hell, he thought, shaking his head. Guess I'll be taking that refresher course on Dr. Seuss after all.

21

"*A*lex? Hi, it's me."

"Cass! How'd it go today?" Cassie could tell from her brother's voice that she hadn't awakened him. No surprise: Alex rarely bothered to sleep.

Cassie curled her legs under the smooth cotton sheets of her bed. It was almost midnight, and she'd finally gotten to take her bath and turn in, so tired she'd almost crawled into her bed. But before switching off the light, she'd reached for the phone. She'd wanted to call Alex and share her success. Cassie couldn't explain it clearly, but a gnawing fear was growing inside her that she was losing him. His voice had sounded so far away the last few times they'd talked. Already, Cassie had invited him to come for a visit, but hadn't succeeded in pinning him down to a date. He kept rattling off one excuse after another.

"Alex, he was fantastic! We had a wee bit of trouble in the first class. We're still getting used to each other, after all . . . But Alex, guess what? We won the Grand Prix. We had the only clean round!"

"Cass, that's great. I knew you could do it."

"It was only a small show, you know, a Saturday event.

Still, there were some decent riders there. Pamela, Caleb's ex, showed up, too, but I didn't let that spoil it."

"She did? How'd she react to finding out you're riding her horse?"

"He's practically Caleb's . . . I'm sure you can imagine her reaction. Snide, rude, threatening. Started going on about her 'investment' and 'property' and contacting her lawyer. How could someone think of a horse like Orion as an investment?"

She got no response from her brother to her question. Nothing but the background clicks of the long-distance call, until at last Alex remarked, "Sounds like typical ex-wife stuff to me. Don't worry about it Cass, just go out and do what you do best. I know you're going to cream them at the bigger shows, too."

Cassie laughed. "Maybe. That would be nice. Now, tell me what's up with you."

"Same old stuff, but I closed a big deal yesterday that's been dragging on for months. All of the sudden, my schedule's opened up. I was wondering whether I could talk the twins and Thompson into coming for a visit next week. They could fly in on Monday and stay through the weekend." The line went silent once again until Alex said softly, "I really miss them, Cass."

This was as big an admission as she'd ever get from her older brother. She didn't hesitate an instant. If her brother was hurting, missing his family even a fraction as much as they were missing him, the twins could skip at least a few days of school. It wasn't as if they were going to flunk kindergarten.

"They're going to be out of control, jumping up and down all week with excitement, Alex. I just wish I could come, too. When will *I* get to see you?"

"I promise I'll try to get down there soon, Cass. But I've got some good news on that front. I think I've got it all arranged to take a few days off to see you ride in the

Classic. I called Great-aunt Grace this week. She still seems to have all her marbles 'cause she knew who I was and insisted that I stay with her. She even wanted Jamie and Sophie to come along."

"Gosh, she really remembered you? She must be ninety if she's a day."

"Actually, I think she's older. But I've kept in touch, you know. After all, I was named after Great-uncle Alex."

"Well, that's great news. And Diana? She'll be staying there, too?"

"Oh, I don't think I'll impose on Aunt Grace *that* much. Diana can always stay with some friends. She's got her pick of homes in the Hamptons. But as you can imagine, with Diana there's always a price. I promised to reserve an entire table at the Grand Prix tent. You know how she is."

"Yeah," she replied dryly. "Nothing like spending several thousand dollars and change to cheer her up. Well, at least she'll be smiling for all those society photographers milling about."

Alex laughed. "She's got some good points, Cass."

Cassie rolled her eyes. Sure, she thought, they were located just south of her shoulders. Personally, she considered Diana a first-class witch who'd managed to snag Alex and was hanging on for dear life. It was amazing how unperturbed he seemed by Diana's blatant devotion to wealth and ostentation. Didn't he ever wonder if Diana loved him for himself or for his wealth? Cassie sincerely hoped her tenure as Alex's lover didn't last long. But Cassie knew better than to stick her nose into Alex's affairs. It wasn't as if her handsome brother hadn't plenty of experience handling women.

They chatted a while more, Alex telling her he'd arrange the airplane reservations and get back in touch with her tomorrow with the flight information. Cassie hung up the phone and reached to turn off the light.

As she was drifting off to sleep, the thought came to her

that now she had no excuse to back out of the trip to U. Penn with Caleb.

"Tod? Hey, it's Caleb."

"Caleb. Good to hear from you. How's that mare you were telling me about? You still bringing her?"

"Yeah, that's what I was calling about. I was wondering if early next week was okay with you."

"Give me a minute to check . . . how does Tuesday sound? My calendar's free and I know Delia and I aren't doing anything that evening."

"Tuesday's fine. How's Delia doing, by the way?"

"She's just great. Complaining a bit that she doesn't know which is more swollen, her ankles or her belly. But you know, I really like the look on her."

Caleb laughed. "I can't wait to see her and the kids."

"You'll stay with us for the night before you head back."

"That's a lot to ask, Tod, with Delia pregnant and all. And I'm going to be bringing someone with me."

"Yeah? Who?"

Caleb heard the sharpened interest in his friend's voice. Delia and Tod were always trying to hook him up with women. Ever since Pamela.

"Her name's Cassie Miller. She owns the mare. She's also Five Oaks's new rider and trainer. Got her showing Orion."

Tod's whistle came long and clear over the connection. "Must be a good rider."

"They won their first Grand Prix last weekend."

"Congratulations, buddy."

"Thanks."

"So what's she like?"

"Cassie?"

"No, Esther Williams. Come on, Caleb, give."

"She's . . . well, she's different."

"What, she got three eyes?"

"Get outta here. She's beautiful enough to make you sweat. No, I mean *she's different*. I thought she was going to be one way and she turned out to be . . . more. I didn't expect it somehow."

"Oh. Now I get you. So, we get one bedroom ready or two?"

The seconds ticked as Tod waited for his friend's response.

Caleb leaned back in the padded leather chair behind his desk. Cassie had found him early this morning, just as he was heading off to pick up the morning paper. Marched right up to him, doing a fair imitation of a marine cadet. She'd halted, a foot away, but hadn't been able to bring her eyes any higher than the third button on his comfortably worn polo shirt.

"I can come to Pennsylvania when you drop off Hot Lips at the clinic." She'd muttered the words, acting like the prospect held as much pleasure as facing a firing squad.

Before he'd even had time to reply to her abrupt announcement, she'd fled the field. Yeah, she'd hightailed it back to the house before he could even get a good morning out of her.

"Hello, Wells, you still there? Look, if you need some more time to think this through, you can call me back in an hour or so. Don't want to rush you." Tod's voice was gleeful, relishing Caleb's unexpected hesitancy.

Caleb sighed. "Better make that two bedrooms, Tod."

He knew that if he told Tod to set up one bedroom, he could finesse the situation so that Cassie would feel too embarrassed and awkward to raise a fuss in front of their host and hostess.

Hell, from the way she'd acted this morning, it was pretty clear she'd convinced herself that by agreeing to go with him she was letting him take one giant step closer to her bed.

Otherwise she wouldn't have been as nervous as a cat trapped in a room full of rocking chairs.

If he forced the issue, he might get the sex, but then she'd be gone in a flash. So he'd wait. He'd wait for her to come willingly, eager for the pleasure she'd find in his arms.

Tod's voice spoke in his ear. "Hold on just a minute, I think there's something wrong with the connection. Did I hear you, Caleb Wells, the Casanova of Virginia, the heart-throb of Pennsylvania, say two bedrooms?"

"Funny, Harper, very funny. Maybe I should repeat it, in case you've gone deaf as well as stupid. Two bedrooms."

"No shit. Jesus, I can't wait to meet this paragon."

When Thompson learned of Alex's plan to fly the twins and her to New York for a visit, she'd tamped down hard on the whoop of joy that surged up inside her.

Hallelujah!

For the past two weeks, she'd been trying to figure out a way to get Cassie and Caleb alone, without the constant threat of someone barging in and interrupting. She'd racked her brains, considering and discarding everything, from bomb threats to telephone calls from long-lost relatives. After witnessing Alex's barely veiled hostility toward Caleb, she'd certainly never thought she'd get any assistance from *that* corner.

Alex must really be missing those kids something fierce.

Well, it would do everyone a world of good, she thought. The twins needed to see their uncle as much as he needed to see them. And Cassie needed some time alone, enough time to step back a moment and take a good long look at all the wonderful things she was letting pass her by. And all she could have if she didn't throw the chance away.

She whistled as her quick hands folded Sophie and Jamie's clothes into two neat towers, her mind busily checking off items on the list she'd compiled of things to do before leaving next Monday.

A large, wet nose brushed against her hip, almost causing Thompson heart failure. Finnegan! My God, she had to talk to Caleb and Francis and make sure the dog would be taken care of. She wondered if he might be healed enough now to manage stairs. If not, she'd just insist that Francis come and sleep here on the night Cassie was in Pennsylvania. She knew Cassie too well not to realize she'd seize any fool excuse not to go to Pennsylvania with Caleb—babysitting a boxer, for instance—and stick to it, ruining what Thompson considered a golden opportunity. That girl could be so stubborn.

The thought of Finnegan gone from the house gave her a moment's pause. She'd come to enjoy those visits from Francis O'Mally quite a bit. *Well,* she thought philosophically, *this would reveal Francis' true feelings.* If he continued his visits to the house even after Finnegan was gone, that would be a good indication that he found her at least as appealing as a drooling boxer.

Cassie struggled through the week. She succeeded only by closing her mind to everything except Sophie, Jamie, and the horses she was riding in preparation for this coming weekend's show. It was the only way to prevent herself from turning into a babbling bundle of nerves. She avoided Caleb at all costs. Just seeing him at a distance had bubbles of hysteria rising up inside her. This stupid trip to Pennsylvania was taking on gargantuan proportions in her fevered imagination. For her peace of mind alone, she should have had the good sense to refuse.

While the kids were at school in the mornings, she rode. Her training with Orion from now through the rest of the show season was focused on smoothing out rough spots they encountered during the weekend competitions. Cassie and Hank were careful to devise workouts that didn't overtax or fatigue the stallion. The stress and physical demands of showing alone were enough to injure a horse. The keys to a successful season were guarding against injury, over-training, and the very real risk of burnout.

By early afternoons she was ready for Jamie and Sophie. With the warm spring weather, Cassie found, to her dismay, that even after their daily riding lessons, the twins were still raring to go. Recently, Jamie had developed a passion for baseball. So Cassie had obligingly driven them into town one afternoon and outfitted both Jamie and his sister with miniature mitts, wide-barrel plastic bats, tennis balls, and a T-ball stand.

Baseball practice became an instant success. On a couple of afternoons, Cassie and the twins managed to coax Thompson out of the house and convince her to cover third base. Everyone batted, the twins shouting encouragement whenever Thompson hit a homer and had to tear around the bases.

Near the end of that week, Caleb came home while a particularly energetic game was in progress. Jamie's excited shrieks met him as he climbed out of his truck, watching as Cassie and Thompson tried to tag the little boy in a squeeze play.

Jamie made a desperate dive for the dishtowel that was third base.

"Safe! I'm safe," he yelled triumphantly, hopping up and down on the towel. "Now it's Mommy's turn. Bring me home, 'kay Mommy!"

"I'll try my best, but Sophie's a mean first baseman. It's tough getting past her."

Cassie picked up the bat and walked to the batter's box. The T was set so low her swing resembled a golf swing as much as anything. With a hard thwack, Cassie sent the bright yellow tennis ball zooming, a line drive up second. From their respective positions on first and shortstop,

Sophie and Thompson both went chasing after the ball, shouting frantic encouragement to each other as they ran. Jamie, his short legs moving like little pistons, flew toward home and, in a grand, but wholly unnecessary gesture, slid into home plate.

The scene unfolded like a marvelous panorama, Caleb's eyes riveted to the running, laughing figure of Cassie. Barefoot, in blue jeans, and a lavender tank top, her feet skimmed the ground, her long wavy hair streaming behind her, a glorious golden banner.

It was almost imperceptible, the way she slowed down as she approached second base, Sophie running toward her with all her might, her small hand clutching the tennis ball. She timed it perfectly, so that Sophie had the thrill, the glory, of tagging her mother out inches away from the base.

"Oooh, you got me, you little stinker! Just wait 'til you get up to bat. No mercy." Laughing, Cassie lifted Sophie high in the air and tumbled to the ground with her, the two of them laughing and rolling together in the green grass of his parents' lawn.

Jamie, unable to resist the fun, threw himself down and a new game began: A tickling contest with Jamie and Sophie teaming up to pin Cassie to the ground. There she was, lying on the ground, tears of laughter streaming down her face, shouting uncle and enough as the twins swarmed over her, busy as ants, their fingers tickling away.

It hit him then with the force of a sledgehammer to the solar plexus. The blow left him stunned, reeling.

He loved her.

He loved her with an intensity, a wholeness, a completeness he'd never even begun to feel for anyone else before.

He loved her for who she was, what she was trying to do with her life, and how damned hard she was striving to make it work.

He stood, incapable of action, as the words *I love her*

sent shock waves through his system. They pummeled his brain, his vitals, his heart. Had he been able to escape, he would have seized the chance, but Thompson's cheerful cry of, "Look, it's Caleb," rendered the possibility tenuous at best.

With the typical fickleness of five-year-olds, Jamie and Sophie left their mother lying on the ground in favor of this new source of entertainment. Scrambling to their feet, they rushed him, flinging their arms around his legs.

"Caleb, Caleb. We're playing baseball. Wanna play too?"

He cleared his throat, unsure of words, speech, sound. His voice came out rusty, as if unused for decades. "The strangest baseball game I've ever seen. You sure you weren't playing rugby?"

"No, silly."

Then, "What's rugby?" Sophie and Jamie inquired simultaneously.

"A game you two are already experts at," Cassie replied, dusting off bits of grass from the seat of her jeans. "I've got some stuff to organize in the house. Sophie and Jamie, you have a half hour before it's bath and supper time."

He was happy to let her go. Glad that he didn't have to deal with her presence right now, when his emotions were so new and volatile within him.

Instead, he turned his attention back to the children, to their faces so open, so eager for the fun to begin again. This he could handle.

"Right, seems to me, you guys are good enough to take this game to a higher level. What we need to do, is to work on your pitching technique. That's it, Sophie, you and your brother grab some of those balls on the ground there. Okay, now, let me see your windup."

Hank truly couldn't figure out what to make of all this. Here they were, on what had been in Hank's opinion a

pretty successful Saturday, with both Orion and Limelight
going well for Cassie, and what were they doing? Standing
around like dumb clucks, acting like they'd been dragged
here against their wills. At least Cassie had ridden fine.
Without a doubt, the competition had been more intense
than the previous week's. This was a significantly larger
show. But she'd pulled off a fifth place with Orion in the
jumping class and a second with Limelight in the pre-
jumpers.

Then, she'd done just great in the Grand Prix with only
eight faults. The two poles they'd nicked Hank was convinced were ready to tumble anyway. It was just bad luck
that several other riders had ridden clear.

That was how it went sometimes in show jumping. Both
Caleb and Cassie knew that. So what in blazes was wrong
with them?

He shrugged his shoulders as he supervised Tony loading first Limelight and then Orion into the van for the drive
back to Five Oaks. At this point, he was almost glad that
Caleb and Cassie were leaving early on Tuesday. Good rid-
dance. He was losing all patience with this kind of foolish-
ness.

Cassie accepted Melissa's invitation to dinner at their
house that Monday night as a drowning man would a buoy
tossed to him. Earlier, she'd driven Thompson and the
twins to the airport, overriding Thompson's objections, and
she dreaded the moment when she'd have to return to the
house and be left all alone to worry about tomorrow.

Caleb didn't join them. He'd spent the entire day at the
Animal Hospital, so that he could take both Tuesday afternoon and Wednesday off for the trip to Pennsylvania. She
refused to wonder what he might be doing tonight.

It was a lovely dinner. Melissa and Hank welcomed
her with the casualness befitting a family member, serv-

ing a delicious vegetable lasagna out on the porch with the cheerful glow of citronella candles to light their dinner. They entertained her with stories of the early days at Five Oaks, when they were just starting out in the business. Cassie was truly sorry when the evening came to an end.

She nearly jumped a foot when his voice called out to her in the darkness. The moon, not quite full, illuminated the path before her. A sprinkling of stars were out, but the house before her stood silent and dark. The thought hadn't even crossed her mind to turn on any lights when she'd left earlier in the day.

"Sorry if I scared you."

"Of course you scared me," she retorted angrily. Her heart was still racing, but for a different reason now. "It's pitch-black out. What were you doing, skulking around in the bushes?"

"Actually, I only returned a few minutes ago, myself. Your lights were off, your car wasn't around. As your well-being is my highest priority, I was debating whether I should go and turn your porch light on, or let you stumble around in the dark, when you happened to drive up." His words dripped sarcasm, his voice as hostile as Cassie's had been. Clearly, he was more than ready to pick a fight. For some absurd reason, that put her at ease.

"Oh. Well, I'm fine."

"Yeah, I can see that. Good night." She heard him move off in the darkness and stood for a minute, surprised that he hadn't even made a move to kiss her, or *anything*.

Okay, so she'd admit she was scared witless he was going to try to seduce her now that they were alone together, but she hadn't exactly wanted him to avoid her like she had the plague either.

"Caleb?" she called to him tentatively.

"What?" Now his voice sounded strained, edgy. Guiltily, she realized that she hadn't even considered how tired he must be, putting in the extra hours at the hospital just so that he could make the trip tomorrow.

"What time should I have Hot Lips ready?"

"The drive'll take about five hours. I've got a few patients to see in the morning. Can you have her ready by noon?"

"Of course."

"You know, Cassie, if you don't want to come, it's no big deal. I can handle the drive myself."

Why was he suddenly giving her a chance to back out? Didn't he want her to go with him? In anyone else, Cassie would have recognized the perversity of her feelings. Rather than gracefully accepting the opportunity he was providing, she now wished for nothing more than proof of his desire for her company.

"Don't you want me to come? Will it be inconvenient?"

He gave a strangled sound of exasperation. "Look, I just thought you might be feeling uncomfortable about traveling with me alone. And I know how exhausting competing every weekend is. Maybe you'd appreciate a little time to yourself, that's all."

"Oh," she said again. Annoyed with her less than brilliant response, she continued. "Well, I'd like to take her. See where she's going and everything."

"Fine. Great. See you at noon." He vanished into the darkness. Without having shown his face. Without having said he wanted her to come.

Damn. He wished she'd said no.

It wasn't that he didn't *want* her to go. Hell, he wanted to spend every second of the day with her. As well as the night.

But he loved her. And it scared the daylights out of him.

He'd promised himself he wouldn't open himself up to that kind of pain, that kind of hurt again. But somehow she'd snuck past his defenses. He figured he'd eventually sort it all out, that he'd tell her about the way he felt. But not now. Not when he was still feeling as if he'd just jumped out of an airplane with no parachute.

22

Christ, this was turning out to be a rotten day. First, Pamela had caught him as he was about to leave for the hospital. He should have followed his instincts and let the machine pick up, but as bad luck would have it, he'd lifted the receiver and got stuck with an eight-o'clock-in-the-morning conversation with his least favorite person in the whole world.

She'd immediately started in on him, wanting to know why he hadn't called her. Then she'd started badgering him about meeting him that afternoon, to "discuss" Orion's progress. Caleb couldn't believe she actually thought he fell for her transparent games. Pamela didn't care about the horse, she just wanted to yank Caleb's chain—and see whether it was attached to his dick in the process.

Even if he hadn't had an excuse, he'd have found one.

"Sorry. Can't do it. I have to go out of town."

"What for?"

"Not that it's any of your business, but I've got to take a horse to U. Penn for aquatherapy."

"Oh, what a shame. An injured leg?" Pamela had been his wife long enough to have learned that much.

"Yes."

"One of Hank's horses?"

"No."

"Mmm, then, let me guess. Oh, I know . . . It must belong to that new girlfriend of yours. That *fabulous* rider. So, she can't even keep her own horse sound? My, my . . ."

"Knock it off, Pamela," he interrupted with icy disdain. "Her mare most likely injured herself before Cassie even purchased her."

"But you can't be certain, can you? Really, Caleb, you're taking a terrible risk. Rather, you're making me take a terrible risk. Perhaps you should consider getting a new rider."

"Cassie stays." Let her chew on that for a while, he thought bitterly. But he felt a nagging worry when she merely laughed.

"Oh, Caleb, you always did think with your cock. Someday that's going to get you into a whole lot of trouble." She'd made it sound like a promise.

Yeah, the phone call had certainly set the tone for the day. And now this. With increasing concern, Caleb finished examining the dog. Seconds passed as his right hand held the stethoscope pressed against the chest of a gently panting, long-haired collie. Already certain of what he would hear, he moved the stethoscope to the dog's stomach.

He removed the stethoscope from his ears. "You said that Belle isn't spayed, Mrs. Kline? Do you know when her last heat was?"

"Oh, some time ago. I can't remember exactly. We haven't spayed her because we thought we might want to breed her sometime. She's so pretty and she's got a pedigree that's chock full of champions."

Belle's owner didn't even realize her dog had gotten pregnant. In Caleb's experience, that was often a really bad sign. Dog owners didn't like those kind of surprises. Why,

Caleb asked himself, did owners opt not to spay or neuter their dogs on the off chance that later on they might like a basketful of cute puppies? Lord save him from amateur breeders.

"Well, Mrs. Kline, it looks like your wish came true. Your dog's about halfway through her gestation. The puppies will be born next month. Any idea who the sire might be?"

"But, but, that's impossible," Mrs. Kline objected, clearly aghast. "We've been so careful when she goes into heat."

"Does she go out alone at night to relieve herself?"

"Why, yes. But we've got her in a fence. We leave her there lots of times. It's a strong, wooden fence."

"How high?"

Mrs. Kline raised her hand to roughly waist level. Caleb counted to twenty, fighting to keep his anger under control. Didn't this pea-brain know there were animal rescue centers full of unwanted, abandoned puppies, many of them destined to be put down?

Teeth clenched, Caleb enunciated his words carefully. "Mrs. Kline, when a female's in heat, unneutered male dogs will sometimes travel miles to mate, attracted by her scent. You don't honestly think a three-and-a-half-foot fence is going to deter them?"

Mrs. Kline's face crumpled. "Oh, Lord, what am I going to do? This is terrible. Who knows what the puppies will look like?"

Caleb impatiently passed the lady a box of Kleenex, not bothering to speak until she'd finished blowing her nose. "Mrs. Kline. I'm going to give you some supplementary vitamin pills for Belle to take. You'll need to increase her food, make sure she stays calm and stress free. We'll talk in a couple of weeks as Belle gets closer to term."

Mrs. Kline nodded her head feebly, still sniffing into her tissue. Caleb leaned down to scratch the dog behind the ear. Belle's tail swished against the linoleum. A fine dog, doubtless more intelligent than her owners. Straightening, he jotted some notes in Belle's folder and continued his instructions.

"After she's birthed her puppies, I'll see what I can do about helping you place them in good, responsible homes. In return, I strongly urge you to consider spaying Belle. If you want to see cute puppies, either make an appointment with your breeder to see a new litter or go to an animal shelter. There are plenty of cute ones there, too. Have a good day, Mrs. Kline."

Caleb closed the examining room door behind him, feeling as if the smoke was still pouring out of his ears, he was so angry. Shaking his head, he glanced at his watch. Ten to twelve. No way he was going to be on time picking up Cassie at Five Oaks.

"Joyce, could you please get some high-potency vitamins for Belle? That fool woman let the dog get pregnant. You'll probably need to make sure the dog's records are in order, too. I doubt Mrs. Kline will continue to use our services."

"You think she'll take her to another vet?"

"Yeah, well, I wasn't at my most sympathetic. Oh, while you're at it, dig out that xeroxed article on what happens to abandoned dogs. Make sure she gets it with her bill. Got to run. Sorry to leave you with this mess." He gave her a crooked smile.

"Not to worry, Caleb. Derek's here for the rest of the afternoon, and both he and Mark are working tomorrow."

"Joyce, you're a wonder. What would I do without you?"

She laughed. "Just remember that when you're writing out the Christmas bonuses!"

Caleb grinned and winked. "I will, I promise. But don't you think your husband's going to get mighty suspicious?"

Her eyes lit up with mischief. "That's the point, Caleb."

Cassie had Hot Lips ready and waiting by the time Caleb pulled into the spot where he habitually parked his truck at Five Oaks. Twenty minutes later they were on the road, Hot Lips having loaded into the van without kicking up too much fuss. An unexpected bonus, considering the mare's high spirits at finally being outside after the long weeks she'd spent confined to stall rest. The short periods of hand walking Cassie'd given the mare were certainly not enough to calm her thoroughbred temperament, either.

"You want to drive first or shall I?" Caleb inquired, the first sentence he'd spoken after a curt hello. For her part, Cassie hadn't been exactly loquacious either.

"I'll drive."

She'd dressed in slim black pants, black paddock boots, and a black sleeveless mock turtleneck. Her hair was raked back tightly into a bun at the nape of her neck. Dark sunglasses shielding her eyes completed the outfit. There was no denying she looked stunning, but Caleb didn't like it. To him, she reminded him of the way she'd acted when they first met. Cool, beautiful, and unapproachable. Ice Case Cassie.

Just as well, he thought, shrugging his shoulders as he made his way to the passenger side. She walked past him, inches away, as if he didn't exist.

Nettled, Caleb spoke. "So, we going to a funeral or did you get a job offer from the Mob?"

Cassie stopped and gave him a where are you hiding your spaceship look. "What are you talking about?"

"What's with the black stuff?"

"Get a life, Wells," she snapped before slamming the driver's side door and starting the engine.

I had a life before you showed up, he thought sourly. I liked it just fine. Everything was basically okay, just the way I wanted it. And now, well . . . *shit*.

"Stop the car a second. Now."

Cassie slammed on the brakes. "What's the matter with

you? You've . . ." Her next words were cut short as Caleb hauled her over to him, and kissed her fiercely, thoroughly, and over and over again.

Cassie's toes were curling by the time they broke apart and sat staring at each other, their breath coming in short, irregular pants in the confines of the Jeep.

Caleb looked at her with a happy grin. Her hair was loose, strands tumbling chaotically around her face. Her cheeks were flushed, and her lips, her lips were deliciously wet, still parted, breath unsteady. He knew that behind her sunglasses, her eyes would be a deep, shining blue, ever so slightly out of focus from passion.

That was the look he really liked on her.

"Okay, Slim, I think we're ready now."

Shaking her head, Cassie eased the Jeep forward, her front teeth biting down on her lip to keep from smiling.

The lawyer escorted Pamela to the bank of elevators outside the reception area of the law firm Pamela had retained for her divorce. It suited her, this firm, and all it represented. Money, elegance, and power. It had gotten her Orion from Caleb's hands with breathless ease, and now it had made her a sizable mountain of money. Even her prodigious spending habits wouldn't put a dent in a sum this large for quite some time.

Pamela flashed her lawyer what she liked to consider her signature smile. The instantaneous male reaction she read in his face was gratifying, and wholly expected. Fleetingly, Pamela considered inviting him to bed. She rejected the thought just as quickly. The poor man simply wasn't attractive enough. Only beautiful things turned her on. Lowering her lashes, she feigned a coyness utterly foreign to her. These lawyers were clever, but their area of expertise was limited.

Extending her hand gracefully, Pamela let the smile linger on her lips. "Thank you so much for all your help,

Alden. I really appreciate your resolving an intolerable situation so efficiently." Just for the fun of it, she let her gaze linger on his face, widening her eyes a touch for added effect.

Alden Whittaker straightened his spine. She didn't have to look to know that other parts of him were standing at attention, too. "I'm happy that we could be of assistance, Mrs. Ross. We were especially fortunate that an interested party presented itself so quickly. That was like magic."

"Magic?" Pamela purred in disbelief. "Alden, this surely means you haven't spent enough time in Virginia's horse country. Rumors and speculation fly just as fast there as they do on Wall Street. I imagine the TLM Group had reports on Orion for some time and were just waiting for an indication that I'd be interested in selling." And I did. And I have, she thought with a rush of excitement flooding her veins.

"Perhaps, Mrs. Ross," Alden Whittaker acknowledged with a somewhat stiff smile. The lawyer doubtless didn't appreciate being contradicted. "As you know, I've given instructions for the transfer of funds to be made immediately. You'll be able to verify the transfer by three o'clock this afternoon with your personal banker."

How lovely. "Well, I suppose that's it, then."

"Yes, except for notifying your ex-husband. We'll send him a letter by express mail informing him of the sale. Is there anything else I can assist you with before I fly back to New York?"

"No, thank you, Alden, what you've done is perfect. Thank you, and good-bye." Pamela's smile had turned into a low, throaty laugh as she stepped into the elevator. Yes, the letter would be waiting for Caleb when he got home, but she'd so enjoy giving him the news personally, face to face.

Leaving the law firm's offices in Washington's Columbia Square Building on Thirteenth Street, Pamela paused momentarily on the sidewalk, letting the anticipation build inside her. Cartier or Tiffany? she wondered. Which store would she prefer to begin spending an indecently large sum of money in, knowing that she'd have tons more after she finished shopping. She already knew what she'd buy: a rock. Surely a deal like this should be celebrated, commemorated with a really big, glittery stone. A stone for a stud.

She loved how it had been so quick, like that first, wild fuck she'd had with Caleb. But this time she'd screwed him without his even knowing it. And it was watertight, one-hundred proof legal, all there in fine print. It had only taken a word in her lawyer's ear, and within a week's time, she'd had an offer the size of which had caused a total meltdown of her insides.

Pamela felt great.

And Caleb was going to feel really bad.

23

*I*t was ridiculous and irrational, but nonetheless she'd
been nervous about meeting Caleb's friends, worrying
she'd be tongue-tied and awkward around them. But they'd
been wonderful.

Tod Harper was waiting for them at the equine center
run by the University of Pennsylvania veterinary school.
Lending a hand, he helped them unload Hot Lips from
the van, directing them to an empty box stall. Tod and
Caleb held the mare's halter while Cassie unwrapped her
bandages.

"So, Cassie, tell me about your mare. She's a lovely-
looking animal."

Cassie lifted her head to smile gratefully at Tod Harper.
U. Penn's reputation was such that some of the finest horses
in the country came to be treated here. It was awfully kind of
him to bother complimenting her on Hot Lips's looks.
Briefly, she described Hot Lips's habit of bucking and crow
hopping the first fifteen minutes someone rode her, as if she
were the toughest draw on the rodeo circuit.

"Caleb isn't sure if the injury happened while she was
at the track or after I bought her. Unfortunately, I'm afraid

that though she was getting better behaved with me, she was persisting in putting on quite a show."

"Well, I'd like to take a look at how the leg's healed. I've got the sonogram machine set up, ready, and waiting."

Cassie grabbed the mare's lead and followed Tod Harper to some nearby cross ties. She waited while he knelt down beside Hot Lips's foreleg. No one spoke as Tod carefully examined her. Finally he stood, patting the horse's shoulder before speaking.

"Seems to have healed just fine, Caleb. No swelling, no heat. And nothing turned up on the screen to worry about. So, it's safe to take the next step in her rehabilitation. As I'm sure you know, the aqua tank is terrific for tendon injuries."

"She's probably going to be quite a handful."

"Oh, we've had plenty of experience with hot-blooded thoroughbreds. Get racehorses in here all the time. Don't worry, she's going to get so much swimming, she'll calm down quick enough. When you come back to pick her up, you'll think you own a seahorse."

"That would be a new experience, all right." Cassie laughed as she unclipped her mare from the ties and led her back to the stall. "I'm mainly concerned about what to do when she's back on dry land. I'm afraid she'll reinjure herself as soon as I start riding her again."

"You say her antics continued pretty much unabated after she left the track?"

"Yes, unfortunately. She does eventually calm down, then she's a really nice mover."

"Well, I'm assuming you've had her thoroughly vetted, so it's not a physical ailment that's causing her discomfort and pain." Cassie nodded and he continued. "Then I suggest you treat it as a behavioral situation. You have to do something to interrupt the cycle. Change the pattern on her so the need to act up is eliminated."

"Do you mean like altering her schedule, or something?" Cassie asked, puzzled.

"Well, that would be a place to start. You'll need to look at what you're doing with her, analyzing it carefully. For instance, when's her turnout time in relation to when you ride her? Does she come back to the barn and sit around for a few hours, getting all revved up again? Maybe she needs a good, ten minute canter right off the bat when you get her into the ring. Unorthodox definitely, but ultimately better than having her buck and throw herself around 'til she's settled. It might be something absurdly simple that ends up calming her down. You'll just have to experiment."

"Thanks a lot, Tod. I should have thought of these things myself." From the look on Cassie's face, one would have thought Tod had just given her the moon.

Tod smiled. He appreciated the fact that she wasn't acting as if she was some know-it-all equestrian and he nothing but the doctor called in to administer the pills.

"Sometimes you need a little distance to be able to see the possible solution, that's all. It's nothing you couldn't have worked out for yourself," he added modestly.

"It does sound good, though, Tod. I wish I'd had that kind of advice for Cassie. What have you been reading lately, some new journal?"

"Hell, no, Cal. I've been reading Dr. Spock. Amazing how his ideas apply to all kinds of stuff."

They had a fun, rather disorganized dinner with Cassie and Caleb playing blocks with the two Harper children, while Tod barbecued ribs and Delia fixed an enormous salad. Because this was a special occasion, and "Uncle" Caleb was visiting, Delia had allowed the kids to stay up late. By the time dinner was on the table, the children were sprawled on the living room sofas, fast asleep.

"No, Delia don't get up, just tell me where the dessert is and I'll bring it in." Cassie was already clearing the dishes before the other woman could object.

Delia gave a rueful smile. "You've got me at a distinct disadvantage, Cassie. I haven't been able to move that fast in about five months." She glanced down at her swollen belly. "Though it's beginning to feel more like five years. There's a cake on the counter. Plates could be just about anywhere in that mess. "

"You really look terrific, Dee. In my humble opinion, you and Demi Moore have given motherhood a whole new meaning. And don't try to con us into believing you don't have Tod waiting on you hand and foot." Caleb leaned back in his chair, smiling fondly at her. "We all know he worships the ground you walk on."

"And rightly so." Delia teased back. "But it's not Tod who's the problem. It's those two rascals. An octopus would have a hard time picking up after these kids and instead I sit around feeling like a beached whale."

Cassie brought in the dessert and four plates she'd found in the cupboard. They sat around discussing kids, horses, and veterinary life as Caleb and Tod set about devouring the chocolate cake Delia had baked.

As the conversation started to wind down, Caleb stood and pushed back his chair. "Dee, that was delicious. Thank you. Tod, let me give you a hand carrying Joshua and Allie upstairs."

"Sounds good. Delia, sweet, go on and put your feet up. Caleb and I will clean up the dishes later."

"Whatever you say, honey," Delia agreed with alacrity, thrilled to escape the disaster in the kitchen. Her back was killing her; besides, she was dying for a chance to have a heart-to-heart chat with Cassie Miller.

"I like her, Cal," Tod whispered in the darkened bedroom, gently depositing his sleeping daughter on the lower bed of the bunkbed she was sharing with her older brother for the night.

"Yeah. I guess I do, too."

"Yeah? Glad to hear it. I was beginning to worry you were suffering from terminal stupidity when it came to women."

Caleb snorted in the darkness. Tod grinned and continued. "I've noticed she's not too hard on the eyes, either."

"Yeah, I thought you might."

"But what really astonishes me is that she seems to be, uh, interested in you."

"Those faculty meetings you attend must be dulling your wits. A couple of years ago you used to be kind of sharp, and a hell of a lot funnier."

Cassie eventually crept upstairs to the brightly painted bedroom, decorated with a wild kingdom of stuffed animals, and large, plastic containers bursting with toys, crayons, and children's books. She was feeling as if she'd just survived an interrogation that would have made the Secret Service proud. Perhaps that was a slight exaggeration. That Delia Harper had asked and probed, ever so delicately, ever so kindly, about practically every aspect of Cassie's life was not. Ordinarily, Cassie would have closed up like a clam, but she found herself talking freely enough, mainly because she sensed how much Delia and Tod cared for Caleb.

Delia did her fair share of talking, too. From her description, Caleb began to sound like some kind of latter-day saint, a position to which Cassie was certain Caleb did not aspire. But she was more than happy to listen to her sing the praises of the man with whom, Cassie would admit only to herself, she was falling head over heels in love.

She'd been tossing and squirming, trying to find a comfortable position on the narrow single bed when a light knock sounded on the door. Rising, she went to open it. Caleb was there, his tall form backlit by the hall light.

Cassie was wearing a T-shirt that was a couple of sizes

too big, with the words Just Do It across her chest. In one swift, sweeping glance, his eyes took in her long slim legs, her bare toes curling into the weave of the wall-to-wall carpet. The tantalizing thought crossed his mind that he, too, could just do it, just back her up, 'til the backs of her knees brushed against the twin bed frame and they were lying together, limbs all atangle. Then he could make really slow, quiet love to her all night, swallowing her moans of pleasure, careful not to disturb the sleeping Harpers.

"Don't, Caleb." Her voice was husky. Pleading.

"Don't what?"

"Don't look at me like that."

"Like what?"

She stamped her barefoot with impatience. "Cut it out. You know perfectly well how you were looking . . . like, like I'm that fourth slice of chocolate cake, or something. No way, not with our hosts in the room next door."

"Ah, Slim. I'm sure you're better than chocolate cake."

"Fine, then. Appetizer, main course. Whatever. You've had enough."

"That's where you are absolutely wrong, Cassie sweet. I'm beginning to think I could never have enough." He held up his hands to stop her words of protest. "All right, all right, I get the point. I just came in to say good night. Honest."

"Good night," she said softly.

He stepped across the threshold and their lips met and clung. He lifted his head and gave her an enchantingly crooked smile. "Better go before I'm too famished. Sweet dreams, Slim."

Cassie was deeply touched by the spontaneous hug Delia gave her the next morning as they were all gathered outside the house, Cassie and Caleb ready to head back down to Virginia.

"Make sure you come with Caleb when your mare's all

set to go. It's nice to have another woman around to balance things out."

"I'll try," Cassie promised. Turning to Tod, she said, "Thank you so much for putting me up. It was really great to meet you."

"We were delighted to have you, Cassie. I'll keep you posted on how Hot Lips is coming along. Caleb tells me you'll be riding in the Hampton Classic in August. Good Luck. I've always loved that show. If we can work out the logistics, you might be able to pick up your mare on the way back down to Five Oaks. Or we can keep her a few extra weeks if your schedule's too crazy."

"Thanks so much. For everything."

Tod turned to his old friend and extended his hand. Caleb grasped it. "Good to see you, Cal. Remember, we want you back real soon."

"You got it." Caleb turned to Delia standing beside him and drew her into his arms for a warm hug. "Delia, take care of yourself. I'm looking forward to meeting the new addition to the Harper family."

"So am I! You take care, too. Don't work too hard."

Then Caleb had hugged Joshua and little Allie, both decked out in matching Orioles' sweatshirts, a present Caleb had given them the night before.

They rolled into the drive of Five Oaks by midafternoon.

The drive back had flown by with Caleb and Cassie listening to the radio, laughing, shooting the breeze. It had been so fun and easy. Cassie felt truly happy, a giddy joy bubbling up inside her. As if she were a teenager out with her first love. Thinking, just maybe, that her love might be returned.

"I'm going to find Hank, see how everything went with Midnight. We had Gaspar cover her yesterday," Caleb offered as they walked together toward the main barn.

"I was planning on checking how Topper and Pip are doing, maybe letting them out in the bottom pasture if Raff can spare it. Then I thought I'd take Arrow and Silverspoon out for a short spin." Because of the trip, she'd cut her exercise schedule in half, giving both Orion and Limelight the day off, but the younger horses still needed a workout.

"Sounds good." Caleb slowed his steps to a halt and stood in the driveway, his legs slightly apart, his hands thrust into the front pockets of his Levi's. Startled, Cassie turned to look at him inquisitively.

He cleared his throat. "Uh, I was wondering whether you'd like to go out to dinner with me, maybe see a movie."

"Tonight?"

"Yeah, tonight. Please, if you don't feel like it, don't say you have to wash your hair. I swear, I'll never recover from the humiliation."

She laughed, remembering the first time she'd said that to him. "I'd like to, honestly. Yes," she repeated, nodding her head, her eyes shining. "Yes, I'd like that."

"Good. Great. How does seven sound to you?"

"Fine."

"Okay, then." His smile was boyish and charming, his hands still balled in his pockets. "See you, Slim."

Now she knew what they meant by the expression *walking ten feet off the ground.* She felt as if she might literally float away.

He'd asked her out on a date! She laughed and hugged herself, not caring if someone from the stable should see her and think her completely off her rocker. She had to get a hold of herself before she rode Arrow and Silverspoon, though. Otherwise, she'd be floating all right, but she'd land with a hard thud.

*   *   *

Caleb was grinning like a sap.

She'd said yes!

Okay, so it was only dinner and a movie, but maybe, just maybe, if Lady Luck were smiling at him, it might blossom into something more. God, it seemed as if from the moment he'd laid eyes on Cassie, he'd been in a constant state of arousal. Somebody had to take pity on him soon.

"Hey, Caleb. How'd the trip go? Hot Lips behave herself?"

"Hank. Glad I found you. The trip was great. That place is something else. Amazing facilities. Hot Lips did fine on the trip, too. They'll be starting therapy on her today."

"Cassie must be real pleased about that. Where is she, by the way?"

"She's doing some stuff with the ponies, then she was planning on riding the four-year-olds. I was hunting you down to find out how it went with Midnight and Gaspar."

"Not as smoothly as your trip, I'm afraid. Come with me over to the barn. Midnight's got a nasty cut on her. It didn't need stitches, but I'd like to have you check her just the same."

"Let me get my bag from the truck."

"Okay, meet me at her stall. By the way, I got some other bad news."

"What?"

"Pamela's called about four times since you left yesterday. Unfortunately, I lost my temper at the fourth call and stupidly let it slip that you were coming back some time this afternoon. Sorry about that, Caleb."

"Damn it to hell!" Caleb cursed heatedly. "Doesn't that woman know what divorced means? No, it's all right, Hank. It's not your fault. I can handle her. That is, if I can't find a good enough hiding place."

*   *   *

"There's not any serious damage, the cuts are all superficial, except for this gash on her shoulder here. I'm going to clean it up a little more for good measure and douse it with antiseptic powder. She'll have a scar, though, Hank."

"Yeah, and such a pretty lady," Hank said regretfully.

Caleb worked slowly and carefully, cleaning the ugly red flesh on the broodmare's right shoulder.

"Did Gaspar do his job?"

"Yeah, though she put up a fuss at first. Struck out at him with her hooves a couple of times. That's when she got hurt. We tried to separate them, to check her for injuries, but before we could, he'd mounted her."

"I hope it did the trick. If it hasn't, we'll have to wait for her next heat. I don't want her in the pen again until that wound is healed."

"We'll keep our fingers crossed."

"And how did Gaspar come out of this? I'd better go see what shape he's in, too."

"He looked okay to me when I checked him afterwards, but you've seen him in action. He's always so happy after he's serviced a mare. Like the cock of the walk." Hank grinned, shaking his head.

"I can understand that. Probably wouldn't have felt it if Midnight's hooves did make contact, the poor bastard was so excited. You want to come along?"

"No." Hank shook his head. "I got some phone calls to make." He brightened as a thought occurred to him. "Hey, maybe if the phone's busy for a while, Pamela will give up and leave you alone."

"There's always the hope."

How he'd ever found her voice sexy, he couldn't imagine. Right now, hearing her call out, "Caleb, are you in here?" in that slightly breathless trill was as irritating as fingernails raking down a chalkboard.

For a second he seriously debated ducking into one of

the stallion's stalls, but discarded the idea quickly enough.
First of all, it was bloody dangerous. Most of the stallions
were well-mannered, but getting the shit kicked out of him
wasn't totally out of the question, especially if the stallion
couldn't figure out what the hell Caleb was doing there.
Second, it wouldn't get rid of Pamela. She'd just lie in wait
for him like some venomous spider.

He didn't respond to her call, knowing she'd see him
soon enough. Instead, he entered Gaspar's stall and
brought the stallion out, hooking him up to the closest
cross ties. The click of her heels sounded against the
cement floor.

Annoyed, he turned to face her. "What is it, Pamela?
I'm a little busy right now."

She smiled that slow, practiced smile. He stared back at
her, his expression one of total boredom. She was dressed
to the nines. Tight white pants, probably one size too
small, no, make that two, and a vividly printed silk shirt he
assumed was purchased from Hermes, Versace, or one of
those places. Wherever she'd gotten it, she obviously
hadn't thought it was worth buttoning, and had instead
simply tied it under her breasts, the tails tickling her bare
mid-rif. Nestled in the valley of her breasts, an obscenely
large diamond rubbed her flesh. Jesus. He couldn't even
imagine what she'd done for that piece of jewelry. He eyed
her with distaste. Did she really think he cared that she was
braless? How utterly pathetic.

"Caleb, I must talk with you about Orion. I tried calling
your office to find out when you'd be returning, and that
beastly secretary wouldn't tell me a thing. The lying hag. I
was forced to call Hank, who's *always* disliked me, and he
kept brushing me off, as if I have no right to speak to you."

"He's absolutely right. Let me explain this to you once
more. We are divorced. If you want to reach me, why don't
you use that lawyer of yours?"

Pamela smiled, "Caleb, you don't really want that . . ."

"Look, Pamela, whatever it is, I don't want to hear it. Will you please leave now, I need to examine this horse."

"No. I have to talk to you. The contract for Orion you signed states that . . ."

"States that you have the right to bleed me each month for more years than most people pay for their homes. What else is new?" he asked, shrugging his shoulders and turning to the injured horse, refusing to pay Pamela any more attention. He figured she'd last about five minutes before she went away. Pamela hated being ignored.

Blocking her from his mind, Caleb set to work, his large hands moving over the stallion's body, probing gently for any sign of pain. The horse flinched, shifting restlessly, as Caleb's fingers moved carefully over the horse's deep chest. Caleb could feel where the flesh was swollen and bruised.

"She got you good, didn't she, big guy?" Caleb murmured softly. He bent to grasp the stallion's leg, closing around the knee joint and pulling the leg forward and up, checking for any sign of deeper tissue damage. From behind, he heard Pamela's voice cry out. Startled, he lowered Gaspar's hoof back to the ground.

"Ow! Caleb, I think I've got something in my eye. Ow! Please, can you look at it?"

He bit back an oath, and reluctantly turned to see what his ex-wife wanted now.

She was glad she'd made the decision to ride Arrow and Silverspoon lightly today. The thought of going out with Caleb tonight had her too distracted to do more than exercise them on the flat and over a few low fences. Just enough to have them paying attention to her for a little while. Just enough to make her feel as if she weren't a total delinquent.

After sitting immobile in the Jeep for so many hours, the exercise had loosened her up, too. Now she was looking forward to indulging in a long, hot bath. First, though, a quick stop at the stallions' barn, so she could say hi to Orion, see whether the stallion had missed her.

"I can't see anything in your eye, Pamela. Blink a few times and I'm sure it will go away."

"But there's *something* there! Look closer."

Caleb angled his head once more to stare at his ex-wife's mascara'd eye. His hands framed her face, holding it steady, finding nothing. He gritted his teeth. "Listen. There's nothing there. Just blink your goddamn eye."

Pamela smiled, her lips parting to reveal her white, polished teeth. She blinked. Her body shivered in surprised delight. He could feel it brushing against him. He hadn't realized they were standing so close.

"Oh, it's gone. You were right. Thank you." Blinking rapidly, she said coyly, "I'd almost forgotten how sweet you can be." And pressed a quick, unexpected kiss against his lips. Before he could shove her away, she stepped back. "Well, I guess we can chat later. I've got to run." She lifted her hand to his jaw, the key chain to her Lamborghini dangling from her finger. It dropped to the ground with a soft, metallic clink. "Oops. How clumsy."

As if in slow motion, she dropped to her knees in front of him. Then suddenly, as if she'd lost her balance, hands reached out, closing around Caleb's belt buckle. Pamela looked up and smiled.

A gasp of pain.

Seconds too late, the whole charade became sickeningly clear in Caleb's mind. While he had been busy with Gaspar, Pamela must have heard the sound of footsteps approaching. Whipping his head around, he was just in time to see Cassie running out of the barn. Running as if she couldn't get away fast enough. He made to follow her, but Pamela stopped him, her nails digging like vicious claws into his thighs.

Cold fury washed over him. Reaching down, he grabbed the silk fabric clinging to her shoulders and hauled her to her feet.

"You deceitful witch. You set me up, didn't you?"

"Oh, heavens, was that your girlfriend, Caleb?" Her voice sweet as candy, her concern equally artificial. "I thought she looked familiar, even from this distance."

Caleb shook her like a terrier would a rat. "You *knew* she was watching, didn't you?"

"No, I didn't," she lied. "But I'm glad she walked in. Now she'll know you're not hers. Anyway, you always loved my mouth on you, remember, Caleb? Ow! You're hurting me!"

Pamela cried out as Caleb shook her again. This time fear threaded her voice. "Let go of me or I'll have you charged with assault. Then you'll really be in a jam. Stuck in jail, no girlfriend, no stallion. What a pity."

"What the hell are you taking about?" Caleb demanded, furiously, aware of dread flooding him.

Her face flushed, she laughed. "Oh, Caleb, I'm afraid you made some very costly, very stupid mistakes. You and Hank should have been a little more careful when you hired Cassie Miller. Without my express agreement, you violated the terms of our contract. It's all there, take a look when you get home. And believe me, you don't stand a chance in court. No, the only thing that can save your horse is me. I have a buyer all lined up. All I have to do is say the word and you no longer have a stallion to play horsey with . . . Of course, I could change my mind." Pamela's eyes locked with Caleb's as she took a step forward, her body pressing against his. Her nipples hard with excitement.

Her lids lowered like dark shutters as her lips moved closer to his. "Get rid of Cassie Miller and be real nice to me, just the way I like, and maybe I'll forget the whole thing."

A hair's breath away, Caleb pushed her back, leaving Pamela teetering to regain her balance. He looked at her, his face etched in stone. "You seem confused, Pamela. You're the one whose talents lie in whoring. And sad to say, you've sorely overestimated your charms. Damned if I can understand what I ever saw in you. But I thank God good old Ross came along, and took you off of my hands."

"Why you bastard," she cried, venom flashing in her eyes. "And isn't it a shame I twisted the truth a bit just now. A little fib, really. News flash for you, lover: I *already* sold your beloved stallion this afternoon. You can kiss your pathetic dreams good-bye."

Pamela made to spin on her high heels and leave, but Caleb was too quick for her. He grabbed her, his fingers crushing the silk of her shirt as he hauled her off her feet, lifting until her toes brushed the cement.

"Pamela, you're a nasty piece of trash. You may have sold Orion and there may be nothing I can do to stop it. But I swear, if you ever come near me again, I'm going to drag your ass in court and slap you with a restraining order."

"You wouldn't dare. They'd never believe anything you said about me."

"What about stalking, Pamela? I'm pretty certain I could line up witnesses around the block to prove it."

"You wouldn't dare. It'd never stand up in court," she repeated, this time with less conviction as she stared at the terrifying expression on his face.

"I wouldn't put it to the test, if I were you. Moreover, I bet Ross might believe me all too easily. And there'd go your gravy train. It's funny how word about your kind of sick behavior always spreads like wildfire through a town this small. Now get the hell out of my sight. Forever."

*H*e found her just where he'd imagined, huddled in her old pony's stall, bawling her eyes out. Curled into a tight ball of misery, she looked so forlorn, without even the presence of her pony to comfort her.

He laid a hand on her shoulder, his heart aching at the thought that he'd involuntarily caused her tears.

She flinched, recognizing his touch. "Get away from me. How dare you touch me."

"Cassie, I need to explain . . ."

"I said, *get away!*" she cried, her face streaming tears. "How *could* you let her? I thought you . . ."

"Wait a minute," he interrupted, bending low to bring his face close to hers. "You don't mean to tell me you fell for that act of Pamela's?"

"Dear God, what do you expect me to think, after what I saw back there?" she shot back. "Just how stupid do you think I am, Caleb? That I don't know what's going on when a woman's down on her knees, unbuckling a man's belt? Maybe I should have stuck around to make sure, is that what you mean? Then I wouldn't have missed the final

act!" She wrenched her shoulder free from his grasp, sobbing uncontrollably.

Urgently, he pulled her back, forcing her to look at him
once more. "Cassie, listen to me, please. She was playing a
game. She likes games. Especially those kinds. It wouldn't
have taken her a second to decide to amuse herself when
she saw you walk into the barn. She likes to cause trouble."
As willful and devastatingly destructive as a tornado.

"I don't believe you." The stark, anguished words hung
in the air between them.

She dropped her head, refusing to see.

He rocked back on his heels, the pain of her words slicing through him with the ease of a knife.

Slowly, anger began to grow inside him again, fueled by
the gross injustice of it all, by Pamela's treachery, by
Cassie's lack of faith. His voice changed, still low, but now
laced with bitterness, each syllable coldly uttered. "So, Slim.
You saw it all. Saw quite enough to realize that I've just
been amusing myself, trying to talk you into my bed. But
sick, horny, moral deviant that I am, I decide to have my ex-
wife give me a blow job in the middle of my partner's barn,
'cause waiting around for you to drop your pants was getting
a mite boring. Sure. Sounds good. But hell, who knows,
with the recent progress I was making with you, I might just
have been able to score twice in one day."

His hand reached up, grasping her chin, forcing her to
meet his gaze. "Tell me. Is that what you really think of
me, Cassie?"

Her gaze slid away.

He dropped his hand. He rose, looking at her huddled
form with bleak detachment. It was a damned shame he
loved her so much.

"Yeah, well, I'm outta here. Have a nice life."

Hours could have passed as she lay crumpled in the corner of the stall, crying, castigating herself with Caleb's

words, repeating them to herself over and over again. Each time coupled with a different memory of Caleb to torment her. His laughter, his teasing seductions, always giving pleasure as much as receiving it. The incredible patience he'd shown to the twins, to her. As each memory assailed her, the question of whether she could have unjustly accused Caleb haunted her. And if so, how in the world could she win his forgiveness?

More than a full fifteen minutes passed before Melissa could begin to comprehend what was wrong with Cassie. She'd assumed the worst. Her heart had pounded with frantic worry as she fired out questions. Cassie's incoherent and disjointed words, further garbled by her tears made the answers almost impossible to decipher. But the violent shake of Cassie's head when she'd asked one of her questions eased Melissa's fear somewhat. At least no one had died.

It was only when Melissa caught the words *Pamela and Caleb* that a glimmer of understanding dawned. Frowning, she made a noise of sympathy and rose to fill a glass with cold water at the kitchen sink.

"Here, Cassie. Drink this very slowly. It'll help. And don't forget to breathe."

Melissa sat back down in the chair opposite Cassie's and waited for the tears to subside. The girl looked a wreck, a miserable wreck. She shook her head, already suspecting the gist of what she was about to hear. She listened in silence, placing a hand over Cassie's, watching the tears begin again as Cassie repeated Caleb's parting words.

"Shh, now, it's all right," Melissa soothed, praying she spoke the truth. Suddenly angry, she banged her fist hard against the top of the table, causing Cassie to start.

"That blasted Pamela! I have never been so tempted to do violence to someone before, and I am *not* a violent person! I wish she'd get out of town. Move to Hollywood or

Miami and cat around there. That woman has been nothing but trouble for Caleb. Still . . ." she sighed, the sound causing Cassie to grow quiet, awaiting Melissa's next words with a mixture of despair and apprehension. "Still, Cassie, as bad as it looked, you should have trusted him. Do you really think Caleb would act that way, that he would treat you so callously? Or me? Or Hank? Don't you see how he looks at you?"

"I know, or I thought I was beginning to know. But when I saw them together, it seemed so, so carnal . . . God, she's so beautiful. And I just freaked. I couldn't think straight, because the only thing in my mind was the two of them together. I guess that's what she intended. Oh, Melissa, what should I do?" she cried, feeling the hopelessness of the situation.

"You've got to talk to him," Melissa replied matter-of-factly. "He must be terribly hurt, I don't think you realize how important you've become. I'm not even certain he's aware of it. You've got to hope he can forgive you. 'Cause, honey, you need to remember, his pride and honor were about all he had left after his marriage to Pamela. You did a major number on both of them today."

25

There were crickets chirping in the night air. The sound was incessant, violent. To her, it seemed an ominous sound, echoing the terrible fear in her heart.

She raised her arm, hesitated and lowered it again. For the third time. Stalling, as she'd been stalling for the past two hours.

Melissa had driven her directly home, making sure to instruct Cassie to take a bath and pull herself together, and not to skimp on the makeup; Cassie wasn't exactly looking her best right now. A brandy might be a good idea, too.

Cassie hadn't dared to glance in the direction of Caleb's house when she returned, so she'd entered the larger, empty one with no one to greet her, not even the dog, Finnegan.

It was a horrible shock when she turned on the bathroom light and caught her reflection in the mirror. Medusa couldn't have been more petrifying a sight. Was that really her?

So she'd sat in the steaming bubble bath for what seemed an age, a cucumber mask covering her face, until she could have easily been mistaken for a stewed prune gone moldy.

Next, she went for the bracing, ice-cold shower, scrubbing her shivering body until it tingled, shampooing her hair countless more times than even the label recommended. Cassie knew enough popular psychology to recognize her behavior as falling into some kind of obsessive or compulsive category, but she was filled with the desperate need to wash her self away.

To emerge new, clean, and strong.

And at least she didn't look so incredibly awful any more.

Another hour slipped by as she lotioned and perfumed herself, then dried her hair, making it shine and fall about her in golden waves. She took a barrette and clipped a few strands back, allowing the rest to fall down her back.

She dressed with seduction in mind. But also to please herself, determined that she be armed with as many weapons and as much self-confidence at her disposal as possible in her battle to win Caleb back.

Because she was terrified she'd lost him.

This time, she tried a different approach. Closing her eyes, she took a deep breath, picturing Caleb's smiling face as she lifted her hand and rapped her knuckles hard on the wooden door. In the seconds that followed, she held her breath, willing him to answer her knock.

She knew he was home. The windows of the converted carriage house were illuminated with a faint glow, and every now and then, she caught a note of music that escaped and drifted out into the evening air.

The door opened with a jerk. Caleb stood before her. Her eyes widened involuntarily as she took in his appearance. Disheveled was the first word that crossed her mind. Drunk was the second. She swallowed hard.

He was shirtless. Half hysterically, Cassie realized she'd

never even seen him without a shirt before, simply learned the sculpted contours of his body through her touch. What a sight she'd been deprived of. He was so very beautiful. Perfectly proportioned, lean, honed muscle. Her eyes traveled down his broad chest to where a narrow line of dark hair descended, disappearing behind the fabric of his jeans. Her eyes flew upwards, shying away from the sight of that top button, and the raw memories of this afternoon.

Color flooded her cheeks. How many seconds had she stood there, raptly cataloging Caleb's assets? God, she had to pull herself together. She forced her eyes to meet his.

Caleb's face was a blank mask, his eyes equally unrevealing. His tall, muscular body planted just behind the threshold, not close, yet clearly barring her from entering his home.

"Go away."

"Caleb." Her voice trembled, so she swallowed and began again. "Caleb, please. I need to talk with you."

"Go away. I'm not nearly as drunk as I want to be, and you're interrupting."

The door slammed shut in her face, hard enough for her to feel the woosh of air following it cool her heated cheeks.

Unshed tears stung the back of her eyes as she stepped forward and knocked again. Nothing. Damn him, why wouldn't he open the door? Frustrated, she banged harder.

From inside the house, the music playing on the stereo grew louder, the notes mocking her in their clarity. Fine, so he intended to drown out the sound of her knocking with music, just as he intended to drown his hurt and anger with a bottle of whiskey.

Well, desperate times called for desperate measures. Cassie refused to give in to despair. If Caleb wouldn't invite her through his front door, she'd get in another way.

He sank deeper into the cushion of the large black leather chair in his living room, sipping slowly, letting the amber liquid fill his mouth before it slid down, like a river of fire, into his belly. He supposed she'd gone away. Of course, he'd known she would come. She'd had to. That was the way these things worked, right? So she'd come and now she could just leave him alone.

He drank again. *Shit.* He realized that he'd be the one who'd have to leave. Had to get out of here. He'd call the hospital tomorrow and tell them he was taking an early vacation. What did it matter if it screwed things up for a while. He was the head partner, after all. They could deal with it until he felt like coming back.

He reached forward, carefully, studiously pouring more whiskey into his empty glass, his long legs stretched out next to the bottle. His bare foot brushed the sharp edge of crisp white letter paper, dated today, informing him of Orion's sale, transfer of ownership effective immediately, to a private group with the acronym TLM. He knew he'd never need to read the letter again. The printed words were etched like acid in his mind, which no amount of alcohol could wash away.

Leaning back, he stared at his toes, not seeing them. Yeah, he had to go away. Didn't matter where the fuck he went. Didn't matter at all, just as long as he was gone. He'd drive to Washington National and hop a plane to God knows where.

No way was he going to stay here, near her.

Seeing her. Wanting her despite it all. Wanting her despite the fact that he knew it was over. Over before it had even begun.

All he had to do now was drink until he passed out. Simple enough. Hopefully, he'd be so sick tomorrow morning he wouldn't even be able to remember his own name, let alone hers.

Van Morrison's *Moondance* album came on. Perverse, masochistic bastard that he was, he'd added that CD to the stack and now the song came back to torture him with memories of Cassie, so very beautiful, standing next to his stallion in the dusty light of the barn. Looking like an angel. Killing him.

He closed his eyes.

Cassie crept around the perimeter of the house, fully aware she'd have made a lousy cat burglar, feeling increasingly foolish with each passing second. She hadn't found a single entry she could breach. All the windows she'd passed so far had been too high, except for the enormous picture window in the back. No matter how drunk he was, she doubted she'd be able to climb in through there without Caleb noticing her pretty quick.

No, she had to get in without his seeing her. That way, he'd have a much harder time throwing her out—she hoped. Rounding the corner as stealthily as possible, she nevertheless whispered a fierce, "Yes!" in triumph as she spied a wide, rectangular window, a fraction above shoulder height. She pressed her face against the screen. The interior was pitch black, offering no clue to what room she was peering into. But at least the window was open and was a new one at that, sliding horizontally, rather than up and down.

Bless Caleb's parents for renovating the house and doing the windows, too.

The screen wouldn't budge. She pressed, tried sliding it, banged as hard as she dared. Nothing!

Her head pounding with frustration, she dropped it forward heavily against the dratted screen, pulling her hair. Inspiration struck. Reaching around, she fumbled with the metal clasp at the back of her head. Releasing it, she ran her index finger along its edge and set to work.

He was sprawled in an oversized black leather chair. From the soft glow of the standing lamp in the corner, she could make out the bottle of whiskey, and his bare feet, crossed one over the other, resting next to it. She stepped closer. His head was angled up toward the ceiling, his neck pressed back against the edge of the chair.

Another step now, near enough now to see his face. His eyes were closed. Oh, no! Panic shot through her. Please God, not asleep!

Alarm bolstered her courage. She cleared her throat. "Caleb, I need to speak with you. Please, can you look at me?"

He heard her voice, but didn't bother to open his eyes. Anyone who'd drunk as much as he would be hearing things. He let himself drift away once more into Van the Man's "Mystic."

A hand shook his shoulder, jostling his eyes open. "Caleb, you've got to wake up. It's me, Cassie. I need to talk with you."

He stared at her in silence, not quite sure whether he was delusional or just dreaming. Not that he particularly cared one way or the other. He closed his eyes.

She shook him again, more roughly this time. Annoyed, he brushed her hand off. She felt real, but then again, he was real drunk. Maybe she'd leave him alone if he told her to go away.

"No, I won't. Caleb, I'm really sorry I hurt you. I should have believed you. It wasn't your fault."

He wasn't listening. He was trying to solve a really big puzzle. Front door was locked. He was sure of it.

"Go away," he repeated, just to see if it might work this time.

"No. I won't leave until you've forgiven me."

"Fine, I forgive you. Go away."

"No. I need to talk to you."

"How the hell did you get in here? Front door's locked."

"I know. I had to climb in through your bathroom window. Caleb, I'm really sorry, but I broke your screen."

He was listening now. He stared at her, blinking owlishly. "Say that again."

She took a deep breath and let it out slowly, striving for patience. This conversation wasn't going at all the way she'd imagined it. "I ripped your screen when I came in through the bathroom window. I'll be happy to pay for it, but I really needed to . . ."

His laughter erupted, loud, uncontrolled. His knees closed about him like a folding chair, as he wrapped his arms around his middle. Caleb's paroxysms of mirth continued as Cassie stood there, wishing she weren't in love with such a total fool, a drunk one at that.

Finally, he managed to speak. Laughter still shaking his voice, "You . . . you came in through the bathroom window. God Almighty, Slim, that is just about the most romantic thing I've ever heard." He sang a line from the Beatles' tune. Horribly off-key. Succeeding only in setting himself off again, until wiping the tears from his eyes, he stood.

Holding a hand in front of him, he ordered, "Wait here. This I've got to see."

The first step was more of a lurch than anything. Then, recovering his balance, he headed off in the direction of the bathroom.

Yup. She'd really done it. He looked at the neatly torn screen hanging like a flag on a windless day, then at the dirty shoe prints soiling his white porcelain bathtub. He grinned. Probably had no idea where she'd end up when she hauled herself through. Pretty gutsy of her, he'd give her that much credit.

What the hell, maybe he was being too harsh on her. If the tables had been turned and he'd caught Cassie in such a compromising situation, finding some man kneeling with his hands up her skirt, would he have believed her, never suffering even a moment of doubt and hurt?

He turned to the sink and yanked the cold water on full blast, plugging the basin drain. Water rose quickly until he twisted the knob shut before plunging in his head. The cold water hurt, stinging him like needles, making him gasp, spewing water. Still, he continued dunking his head repeatedly, feeling the water slosh about his feet, the tiles underneath him turning slick as an ice rink.

Finally, he grabbed a bath towel and buried his face in it, rubbing briskly. He brushed his teeth, then pulled open the medicine cabinet door. He grabbed a bottle of aspirin, popping two, not really thinking they'd do any good, but figuring it was better than nothing. Then he reached for the bottle of Listerine and poured about half of it into his mouth, gargling, swishing, spitting. He closed the top, shutting the medicine cabinet once more. It wasn't worth the bother looking at his reflection. He couldn't look like anything but shit.

She was afraid he'd gone and passed out in the bathroom or wherever he'd stumbled off to. Shouldn't she go in and make sure he was okay, wasn't lying concussed, perhaps bleeding on the floor? She dropped her head against the coolness of the window pane, staring blindly out at the trees shimmering in the night breeze. How could this day have started out so differently? She'd been so happy a mere twelve hours ago. Funny how a world could change so quickly. She should be used to it by now, but she kept getting caught off guard. If only . . .

She turned, sensing he'd come into the room. She spoke quickly, determined he at least hear her apology. She had to try to make it right.

"Caleb, I know how much I hurt you this afternoon . . ."

"It's okay, Cassie, I forgive you."

"That's what you said before. But you didn't mean it." Not believing he meant it now.

He smiled. "No, I didn't mean it. I just wanted you gone. I was pretty drunk. Probably still am. But this time, I do mean it. I understand how you might have thought . . ."

"No, no. I was being horribly unfair. It's just," her voice dropped. "It's just that I was . . . jealous." Her voice faded into the quiet of the room.

He stepped forward, unsure. He moved close, close enough to read her lips in the half-light if necessary. Close enough to feel the whisper of her words on his flesh.

He might have been talking to a queen, his tone was so polite, his words so careful. "Excuse me, but would you remind repeating what you said? I must still have water in my ears." His hand lifted to his damp hair in explanation.

Her heart thundered inside her chest like a violent storm. She drew in a calming breath. Her words came out, a hushed confession. "I was jealous. I wanted to be her, to be every woman you'd ever looked at, ever touched. I wanted to be the only one."

He closed his eyes. The power of her words sinking deep into his heart. Healing him. Enriching him beyond his wildest dreams. He cleared his throat. He had to tell her.

"Cassie, there's more. She sold Orion."

"What? She sold Orion?" Her voice, though quiet, cracked with disbelief.

"Yes. I don't know what will happen now."

She was silent, absorbing the implications of what he'd told her before speaking, forming the words carefully. "She sold him."

"Yes. I'm sorry."

"She sold him. Oh, Caleb, I'm so sorry." Then, "But that means she's gone."

"Yes."

The slow smile transformed her face. "She's gone, so . . . it's just you and me. Alone. Together . . ."

His breath lodged somewhere in his chest as he heard her repeat the words he'd spoken to her that first night, so long ago. In concert they moved toward each other, stopping mere inches away. He felt the shift of her body, her hands reaching out to bridge that small gap. Seeking, caressing the ridge of muscle and bone that was his ribcage. He felt her cool, soft lips press against his heated flesh, felt the space that separated their bodies as intolerable. His arms circled about her, bringing her where he needed her for . . . forever.

There was no hurry.

They allowed their hands and mouths to roam freely, Cassie's clothes slipping one by one to the floor accompanied by the sound of soft whispers and sighs.

She stood naked before him, a pale pool of silk lapping at her feet.

He let his eyes drink in the perfection of her body. The long, delicious length of her legs, crowned by the triangle of short, golden curls at the apex of her thighs. Up past the shadowed indentation of her belly button, to the breasts he'd dreamed of, the rosy pink nipples tight with arousal, with desire for him. The sight of her was far more potent than anything he had consumed in his life.

"Take off your earrings."

Cassie's eyes widened. "Why?" she asked, her voice a mere whisper as she lifted suddenly clumsy fingers to her lobes.

"Because I want to be able to taste every inch of you."

Her body began to tremble.

The earrings dropped, sinking into the silken pile, forgotten, as Caleb swept her into his arms and carried her to his bedroom. Slowly, he lowered her near the foot of his king-size bed. Her eyes slid from him to take in the enormous bed, returning quickly, shyly, a slight flush staining her face.

"Shh, shh . . ." He soothed, his hand stroking the golden waves of her hair. "We've got all the time in the world."

"I know. It's silly to be nervous," she replied quietly, giving him a tremulous smile. She wasn't about to tell him how grossly inadequate she felt. What if she didn't please him? She'd only had one lover, Brad, and truth be told, she wasn't so sure she'd enjoyed the experience all that much. Anyway, it had been so long ago, she'd probably forgotten how.

Instead, she blurted out an entirely different concern, one that was becoming a huge preoccupation. "Caleb, did you know your pants are still on?"

He laughed low in his throat. "Yeah, I thought that might help keep things a bit more under control. Would you like me to take them off?"

She nodded solemnly, her eyes as wide as the ocean. Smiling, Caleb pressed his lips against her brow, making no move to do so. Instead, he kept kissing her, rediscovering the sensitive places along the slender column of her neck, behind the delicate shell of her ear. His hands moved leisurely over her breasts, lifting, squeezing, his thumbs passing back and forth across the sensitive buds of her nipples.

She moaned, a low helpless sound that drove him wild. Intoxicated from the sensations he aroused, her hands moved restlessly, kneading muscles, testing flesh, dropping lower. Finally, his hand sought hers, clasping it, guiding her to the front of his jeans. Holding her there.

"Cassie, sweet, do you know what you do to me? Touch me. Feel what you do to me. Please."

Her breath stalled in her throat as her fingers did his bidding, slipping between the folds of denim, releasing each metal button, one after the other.

Pausing.

Easing the fabric wider. Feeling the heavy pounding of his heart against her forehead as she pressed against his chest. Mesmerized, she watched the progress of her hands. As he waited.

She released him. He sprang into her hands, hot and hard. Entranced, she glided her hands along his shaft, learning him, delighting in the wonder of him, her previous fears eclipsed by the sheer masculine beauty offered to her.

Sweat beaded his brow, each muscle in his body tight, throbbing with need. She was destroying him, her hands an instrument of pleasure so intense it bordered on pain. He couldn't last if she kept this up much longer. His hands gripped her elbows, squeezing, momentarily stilling her hands.

His voice, rough with need, pleaded. "Cassie, I'm sorry . . . But, I can't take much more . . . I need you now. Let me come inside you."

His words thrilled her. In response, her fingers flexed, testing, and hearing the hiss of his indrawn breath, she exulted in her power over him. Her eyes lifted to his dark glittering ones, her small smile of satisfaction bewitching.

"I'm glad," she said simply, rising on her toes to kiss the corner of his mouth.

With his need spinning dangerously out of control, Caleb hated waiting even a second longer, but knew he had to. He wouldn't rush her.

Succumbing to temptation, her lips wandered over the warm expanse of flesh where his chest met the smooth, rounded curve of his shoulder. The tip of her tongue traced an invisible, meandering path, its pink, cooling wetness dragging slowly against him. The sensation nearly driving him mad. He didn't know whether to laugh or groan.

God, she was so sweet and he needed to be inside her so bad. Moving, Caleb bowed his head, inhaling the fragrance of honeysuckle from the delicate hollow of her collar bone, knowing that he'd never smell that scent again without thinking of her.

"Caleb," her soft whisper reached him. "Please, I want to feel you. Please make love to me."

A slow, devastatingly beautiful smile lit his features, robbing her of breath. His words were a husky promise against her lips. "Your wish is my command."

His mouth swooped down to capture, his arms shifted and cradled, laying her on his bed.

The crisp cotton of the sheets, so cool against her flushed skin, caused an instinctive shimmy, the friction delicious. Above her, Caleb groaned low in his throat, the sinuous movement of her body unraveling him. Luring him, like a siren's song.

"You're the most beautiful sight I've ever seen," he whispered, his voice rough. He moved toward her, slipping a hand under the small of her back, arching her toward him, lifting her until she kneeled on the mattress, facing him.

"I've never wanted anyone as much as I want you right now." His erection brushed the nest of her curls. With an inarticulate sound of happiness, Cassie wrapped her arms about his neck, drawing him down. Glorying in the solid weight of him.

They moved, twisting, turning, heated flesh against silken curves. His kisses devoured, roaming freely over her body, feeding, then hungering anew until she writhed against him, her body no longer hers to control.

"Caleb . . ." she begged, incoherent. Needing so much.

He rolled, pulling her arms up high over her head, bracing his weight on his elbows. Staring down at her flushed face, his eyes glittered, reflecting his arousal. His hips flexed. Testing, promising. Shivering in reaction, Cassie's legs opened, trembling underneath his. Bringing him closer. Her need spinning, escalating, like some mad law of physics.

His assault was merciless, a wildfire that spread through her body. Its tongues licking greedily across her body. His hands, his mouth relentless, moving over her, down the length of her, stopping only to tease, to torment, to delight. Making her writhe as he claimed every inch of her body as his own. Blindly, she reached, her hands guiding him where she needed him so desperately now. Her slender thighs opening wider, bidding him welcome.

He felt the slick, wet heat of her against his shaft and tamped down on the tearing impulse to slam into her. Rocketing them both into sweet oblivion.

His eyes held Cassie's captive as he pressed, sliding slowly, inexorably. Tremors racked his straining muscles, as rivulets of sweat ran down his shoulders and back. A low groan tore from his throat, the sound as harsh as his labored breathing as he filled her, completing her. Every atom of his being fixed on her incredible tightness. Stretching, pulsing to accommodate him. The feel of her was beyond his wildest imagination. So impossibly exquisite. Muscles bunching, his hips flexed pushing deeper, and he withdrew.

The rhythm began. The rhythm of his hips pumping slowly, a controlled cadence. Bringing her higher and higher. Drawing forth helpless gasps of pleasure, throaty moans of enchantment. Refusing to hurry, wanting to prolong every second of sensation, every inch of pleasure he gave her.

Her nails clung, digging helplessly into his shoulders. Her hips arched to meet him, to deepen his every thrust. He was taking her to places she'd never been, forcing her to climb higher and higher. The pleasure of the ascent flooded her mind, flooded her soul, setting them deliriously awhirl.

Cassie looked up into Caleb's eyes, glimmering like dark stones, watching her, watching the pleasure he gave her. Absorbing it, sharing it.

She had to tell him, now, before she was lost. "Caleb . . ." Her voice, turned into a soft cry, torn from her as his hips flexed, rocking deliciously. So deep inside her, touching her very core. Staying deep. Just staying.

She was so close. He could feel it in the tremors shaking her, see it in the glazed fever of her eyes, hear it in the desperate pitch of her voice calling his name.

Not just yet. He wanted her higher, higher still. He

wanted to give her everything, the moon and all the stars.
He wanted her to touch them.

Oh, God, what was he doing to her? He'd stopped,
buried deep inside her. Now he was lifting her, drawing her
legs around his waist. Pinning her. His hot, hard thickness
imbedded as she throbbed and pulsed around him. She
moaned loudly, the tension unbearable. Feeling the first
shockwave of her climax rushing over her, words tumbled
forth, so desperate was she to say them: *"Caleb, Caleb, I
love you!"*

Their eyes locked. With a fierce, yet achingly tender
smile, he gave her what she needed, what she was dying
for: the tiniest push. Cassie's climax ripped through her at
the feel of him brushing, caressing her womb.

Not yet ready to let himself go, Caleb rolled his hips
infinitesimally. "I'm real glad to hear you say that, Slim.
Because . . ." he whispered, loving her breathless moan as
he moved inside her, her tremors continuing to squeeze and
pull at him. "Because . . ." he repeated, withdrawing now,
the clamp of her muscles gripping him deliciously, until
just the tip of his shaft remained inside her.

Caleb looked down at her, so beautiful, so gloriously
naked, and so well-loved his heart ached. "Because, you
know," his mouth catching hers, swallowing her soft cries.
"Because you know, I love you, too. And I hate flying
solo." With that, he dropped his hips, thrusting deeply,
watching her face as a scream of pleasure was torn from
her throat. Joy flooded him at the sight of Cassie locked
once more in the throes of passion. This time he joined her
in her ecstatic flight, rushing toward her very soul.

Slowly, softly, they floated back down to earth.

Cassie lay, eyes closed, languid, replete, drugged with
happiness. She smiled sleepily as she felt Caleb roll to his
side, drawing her body close, his penis still deep inside her.
She sighed, burrowing her head under the dark stubble of

his chin, summoning just enough energy to raise her hand and lay it against his sweat-slicked chest, the heavy thud of his heart against her palm.

She felt him lift her hand, gently bringing each finger to his lips, bathing them with a soft kiss. She made a mewling sound in her throat, as a kitten might, her lids too weighted to open.

"Cassie." His voice rumbled against her face.

"Mmm."

"Cassie, I love you. Truly, madly, deeply."

"Mmm. Love you, too." Her words slurred with fatigue.

His fingers lifted hers again, his mouth brushing her knuckles lightly. "Cassie, I think we should get married. Will you marry me, love?"

"Mmm."

"Uh, sweetheart, was that a 'yes mmm' or a 'no mmm'?"

No response.

"Please, Slim, Do you want to marry me? . . . Cassie?"

She mumbled something in sleepy irritation. As if he were a particularly pesky fly, buzzing about. Shifting restlessly, she hitched her leg over his thigh, pushing him over so he lay on his back. His body her new mattress. Asleep already.

Caleb stared at the ceiling of his bedroom, Cassie's soft, even breathing fanning his skin, his fingers stroking lazy patterns across the silken length of her back. He was grinning, he knew, like an utter fool. Like a fool in love.

She was dreaming. Floating on a cloud, its warm, beguiling wetness brushing her belly, caressing her hip bones, moving down as she squirmed in anticipation, wanting it to move . . . closer. A delicious warmth, it fanned across the sensitive flesh of her inner thigh. Impatient for the touch, for the heat, she twisted restlessly against it.

It engulfed her. Hot, consuming, demanding. And she exploded, shattering into a thousand pieces of light, trembling as he soothed and stroked. Then stirring her once more as his mouth moved now to her breasts, suckling gently. Drawing the knot inside her tighter and tighter. Climaxing again as he surged into her, sending her flying, soaring back into the starry night.

She was too sleepy to agonize over any morning-after awkwardness. It helped, too, that there was the rather unique distraction of Caleb's erection pressing insistently against the back of her thighs as his hands amused themselves elsewhere. Idly playing over her breasts. Cupping, squeezing, lifting. Making her squirm against him.

"Caleb, are you awake?" Not a hundred percent certain about his sleep habits. Suspecting, perhaps, that Caleb was fully capable of making love asleep or awake, or that maybe he just never slept. He certainly hadn't seemed to last night.

"Yeah, I'm awake. Can't you tell? Feeling pretty good, actually." His arm snaked down to her middle, pulling her more fully against him, his erection sliding between her thighs, rubbing her cleft.

She shivered, her nerve endings running wild. "Caleb, don't you think we better get up?"

"Slim," he nuzzled the column of her throat. "I've been up for hours, now." His teeth opened over the muscle of her shoulder, biting down gently. She moaned low in her throat, her hips pushing backwards, rubbing against him, helpless to resist the hunger he so effortlessly aroused.

Shifting suddenly, Caleb rolled onto his back. Then, amazing Cassie yet again at his effortless strength, he lifted her, holding her above him as if she weighed no more than rag doll. Her breath caught as he lowered her slowly. Of their own accord, her knees parted until she rested, quivering, suspended above his straining erection. Caleb waited, watching her eyes drink in the erotic sight. As he raised his hips fractionally, her eyes grew even larger.

"Cassie, love," he began, the tip of his penis just grazing her nest of curls, "I was hoping maybe you could take me for a ride."

Dying from pleasure as Cassie sank slowly down and proceeded to do just that.

26

*H*ank chuckled, watching his wife brush her hair in the mirror. "Who'd have ever guessed that Pamela's machinations might actually bring about some good?"

"You mean with Orion?"

Hank nodded. "Yeah. Damnedest thing, the day after Caleb got that letter from the lawyer, we received yet another letter, this time from TLM, the private group that bought Orion. It instructed us that unless they notified us specifically, not to change a thing in terms of Orion's training, or showing schedule, and that Cassie should stay on as his rider."

"Sounds like whoever's in charge is a smart person and must realize what a winning combination Cassie and Orion are."

"Yeah, but it's weird. People aren't usually like that. They spend a small fortune on something; well then, they can't resist going and fiddling with it, messing around. Like I said, it's the damnedest thing."

Melissa gave a small shrug of her shoulders. Hank watched how the slender straps of her nightgown slid across her bare skin.

"And how are Caleb and Cassie doing?"

Hank's face split into a wide grin. "Those two? Utterly amazing. Remember last week at the show? How I told you they were acting about as mature as teenagers: moody, talkative as rocks, and about as much fun to be with. Boy, oh boy, what a difference one week can make! Now they're acting about as *silly* as teenagers. You know, I walked in on them noodling in the tack room the other day? Thank God Caleb hadn't gotten around to undressing her . . ."

"Hank, you know Caleb has more self-control than that. He was probably just stealing a few kisses."

"Don't bet the farm on that one, love. The way he looks at her these days, reminds me exactly of how I felt when I fell in love with you. Yeah, I think it was a mighty good thing I barged in when I did."

"It's not affecting Cassie or Caleb's work, is it? The horses are coming along fine?"

"Of course not, she's a pro. Orion did great today. Beat out some pretty good horses." He grinned, remembering the excitement of the day. "After the class, Rob Buchanan came up and offered us a neat pile of money for him. Caleb threw back his head and laughed. Said unfortunately, Rob was too late. Then Cassie, bless her horsewoman's soul, she gave him that pretty smile of hers. Told him to come by and check out Arrow, that he was showing lots of potential. If he telephones, I thought I might suggest he look at Limelight, too."

"Knowing Rob, I expect you'll be getting a call about eight o'clock tomorrow morning."

"Certainly hope so. He's always done well by our horses."

Melissa laid her brush on the old-fashioned vanity that had belonged to her grandmother and smiled, catching and holding Hank's gaze in the reflection of the mirror. A tiny shake of her head caused her dark hair to sway. Her mouth lifted in a small smile as she watched her husband absorb the sight of her, thrilled by the instant spark of desire that flared in his eye. Sharing it.

She rose, turned, and approached him slowly, letting her hips sway ever so slightly, causing the sheer cotton gown to float about her calves. She knelt down next to the upholstered chair where he sat. He went still as a rock. But she could feel the weight of his eyes locked on the pale outline of her breasts.She smiled, pressing closer, letting him feel them, too. "You know, Hank, honey, all this talk of noodling . . ."

"No, Caleb. You *can't*. Not again."

"Aw, come on, Slim, please. Let me." The words whispered against her coaxingly, his tongue tracing the shell of her ear. Her neck arched reflexively, setting her insides aquiver. A moan escaped her. Half-heartedly, she pleaded with him, her voice sounding thin and reedy to her ears. "Two times is more than enough, honestly."

"Slim, my love, don't you know you can never have too much of a good thing?" His hands smoothed upwards, traveling the length of her arms, coming to rest on her shoulders. The angle of his head shifted behind her, his breath fanning the delicate line of her jaw.

"*Let me*. Thompson and the kids'll be back tomorrow. Who knows how long it will be before I get to do this again?"

"Oh, all right," she grumbled peevishly. Geez Louise, the man was stubborn as a mule.

He rewarded her with a kiss. "You're a pal, Slim. Now, hold still and close your eyes."

Obediently, Cassie shut her eyes. Tight this time. Last time, Caleb had used too much shampoo. When she'd complained the bubbles were getting in her eyes, he'd gone and dunked her. With no warning. In her own jacuzzi, too.

The bathroom was a total disaster. Of course, most of that was from their lovemaking. The waves had started

rolling over the sides, both Cassie and Caleb too preoccu-
pied to notice at the time, Cassie busy experiencing her
very own, internal tsunami caused by Caleb's wicked
mouth.

She leaned back into his chest as his fingers worked
through her thick, soapy mass of hair, massaging. Making
her feel pampered and adored. She was so happy, at times
she wondered whether she should pinch herself, as though
such happiness could only be a dream. True, Caleb hadn't
yet spoken to her of marriage, but knowing how disastrous
his previous one had been, she didn't want to push him.
She was happy just to be with him.

He loved the feel of her next to him. Even when they
weren't making love. Merely touching her did something
to his insides he'd never experienced before.

An unexpected and somewhat bewildering surprise.

He'd never had a moment's doubt how good the physical act would be between them. With the experience of a
true connoisseur, he'd needed only that first glance at
Cassie, standing half-naked in Hank's office, to know
they'd get along like wild fire in bed. Her beautiful body
alone was enough to make a man happy for a couple of
eons.

But he was discovering there was more to it. So much
more than simply having four-star sex with a gorgeous
woman. It was all the other things that were keeping him
hard and aching, needing her time after time: Those breathless little moans she made when he pleased her, the way
she curled up like a child, seeking the warmth and comfort
of his body as she slept, the way she drove him wild with
just a smile and a flick of her tongue.

And never had he experienced this degree of pleasure
from the mundane stuff. From such a simple act as watching the soapy lather slide down her silken shoulders, down
the straight, elegant line of her spine. Solely because it was
Cassie's shoulders, Cassie's spine. He didn't understand

the emotions she called forth. To put it crudely, he'd always thought of love in terms of his groin. Yet with each hour they spent together, it was becoming increasingly clear that with Cassie, love involved every particle of his being.

A big glob of lather dropped from his hand into the warm bath water, chasing away his moment of introspection. Time for the fun to begin again. Pressing down on her shoulders Caleb whispered his command.

"Ready, Slim? Down you go." His face was split in a boyish grin. He really loved this part, the feel of her wet torso sliding down his body, her hair brushing against his groin. Somehow, they'd gotten distracted from the hair washing a couple of times, but he was having such a good time pleading, cajoling, and squabbling happily with her that he was fully prepared to do whatever it took for a three-peat.

A groan escaped his lips as her thick, wet hair rubbed back and forth against his erection. Knowing she was torturing him on purpose, his imagination immediately began devising all manners of sensual retaliation. Anticipating happily just how he'd convince her of the benefits of conditioner.

27

"Come on Cassie, this is utter crap." Caleb's tone was curt, impatient, revealing his exasperation.

They'd been arguing, going round and round in circles for the past half hour. Actually, to be precise, they'd been saying essentially the same thing to each other for close to a month now.

He was damn tired of it.

He wanted her to cave in and be done with it.

"No, it's not. I'm sorry, but I'm just not going to do it." She felt sick inside, but her reply to Caleb was implacable. She refused to back down, hated the fact that it had come to this: their first full-blown argument. But she knew she had to stand her ground.

"Can't you see how hare-brained this is? You say you're willing to come and sleep in my bed on *some* nights, but not every night? Where's the logic behind this? Where?"

"It doesn't have to be logical to you for me to know it's right."

Caleb rolled his eyes. Feminine reasoning was so skewed it was a wonder the two sexes ever got past hello with each other. Bloody Hell, it wasn't as if everybody wasn't aware of what was going on. At least everybody who mattered.

Over a month had passed since Cassie and Caleb had first made love. Upon her return from New York with the twins, it had taken all of thirty seconds for Thompson to size up the situation. Ever since, she'd been all smiles, cooking Caleb his favorite dishes so often, he worried at times that he was in imminent danger of becoming a fat slob.

Indeed, Thompson was so thrilled, she kept inventing as many excuses as possible to get Jamie and Sophie out of the house so that Caleb and Cassie could have time alone together. She hadn't been shy about sharing the happy news, either. She must have been on the horn to Francis O'Mally in the blink of an eye, updating her gentleman friend on the romance blossoming at Hay Fever Farm.

Caleb had been struck dumb the afternoon O'Mally had walked right up to him on Main Street and had given Caleb a quick, friendly jab in the ribs with his elbow.

"Nice going there, son," he'd smiled, winking broadly. "Here's hoping you're starting a trend over at your place. Cassie and Bessie are two of the finest women I've ever met."

Even Finnegan, walking with no sign of a limp, had been grinning from ear to ear, a stream of drool hanging from his mouth all the way to the sidewalk.

Hell, as far as Caleb could tell, Jamie and Sophie also knew what was going on. Caleb could only guess (actually too chicken to come right out and ask them what they thought, terrified of the zillion questions most likely fermenting in their five-year-old heads). But he'd caught enough whispered giggles about Mommy's boyfriend and drawn out exclamations of in love to realize that they were keeping close tabs on Cassie and him. He was just grateful they hadn't started chanting that children's ditty about kissing in a tree.

But they'd been deeply fascinated, as only small children can be, when last Sunday evening Caleb had carried a sleeping Cassie in from the car and up the stairs to her bedroom. Keenly aware of the four eyes, round as saucers, watching his every move, he'd refrained from pulling off her show britches to make her more comfortable. Instead, he'd contented himself with slipping off her sneakers and laying a light blanket on top of her sleeping form.

He'd turned and quietly left the room, laying a finger to his lips. "Shh. Let's let your mom sleep."

"Why'd you have to carry her, Caleb? She's too big to be carried," Jamie had demanded as soon as the door was closed.

"She rode in a lot of classes today, on three different horses, Jamie. It was a big, important show today. A really long day. Your mom was pretty beat. I thought it would be nice for her to sleep a little longer. Besides, she doesn't weigh that much more than the two of you put together. You guys are monsters!"

That evening he'd been more than willing to spend the next ten minutes distracting the twins, picking each child up, letting them argue over which one was the heaviest.

But he wasn't willing to sleep alone anymore.

He wanted her next to him, curled snug within his arms, skin touching skin. Not just on select nights, but every night.

It had been a mistake not to speak up as soon as the twins and Thompson had returned from New York. He'd thought it better to go easy, not make Cassie uncomfortable. Everything was new, and she had more to adjust to on her end than he.

But after two weeks of this nonsense, of these on-and-off trysts at his house, he'd started to grow restless. When he'd broached the subject with Cassie, however, she'd mumbled something about being in the house in case the kids needed her. Thinking it might make things easier, he'd immediately offered to sleep at her house. She'd looked at him as if he were a Martian. What if Sophie should awaken from a nightmare and come looking for her?

"Well, what about Thompson? They love her. They can go to her room in the middle of the night."

"Of course they love her, but I'm their mother. I have to be there," she'd replied impatiently. "I probably shouldn't even be spending the entire night with you, but I want to . . ." Her cheeks had turned bright red with embarrassment. "And, well, I'm not getting a lot of sleep as it is. I can't afford to lose any more going back and forth between the houses in the middle of the night."

The hell of it was, she was telling the truth. They'd moved up, competing in the big shows now, often bringing Silverspoon in addition to Orion and Limelight. If Hank hadn't just negotiated a honey of a deal last week, selling Arrow to Rob Buchanan, she'd be riding Arrow, too. Even with only three horses to show, Cassie was working nonstop. A show every weekend, plus all the training she put in during the week, to say her schedule was grueling was no exaggeration.

Only three weeks remained until they left for the Hampton Classic. Caleb knew that right now was the crunch period. In a week, after this next show, Cassie would begin a taper for Orion and Limelight, toning down the intensity of their workouts, hoping to peak at the Classic. He knew, too, that Orion's sale had put extra pressure on Cassie. She felt that if she didn't perform well with him, she'd be out of a job with her invisible new owners. She was pushing herself to the max. Riding hard all day, being a mother, being his lover. Doing it all so beautifully.

He was well aware the solution to his problem was staring him in the face.

Ask her to marry him again.

It hadn't taken him long to realize that Cassie had been far too exhausted from the tumultuous day as well as from the passion of their lovemaking that night, for her to have heard, let alone have remembered, that as they lay in bed, sated and sleepy, Caleb had proposed. And shamed as he was to admit it, after that first night, the words hadn't crossed his lips a second time.

The feeling of dread at the idea of marrying still held him captive. When Cassie hadn't mentioned the despised *M* word, he'd breathed a sigh of relief, thinking that he could have everything the way he wanted it, until he felt like changing it.

He could propose when he no longer felt quite so queasy just thinking of it.

Of course, he hadn't expected that Cassie would resist him in any way. Making him detest the nights spent alone, away from her. That his need for her would overcome any lingering reluctance to marry. She had become too damned important to him.

So the previous week, he'd roared up the interstate to Washington, a slip of paper with Cassie's ring size tucked in his pocket. Wanting something special, he'd made an appointment at an exclusive jeweler to have a ring specially designed.

He was even ready to pop the question now, before he returned to pick up the ring. But proposing in the middle of an argument hardly seemed romantic, and it reeked of opportunism.

He had to tell her how much he loved her, and it had to be done just right. She deserved the perfect setting.

"Okay, Slim," he sighed heavily. "I won't push you any more. We'll do it your way." He looked across at her, sitting on the porch swing, her knees drawn tight against her chest in an unconscious gesture of defense. His eyes sought hers, the deep shadows of the porch impeding him. He closed the distance between them, dropping down on his haunches, reaching out to clasp her hands in his.

He looked up, able now to see the sadness dimming her

eyes. "Slim, I'm sorry. Please don't be blue. I promise I'll stop badgering you. It's just that when it comes to you, I want it all. I'm greedy." Drawing their entwined hands toward his mouth, he opened her palm, pressing his mouth to its center.

Cassie closed her eyes, keeping back the tears that threatened to spill. Refusing to cry.

It *was* the right thing to do. She was a mother. Her children necessarily affected her behavior, her choices. She'd been so naive, thinking she could be happy just being with him. She was. But it was all terribly more complex. Conflicted.

Sighing inwardly, she told herself she should be grateful that Caleb wasn't like Brad, that he hadn't forced her to choose between him and the twins. He was sensitive enough to realize how important the children were to her. And she knew how deeply, how truly he cared for them.

Dear Lord, she loved him so much. And she was sure that he loved her, too. But not enough, apparently. Not enough to want to marry her. Days had turned into weeks, Caleb making passionate love to her time and time again. Each time binding her closer to him. But never mentioning marriage. It wasn't a topic she felt she herself could bring up. Her experience with Brad had made Cassie overly sensitive to the issue of marriage. Cassie would only consider marrying a man as eager to be a parent to Jamie and Sophie as she was. Moreover, after being so mistaken with Brad, she refused to assume eagerness. And so she'd been waiting for Caleb to propose. How long could she continue waiting?

It was ironic. Ever since she'd realized that Orion was owned by Pamela, a part of her had acknowledged the possibility that she might have to leave, that she wouldn't be able to stay on at Five Oaks. How sad that the reason she'd have to go would be the man she was desperately in love with.

And now it had come to this. He probably thought that

when she insisted on sleeping apart from him, she was being some kind of tease, trying to manipulate him, like Pamela had.

She wasn't. She was simply desperately afraid of losing herself. Of being unable to survive without him. Those cold, empty nights she spent without Caleb were a sharp, bitter pill she forced herself to take, her personal dose of reality. Just in case. Oh well, at least she hadn't caved in, she thought with a sigh, determined to chase her black thoughts away and put their argument behind them.

Hands still touching, Caleb felt a tiny, involuntary shudder run through her, and lifted a dark brow in inquiry.

"What's wrong? Are you cold?" His hands moved up her arms, rubbing her skin.

She offered up a small smile. "No, it's nothing." Her voice dropped to a low whisper. "Caleb, can we go to your house? I'd like to spend the night with you if I may."

Their eyes locked, saying all that their hearts couldn't. In a fluid motion, Caleb rose to his feet, bringing her with him, off the swing and into his arms. They stood, locked in each other's embrace, sharing the comfort they found there. Wordlessly, he led her into the night.

She undressed for him. Each garment shed with the delicacy of a leaf falling, twirling to the ground. Revealing the beauty of her body, layer by layer.

Transfixed, caught fast in the spell she wove, he watched her approach. Curling in glorious waves about her shoulders, her hair was like a golden nimbus. Her breasts trembled as she moved, teasing him with their perfection. Their texture like silk, their taste like honey. He knew her so well, and yet his hunger for her remained as keen as a dagger's edge. He knew, too, that it would never dull.

As her hands touched him, his breath rushed out, unaware until that moment he'd been holding it. His only focus, her. His heart ached at the bittersweet melancholy that enveloped her tonight, aware their argument had caused it, desperate to make it right. As he fumbled with the buttons on his shirt, her hands brushed his aside; her quiet "Let me" caused his hands to drop passively to his sides. With excruciating slowness, she peeled away his shirt, tugging the material off his shoulders, bringing her mouth against the warm, resilient skin. Her indulgent tongue bathed him, absorbing the salty, masculine taste of him. Moving lower.

The muscles of his abdomen tensed, the ridges in sharp relief, Caleb's breath labored as her own fanned softly across his belly, her tongue dipping into the shallow circle of his belly button. His erection throbbed, straining, dying for her touch.

Cassie's hands moved to his jeans, her heart pounding in anticipation as liquid heat pooled within her. Knowing what she would find. Nothing could ever be more arousing to her than knowing he was hers. That she made him the way she would find him. Hot and heavy for her.

The sight was incredible. Unbearable. Cassie on her knees before him. Her nipples, tight with desire, just visible through the golden curtain of her hair. He watched enviously as her hair brushed, as if caressing, their pink tips. Lower still, her hands were stroking him, her mouth inches away. Coming nearer.

His hands dug into her hair, halting her. His words scratchy and rough, tearing at his throat like sandpaper. "Cassie, Cassie, I'm too close . . . I can't . . ."

Her eyes glittered up at him in the semidarkness. His skin felt the whisper of her breath as her mouth moved once more, meeting him. Humbling him. Destroying him as he shattered into a thousand pieces, helpless to resist.

By the second shrill ring, Caleb's arm had stretched out, snatching the receiver from its cradle, not willing to risk a third ring disturbing Cassie from her sleep. He glanced down at her lying against him, her head pillowed against his chest, her breathing unchanged.

"Yes," he answered, turning his head slightly, checking the glowing hands of his alarm clock. One-fifteen in the morning. This better be good, he thought irritably.

"Caleb. Matt here. Sorry to wake you. It's Mrs. Kline. Says it can't wait 'til morning, that you've got to call her. She sounds close to hysteria, otherwise I'd have waited."

Caleb sighed heavily. "No, you did right, Matt. Give me her number." Caleb repeated the numbers to make sure he'd heard them correctly and hung up, punching them in immediately. Mrs. Kline's voice answered on the first ring.

"Dr. Wells? Oh, thank goodness!" Matt Dupre had got it right. Even saying hello was setting her voice trembling with nerves.

"What seems to be the problem, Mrs. Kline?"

"Belle's gone into labor. She's already past term and something seems terribly wrong. She's been whimpering and panting all night, but nothing's happening. She looks awful."

"Mrs. Kline, this is her first litter. Sometimes these things take a while."

"But I just know there's something wrong! My husband's out of town and I'm alone." Her voice had risen, a thin wail that attacked his eardrum.

Wincing, Caleb tried again. "Mrs. Kline. I really think you need to relax . . ."

"Relax? How can I relax when my poor dog may be dying in front of my eyes? Dr. Wells, you've *got* to come. You've got to help her."

"All right. Okay. Listen, would you please stop crying? Mrs. Kline," Caleb ground out. "I can't hear your address if you're crying so loudly. Say it again. Slowly. Right. I'll be there in fifteen minutes." He replaced the receiver, the sound of plastic hitting plastic an audible click in the darkness.

Several seconds passed as he lay in the darkness, stealing this short time to enjoy the sensation of her lying next to him. Finally, he moved his arms carefully as possible, intending to lift her body away from him. Annoyed at having to leave her alone.

"It's all right, I'm awake." Cassie's throaty voice reassured him. "Who was that?"

"A client. Her dog's in labor and she's convinced it's in distress." His hand reached up to stroke her hair. "I'm sorry, but I've got to go. I'm on call tonight."

"It's okay, I understand. . . . But"—she lifted her head—"Caleb, do you think I could come with you?"

He rolled, turning to the side to face her, straining to read her features in the dark. "Sweetheart, it's past one. You sure you want to go? It's probably nothing, the puppies won't even be close to being delivered."

"That doesn't matter. I just want to be with you . . ."

He was quiet, remembering their earlier argument, followed by the maddeningly sweet hours they had spent locked in each other's arms.

Hell, he didn't want to be away from her, either. And it wasn't as if he gave a damn whether Mrs. Kline was offended by her unorthodox presence or not.

He dropped a light kiss on the top of her head. "Sure, it'd be great." He swung his legs out of bed, extending a hand to pull her up. "That way you can help distract the wretch."

"The dog?"

"No," he replied, reaching for his jeans. "The owner."

Cassie sat quietly on the floor, not far from where Caleb was positioned, watching him examine Belle. Gently, he eased his fingers inside, probing carefully, not wanting to agitate the dog any further.

From the corner of the room, Mrs. Kline also stood watching. Her hand was pressed tight against her mouth.

She'd been that way ever since Caleb had bluntly informed her she'd have to leave the room if she didn't stop carrying on so. Her cries were only adding to the dog's distress.

Caleb lifted his head slightly, addressing the older woman. "Belle's doing fine. The first pup has its head locked in. It's a bit big, but she should be able to push him out without too much problem." He withdrew his hands from the dog's posterior.

"Can't you do something? Can't you pull them out?"

Caleb gave a quick shake of his dark head as he rose to his feet to wash his hands in the adjacent bathroom. "Belle's doing great on her own, Mrs. Kline. Her contractions are hard and strong. She's not giving up the fight yet. I always try to let the birth process take its natural course. It's really better for the animals that way." He dried his hands on the guest towel and turned back to face them, his eyes scanning the room.

"You've got everything set up nicely here," he offered, feeling the woman deserved some credit. "The pups'll be along soon enough."

"But . . . you're not going to leave now, are you?"

"Mrs. Kline, it's past two o'clock in the morning. I'm afraid we can't stay any longer."

"Oh, please, *please.*" Tears had welled up in the woman's eyes. She turned imploringly to Cassie, hoping for a sympathetic face.

Cassie looked at the collie as she lay, sides heaving, her large dark eyes staring forward. She was a lovely dog. "I've never seen puppies being born," she said simply.

Caleb sighed, raising a hand to massage the back of his neck. That settled it then. "Mrs. Kline, could we trouble you for a cup of coffee while we wait?"

Beaming, Mrs. Kline hurried toward the back of the house.

*   *   *

Caleb uttered a short whisper of thanks at Belle's sudden change of breathing some forty-five minutes later. He dropped down from his seat on the wooden chair and crouched by the dog, lifting her tail. The dog was straining mightily, and Caleb could just make out the dark tiny spot of a muzzle.

"Thatta girl, Belle, a couple more pushes and you'll be home free." He felt, rather than saw, Cassie join him beside the dog, observing intently, waiting with bated breath until at last a pup emerged, slipping into Caleb's waiting hands.

Cassie's heart squeezed tight at the sight before her, the tiny, fragile pup, slick with birth fluid, cradled in Caleb's hand. Just seeing the gentle way he handled the pup, how soothingly he spoke to the laboring dog, filled Cassie with love and pride. What an incredible man he was.

His attention centered on the newborn pup, he placed it gently on the large, fluffy beach towel Mrs. Kline had provided.

"The next one'll be here soon," he said, aware now of Mrs. Kline's approach, her presence hovering over them. "Looks like a fine pup, Mrs. Kline. Let's see how many she gives you."

Cassie's eyes were glued to the sight of the minuscule creature, so tiny even she could have held it in one hand. Its eyes were shut tight. Its body so still, just a slight tremor shaking it as it breathed.

"Here comes the next one, Cassie."

Eagerly, she witnessed the process again, at the miracle taking place in front of her. Thrilled when a second miniature form was placed on the fluffy towel.

Soon there was a third. Slowly, the collie's breathing began to ease. She lay quietly, panting lightly.

Caleb watched her, saying nothing. Then, reaching out to stroke the dog's thick coat, he said, "It looks like Belle's litter might be small, Mrs. Kline. I'll examine her again in a minute, just to be certain. If that's the lot, I'll clean her up so she can begin the job of mothering." He gave Cassie a surreptitious wink, dropping his voice to a whisper so that only she could hear. "The really hard part."

Cassie blushed, ducking her head.

"Shouldn't a dog her size have more than three puppies?" Mrs. Kline asked.

Caleb shrugged. "It's her first litter. And we don't know who the sire was. Could have been a big dog. In any case, litter sizes are unpredictable. A dog might birth six pups one time, and the next, thirteen."

"Well, I guess I shouldn't complain. It'll be easier to find homes for three than six."

Caleb stared at her, truly astounded. "Mrs. Kline, are you telling me you're not planning on keeping any of these puppies, not even one?"

"Oh, no," she replied airily. "My husband and I talked it over. We really prefer pure breeds. As you said, we won't be able to tell who the sire was, it could have been a mongrel. We'll wait until she can give us some pedigree puppies. Like her."

"I see." He was pleased with how even his voice sounded. Obviously that lecture he'd given her on spaying Belle hadn't made much of an impression. He might as well have been talking to a wall. It wasn't hard to discern from Cassie's sudden, unnatural stillness that she, too, was shocked by the woman's attitude.

Mrs. Kline smiled brightly, unconcerned with the callousness of her previous words. "But I'm counting on you, Dr. Wells, to find good homes for them." She wagged her finger in his direction as if he were some sort of delinquent child. "Now, remember, you promised."

"I haven't forgotten," he replied curtly. "Mrs. Kline, Belle's going to need some water soon and a bowl of food later on. Please make sure you keep feeding her the high calorie food I prescribed until the puppies are ready to be weaned. I'll just examine her now while you're getting the water."

Grimly, he set to work. Well, he consoled himself, at the very least he could find decent owners for these puppies, some with brains in their heads.

"It's as I thought. Her uterus is empty. I'm just going to clean up the remains of her after-birth."

When Caleb left the room momentarily to wash his hands once more, Cassie remained captivated, staring at the mass of dark bodies. Less than a minute passed before Belle began to wiggle toward them, her long, pointed muzzle sniffing, then licking her puppies' damp bodies. Mrs. Kline's words echoed repeatedly in her mind. Caleb's body brushed hers as he knelt down beside her, also watching the new mother inspect her pups.

"Caleb," Cassie spoke softly, so as not to disturb Belle. "Do you think it would be all right if we took one or two of the pups? Would they be okay with the twins?"

He stared. Her face was animated with excitement at the idea, her eyes bright. How could he have been this lucky to find a woman so lovely, both inside and out?

Caleb reached across and let his fingers run across the smoothness of her cheek. Sitting back, he said with a smile, "Let me see what the puppies look like in a few weeks' time. When they're a bit bigger, I'll be able to see how they play, maybe even take a stab at guessing the breed of the male. We've got to be sure they're right for you. There are some breeds you don't want to mess with, Cass, especially when you have small children. You'd just be asking for heartbreak, otherwise."

"But if they're okay? Do you think . . ."

He interrupted, kissing her lingeringly. Lifting his head, he smiled, answering, "Yeah, I think so. Hey, Slim . . . anybody ever tell you you're a real softie?"

She shook her head in denial. Then she looked again at the squirming little bodies being washed by their mother.

"It was pretty special, seeing those puppies being born. I've always liked dogs, lots of different kinds . . ."

"It's a shame Mrs. Kline doesn't have your heart or your generosity. Come on, let's get out of here. You need to take me home before I break a cherished rule of etiquette here in Virginia and throttle our hostess."

28

She snuck out of the house silently as a shadow, before even the dawn had shown its face. The quiet darkness soothed. All she needed was an hour alone. An hour to gather her thoughts, to prepare herself mentally for the trip ahead, for the chaos and excitement to come.

This was it.

They were leaving at six-thirty sharp, barring any unforeseen delays. Loading Orion and Limelight and heading off to the Hamptons. To the Classic.

She thought they just might be able to pull it off. And she wanted it so badly, it was scary.

Oh, she didn't necessarily expect that they were going to go out and win the Grand Prix. Orion was still young. If he didn't get it this year, she knew in her heart that his day would come. He was destined for great things. But she was hoping to do right by him. To give him that fighting chance, to shine brightly amidst the glitter and sparkle of what was one of the most prestigious shows in the Northeast. She wanted it for him, for Caleb, for Hank. And, yes, for herself, too. As of yet, she hadn't met the new owners who had purchased Orion, didn't know when they'd put in an appearance. But they had given her the chance to take an incredible horse to the Classic and she wanted to prove to them what she could do.

For Cassie, the Classic was different from any of the other shows they'd competed at this summer. She was going home. Riding at a show where she'd literally cut her baby teeth. She'd never mentioned it to Hank or Caleb, but some of her earliest moments of glory had occurred at the Classic. Before her father had died, there'd been a box that Cassie's mother had stored in the attic of her parents' home with all of Cassie's childhood ribbons that Cassie occasionally enjoyed rummaging through. Way down at the very bottom were the faded ribbons she'd received in the lead-line class at the Hampton Classic, won when she must have been all of five years old. No older than Sophie and Jamie, she thought with a smile.

There were the memories. And now, in the present, there were her fellow rivals. She knew them well. Sam Waters would be there, among many others. Truly great riders, truly great horses. As competitive as she was, Cassie couldn't help but want Orion and herself to be in top form, pitting themselves against some of the best equestrians in the country.

As a team, she and Orion had come a long way in an exceedingly short period of time. She'd been lucky things had clicked so well between the two of them. With each passing day, she was understanding the horse's temperament better and better. He was an intelligent animal. When he didn't like something, he made it abundantly clear. This season, Cassie had worked hard, building his confidence, showing the horse that he could handle just about anything a course designer threw at them. Even so, the Hampton Classic's Grand Prix course was renowned, not only for its beauty, but also for the difficulty and challenge of its fences. Oxers, walls, ditches, windmills. And one couldn't forget the water jumps.

The water jumps alone had been the literal downfall of many a rider. Getting a horse to clear a twelve-to-fourteen-foot expanse of water could be a lot trickier than simply getting it to jump up and over a formidably high obstacle. Better riders than she had been stymied by the Classic's water jumps.

While she sat, staring blindly at the mirrorlike surface of the frog pond, a symphony had begun all around her, birds chirping and warbling loudly from the treetops. It played on, unnoticed by Cassie, her thoughts still on the days to come. She remained there, at the water's edge, striving for calm, equally determined to keep it. At least until she made it to Grand Prix Sunday.

Route 27 was a nightmare. After leaving the exit on the Long Island Expressway, Route 27 served as the main artery to eastern Long Island. It cut a straight path through the Hamptons right out to Montauk, the Island's eastern tip.

But with Route 27, straight didn't mean fast. During the summer months, traffic became so congested with vacationers, summer renters, and day-trippers, that cars were forced to slow to a crawl, inching along the two-lane road. While Cassie was familiar with a few of the back roads the locals used as short-cuts to avoid the horrors of 27, unfortunately the horse van was simply too big to negotiate the smaller roads or the train overpasses that crisscrossed above them.

So they sat. Stuck. Sweating. Staring at the back of Five Oaks's van which they'd been following for the past four-hundred miles or so. Cassie could only thank God that she'd been smart enough to send Thompson, Jamie, and Sophie by plane to New York to rendezvous with Alex. She could just imagine how major, how monumental a disaster it would have been, having two fidgety five-year-olds stuck in the back seat for this long a drive. Most likely, Cassie would have thrown in the towel, insisting they turn around somewhere in southern New Jersey.

Even without Jamie and Sophie antsy and bickering at each other, the trip was incredibly frustrating. It was cruel, mental torture, knowing that you could probably walk to your destination faster than these cars pathetically slithering along with all the speed of a dying snake. Their car was just a tiny metallic dot along the endless line of traffic into the Hamptons.

"What are all these people *doing* here?" Caleb's patience, too, was wearing extremely thin.

"They're escaping from New York," Hank responded, with far more equanimity. He had the plum seat—stretched out along the back, legs up, a pillow for his neck, a can of soda propped against his stomach. "Just like in the movie. Don't you remember that film with what's his name—Snake Plisken?"

"Naw, Hank, I'm pretty sure what we're seeing here is *Deep Impact*, but the dumb clucks are all going in the wrong direction. This . . ." Caleb said, waving a hand at the potato fields sprinkled liberally with expensive, oversized summer homes, "all this is ground zero."

"Well, in that case, we can just hope that a tidal wave is gonna come real soon and put us out of our misery. Cassie, keep your eyes peeled."

"No problem. I'll just look out for the only thing moving at a decent speed."

Inch by inch they rolled through the town of Watermill, and then finally into Bridgehampton, home of the Hampton Classic. Cassie sat forward expectantly, her eyes scanning the highway. "Caleb, the turnoff's going to be up on your left, Snake Hollow Road. I hope Raff sees it."

"Slim, at the speed we're rolling, Raff would have to be sitting with his eyes shut tight to miss it."

Cassie needn't have worried. A police patrolman was

directing all the horse vans, indicating the road with a practiced flick of his forearm. Since the opening day at the Classic, there had been such a constant stream of trailers coming through that in order to accommodate the surplus traffic, select roads leading to the show grounds had been closed to all other traffic.

It was like being newly sprung from jail, Cassie thought, stretching, raising her arms high above her head, twisting her torso left and right, taking it all in.

All around, the Classic was already in full swing, the show having started the previous day. The hustle and bustle of activity, riders coming and going, vans moving in and out, the enormous, brightly striped tents—all added to the feeling of a wondrous carnival come to town.

Cassie's first classes with Orion and Limelight were scheduled for the following morning. But before then, there was tons to be done. Hours would pass spent unloading the horses, walking them, longeing them lightly, then watering and feeding them. That was the easy, straightforward part, dealing with the animals. The show coordinators also had to be contacted, vaccination records and other paperwork presented, exhibitor passes for the show grounds procured.

Then the stalls had to be checked and prepared, bedding, hay, and bags of grain unloaded. For the two horses, Limelight and Orion, they'd been obliged to reserve four stalls. Limelight would get one. Orion would be placed in the middle stall, an empty one on either side. Hank and Caleb had wanted to minimize as much as possible the chance for Orion to kick up a fuss. Isolating him was their best guarantee.

"Cassie, you and Caleb deal with the horses. Raff, you come with me. We'll find out where our stalls are, make sure there are no screwups with the arrangements. Tony and Mike, stay with the van and help unload. Raff and I will come back as soon as we can." Hank was in his military mode, with everyone following his orders as quickly and efficiently as they could. Knowing it was the only way they'd ever get through the myriad of chores.

Cassie and Caleb got down to work. Caleb went for the stallion first, unloading Orion and then handing him over to Tony so Cassie could unwrap his bandages. Then repeating the process all over again with Limelight given to Mike.

That much accomplished, Caleb held both horses' leads while Cassie ran to fetch the longe lines stored away in the tack box in the back of the van.

After threading the longes through the horses' halters and eyeing the way Orion was refusing to keep all four hooves on the ground, Cassie suggested, "You should probably take Orion, Caleb. He's really wound up right now. This place is pretty busy."

"Good idea. I don't want him tossing you around."

Cassie watched as Caleb held the line tight beneath the stallion's halter, keeping him under firm control. Sometimes being six-foot-two had definite advantages.

Limelight was feeling perky, too. The long ride in the van had affected even the gelding's more mellow disposition. Both horses were in sore need of exercise to release all that energy.

They spent the next hour walking, longeing, then walking the horses some more, letting them work out their extra energy and high spirits as much as possible. That was the biggest drawback to these week-long horse shows. The horses were deprived of their normal pastures to run in, where steam could be blown off naturally.

Horses needed freedom in addition to the exercise that longeing and riding offered. Cassie knew that by the end of the week, they were all, humans as well as horses, going to be longing for Five Oaks's acres of fenced pasture.

For their own accommodations, Hank had picked a place called Cozy Cabins. A convenient location, the motel was located about four miles from the showgrounds. And they'd advertised kitchenettes. Having a snack at midnight or breakfast before dawn was an essential criterion, one Cassie had insisted on.

Hank was sharing a cabin with Rafflael. Tony and Mike, the two grooms, would remain on the show grounds, sleeping on fold-out cots in the van, near the horses in case of emergency.

Cassie and Caleb would be staying at Cozy Cabins, too, sharing a cabin of their own. Because of their recent argument over the topic of sleeping arrangements, Caleb had been uncertain how Cassie would react to the idea of sleeping together rather than Caleb bunking with Hank and Raffael. So he'd approached her with a certain amount of trepidation. He'd been thrilled, though a bit baffled, when she'd merely smiled and said, "Of course," offering no further explanation.

He wished he could figure out how women's minds worked.

But he certainly wasn't about to look a gift horse in the mouth. This way, he'd have a better chance at stealing her away to the beach one night, the engagement ring nestled in its velvet-covered box, snug in his front pocket, and he could pop the question.

Moonlight and diamonds for Cassie, that's what he wanted.

It was close to eight at night by the time they carried their duffel bags in from the Jeep. Cassie had extra stuff, too. A garment bag loaded with riding jackets, breeches, and pressed rat-catchers: those button-down, cotton shirts with collars that looked similar to a cleric's worn by the female competitors at horse shows. Another bag carried her field boots and hunt cap. Hank had reserved their cabins next door to each other as everyone's comings and goings would often be synchronized.

Before he disappeared into his own cabin to unpack and wash off the day's grime, Hank paused, addressing Caleb. "I've got to call Melissa. Let her know we got here safe and sound."

Melissa had volunteered to stay and supervise the running of Five Oaks. Although she was sad not to see Cassie and Orion compete, she knew how worried Hank would be, were someone else left in charge.

"Give her my love. Tell her we miss her already. Cassie's going to call her brother, too. They're out here, somewhere nearby."

"You guys interested in grabbing something to eat a little later?"

"Sounds good. I'm starving."

"Well, just give a knock when you're ready, then."

"Sorry it's so late, Alex, I hope you weren't worried. The traffic was a disaster, we didn't get in until midafternoon. Then we had to get the horses settled. How are you doing? The kids behaving at Aunt Grace's?"

"They've been super. Great-aunt Grace is completely charmed. The kids spent all day at the beach, had the time of their lives."

"I'm so glad. They would have been just miserable, sitting in that car all day."

"So when's your first class tomorrow? When should the fans arrive?"

"Tomorrow morning. But come when you like. I've gotten passes for all of you, Diana included. Keep an eye open for Hank, he'll give them to you, if I'm not around. And don't forget those wrist bands for the Grand Prix tent. I tend to doubt Diana would find it amusing being bounced from the tent by one of the security guards."

"Don't worry about us, or Diana. You've got enough on your plate . . ." Cassie heard Alex sigh heavily into the phone. "But speaking of plates, that reminds me. There's this party Diana's all fired up about."

"The exhibitor/patron party?"

"No, I think it's another, even swankier party. It's at some director's house. But apparently, coming with a rider from the Classic puts you at the top of the heap. Would you mind, Cass?"

Cassie sighed in return. "Sure, I'll go, but you'll have to count on including Caleb and Hank. They're my excuse to duck out early." Alex's laugh came over the line. "When is this party anyway?"

"Saturday night."

"What? Before the Grand Prix!" Diana certainly had nerve. What did she think, that Cassie typically partied all night before an event like this? What had she gotten herself into? "Listen, Alex, I'll agree to go for a drink at the cocktail, but then I'm ditching you. By that time I'm sure Diana will have found loads of people more interesting than us lowly equestrians."

"Fine by me, Cassie. You're a love to do this. I'm not into this stuff, either, but Diana's been talking about it for the past month. She's convinced there's a certain cachet walking into this bash with one of the top competitors."

At Cassie's snort of disgust, Alex said, "I know, ridiculous, but take it as a compliment. At least Diana has recognized what a good rider you are."

"Alex, I can't tell you how much that means to me."

He laughed. "Don't be a brat, sis. Anyway, I want to enjoy myself with the kids this week. I'd never hear the end of it if she misses out on the big party of the season."

"So this is like a preemptive strike, huh?"

"Yeah. I'm not going to hang around there too long, either. If I can't drag her away at a reasonable time, I've told her she'll have to find her own way home."

"Oh, you mean, who you leave with is different from who you show up with?"

"Now you're catching on. You'll be a socialite in a few short lessons."

"Oh, please, save me."

"Good night, Cass. And good luck. We'll be cheering for you. Love you."

"Love you, too. 'Bye."

Alex Miller dropped the receiver back in its cradle, grimacing. Christ, he hated roping Cassie into these sorts of events. It shouldn't be her problem, too, that Diana was becoming increasingly tiresome, doing her level best to manipulate him as often as possible.

These days, Alex simply didn't give a damn what kind of a pain in the neck Diana was. Maybe he was suffering from some sort of delayed shock, a numbing grief. When Tom and Dad and Lisa had died, he'd thrown himself into work, his only concern making piles of money and taking care of Cassie and the twins. He guessed he'd succeeded there.

He'd made more money than he had use for and now Cassie had a stallion most breeders dreamed about. And Cassie seemed to be doing great. She sounded happy and the twins were obviously thriving. Yes, he'd succeeded just great: they didn't need him anymore.

So what was he left with? An intense love for his family. Piles of money, that hadn't diminished even after the purchase of Orion when Alex transferred a small fortune into Pamela Ross's open hands. He also had a job that symbolized power and control. And a mistress, a lover, or whatever she wanted to call herself, who was becoming increasingly stale—no matter how imaginative she tried to be in bed.

So why not give Diana her walking papers? He was good at that. After all, he'd more than enough practice.

It all came back to that numbness inside him. If he couldn't feel anything, why should he possibly care one way or another about Diana's manipulations? And while his soul might be frozen colder than Antarctica, his thirty-year-old body seemed to be functioning just fine. In that respect, Diana served those needs admirably, top of the class. Besides, she was easy to understand. Indeed, they understood each other only too well. He used her body, she used his money and social position. Yeah, thought Alex cynically. He simply was a traditionalist, following a tried-and-true exchange that had existed for centuries between the two sexes.

No way was he going to trouble his little sister with the mess his private life had become.

29

The rain started as they were pulling into the parking lot of the restaurant Cassie had recommended. Big, fat drops fell, splattering against their skin. They looked at each other, silent.

Just great, thought Caleb. What *was* it with this place? So far, he'd seen nothing but traffic jams, rude drivers, and highway. Now rain. So much for taking Cassie on a picturesque moonlight stroll, ocean waves lapping gently at their feet.

Caleb's mood, which had improved significantly after a few cold beers accompanied by a delicious bowl of steamed mussels, plummeted again once they stepped outside. Rain was coming down in earnest. Straight sheets of the stuff.

"Hope this tapers off by tomorrow." Hank spoke, giving voice to everyone's chief concern.

They drove back to the motel, rain pounding the car, filling the silence.

The rain kept on. It drummed, tapping a staccato beat on the roof of the cabin as Caleb and Cassie made slow, quiet love, their voices hushed by its sound. Moving against each other, they murmured tender words, afterwards drifting off, wrapped in each others' arms. They slept, rain falling steadily.

Riders acknowledged each other glumly, forced to peer intently through the rain from underneath the voluminous hoods of their ponchos. It wasn't easy guessing identities with everyone covered from head to foot in rubber and oilskins. For those standing with their mounts, sometimes looking at the horse made it easier, then all one had to do was match horse with rider. Everywhere there were complaints, but especially by the in-gate.

"Watch it when you're up. The footing's a bitch and it's so damn foggy the fences jump out at you."

"Tough round."

A short, bitter laugh. "You can say that again. No traction whatsoever. I'm just happy we got out of that mess with only eight faults and a time penalty."

Cassie was standing nearby, listening to the disheartened comments of the riders as they passed. No doubt about it, it looked good and nasty out there. She shrugged inside her slicker, then glanced up, feeling the cold rain hit her face. What she saw only depressed her more: not a single break in the cloud-covered sky.

"That you, Cassie, underneath that cap?" a familiar voice inquired.

She spun around, her spirits lifting for the first time since awakening this morning to a thoroughly drenched world. "Sam! I was hoping I'd run into you today!" She gave the older man a fierce, wet hug. "How are you? You look great."

"Been doing real well. Got some nice horses coming up—you'll recognize a couple of them. And how about you? How's life in Virginia treating you?"

"I love it. Hank Sawyer's just great. I never got to thank you for putting in a good word for me."

Sam Waters waved his hand, brushing away her thanks. "You'd have gotten the job anyway. Hank come down with you?"

"He should be coming back any moment. He and his partner, Caleb Wells, went to get my horse. I wanted to stay here and watch the rounds. Footing's getting real messy, Sam."

"Yeah, I've been watching from over there. A real bitch. If you want my advice, Cassie, take it slow. Forget about the clock. This is just the jumping class. Be real conservative."

"Thanks. Let's cross our fingers that this clears by Sunday."

"They're going to have to postpone classes if it doesn't stop sooner than that. The course is at the limit of ridability now. Just look at the ground already."

He was right. The ground was becoming pitted and gouged, the horses' hooves having dug deep into the sodden turf. Both watched glumly as another rider trotted out to brave the course.

Cassie was up on Limelight first. The class was so big, with so many riders, she'd had ample time to cringe at disastrous rides as well as marvel at feats of brilliance.

"You sure you want to go through with this, Cassie? If you want to scratch . . ."

"No, Caleb. Don't worry, I'm going to go real easy out there. We've got to take a look at these jumps sooner or later. I'd rather it was before Friday's qualifying class."

Nodding reluctantly, Caleb pulled her into his arms, giving her a brief, hard kiss before letting her go. "Good luck, Slim. Be careful."

"I will. I promise."

He helped her mount Limelight, the dapple grey's hindquarters still protected by a large plastic poncho.

Waiting until the very last minute, Caleb pulled it back, off her horse as she trotted into the show ring.

Standing there with the dripping wet poncho in his hands, he stared after her. Damn, he hated this rain.

They were right. The footing was slippery. Cassie kept Limelight's pace tightly controlled. Just sixteen fences, she repeated to herself like a litany. Take them one at a time, make those corners nice and wide and easy. Don't think about the clock, just forget it. It doesn't matter.

Limelight was such a brave horse. So willing. But it was nerve-rackingly tricky, especially when his hooves kept sliding, both on the take-off *and* the landing. All too soon, Cassie heard the muffled thud of rails falling to the saturated ground behind them, a sound that was repeated again and again.

When it was over, she could only breathe a huge sigh of relief. All things considered, Limelight had done a terrific job. Fifteen faults, including the time penalty, certainly wasn't anything to write home about, but on a day like today, she was happy enough to take it. Limelight hadn't shied away from any of the imposing fences, and they'd avoided injury. She wasn't going to ask for more than that under these rotten conditions.

She trotted back to Caleb and Hank, her white britches wet, brown splotches of mud clinging to them. Limelight's perfectly groomed coat was now streaked with sweat and mud. Mike and Tony, waiting alongside Caleb and Hank, immediately went to work, taking the gelding by the reins, covering his steaming body with a cooler. Knowing Limelight wouldn't qualify in the event of a jump-off, they led him back to the stabling area to dry him off and rub him down.

Caleb turned to Cassie and pressed a cup of steaming tea into her hand. "Drink this, Cassie. Your lips are blue."

Nodding her head tightly in thanks, she sipped the hot, slightly sweetened liquid. "He tried really hard," she mumbled between sips. "I hate to say it, but I'm grateful I won't be in a jump-off with him. I'll be more than glad to call it a day after my ride with Orion." Using an expression she rarely allowed to pass her lips, Cassie finished, enunciating clearly, "This weather bites the big one."

Caleb and Hank laughed. "Damn straight. You did fine. You know, we've been hearing rumors going round that the judges are considering stopping the class for a rain delay and continuing it tomorrow."

"I'd just as soon get it over with and let Orion and Limelight rest tomorrow. Two days in a row of fences this high and courses this difficult is a lot . . ."

"Well, there are about seven riders before you're up again. I guess if they're going to call it, we'll know soon."

"Where's Orion?"

"Raff's out longeing him. Should be here any second."

"Cassie, you want anything before you go back out there? You hungry?"

"No, thanks, Hank. It's too early, even for my junk food addiction. Think you can round up some windshield wipers, though? They might come in handy."

Hank laughed. "Thatta girl. Keep your sense of humor up, you need one on a day like today. Here come Raff and Orion now. You plan to hop on him, warm him up a bit more?"

"Yes. I feel pretty soaked, I need to keep warm, too. I'll trot him around a bit, away from this crowd. Can you call me when I'm on deck?"

Caleb walked Cassie over to the stallion. Today, his mane was unbraided. They were saving the braids for Sunday's Grand Prix, should Cassie and the stallion make it that far. The stallion was pawing the mud with his hoof, shaking his head, his mane slapping, thick and wet against his muscular neck. Clearly, he was impatient at being asked to stand for even a minute in this cold, stinging rain.

"Hey, big guy, you look as happy as the rest of us out here. A real happy camper," Caleb said, patting the stallion's rain-streaked neck as he pulled down the stirrups on his side of the saddle.

"Well, at least there aren't any psychedelic railings out there," Cassie said, remembering that first spring outing with Orion in the show jumping ring. How long ago that seemed. "Everything's supremely tasteful here at the Classic. Nothing to offend your delicate sensibilities, Orion."

Caleb chuckled and gave her a leg up. Cassie settled herself in the saddle, feeling the clammy wetness of her breeches cling to her skin. Her gloves were soaking, too. But in this weather she didn't dare ride without them. The leather reins would be too slick to hold barehanded.

"Looks like your wish will be granted, Slim. I don't think they're going to postpone the class. Tell you what, after you get through this course, it's my treat for the hot dogs. Just 'cause I'm a really great guy."

Cassie grinned back at him, grateful for the banter. She needed the distraction. "Last of the big-time spenders, huh? You're on, Wells. Hope you brought your Visa. This is the Hamptons, after all."

She laughed when Caleb patted his pockets with an exaggerated look of horror. A smile still hovering on her lips, she rode off hoping for even a patch of decent footing to warm up in.

No, Orion was definitely not a happy camper. Just barely manageable, he was communicating his displeasure to the world through the angry twitching of his ears and the sudden, abrupt swiveling of his hindquarters as he took vicious aim at passing horses. Orion was telling her loud and clear that he was going to be a handful out on the course.

Well, show time. Hank had just waved to her, signaling that they were up. Drawing a deep breath, Cassie guided the stallion into the ring.

Same story, Cassie. Same story, different horse, she amended to herself, keenly aware of Orion's powerful stride as she moved him into a canter, feeling the horse's rising excitement as he sighted their first fence, a brush jump of potted evergreens, topped with a bright green and white striped pole.

There was such incredible strength underneath her. Gathering, soaring, landing, and . . . bucking.

Right, thought Cassie, this is great, as she was jolted suddenly, unpleasantly, the stallion's hindquarters lifting and kicking the air behind him as they galloped along. Orion's having a temper tantrum. Hope he doesn't destroy the fences, too. They continued on, Orion alternately straining at the bit, rushing the approaching jumps, landing, then bucking violently, as gifted and temperamental as a genius. And about as controllable.

Her arms were trembling now from the effort of holding him back, keeping him in check, as they negotiated the slippery footing. The course seemed endless as Cassie worked to keep her mount jumping safely.

The triple combination loomed before them.

Three striped verticals. Huge, and growing larger with each galloping stride.

As if suddenly elected chairman of the board, Orion made a split-second decision, without bothering to let Cassie in on it. So fast, so powerful, he leapt, hurtling his body high over the first jump of the combination. Taking off from a distance so great, it might as well have been another continent away.

He continued, soaring, as if he wanted to swallow all three jumps whole. Not needing to land between them. The world whooshed by. During that mad rush, she somehow lost contact with the stallion's body. All too suddenly, Cassie realized she was flying alone and about to crash.

Instinctively she rolled, curling herself into a tight ball, protecting her fragile body.

Then crashing. Slamming into the soft mud, going deeper, into the hard ground.

For seconds she lay immobile, shakily assessing the damage. Nothing seemed broken. No tearing, shooting pain. Just a dull, *throbbing* pain. She could live with that.

Gingerly, painfully, she uncurled herself, turning over from her side to her knees, moving carefully, regaining control of her muscles little by little. Her sole objective at the moment being to struggle back onto her feet and try to catch Orion.

She couldn't recall hearing any terrifying crashing sounds as she'd hit the ground, so she assumed the stallion was unhurt, that he'd cleared the jump safely and was somewhere nearby. She prayed he was unhurt.

She'd made it to her knees by the time Caleb reached her. Having run, as if in a race for his life, through the muddy field to reach her fallen, motionless body. Sprinting even faster as he saw her begin the arduous process of regaining her feet.

It would have been difficult to judge whose face was paler with shock and fright.

"Cassie, Cassie, Jesus, are you all right? Don't," he ordered fiercely. "Don't move, just lie back. Let me make sure nothing's broken."

Too weak to do otherwise, she obeyed his authoritative command. His dark eyes searched her face, gauging her reaction as his hands traveled slowly, methodically over her neck, her shoulders, her limbs, probing carefully.

Cassie submitted for a few seconds, before saying, "I'm really fine, Caleb. Really." Her head, too, was already feeling somewhat clearer. "Just help me get to my feet." She lifted her shoulders off the wet ground, struggling to sit up.

"Fuck that," Caleb replied harshly, still terrified, his heart still pounding with dread. He scooped her up into his arms, cradling her against his chest as if she were no bigger than Sophie.

"Caleb," Cassie demanded through gritted teeth. "Stop right now and put me down. You've got to let me walk out of this ring on my own two feet. Do you hear me? You've got to."

He looked deep into her eyes, recognizing the fierce pride in them. Slowly, wordlessly, he lowered her feet until they touched the muddy ground.

"Thank you," she whispered softly.

Alex had seen the fall from his reserved table underneath the Grand Prix tent. He thanked God that Thompson and the kids had missed it. Not having realized Cassie was due to ride again so soon, he'd suggested that Thompson and the twins go and look at the llamas and miniature horses on display in the far corner of the tent.

His chair had flown backwards, thudding to the ground as Alex rushed to the railing, ducking, running, desperate to reach his sister lying on the ground. From the corner of his eye, he'd seen Caleb Wells tearing across the Grand Prix ring. Caleb reached her first, falling to his knees beside Cassie, his body bowed over her, his hands moving over her, obviously checking for injuries.

He'd almost caught up to them when he saw Wells reach out and lift Cassie into his arms, carrying her a mere three paces before coming to a halt . . . then gently depositing her. Then he saw them both begin to walk, side by side, Wells's arm behind her back, lending support.

Cassie was covered from head to foot in mud. She was moving stiffly, her face pinched with strain. Not yet having noticed Alex's approach, she turned her head to say something to Wells. Alex's gaze followed, lighting on Caleb's face.

Surprised to see it was as white as a bleached sheet.

Finally, he intercepted them. His chest tight with worry, he opened his arms. Wordlessly, Cassie stepped into her brother's embrace. Alex held her, stroking his open hand up and down her back, feeling the tremors that still shook her body. Caleb stood by silently watching.

Giving her a final reassuring squeeze, Alex released his arms. With a shaky smile, Cassie said, "We've got to get out of here and let another rider try his luck. I'm glad you were here, Alex," she finished simply, as they began walking toward the gate.

"Me, too, Cass."

Not far from the in-gate, all five of them converged, Hank with Orion in tow finally catching up. His face somber, Hank held Orion's reins out to Cassie. Their eyes met, hers expressing thanks as she accepted them.

They continued on, walking as quickly as Cassie could manage, needing to leave the ring so the course would be clear for the next rider. The pain in her battered body growing with every step, it was an effort just to make her legs carry her across the field. Hoping that perhaps talking would help distract her, Cassie asked, "Did you check Orion, Hank? I didn't hear him hitting anything."

"He's fine. Not a scratch on him. Went and found some grass in the far corner to munch on while he waited for someone to come and get him." His voice gruff, he asked, "The important question is, how about you? That was quite a fall, Cassie. No parachute, either."

"Yeah, Cass," Alex chimed in. "You sure you're okay?"

Cassie nodded carefully. "I'm okay, really. Nothing ice packs, a hot bath, and a bottle of aspirin won't cure."

"You think we should take her to the hospital?" Alex asked Caleb, ignoring his sister. He still wasn't close to liking Wells. But oddly enough, now, after seeing the fear still lingering stark in Caleb's eyes, he trusted him. Perhaps someday he'd get around to liking him, too.

Caleb hesitated and then shook his head. "Nothing seems broken. She's walking, she's lucid. Cassie would let us know if she were hurting . . . Am I right, Slim?"

"Yes, Dr. Wells. Not that you'd get me to a hospital, anyway. Hate them."

Caleb tugged gently on her elbow, pulling her to a stop. His index finger reached and lifted her chin as his eyes searched her mud-streaked face. Loving her so much.

He gave a small smile, the corners of his mouth lifting. "And here I always thought it would be nice to have a patient who talked back." His mouth descended, soft and warm, lightly caressing. Needing to touch her so badly, to reassure himself she had truly escaped harm.

So, that was the way the wind blew, Alex thought to himself, watching Caleb claim his sister's lips in a tender kiss. Cassie had been careful not to mention any romantic involvement with Caleb. It wasn't as if he hadn't expected it. But if what Alex witnessed during the past few minutes was any indication, then it was obvious Caleb's feelings for Cassie ran far deeper than Alex would have guessed possible. Perhaps Caleb Wells did have some redeeming qualities after all.

Sam Waters was waiting by the in-gate. "Tough break, Cassie. You'll get 'em Friday."

"Thanks, Sam," Cassie replied, grateful for her old friend's support. Right now she was feeling about as resilient and self-confident as a wet noodle.

Alex left them, intending to head off Thompson and the twins before they saw Cassie in her present condition. He and Cassie had agreed there was no sense in scaring them. With Cassie still plastered in mud, the nastiness of her spill was all too obvious. After she'd had time to recover and rest, Cassie could meet them later for dinner and some quiet relaxation.

Cassie was just as glad to be spared the countless questions the sight of her ruined riding clothes would raise. Her muscles were screaming, and the rest of her body felt like it was one huge punching bag, and the reigning world champion had just finished a pummeling session with her.

"Take her back to the motel, Caleb," Hank suggested quietly as Alex kissed his sister good-bye. "We'll handle things on this end for the rest of the afternoon. If this damn rain lets up, I'll go out and longe Orion again. Calm him down a bit."

Caleb nodded. "Thanks, Hank. I'd like to make sure she's really okay. I'll come back and pick you up about six, we can grab some dinner then."

30

"*W*ait. Let me get this straight. Yesterday you fell. Today, your shoulder and side still look like a really big, really ugly abstract painting, and you want to go and school both Orion and Limelight over some fences?" His tone was incredulous.

Cassie ground her teeth in frustration. She loved Caleb so much. But she was going to go nuts if he kept this up. He was acting worse than a mother hen.

She spoke carefully, as if she were trying to explain quantum mechanics to Jamie. "Friday is the Grand Prix qualifier. I've got to get back on and ride before then. Caleb, this is my job. This is what I do." She turned imploringly to the older man. "Hank, help me out on this, please."

"Hate to say it, Caleb, but she's got a point. She'll be even stiffer if she waits 'til tomorrow or Friday to ride."

"Hank, have you seen what her shoulders and ribs look like?"

"I only fell and bruised myself," she muttered defensively.

Hank looked at Caleb, then at Cassie, concern and

understanding at war inside him. Finally he replied heavily. "I know it's no worse than some really bad bruising, but Cassie, it's only fair I should warn you, I'm going to watch you like a hawk out there. Nothing is worth your seriously injuring yourself."

"I realize that, Hank." Her voice was quiet. "I've got two small children who need me. I don't take risks unnecessarily. But this sport, like a lot of things in life, has its dangers. You just can't shy away from them."

Caleb stared at her bent head, filled with a sense of helpless frustration. What could he say? He knew she was right. And the hell of it was, if he refused her this, then he was denying her the right to do something she truly loved and excelled at. It would be demeaning, too. Cassie's courage was one of the many qualities he admired and respected in her. He couldn't love her, then turn around and ride roughshod when she displayed that courage. He realized, too, that if the shoe were on the other foot, he'd go out and prepare just as thoroughly for Friday's class. But it wasn't, and the memory of her fall still had him breaking out into a cold sweat.

She'd made it.

It hadn't been pretty. Down right ugly, in fact, but she'd managed to squeak by. She'd ridden in the Grand Prix qualifier today and done well enough to go on. The day's qualifying event had been downright wicked. What was scarier was that she knew it was just the appetizer. Sunday's course would require even greater skill and finesse. Still bruised and sore from her spill earlier in the week, she was feeling pretty low on both.

Cassie had ridden the course twice, first on Orion, then on top of Limelight. With Orion, she'd felt unnaturally tense, unable to get in the groove. That flow athletes often find during their best performances was noticeably absent. Cassie's round had been so rocky, she'd almost blown it

completely when they'd come up against that triple combination. This time, however, Orion had saved her from herself. Finding the right spot and jumping easily, smoothly.
One, two, three.

But Orion hadn't been able to help her with her next
blunder. It had been a stupid mistake, holding him back,
freezing up, until he had gotten way too close to the watermill jump. Unable to get the height, Orion's front hooves
had smashed into the poles, knocking them down.

Cassie knew she was entirely to blame. She hadn't listened to her horse, she hadn't believed in him. And they'd
paid for it. It cost them seven faults, four faults for the
knockdown and an additional three points as a time
penalty. Another mistake she could claim: She'd stupidly,
ruthlessly held Orion back, slowing his pace until they
were going about as fast as that traffic jam back there on
Route 27.

Things had started off marginally better with Limelight,
at least until they came up against the second of the two
big water jumps on the course. Like many horses in the
class, Limelight wasn't able to make the distance over that
fourteen-foot pool of water. He landed early, hitting the
water, thoroughly rattled when forced to scramble for his
footing. Their pace, fine up until that point, simply fizzled
out, and they'd headed into the next jump moving far too
slowly. With his smaller frame, Limelight just didn't have
the kind of awesome power to draw on that Orion did. He
did his best to clear the fence, but couldn't get sufficient
height. Eight faults for that ride.

Well, it was done. Both horses had qualified for the
Grand Prix this Sunday. It had been pure luck her rounds
weren't as fault riddled as some of the others. She just hoped
she'd be able to get her act together by Grand Prix Sunday.

She wanted to go to this exhibitors' party like she
wanted a root canal, but she'd made a promise to Alex.

He'd been an angel these past few days. Taking Jamie and Sophie all over the Hamptons. They'd visited everything, from the Montauk Lighthouse to Sag Harbor's picturesque village and beautiful homes. Thanks to Alex, Jamie and Sophie were having a blast. When they weren't sightseeing, they were racing around on the beaches, visiting the horses at the Classic, and buying penny candy by the pound. Uncle Alex was keeping them hopping day and night—keeping them far too busy to wonder why their mother winced every time she made a sudden movement.

And she owed Alex big time for his unexpected discretion. He hadn't said a word when he found out that she and Caleb were sharing a motel room. She'd been half-expecting him to draw her aside for another one of his lectures on Caleb's debased character, but he hadn't. Instead, he'd leveled a long look at Caleb, seemingly satisfied when Caleb unflinchingly returned his stare. For that alone she was willing to go to this blasted event.

After the show, she'd explain to him how it was between her and Caleb. Right now, all she could really think about was tomorrow's ride.

That and Caleb's hands, running lazily over her breasts.

They were lying on their sides facing each other. Cassie could only lie comfortably on one side, her other one was still too bruised and sore. Caleb had hustled her into bed as soon as they'd reached the motel, claiming that she needed to rest as much as possible before tomorrow's Grand Prix.

Caleb's idea of rest was decidedly, deliciously different. "Slim." His voice was muffled, coming from the valley he was busy exploring, his mouth kissing the warm, fragrant flesh between her breasts.

"Mmm, what?"

"Let's blow this party off. We'll make up some really good excuse, like you don't have a thing to wear, and then you and I will sneak off to the beach. It's warm out tonight, looks like there will be plenty of stars." He paused, indulging himself, his tongue traveling leisurely along the underside of her breast, bathing it, then tickling it dry with his breath. "I'd like to be with you under all those stars, Slim."

She was torn. His suggestion sounded so lovely, so romantic. She wanted to say yes so badly. All this week, they'd been frantically busy at the show. By the end of each day, she'd been so worn out and achy that the most she could summon the energy for was to spend time with Sophie and Jamie. Cassie and Caleb hadn't even caught a glimpse of that endless expanse of blue.

She loved the sea, too. Nothing sounded sweeter than sharing a star-filled night on the beach with Caleb's strong arms wrapped around her. But she didn't want to leave Alex with a pouting Diana, either. Nobody deserved that.

Cassie dropped her head, running her fingers through his thick, dark hair. Her lips pressed kisses along his scalp.

"Would you be willing to accept a compromise? We can go to this party for an hour, then duck out and head for the beach."

Caleb was silent, thinking, planning. "I'd be willing to go for that. But, Slim, I'm keeping you on a strict time limit. After sixty minutes, you're mine." A blanket, a bottle of champagne, and the engagement ring tucked in his pocket would help make that true.

Caleb was seething with impatience by the time they arrived at the party. Diana, Alex's girlfriend, had kept them waiting for more than half an hour when Alex, Cassie, and Caleb had driven over to the house she was staying at for the weekend. Caleb had sat, drumming his fingers against the leg of his pants, while Cassie and Alex made polite conversation with Diana's host and hostess. Caleb frankly couldn't be bothered to enter into the conversation. He was way too keyed up, all his thoughts concentrated on the moment when he and Cassie would be alone on the moon-lit beach.

In any case, it was soon all too apparent that Alex Miller didn't know these people, although they seemed to know him, or *of* him. The wife, especially. An over-dressed, overblown blond, the wife kept making these coy, suggestive remarks, until Alex Miller finally leveled her with one cold stare. That killed the small talk quite effec-tively. The last, seemingly interminable, ten minutes were spent in awkward silence, waiting for Miller's girlfriend.

She must have been doing her makeup, Caleb thought to himself when she'd finally made an appearance. She was a looker, all right, he'd give her that. Dark eyes, slashing cheekbones, and a killer body. She'd be right at home on the fashion runway. But Caleb immediately recognized the type of woman wrapped up in that incredible package.

Diana looked like the kind of person who enjoyed mak-ing grand entrances. And also enjoyed keeping others wait-ing. He was almost sorry for Alex Miller. Almost, until he glanced over and saw the expression on Alex's face. His face was a study in a boredom. Gauging Miller's complete and utter indifference, Caleb had a strong hunch Diana could have roared into that living room buck naked, legs wrapped tight around a Harley, and Alex wouldn't have so much as blinked. He wondered if Diana knew she was wasting her energy trying to reel him in.

The party was in full swing by the time they arrived. The crush of people enormous, flowing out of the brightly lit, beach-front cottage—that quaint term used in the Hamptons for what would be a megamansion anywhere else. The crowd of guests was a mix of top riders, trainers, owners, big money, and what Caleb surmised was the Hamptons' beautiful people.

It was pretty clear who was who. The horse people

looked like anybody, some better, some worse. The rich people glittered with that special shine of money. The beautiful people posed, as if presenting their best angles to imaginary paparazzi. Sprinkled among them all, Caleb recognized the stars: movie actors, TV personalities, and some of those people whose faces kept appearing on the covers of magazines. For what reason, Caleb was never quite sure.

Far off in the corner of one of the rooms, he spied Hank speaking with Sam Waters and began to feel marginally better, as if he didn't have to grab Cassie's hand and flee the party this very second. Just as he was about to nudge Cassie, a signal to her that he'd seen Hank, he felt her go stiff as a board.

Surprised, he looked down at her face and saw her eyes were wide with shock. Following the direction of her frozen stare, he picked out from the throng a man with perfect, wavy blond hair who was staring right back at her, a smug smile on his face. Caleb saw him lift a glass in mock salute. Caleb didn't know who the hell he was, but he knew damn well he didn't like the condescending smirk the creep was giving Cassie.

"Who's the bozo with the smile, Cassie?"

"What? Oh, he's no one. Someone I used to know. Let's go get a drink." Lacing her fingers around his forearm, Cassie turned Caleb around, practically dragging him in the opposite direction.

She was flat-out determined to avoid an encounter between Caleb and her ex-fiancé, Brad Gibson.

Caleb kept catching threads of conversation as he moved through the press of bodies, navigating his way between the shifting clumps of people wearing designer clothes and deeply tanned skin. He snagged two glasses of champagne from a passing waiter, following Cassie as she threaded her way in the general direction of Hank and

Sam. When a waiter carrying a gigantic silver platter full of hors d'oeuvres stepped in front of him, Caleb was forced to stop, cut off from Cassie's advancing figure.

Might as well eat something, he thought to himself, eyeing the contents of the tray. With a smile of thanks, he chose a canapé, popped it into his mouth and reached for another. Abrupt laughter off to his right caused his head to turn.

It was a group of six or seven people. Among them he recognized Diana as well as the blond guy Cassie said she knew. They were laughing delightedly as a bone-thin, red-headed woman held forth. Like quite a few other people in that group, the woman's face was slightly flushed. Her voice loud and carrying. It took a few seconds before he realized the woman was describing, in minute and graphic detail, the wonders of colonic irrigation.

"Why, it's just changed my life!" The woman finished with a beatific smile.

Welcome to the Hamptons, Caleb muttered under his breath. Glancing down at the little triangle of toast topped by what he'd previously thought of as pâté, he stepped casually a few feet to the left and dumped it in the tub of a nearby potted plant. Good for the soil, he assured himself as he moved off, intent on catching up with Cassie.

The sooner I get her out of this circus, the better.

Caleb didn't notice the belligerent glare that followed him.

His dark head brushed hers, his lips whispering for her ears alone, "According to my watch, which is unfailingly accurate, you have exactly eight minutes and forty-nine seconds before I drag you out of here and make love to you under the stars."

Only a twitch of her lips gave any indication that she'd heard him. She was staring straight ahead, as if raptly absorbed by Hank's somewhat lengthy account of the exercise program he'd developed for Five Oaks's yearlings.

She relented at last. A grin spread over his face when he felt the tiny nod of her head. Yes! Excitement and anticipation making his heart pound, he continued, his lips still only inches away from her ear, "I'm going to borrow a bottle of champagne from our gracious hosts. There's enough flowing around here, an entire case wouldn't be missed. Why don't you find your brother so we can say good-bye. I'll meet up with you. Remember, the clock is ticking."

Five minutes later he located Alex Miller, surprised to find him alone.

"Hi, did Cassie come over yet?" Caleb asked, his eyes searching the crowd for a glimpse of her. "We were getting ready to leave. Just wanted to say good-bye." Damn. Where was she? The ladies' room, perhaps? He could hardly stand it, so impatient was he to be gone, to be alone with her.

Alex glanced at him sharply. "No, I haven't seen her since we arrived. I was pretty sure she'd be sticking to you like glue, especially when I noticed who else was here. Let's take a look for her. Last time I checked, Brad Gibson was in the other room. Drunk off his ass. Acting like an even bigger fool than he already is."

Brad Gibson. Had he heard that name before? "Who's Brad Gibson?" He asked Alex's back, raising his voice loud enough to be heard.

Alex shot him a curt look over his shoulder. "Cassie's old boyfriend. They were engaged to be married. Pompous fuck. Never liked him."

Suddenly it clicked. Gibson was probably the smirking creep he'd noticed at the beginning of the party. Gut clenching, Caleb's hands fisted at his side. His stride lengthened, keeping pace with Alex Miller's.

"Maybe she's out front. There's a patio leading out to the lawn." Together they'd searched all the rooms without catching sight of her.

They stepped out into the relative quiet of the evening. Daylight had long since faded. Now the night was set aglow, illuminated by brightly colored paper lanterns, citronella flares, and weighted paperbags with candles set inside dotting the perimeter of the patio.

It was a spectacular evening. A faint ocean breeze, mingling with the sweet scent of Cheyenne privet, blew across the immaculately manicured grounds. Overhead, the first stars winked in the darkened sky.

Caleb and Alex heard the voices first. Rather, they heard a single voice, a man's. Loud and aggressive. Recognizing it, Alex was off, his body tense. Taking his cue from Alex, Caleb moved quickly, a cold fury growing inside him as the man's voice became clearer and clearer.

They were at the edge of the light. A slight shift in the wind caused the lanterns to sway, casting Cassie and Brad Gibson into greater relief; a scene that should have been pretty turned repugnant. There, on the perfectly mowed lawn was Cassie standing straight, elegantly slender. Imprisoned by Brad Gibson's restraining hand clamped tight around her forearm, she stood, coolly immobile, a statue. Gibson was leaning forward, invading the space that separated them as he angled his face close to hers, spewing verbal filth. So caught up in his hateful taunts, the two men closing in escaped his notice.

Even slurred, his words rang clearly in the night. "Saw that fall you took this week. Didn't do much better yesterday, did you? I guess you've lost your touch. Not that you were all that good a rider, anyway. Made me wonder exactly what you'd been hired for down in Virginia." Gibson laughed, shaking his head, his blond hair hardly moving in the lantern's light. "Yes, I was definitely puzzled. That is, Cassie, until I saw you with your new boss. It all came back. You know, the thing you're really good at. Lying back and spreading your legs . . ."

Alex lunged, ready to tear Brad Gibson limb from limb. He never got the chance.

With the speed of a panther making his kill, Caleb had already pounced. With one hand, he grabbed Gibson by the front of his shirt, tearing him away from Cassie. The other, now curled into a rock hard fist, plowed into Gibson's face, slamming into his nose with all his might.

Gibson crumpled to the ground, unconscious.

Barks of laughter floated out eerily from the brightly lit house, the sound of the party continuing undisturbed, incongruous with the scene outside. A weird silence descended around the three standing figures, the night and all that had just happened taking on a surreal air.

Seconds ticked by, with no one moving, no one speaking. At last Alex stepped forward, looking down dispassionately at the bloody figure lying on the ground. Out like a light. It was interesting, the way Brad Gibson's nose was no longer quite where it should be. He was curious what the medical term for that was. Already, it was taking on the appearance of a squashed tomato, draped inelegantly off the side of Gibson's face. Major reconstructive surgery, no doubt about it.

Slightly envious of Caleb's handiwork, he angled his head, giving Caleb an inscrutable look. His tone was conversational. "You know, Wells, you might have had the courtesy of letting me take him out. After all, she is my sister."

"True," Caleb nodded agreeably, understanding the other man's feelings completely. The adrenaline was still pumping through his veins as the scene unfolded once more in his mind. Such rage, such an overwhelming need to protect Cassie, the woman he loved. Caleb knew instinctively that Miller had experienced an identical reaction.

Since he'd robbed him of the pleasure of smashing in Gibson's face, Caleb supposed the least he could do was to give Cassie's brother an explanation, an apology of sorts.

"Sorry I stepped in like that. But I figured that since I'm going to marry her, I had, uh, precedence."

"You're going to marry her?"

"Yeah." His teeth flashed in the dark. "Of course, I'd appreciate your permission, as you're her older brother and all."

There, that was perfect, showed lots of tact. Important to respect Miller's position as head of the family. Caleb's eyes dropped back down to the unconscious form, recalling how his fist had connected with Gibson's face. A definite pleasure, he thought. Too bad it had taken just one punch. What a wimp. He wondered if they could just leave him here, merely informing their host that someone was in need of immediate assistance.

Alex spoke again, interrupting his thoughts. "And has Cassie said yes?"

It jolted him, like an electric shock, snapping him out of the bizarre, trancelike state he'd slipped into from the moment he'd seen Gibson standing, his hand a vice grip on Cassie. Realizing his blunder too late, hoping against hope it wasn't as bad as he feared.

It was.

Cassie stepped forward, her eyes shooting fire, her body taught with rage. Truly magnificent in her fury. "No, she hasn't. Gee, I wonder why? Five weeks, *five weeks,* and not a word!" Her words lashed, fueled by righteous indignation. "Then you have the gall, the unmitigated gall, to go and ask my brother for my hand in marriage. And speak about me as if I didn't even exist?"

She was so mad she could spit. Her chest was heaving, rising and falling violently. What incredible nerve, she thought, filled with disgust at Alex and Caleb's exchange. Planning to marry her? Since when? After all those weeks of dying a little with every day that passed and he remained silent? She supposed she should be grateful she'd been informed at all, let alone *asked.* Maybe he'd thought he could just arrange the whole thing with Alex, like they did in the Middle Ages.

Well, she was damned if anyone was going to get away with treating her as if she were of no consequence.

In her opinion, Caleb's lack of consideration was far more offensive than the sight of Brad's destroyed nose. As far as Brad's nose went, if any one had *bothered* to ask, Cassie would have replied that Brad had been asking for a busted nose for some time now.

If she'd cared enough, she'd have given him one herself. But she hadn't. Those drunken words he'd spewed at her, while ugly and vicious, hadn't the power to hurt her. Because she didn't love him. But she loved Caleb, damn him.

With a renewed spurt of anger, Cassie whirled, surprised to find she still held a glass of champagne in her hand. How odd. With a grim smile, she flicked her wrist, splashing the remains of her champagne over Brad's battered face.

Turning to Caleb, her eyes sent him straight to hell. "I hope when Brad comes to, he presses charges. Have fun in jail."

"I take it she hasn't said yes yet," Alex said mildly, watching his sister storm across the lawn. Yes, indeed, his kid sister was truly pissed. He hadn't seen her this mad in years. What a sight she was, he thought proudly.

Oh, God. Caleb rubbed his hands roughly up and down his face, cursing himself viciously. Unable to believe the magnitude of his blunder. How stupid could he have been?

"I was planning on asking her tonight. On the beach. We were heading there now. I've got the ring in my pocket."

Alex noticed Brad Gibson was beginning to stir, moaning feebly. He nudged him with the sole of his shoe, eliciting another moan.

"So, you were a bit . . . premature."

Caleb remained silent. Not bothering with excuses, knowing there weren't any.

"Come on then, we'd better go figure out how you're going to make it up to her."

Caleb paused. His thoughts clearing somewhat, he was torn, unsure what to do about Brad Gibson, whose moans of pain were growing louder with each passing minute.

Seeing Caleb hesitate, Alex Miller spared Brad Gibson a final, scornful glance. "Don't worry about Gibson. Even if he ever figures out what, or who hit him, he won't press charges. He'd rather have a ruined nose than a ruined law practice, which is what he'd get, compliments of yours truly."

As if they were college roommates out together for a night on the town, Alex draped an arm around Caleb's shoulder, drawing him away. After a few yards, he bent, scooping up from the ground Caleb's forgotten bottle of champagne. Caleb had dropped it when he'd charged, needing both hands to properly rearrange Gibson's face. Alex held the bottle aloft as if it were a torch to guide them. "Now then," he said. "What we need is some sound female advice."

But Thompson wasn't giving. When Alex and Caleb returned to Great-aunt Grace's home in Georgica Estates and told Thompson the whole sorry tale, she proceeded to chew the hide off Caleb. Then she left, declaring loudly she'd never have encouraged him in his pursuit of Cassie if she'd suspected just what a nitwit he was.

It was a horrible feeling, having two females he cared about detest him at the same time.

For lack of a better alternative, they were forced to talk it over themselves. Or rather Alex talked, sipping champagne from the bottle Caleb had appropriated earlier, explaining his sister's fierce sense of independence. Waxing increasingly philosophical.

"Cass has wanted to be her own person, handle things by herself for a long time now. You know, or maybe you don't, I offered her a pile of money so she could start her own barn, buy some horses, call her own shots. But she turned me down, preferring to work for you and Hank. I could tell how important it was to her, that she'd gone out and gotten the job. She wanted to make something of it, all by herself."

From across the rustic farmhouse table Alex looked at Caleb, who was sitting dejectedly, his head cradled in his hands, staring down at the wooden grain of the kitchen floorboards. Mute with despair.

Not overly concerned, Alex continued his musing. "So, obviously, Cass must have been a little put out when she heard you asking me for her hand in marriage. Guess that was one of those major life decisions she wanted to make for herself."

Caleb hadn't realized Alex Miller was such a master of understatement. Probably everybody talked this way in those big, New York financial firms. Still Caleb said nothing, his mind like a stuck record, her anger, her fury, playing over and over again. God, he wished he could take back every second of the evening and start afresh. Except maybe the part where his fist connected with Gibson's nose. That he'd keep.

Alex's voice interrupted his thoughts. "Come on, Wells. Snap out of it. No way are you going to win Cassie, or her forgiveness, sitting around here like a kicked dog."

Caleb's head lifted, his hands supporting his chin. He eyed Alex balefully. "Careful there, Miller. I'd watch my language. In my profession that's a really nasty expression."

Alex swept out a hand, bringing the glass of champagne to his lips for a slow sip. "My apologies," he offered as he refilled his empty glass. "But I need you to start paying close attention. I've come up with an idea I think might work. You'll still have to do some serious persuading, some serious groveling, too, but this might help tip the scales in your favor."

He outlined the rudiments of his plan. Listening, Caleb began to sit straighter in his chair, a glimmer of hope kindling inside him. Yeah, he had to hand it to Miller, it was a good idea. Big, a bit silly, and really sweet. Cassie just might soften up enough for him to beg her forgiveness. But the logistics would be damned tricky.

"You really think we can pull that off, on a Sunday morning?" Caleb asked.

"Well, you're going to have to get on the phone at the crack of dawn, and you're going to have to blow a major amount of cash, but then, I'm assuming you know my sister's worth a whole lot more than that."

"Absolutely," he agreed quietly. "I love her so much it hurts." He looked across at Alex. "But I have to admit, Miller, I'm curious why you're helping me. Down in Virginia, you seemed more than eager to tear a piece out of my hide. Why this about-face? Why help me win her back? This is a golden opportunity to blow me clear out of the water."

Alex leaned back in his chair.

"I don't need to blow you out of the water. Not anymore. I'd arranged everything, in case that became necessary, but I won't do it." His even teeth flashed against his lightly tan skin. "I'm even thinking of giving you Orion as a wedding present. I like the symbolism of the gesture, don't you?"

"What the hell do you mean, give me Orion?" Caleb demanded. His eyes narrowed as the recent events began at last to make sense. He asked suddenly, "Wait, do you mean . . . did Cassie?"

Alex raised a hand, stopping him. "No, she never knew, although I'm surprised she didn't recognize it. She's aware I created the TLM Group after the accident. Acronym for

Tom and Lisa Miller. It's a fund I use for a lot of different investments, special charities. Cassie probably would have figured it out eventually. I suppose at the time," Alex finished blandly, "she was fairly distracted, what with one thing and another."

Caleb coughed. "Yeah, a lot's been happening during the last month." He looked across the table in bemusement at Cassie's brother. "I admit to shock. You could have taken away everything I love but now instead you're helping me."

Alex's sharp, chiseled features assessed Caleb with careful scrutiny. A quiet laugh escaped his lips. "I agree, it does seem wildly out of character, suspicious, even. Why help you?" he mused. "A few reasons actually." Counting them off, one by one, Alex extended his thumb, his other fingers following, as he reeled off his explanation. "First, back in Virginia, it was hard not to notice how Cassie looked at you. Even then, she was already half in love with you. From the way her face glows now, this evening excluded, of course, I'd say she's as much in love with you as you are with her." Alex's index finger shot out. "Second, I saw how good you were with Jamie and Sophie. You weren't pretending to like them just to get her into your bed. Knowing Cassie as well as I do, I know she couldn't truly love you if the kids weren't important to you. That's why it would have never worked out with Brad. Because of her grief after the accident, it took her way too long to see him for the selfish jerk he was." His middle finger joined the first two. "Third, I saw the expression on your face this Wednesday when Cassie fell off Orion. That said it all." He fell silent a moment, letting his sentence hang in the air. Lifting his champagne glass, he stared at the tiny bubbles rising, exploding. He drank deeply. When at last he looked up again, his blue eyes reminded Caleb of bitter frost on a winter's day. "Fourth, I suddenly find I don't need to go in for the kill, so to speak. Cassie's grown up on me. She doesn't need her big brother to watch out for her. And the final reason I'm suddenly your closest ally, perhaps even your new best friend, is because I love my sister and my niece and nephew more than anything in the world. Myself, I don't have a lot of optimism about ever finding a real and lasting love. If my sister has, I'll move heaven, earth, and hell itself to help her get it and keep it."

31

"Uh, Cassie, don't you think you could maybe, just maybe, find it in your heart to forgive Caleb?"

"Hank," Cassie replied tightly, "I'd really appreciate it if you drop this subject immediately. Even better, don't mention that man's name."

Hank wished he were just about anywhere else on earth right now than in Cassie's Jeep, driving her back to the motel. Christ, he wasn't even sure he understood exactly what had happened back at the party to get her this upset. He'd been confused from the word go, when she'd marched right up and informed him that if he didn't leave the party with her this very second, he could walk back to the motel. Hank had started to ask about Caleb, but she'd interrupted him, telling him that Caleb could go take a hike, for all she cared.

No, Hank thought, glancing over at Cassie, who sat fuming in the passenger seat. He couldn't figure out for the life of him what was going on. And he damn sure didn't want to find out. He missed his wife. Perhaps he could telephone her when they arrived and she could deal with the whole rotten mess.

He pulled into the parking space near the motel cabins. Cassie was out of the car like a shot, slamming the door behind her. She called to him as she fumbled with her key.

"By the way, if Caleb happens to show his face, you'd better tell him he's sleeping in your room. If he tries to get in mine, I swear I'll call the police."

Jesus Christ Almighty, that girl certainly had a temper. "Sure thing, Cassie, I'll be sure to pass that on." Not knowing what else to say, he called out lamely, "Sweet dreams."

If Thompson was taken aback at finding Caleb still sitting in Great-aunt Grace's kitchen at six o'clock the following morning, she was too good a poker player to reveal it. He didn't look as if he'd slept, but his hair was damp. A shower or a predawn dip in the ocean? His bare, sandy feet gave her the answer.

As was his custom, Caleb had immediately stood upon Thompson's entering the room. For a minute, neither spoke.

Then testily, she made a shooing motion with her hand. "Go on, sit down. I can't make breakfast if you're standing in the middle of the kitchen. I suppose you'll want some."

"You still mad at me, Bessie?"

"Yes. That is, unless you managed to get a new brain overnight."

"Ouch. Have pity on me, I know I've been an idiot. Unfortunately it's hard to get a brain transplant on a Saturday night. But luckily Alex lent me his."

"Alex?"

"Yeah. Nice to see surprise on your face, too. He's not such a stiff after all."

"Of course not." Her tone was exasperated.

"Well, you might not have thought he was one, being a woman and all . . ."

"Caleb Wells . . ." Thompson's voice rose warningly.

"Okay, okay. Anyway, he and I talked things over. I

admire the way he cares for his family. And I can't over-
look the fact that he's trying to help me out of the mess I
made with Cassie."

"So what are you going to do?" She tried to ask the
question casually, as if it were only of the mildest interest.

"Bessie, I think you'll like this plan . . ."

Caleb was back on Thompson's most-favored-person
list by the time Alex made his way downstairs for breakfast. Caleb inspected him closely, coming to the conclusion
that Alex must be blessed with a stomach of iron. Not even
a hint of a hangover after having finished that bottle of
champagne all on his own. Indeed, Alex sat down and put
away a breakfast easily as big as Caleb's own.

"So, you all set to make some calls, Caleb?"

"Yeah, I was just telling Bessie about your idea."

"If it meets with Thompson's approval, then I think you
have a shot at success. Let me find the telephone book so
you can start calling around."

Sophie and Jamie were far more enthusiastic than
Thompson had been when they discovered Caleb sitting by
the phone, jotting down numbers, dialing, making arrangements, dialing some more. "What's Caleb doing here,
Uncle Alex?"

"He's arranging a surprise for your mom."

"What kind of surprise?" As excited as if the surprise
were for themselves.

"A big one. It's a secret, so I can't tell. You'll see it
later."

"I know what kind of surprise I'd give her, if I could."

"What's that, Sophie love?"

"I'd get her a dog, 'cause she liked Finnegan almost as
much as me and I miss him lots."

"Me, too," Jamie chimed in.

"Well, I don't think Caleb's going to get a dog for her

today, but now that you mention it, I think you're right. Your mom would like a dog. What kind did you say she'd like?"

Sophie held her arms open wide. "A big one."

"Well, perhaps Caleb can help us with that, too."

"Yippee!" Then, "Wait 'til we tell Aunt Grace! Can we go see her now?"

Caleb had to leave before he had the pleasure of meeting Great-aunt Grace. As Alex had informed him when he came down to the kitchen, Aunt Grace preferred her breakfast and morning paper in bed. It was carried up to her on a bamboo tray with a deep purple hydrangea blossom tucked in a glass vase. The woman who performed this morning ritual was named Tilly, and lived in the house as a companion to the ninety-one-year-old lady.

Caleb was truly sorry he'd missed her. Aunt Grace sounded like quite a character. Alex claimed that despite her advanced years, she was mentally as sharp as a tack. Physically, too. Apparently, the old lady attributed her good health and longevity to the daily walks she took on the beach, rain or shine. Unfortunately, Caleb couldn't afford to wait until the grande dame put in her appearance. He had to get the ball rolling if this thing was going to work.

32

The Hamptons were sparkling brilliantly, gloriously, on Grand Prix Sunday. The sky was an endless sweep of saturated blue, puffy, cotton-ball clouds floating lazily overhead, promising only perfect weather.

On the horse show grounds, the stripes of the colored tents gleamed brightly in the sun. Most dazzling of all, however, was the Grand Prix ring itself. The beauty of the jumps simply breathtaking. They rose up from emerald green grass, massive and high. Around their bases, a florist's fantasy: enormous arrangements of flowers, plants, and shrubs created borders as fantastic and rich as the prestige of the Grand Prix event itself.

"Hey, Hank, how are things going?"

"Where the *hell* have you been? I sat up half the night, expecting to hear from you, wondering whether I'd have to go and bail you out of jail or some other such nonsense."

"Sorry about that. I ended up spending the night where Alex and the twins are staying. There was extra room there, and I figured Cassie wasn't too eager to see me. I tried to call you earlier, but you'd already left for the show grounds."

Hank wasn't in a very forgiving mood. He'd suffered through a lousy night followed by an even lousier morning. It had been a real treat to be with Cassie this morning. Kind of like hanging out in Siberia during the winter months.

"Well, it's real nice of you to bother to show up at all." Sarcasm laced his voice. "Or perhaps you'd forgotten Cassie's due to ride in a couple of hours?" He shook his head in disgust. "You know, I'm beginning to believe all that terrible stuff she was muttering about you last night."

Caleb grinned with all the charm of a schoolboy as he wrapped his arm around the shoulders of his friend and partner. "Hank, I hate to admit it, but I am probably guilty of every heinous crime Cassie lay at my feet last night. But don't you worry. I spent the greater part of last night and all of this morning working on a plan for major redemption. Has she talked about me at all this morning?"

Hank gave a quick negative jerk to his head. "Not a word." He let out a harried breath as he continued. "Caleb, you know I love you like a second son, and I'm really pleased you're going to try to mend your fences with Cassie, but I gotta tell you . . . I am beginning to suffer from massive migraines whenever you and Cassie have one of your tiffs. And . . . I don't think it's anything to laugh at, either."

"Sorry, Hank, really. But I need all the help I can get, from you especially. This operation requires precision timing." He looked at his friend, his expression utterly serious. "I love her, Hank. I want her to be my wife."

Hank's jaw dropped, stunned. "No kidding?" His astonishment was almost comical. "In the Jeep last night, I thought I heard her mention something about someone proposing marriage, but I couldn't figure out whether it was her brother, Alex, who was getting hitched, or someone else."

Caleb had the grace to look chagrined. "Yeah, well, I'll explain that mess to you some other day. But let me fill you in on what I'll need you for later. Like I said, it's the timing that's crucial: it's got to happen just after Cassie's completed her first round with Limelight, but before she's up with Orion."

Her mother used to love that old show tune from *South Pacific,* the one with the lyrics that went, "I'm gonna wash that man right out of my hair." Since last night, she'd taken those words to heart. Caleb was banished, locked from her mind, and her heart. As far as she was concerned, Caleb could take a long walk off the shortest pier in Montauk.

For Cassie, the only thing that remained was the anger.

Such wonderful, righteous anger. She didn't care a fig whether she was being unreasonable or irrational. It was hers, and she embraced it, feeling it flow through her veins, strong and bracing.

33

*S*ometimes it was the little things, the ones one might brush aside as having only trivial importance, that ended up tipping the scales in an event like the Grand Prix. For instance, take the order to go, as it was called in the show-jumping world. With the Grand Prix, the order of the riders was determined by the number of faults the rider had earned from the earlier qualifying event, the rider with the most faults going first.

The Grand Prix class had been whittled down to the thirty best rides. As Cassie's round with Limelight in the qualifying class had racked up eight points, she would be riding early, near the top of the jumping order. Then the others would come after, chasing down her time, trying for an even better round.

It could be a nail-biting kind of experience, riding early in a class, then watching your competitors come hustling after you. Determined to outride you, to outgallop you. Luckily, Cassie would barely have time to watch. Once Limelight's round was under her belt, she would have only minutes to spare, just enough to dismount, regroup mentally, and hop onto Orion's back for a second chance at that all-too elusive, perfect round.

It was a beautiful day, but it certainly didn't seem to be going beautifully for the riders. Horse after horse rode into the ring, exiting a grueling sixty seconds later, with each of their riders' mistakes captured in the bright summer sun, witnessed by a crowd of close to twenty thousand.

No one had yet gone clean, or even close. Shallow cups let poles fall if a hoof so much as grazed them. The two water jumps had already claimed three horses. Tight corners had led to knockdowns and refusals. One ride had been particularly ghastly, causing the crowd to cry out in sympathy and horror. One of the horse's had, instead of clearing the course's double-oxer, landed on top, straddling it. Managing to free himself only after bringing down the entire fence. These sorts of accidents happened in the sport of show jumping. But because today was Grand Prix Sunday, and the competition was riding for a purse of one hundred thousand dollars, the tension heightened unbearably. Each success, each failure stirred the excitement of the crowd.

Now it was time for Limelight. Cassie nodded to Hank. He smiled briefly and gave her a jaunty thumbs-up sign.

She trotted into the ring. Limelight's dapple grey coat glistened in the afternoon sun. His neck arched gracefully, the line emphasized by the neat, dark grey row of braids along his mane. Cassie slowed him to a halt, saluted the judges in their stand, and urged the gelding into the smooth rhythm of his canter.

She couldn't know it, but, as soon as Cassie trotted into the ring, Caleb appeared at Hank's side.

"How's she doing? Nervous?"

"Not that I could tell. Real quiet, real focused."

"I would have given my right arm to be there with her, but I was afraid of lousing things up."

"You might just get your chance to louse things up pretty good if this plan of yours doesn't go like clockwork. I'd sure hate for her to be rattled riding Orion."

"Like Alex said, I'm going to have to do some mighty fast talking."

She was riding Limelight with the precision of an artist, her form perfect and clean, a lesson straight from riding's great masters. She handled her horse with an inner sense of timing that was uncanny. Carefully, she guided the small grey gelding over fence after fence. Giving him time to set up so that he took the fences, his knees tucked tightly underneath him, soaring through the air like a silver rocket, then landing clear.

At the water jump, he didn't even hesitate, flying boldly over the incredible construction built to resemble an ocean dock. His confidence was such that he could have leapt the Long Island Sound.

The murmurs of the crowd grew stronger with each perfectly negotiated jump. By the time Cassie and Limelight reached the water jump, Hank and Caleb were grinning. The thunderous applause for the horse and rider was the music they had dreamt of. Two more fences and they too were clapping, urging her on.

It was great round, by far the best of the day, but even so, Cassie had accumulated a fault and a half as a time penalty. Because she'd allowed Limelight to set up so carefully, she hadn't managed to beat the clock. Still, Cassie's ride put her in first place in the class's standings. Now, she'd just have to go one better, this time with Orion.

Her heart was thumping from exertion and excitement as Cassie trotted back to Hank, only to remember he was alone. Her spirits plummeted and her lips tightened.

Never mind. You did it for yourself, you don't need anyone else. But a niggling voice inside her head replied that it was so much better to share success with someone you loved.

"Congratulations, Cassie. The way things are going today, you may have come up with the winning ride."

"Shame on you, Hank. What about Orion?" Cassie swung her leg over the saddle, slipping gratefully to the ground, even as her aches and bruises descended on her in a rush of pain. She patted Limelight's neck, thrilled with the gelding's accomplishment.

"He was great out there, a real gem. I feel like kicking myself. If I'd been just that much faster . . ."

"You mean like those other riders, tearing around the course, knocking everything in sight? No, you rode it fine. It was beautiful." He cleared his throat as if remembering. "Now, you'd better go fetch Orion. He's back at the stall."

Utterly dumbfounded, Cassie stared. *"What's he doing back there, Hank?* I'm up in about ten minutes!"

As he couldn't answer her question without blowing Caleb's scheme, he settled for a brusque order. "Well, then, you'd better get back there double quick." His lips mumbled a quick prayer as she took off, running toward the far end of the show grounds.

Cassie tore into the stable area, her lungs heaving, a stitch shooting up her side. In all her life competing at horse shows, she'd never missed a class yet. She wasn't about to start today. When she saw him, she stopped so abruptly she almost tripped over her feet. God, he was so tall, so handsome, standing there next to Orion. She stood frozen.

"Cassie, love, if you want this horse, you're first going to have to listen to me apologize."

"Better make it snappy because I'm up in a few minutes . . . Not that I'm interested," she quickly added.

She refused to retreat as he approached. Holding her

ground, she looked up at him defiantly, her jaw set, waiting for him to hand over the reins.

Smiling solemnly, he held them out to her. But when she grasped the reins he refused to relinquish them. Lifting the reins and her clenched hands, he kissed her knuckle softly.

"I was so proud of you out there just now." Feeling her skin shiver beneath his lips, he kissed the knuckle again. "I love you, Cassie. So very much. I'd give anything in the world to take back last night." His eyes met hers, pleading that she believe him.

"I'd been planning on asking you to marry me for some time, wanting it to be perfect for you. Never finding the moment, perhaps too scared to create one. But it tears me apart that I ruined it for you, my love."

Moving closer, he angled his head, his lips brushing her lips, lightly coaxing. Their very gentleness undoing her. "Please, Cassie, forgive me. Let me try to make it up to you."

Desperately, she tried to summon the anger, the outrage, the indignation she'd felt last night. But somehow those emotions paled in comparison to the memory of the crushing loneliness when Caleb hadn't been there, waiting for her by the gate.

"Yes," she said simply, not needing to say more.

Not quite believing his good fortune, he stilled. In the next instant, his arms were wrapped about her, crushing her close, his mouth raining kisses, at last reaching her parted lips. "Oh, God, Cassie, thank you, thank you. I love you so much!" He knew he was flooding her with his love. Never, absolutely never, would he let her go.

"Caleb." She was breathless, unsure of how much time she'd been submerged, still struggling to the surface. "I'm going to be late for my class."

"Right," he agreed, reluctantly controlling himself.

"Let's get going. You've got a huge crowd of fans out there. Did you hear them applauding, roaring for you?"

They were walking quickly out of the stable. Suddenly Caleb pulled Orion to a halt, holding out his hand to give Cassie a leg up. "Come on, love, you'll go faster riding him. Trot over to the in-gate. I'll follow behind. Don't worry, I won't miss your ride."

"Caleb, wait." The unsteady waver in her voice had him searching her face. "Caleb, that last round, on Limelight, I think I did as well as I did because I was so mad at you. But I'm not mad at you now." Her eyes were frantic.

He was silent for a second. "Yeah, I can understand that. It helped block everything out for you." He reached for her hand, pulling it against his lips. "But now, Cassie, you're going to go out there and win because you're the best rider in the whole damn place, you've got the finest horse, and you have a man ready to throw himself at your feet, who will love you until the end of time."

She looked at him, a dazzling smile spreading across her face. "Oh, yeah. Thanks for reminding me."

The smile never left her face.

The only word to describe it was magic, the way she rode Orion. Proving again and again to the crowd just how magnificent a creature he truly was. It was a ride that made the brilliance of the horse and rider, melded together as a team, absolutely thrilling. It left the crowd gasping with awe. Excitement rose with each turn, each stride, each powerful take-off and flawless landing. The spectators were on their feet, cheering them on, as Cassie and Orion headed for the final jump. Orion cleared it, and Cassie galloped him madly, joyfully to the wire. The clock stopped.

"Holy God," said Hank. "That was one to remember." A perfect, crazy, dizzyingly fast round.

They were all waiting for her, tears of laughter and joy moistening their eyes, smiles splitting their faces.

Cassie's eyes searched and found him standing off to the side, shaking his dark head in admiration. His smile, the smile she loved, was achingly tender.

As though in a dream, Cassie dismounted. She hardly noticed Orion being led away by a grinning Raffael. Even Sophie and Jamie, jumping wildly with excitement, barely registered. For the moment her eyes were for Caleb alone. Her breath caught tight in her throat, she watched him approach.

In front of her at last, Caleb dropped to one knee, reaching out to clasp her left hand in his. His voice was warm with love, making her heart pound with joy. "Cassie, my love, I'd like you to look up. Right now."

She blinked, wondering whether she'd heard him correctly.

"Please, Slim, I'd hate for you to miss this." His own eyes drifted upwards, scanning the sky.

Baffled, she obeyed his request, staring up at the sky, not knowing what she was looking for.

Not understanding until the small biplane roared above, trailing a long white banner. Not sure until she read, CASSIE, BE MINE in bold, bright red letters. Not breathing until she felt Caleb slipping the engagement ring on her finger.

She fell to her knees in front of him, laughing and crying. Tears filled her eyes and streamed down her cheeks for Caleb to catch them with his kisses, as he murmured words of love.

"I wanted it perfect for you, Cassie. I love you. Be my wife."

She kissed him softly. With eyes still moist from tears, she smiled. "Caleb, I love you so much, I don't need perfection. The only thing I need is you."

"Love, I hope you'll have me forever."

Hank's deep voice, bursting with laughter and pride, floated down to them. "Uh, Cassie, I hate to interrupt, but I wanted to be the first to congratulate you. You've just won the Grand Prix."

Cassie only smiled, knowing that if she had Caleb's love, she'd won all that truly mattered.

Epilogue

*H*ank had been put in charge of the procession, so as soon as he saw Tod and Delia arrive, he called out cheerfully, "Hi, good morning. Welcome to 'The Peaceable Kingdom.' Hot Lips should be almost ready, Tod. Raffael's just double checking that her braids are perfect." He gave Delia a careful embrace. "So this is young Samuel." He smiled, looking down at the newborn cradled in Delia's arms. "Congratulations."

"Thank you, Hank. Don't you look wonderful. Very dashing," Delia said, taking in his dove grey morning coat.

Hank blushed, fingering the silk tie at his throat. "Thank you. I know I'll feel a little overdressed standing beside Barney, but even that old donkey's going to look good today. Cassie convinced Raff to put a garland of flowers around his neck. Of course he'll probably try to eat it during the middle of the ceremony."

Tod grinned, looking around at the other guests who had begun to congregate, many of them already paired with an animal. "This is truly extraordinary, I've never seen anything quite like it. You know, on the invitation we received, Cassie wrote that she would love it if I could *accompany*

Hot Lips. Until I talked to her and Caleb, I thought *accompany* meant driving her mare here from Pennsylvania."

"Having Hot Lips healthy again has been the icing on the cake, so to speak. Cassie says she owes everything to you, Tod, not only because of the aqua tank, but also because you changed her training approach with Hot Lips. That mare's practically a different horse now. It seems like her wild banshee days are over. There's been a lot of changes around here, all to the good."

Smiling, he thought of Bessie Thompson, who had conceded with a flattering blush, that yes, now everyone could call her Bessie, that being only logical since her new last name was O'Mally. She and Francis O'Mally had eloped three weeks before, an act of passion so exciting, so invigorating, Francis claimed he felt twenty years younger. The old devil. They would soon be moving into Caleb's carriage house. And right here was more good news: Delia Harper with her beautiful baby asleep in her arms. She was rocking him gently.

"I'm so happy for them," she said. "I know it's going to be just beautiful. I can't imagine a ceremony that would suit them so well."

Hank laughed. "You're right. Everyone is thrilled. Though I think we should all be deeply grateful Caleb's not a plumber. Just picture it. We might instead be standing around, each one of us holding our kitchen sinks! If you'll excuse me, I see Francis O'Mally has arrived. He and Finnegan are leading the canine retinue."

By the time the minister had finished reading Saint Francis's "Sermon to the Birds," and had begun the blessing of all the animals assembled, Melissa's handkerchief was a soggy mess. She nudged Hank gently with her elbow. He passed her a second, having brought several, just in case. Glancing up at her husband, she was gratified to see moisture in his eyes, too. It was so lovely, worth every sentimental tear she shed. Melissa's hand searched out Hank's, and they gazed on, fingers intertwined.

Dabbing her eyes as daintily as she could, she smiled mistily at the scene before her. It was a moving experience to stand there, side by side, a congregation arranged in a large circle. Family and friends, coming together, to participate in this joyous ceremony, beginning with the blessing of the many animals in their lives, young and old, big and small. Each person or couple in the gathering was responsible for some kind of creature. Horses of course out in large number: Hot Lips, Limelight, Silverspoon, Arrow, Pip, Topper, and even Barney the donkey. But other animals were present too. Barn and house cats; and dogs, such as Finnegan; and the two eight-week-old-puppies tumbling about Jamie and Sophie's feet. Not to be forgotten was the splendid, snow-white cockatoo perched on the shoulder of Mark Winterer.

The blessing was a magical prelude that set the tone for the ceremony, for when at last the time came for humans and animals to leave the circle they had formed, Caleb and Cassie would be wed, at last man and wife.

Everyone watched as the minister, David Cosgrove, walked slowly around the perimeter, blessing each animal in turn.

Then, he turned toward the center of the ring, and waited, watching the couple who stood before them all.

Cassie was dressed in an ivory gown that ended in a long, flowing train. The dress had belonged to her mother, worn on her wedding day as well. A wreath of miniature roses and baby's breath crowned Cassie's head. She resembled a sylvan princess; the autumn leaves hanging from the trees nearby, her golden bower. Caleb, tall and dark in a formal cutaway, had never looked handsomer or as happy. They stood together, joy shining on their faces.

A movement, and into the circle's center stepped a tall blond man, leading a dark horse. Alex Miller and Orion.

The horse's coat gleamed, his mane decorated with running braids, looped together to form a scalloped edge along his arched neck. Man and horse approached Cassie and Caleb. Embracing them both, Alex held out to them the stallion's lead. As both Cassie and Caleb grasped it, Alex stepped back, taking his place at Jamie and Sophie's side.

Then the minister spoke, his rich tenor reaching everyone. "Beloved friends, beloved family, welcome. Today is a day of great joy. On this day we come together to celebrate the life of Saint Francis and of all God's creatures. This date was chosen with care by Cassie and Caleb. For today, we are invited not only to share in their love of animals, but also to stand as joyful witnesses as they pledge their love for each other. Here, in this large and wondrous circle, we are gathered to bless. And we are gathered to love.

"Before Cassie and Caleb exchange their vows and pledge themselves to each other, there is one last animal to bless. He stands before you all, a symbol of beauty, courage, and life: a giver. It is Orion. Among the many animals Cassie and Caleb love, this dark horse holds a special place in their hearts. For it was through Orion that these two remarkable people came together and found what they were seeking. Through Orion, they received the most precious gift of all: the gift of love."

**Visit the Simon & Schuster
romance Web site:**

www.SimonSaysLove.com

**and sign up for our
romance e-mail updates!**

Keep up on the latest
new romance releases,
author appearances, news, chats,
special offers, and more!
We'll deliver the information
right to your inbox—if it's new,
you'll know about it.

POCKET BOOKS

2800.02